Masters

of the Veil

TO GRACE!

1 !!!!....

THANKS FOR STOPPING BY!

—DAN

Spencer Hill Press

Please visit our website at www.spencerhillpress.com

First Edition: March 2012.

Cohen, Daniel A. 1989
Masters of the Veil: a novel / by Daniel A. Cohen – 1st ed.
p. cm.
Summary:
High school senior Sam Lock accidentally manifests magic for the first time during the big football game. Not only does this destroy his chances for a football scholarship, now sorcerers—both good and evil—are searching for him.

The author acknowledges the copyrighted or trademarked status and trademark owners of the following wordmarks mentioned in this fiction:
La-Z-Boy, Plexiglas, PowerPoint

Cover design by K. Kaynak

ISBN 978-1-937053-02-4 (paperback)
ISBN 978-1-937053-03-1 (e-book)

Printed in the United States of America

Masters of the Veil

of the Veil

Book One of the Veil Trilogy by

Daniel A. Cohen

SPENCER HILL PRESS

Also by Daniel A. Cohen:

The Ancillary's Mark: A Novel
Black Rose (2010)
ISBN 9781935605768

To Stephanie.
May you find happiness under every stone overturned
and along every river followed.

CHAPTER 1

Samuel Lock's fingertips pierced the soft turf up to his first knuckle. His hand, which at that moment supported his entire upper body weight, had been mummy-wrapped with strips of white tape over an array of cuts.

Like his coach always said, "The redder, the better."

The green Carver High helmet with the Grizzly logo barely muffled the screams of the seven thousand cheering fans. The stadium was only supposed to hold five thousand, but this was the championship game and a few rules had been bent. Even Channel Four's reserved portion of the field had been overrun.

As a wide receiver, Sam wasn't the captain of the team, but he might as well have been. Even though Doug was their quarterback, the team really looked up to Sam. At six foot three and two hundred pounds of human iron, Sam was made for football; it was in his blood. Not only were scouts from every major college looking at him, they were looking at him *right now*.

This game—this moment—was the culmination of his entire high school career. His team was good, very good, and he was lucky for it. As Coach DeGrella always said, "The ripest apple still goes unpicked if everyone thinks the tree's dead." This particular tree was full-on green. Right now, they had a great shot at taking the season title. That undefeated record boosted their confidence… and made the pressure all the more brutal.

Skyline High—Carver High's rivals for as far back as anyone could remember—had also come into this game with an undefeated record. Sam had spent time at their games, disguised in a dark hoodie, so he could watch how they moved. The Skyline Hornets played like their mascots—coordinated and ferocious—and they'd set the very same goal as Carver: a Championship win, whatever the cost.

Campy, hand-painted signs peppered the stands: "Lock and Load," "Lock Down the Victory," and Sam Lock's personal favorite, "Lock has the Key to my Heart." Most days he couldn't even walk down the hallway to his locker without getting a kiss on the cheek from a cheerleader—

sometimes even from Samantha Douglas. It was every high school boy's fantasy, and he was living it. Yep, between his athletic talent and his blond-and-blue-eyed good looks, he was pretty much the king of Carver High—and he had the attitude to prove it.

The only problem was the pressure—all those expectations that now piled onto Sam's shoulders.

Talk of football filled the hushed whispers during class, became a not-so-hushed roar in the cafeteria, and even the stoners who snuck away into the bathroom stalls for a smoke rambled on about Carver High's chances against Skyline.

Skyline's jerseys glared an angry yellow under the stadium lights. Sam's eyes zeroed in on the cornerback in front of him. He had to get around him, but the guy was powerful and quick, one of the best he'd come up against.

The scouts are sure getting their money's worth.

The cornerback had been keeping up with him all night, even managing to intercept a crisp pass in the first half. Sam had to do something—and quick—if he wanted to give the town something to brag about for the next year.

The giant scoreboard mocked the hometown fans in big neon numbers. With only thirty seconds left in the second half, the visiting Hornets led twenty-one to seventeen. If Curt hadn't recovered that onside kick, the game would've been over already.

The Grizzlies were in possession on their third down, forty yards from the end zone. Sam already had his route planned out. Doug would fire one of his "bullet" passes twenty yards downfield, which Sam would catch and then run out-of-bounds to stop the clock.

The cornerback is just a feather, and I am a hurricane.

"Red nineteen, red nineteen," Doug bellowed. "Set… Hut, hut, hike!"

Hard pads crunched as the titans of both teams collided. Sam took off. The muscles in his legs strained as he twisted past his opponent and looked for the open spot. The noise of the crowd faded away as his focus narrowed on getting that ball in his hands. He exploded down the field, not holding anything back. Five yards, ten… no one could catch him… fifteen… almost there… TWENTY. Planting his cleat hard into the ground, he turned just as the ball was about to reach him. He caught it with the familiarity of thousands of practices behind him. With the ball secure in his hands, he took a quick step across the sideline.

Screams erupted from the stands. Sam pointed the ball at Coach DeGrella, but that was all—it was too early for celebration. Sam would rejoice only after the win, when the clerk at the corner store would gladly misread the birthdates on the team's IDs and sell the senior players each a six-pack.

It's going to be one heck of a celebration.

2

The clock stopped with eight seconds left in the game. The Grizzlies had time for one final play. Soon enough Sam would have his victory. He would bask in the glow of affection from every girl and the envy of every guy at the school. Only twenty yards to go, and his name would live on in the tales of Carver High forever.

It was going to be so monumental that Sam could already see the statue.

Tracy Goodman's parents had already agreed that she could have as many people over as she wanted, so long as they turned in their car keys at the front door. Only twenty yards to go. Losing was not an option—not for Sam, not for the town of Stanton.

Sam's team raced down the field toward him. After a barrage of chest bumps and head slaps they huddled for the next play.

"The ball goes to Sam," Doug managed to get out between heavy breaths. "It's only right."

Most of the team nodded in agreement. Sam deserved to be the hero.

"Give it to me," the running back said. "I can do it."

"Shut your mouth, Rodney. The ball goes to Sam." Doug slapped a hand on Sam's shoulder. "Ready to make history, Lock?"

"You use that cannon to get the ball into the end zone, and I'll catch it."

Doug nodded. "What play?"

"Post on two. I'll burn him to the outside."

"Couldn't have called it better myself. BREAK."

The players took their positions on the line, warriors setting up to send fear and chaos across the line of scrimmage. The linemen scowled at their opponents with looks that said, "I will crush you like the bug you are, Hornet." Sam took his rightful place on the field as his heart raced.

This was it. The final play of the final game of the final season—until college ball, at least. Sam felt like he was submerged too far underwater, but he refused to let the pressure take over. He would push past the doubt and fear. He had to. The scouts were all watching; the fans were all hoping. If he failed...

Failure isn't an option.

Sam's legs were poised for the initial burst, all his muscles taut, ready to spring. The cornerback was close, just inches away from the line, giving Sam a menacing stare above his mask's wiring.

He's gonna stick on me like his life depends on it.

A surge built inside Sam, a bubbling that pushed energy to his extremities as though every heartbeat delivered a fresh pump of adrenaline. It was bringing out the monster in him.

Coach DeGrella would be so proud.

Energy radiated through him, pulsing outward down the field. His knees began to shake and everything looked a little too red. It felt like crap, but the intensity was just what he needed.

Here we go. Just call the snap.

The pressure held no power over the cornerback. Sam could tell by his stance. He was like a statue, holding steady, waiting to see what Sam was going to do.

Skyline had trained him well.

The noise from the stands had vanished—all Sam could hear was the wind. His heartbeat thudded against his eardrums, almost to the point of making him woozy.

Weird. Doug usually doesn't take this long to snap.

Sam checked his peripherals and saw the rest of the team poised— oddly still—but ready to pounce. Sam wondered if the pressure was getting to be too much for them as well.

His eyes moved back to the cornerback. The guy hadn't budged an inch, the intense scowl still on his face. The glaring yellow jersey flapped in the breeze, but the player didn't move in the slightest. No shifting, no scratching: it was very impressive stuff.

C'mon, Doug, what are you waiting for? Call it! Let's do it!

A few more seconds went by. Sam thought he was going to explode. He wondered if all the adrenaline was messing with his perception of time. His heartbeat was getting louder in his ears. He couldn't take it anymore. He knew he shouldn't get out of his crouch in case of a false start, but something weird was happening.

He stood up straight and surveyed his team.

Doug had his hands low, ready to take the snap, but he wasn't moving. The line in front of him just stood there, like they'd all turned to stone or something.

More pounding filled his head.

Whatever the hell was going on, it wasn't just confined to the field. He twisted around to look at the bleachers. *Like wax figurines.* Some fans had their hands covering their faces; others had outstretched fists. Lips had frozen in mid-yell. Couples clasped their palms together; people held giant foam fingers absolutely still, a few fans had stopped with cups sitting patiently at their lips—no sound and no movement at all. Everyone was just… frozen. Sam couldn't wrap his mind around it. The most important moment of the whole year… and what was happening?

The pounding in his head reached a crescendo; any more and he knew it would burst. His stomach twisted. Had the pressure actually made him go crazy?

Sam lowered into his crouch and stared back into his opponent's eyes. All signs of life had vanished. The intensity was still there, but it was like a photograph. His gaze was stuck in time.

4

Dry heaves pushed up from his gut, and his head felt like it would split at the seams. He gasped as the pounding pressure stopped, leaving the horrible sense that his skull was inflating like a balloon. He brought a hand to his helmet. "What the—"

"HIKE!"

In a flash, everything started moving again.

Life flowed back into everyone. The stadium noise returned in a crashing wave as a bulky lineman threw his weight like a sumo wrestler. The Hornets' defense slid into action, buzzing onward.

But Sam didn't budge.

What just happened? Did anyone else see that?

"Sam, RUN!"

The call snapped him out of his daze. He leapt forward, trying to get to where he was supposed to be to meet the ball.

The momentary lapse was all the cornerback needed. Sam tried to break past, but his opponent was too good, and he was ready. He stuck with Sam, who was already behind schedule.

Sam could see the spot where Doug would throw the ball. He dug deep, but he already knew it was futile. Doug was always so consistent, and the rendezvous was usually flawless.

Sam knew what was going to happen.

He dove, stretching his fingers to their absolute limits, but the ball was too far to the right. The Hornet cornerback snatched the ball out of the air, changed directions, and sprinted down the field.

Sam hadn't been fast enough. He'd hesitated. It was all over.

The gasp from the crowd made his heart sink.

Skyline's cornerback ran the ball in, broke past Carver's fullback, and scored. The buzzer sliced through the shouting from the stands, and Sam felt the shameful cloak of defeat drape his soul.

Ripping off his helmet, he rubbed his forehead with the palm of his hand. Already, boos came from the crowd. He'd disappointed the whole town.

But that can't count. Everyone froze. It doesn't count.

Skyline's team was already downfield, dancing and celebrating in Carver's end zone. The cornerback had been hoisted on his team's shoulders as they piled together and whooped.

It should have been Sam's victory. It should have been *him* spiking the ball.

He ran over to the nearest official.

"You saw that, right?"

The official frowned. "Yeah."

"What happened?"

"It's called choking." The man huffed as he turned to walk away.

The jeers and catcalls swelled from the crowd.

Sam followed after the official. "No, everyone froze up!" he yelled. "You didn't see it?"

"I saw one player freeze up, yes."

"No! It was like everyone turned into statues. You have to do something!"

"Yeah, have a stiff drink on ice and try to forget that shoddy playing I saw out there."

"NO!" Sam shook his head. "I can't be the only one who saw it!"

The official gestured to the crowd. "No, son. Judging by what I hear, the whole town saw it."

The pounding in Sam's head, along with the strange energy, started to return. He pressed a hand against his temple and squeezed his eyes shut. "Sir, you have to—"

"Go home, boy. The game's over."

Sam could feel the fire in the spectators' insults, the pain in their hearts.

Didn't anyone else see what happened?

Sam ran over to Doug. His quarterback groaned as he rubbed the skin on his cheeks.

"Doug, didn't you see that?"

Doug opened his eyes. The corners were wet, with poison lurking behind his gaze. "Don't you dare try to blame this one on me."

Sam was taken aback. "What? No, I mean, didn't you see everyone freeze?"

"It's not my fault."

"You're not listening to me. Everyone froze, I mean *everyone*. They were like statues."

Doug took his hands away from his face and glared at Sam with narrowed eyes.

"Don't you *dare* try to blame this on the team, either. You're the only one who froze up." Doug shook his head and curled his lip. "How could you choke, man? It was all about tonight."

What happened? Was I hallucinating?

"I…"

"Just get out of here." Doug scowled at him. "I don't want to be seen with you, especially when you're about to make up some lie to try and save face."

Sam looked over at the Hornets. They'd huddled together in a ring of ecstatic bodies, jumping up and down in unison.

"That's supposed to be us," Sam said.

"Well, thanks to you, it isn't."

The beating in Sam's head got stronger.

The rest of Sam's team headed toward the locker room like they were going to a wake, their heads hung low. On the sidelines, cheerleaders crammed pom-poms away and wiped glitter paint off their faces.

At the midfield sideline, Channel Four began packing up its gear. Sam rushed over to them just as they were about to put away the large camera.

"Excuse me!"

A cameraman with a goatee looked up, and then frowned in annoyance.

"You have to check the tape on that."

The man turned his back to Sam. "I expected more from you, kid."

"I swear, something crazy happened. You have to look at the tape. Everyone just stopped moving, right before the play."

The man started wrapping up cords. "That's what normally happens on the line."

Sam felt something break within him. Spit sprayed from his mouth as he yelled, "Don't you think I know what happens on the line of scrimmage?"

The man turned back around. "You really think something happened?"

Finally, he was getting through. "Yes! Please, just watch the last play."

The man picked up the camera and opened the side panel, revealing a small screen. He flipped a few switches and rewound the scene to show the last down.

"You see?" Sam asked. "Everyone just stopped moving."

The man looked at Sam with a small amount of compassion. "C'mere."

Sam moved in so he could see the little screen.

"Now watch closely," the cameraman said, "so there can be no doubt."

Sam watched as they all lined up, ready for the last down. Right as Sam got in his crouch, a tiny flash of static warped the scene. Then everything continued—at normal speed, with not even a hiccup in the time stamp. The digitized version of Sam looked around, stunned, for a moment while the game went on around him.

From the viewer's perspective, Sam had choked.

Sam didn't understand. "But, the static. It must have—"

The cameraman threw his hands outward. "Kid, you lost. Stop deluding yourself."

"I swear!" Sam yelled. "Something—"

"Hey!"

Sam turned as the Hornets' cornerback jogged up to him.

"What do you want?" Sam asked.

"You played a heck of a game, man." He reached out a hand. "Best I've been up against by far. It was a great game."

Sam stared at his hand in disgust. "No, it wasn't."

7

The cornerback retracted his hand.

Sam started to feel light. "The game's not over. Something happened."

The cornerback looked up at the scoreboard. "Looks pretty over to me."

"Sam here thinks that you guys cheated somehow," the cameraman said.

Sam felt the anger inside of him taking over. "That's not what I said."

"You calling us cheaters?"

Sam felt like he was going to explode again. "No, it's just that—"

"Whatever, man." The cornerback turned away.

The crazy energy was back. "Hold on." Sam went to grab the cornerback's shoulder.

And then the cornerback was on the ground, yelling in pain.

The stands hushed as thousands of eyes turned in their direction.

The insane energy stopped again, along with the pounding in his head. Only the screams of the cornerback, writhing on the ground in agony, broke the silence.

The Skyline coach ran up. "What the heck happened?"

Sam honestly didn't know. All he'd done was try to grab the kid's shoulder. "I… I just…"

"He hit him." The cameraman's face had gone pale.

"What? No, I—"

"You hit my player?"

Sam stared wide-eyed down at his opponent. "No, I swear, I just grabbed his shoulder and—"

"He hit him, hard," the cameraman said, "really hard."

"I didn't hit him!"

From down near his feet came more screams of pain. The cornerback whimpered and curled in a fetal ball on the grass. Blood seeped through the back of his jersey.

"Back off!" The coach scowled at Sam. "Someone call the medics!"

Sam's hands clenched into fists as he turned to the cameraman. "Why would you lie? I didn't hit him."

The cameraman held up defensive hands. "Don't hit me, too."

The muttering took on a dangerous edge.

"Loser!"

"Leave him alone!"

"How could you?"

Why do they hate me? I didn't do anything wrong!

The Skyline coach bent over his shrieking player. Blood darkened his once-yellow jersey. Sam stumbled backward and kept his hand tight against his forehead as the pounding started up again. In seconds everything had been ruined—his career, his reputation, his life.

Did I really choke? Did I really hit him? No, something weird happened. I wouldn't have...

Everyone—the fans, the players, the cheerleaders—now looked at him like he was some kind of freak. Their animosity swept over him like a tidal wave. Both teams' coaches started toward him. He had to get away. He needed space to think.

Why won't that damn pounding stop?

He grabbed the sides of his head, squeezing like a vice, but the force within his skull wasn't going away.

All he could think to do was run.

He pushed past the cameraman and ran toward the parking lot. He couldn't focus with the full drum line in his ear, but at least he could run fast. Even though his brain might be exploding, the energy filled his body—supercharging it. People jumped out of his way as he flashed through the crowd, and then past them.

Thankfully, no one followed him. At that speed, no one could. Once out of the mayhem, he ripped off his pads and put his jersey back over his t-shirt. He took a deep breath as the throbbing pressure released his cranium, but all of that extra energy drained away with it. His eyelids started getting heavy and his lips went numb.

Am I going to pass out?

He spotted his car over in the corner, sandwiched between two large pick-ups. Just seeing it inspired a bit of relief. He stumbled over and knelt down by the back door. As he dropped, he felt his whole body shutting down. He reached underneath the car and grabbed the spare key duct-taped next to the muffler. His regular set—along with his street clothes—was still in the locker room.

He stripped off the gooey white bands of tape and pulled the key free. His vision went black as he forced himself upright, and he fell against the side of the car. Sam found the unlock button on his key by sense of touch, and slid halfway down against the door before he finally found a handle and maneuvered into the back seat.

Just as he hit the doorlock button on the key, the world went away.

CHAPTER 2

The world went from black to blinding red as Bariv closed his eyes. Once the color faded, he was shown what'd happened. The scene played out behind his closed eyelids while he sat in the damp cave. The flashes made no clear picture, but the snippets revealed power—*real* power—the kind he hadn't seen since…

Bariv traced the swirls on each of his cheeks with his fingertips as he remembered his own first "hiccup." This new one's first hiccup had been much more impressive… and dangerous.

If this had been a normal case, he would've sent May a message in the traditional fashion, but Bariv didn't know when May would be back in her tower, and the boy needed her right now.

Someone else might've felt that hiccup, too.

He braced himself, and then sprinted through the wall. Shielding his eyes against the bright sun, he kept running. After a few strides, his eyes acclimated to the light.

Things on the outside were nearly the same, but the trees looked taller.

How long have I been in there?

He reached his arm skyward and wrote against the clouds.

May. The fountain, immediately.

A flick of his finger signed the emergency message.

Bariv.

His short legs didn't carry him fast enough. May was already there when he arrived, her mouth tight. People were all around, gathering rinsers, but Bariv couldn't worry about that now.

"Even I felt it." May's voice shook. "And I haven't felt one since—"

"I know."

"But what does it mean?"

Bariv reached up and touched the second-skin that covered her hand. Her eyes widened as the knowledge passed to her. "Will he be as powerful as they are?"

"Even more so."

"What if—"

"We can't think about that now. Just get to him before they do, because wherever he ends up, he's going to be extraordinary."

CHAPTER 3

Officer Gaetani had known the Lock family since Sam had been in diapers, and ever since Sam's hands had been big enough to grip the laces there'd been a ball between his fingers. Sam's old man had played pro ball back in the day, and that was all he wanted for the boy. He'd sent Sam to sports camps, worked the kid, starting in the peewee days, until he dropped, and even installed those lights in their backyard so they could run plays after the sun had gone down—all so Sam could make it.

Kid could've done it, too.

Officer Gaetani rubbed a hand across his forehead and sighed. He'd been on-duty during the game and was now glad he hadn't been there to watch the kid's worst nightmare firsthand.

Poor Sam, a slip-up like that's going to cost him everything.

In the station with Curcio and Palazzolo, he stared with hollow eyes as Channel Four News replayed that last, agonizing down of the game.

"Here it comes." Curcio's hand hovered in front of his throat. "Aaaaaand… choke!" He gripped his jugular and made a gurgling sound.

"That's enough." Gaetani frowned. "Give the kid a break."

"Look how confused he looks!" Curcio opened his eyes wide. "'Huh? What do I do? Why is everyone moving so fast?'"

"So the kid messed up." Gaetani sighed. "It's one bad move."

Palazzolo licked doughnut glaze off his fingers. "It's the worst move. Too bad for Sam. You know this town."

Gaetani *did* know. Stanton's priorities were church and football, and which was the religion and which was the pastime were often muddled. This made Sam's inaction akin to blasphemy.

"Kid's old man isn't gonna be too happy." Palazzolo wiped his mouth on the back of one hand, then inspected it for any last traces of doughnut. "Let's hope Pete doesn't hit the bottle too hard tonight… Maybe we should send a car over to the Locks' later, just in case?"

Curcio hit the side of the television with the flat of his hand. "What's with that static? This old piece of junk's got to go. Think the chief'll spring for a new one?"

"It's not the set. I think it's the feed. That thing's only a few years old."

"Gotta love two-bit reporters with one-bit equipment."

"It's not like I want to watch it again, anyway." Gaetani shook his head. "Kid's going to have a hard enough time; he doesn't need this whole town to get on his case."

Curcio wiped some dust off the screen. "Maybe he should've played some football, then. Look at that—just a deer in the headlights."

The door banged against the wall, and the stink of cheap cigars rolled in with Lieutenant McNally. "Be ready in two minutes, boys."

Gaetani frowned. "Ready for what?"

"You three are going over to the Lock house to bring Sam in for questioning."

Curcio chuckled. "I guess playing bad football actually *is* a crime in this town. I always suspected."

"I'm not kidding around," Lieutenant McNally growled. "Get going."

Curcio ran his hands over his pockets. "For what?"

"News didn't catch it, but I got a few calls saying Sam hurt a Skyline player pretty bad."

Gaetani's brows jumped to his hairline. "Sam? There's no way. Kid's brutal on the field, but he would never *deliberately* hurt anyone."

The Lieutenant tapped his wristwatch. "Time is money, and it ain't free."

Huh?

Officer Gaetani gave him a more intense look, taking in details like he would with a suspect. Something was off about the Lieutenant's eyes. Had he been drinking? Or crying? Neither seemed likely. The precinct didn't have the greatest lighting, but they did look... reddish. Strange.

"It's late. Shouldn't we let the kid get some rest and bring him in tomorrow?"

The Lieutenant's leg started to shake. "No."

Normally, the Lieutenant was a look-'em-straight-in-the-eye kind of man, but tonight he kept his gaze away from his fellow officers.

"But Lieutenant—"

The Lieutenant lifted Gaetani out of the seat by the front of his shirt. "Question me one more time, and I'll have you out of here." After an eerily intense glare, the Lieutenant released him. "I believe you're down to one minute."

Gaetani gaped at the man.

What the HELL is wrong with the Lieutenant?

The guy had just... assaulted him for asking a question! And those eyes were definitely red—and not just a bloodshot, one-too-many-sleepless-nights red. The pupils—the parts that should be black—were off.

"What're you waiting for?" Curcio tipped his head toward the door. "Let's get moving."

"Uh… sure."

"And get back ASAP. No screwing around." The Lieutenant slammed the door behind him.

Gaetani frowned. Maybe it was just a trick of the light, but eyes were not supposed to look like that. The Lieutenant had never been a violent man. Maybe he'd had some money riding on the game?

Curcio tossed Gaetani a set of keys. "You're driving."

"Fine, but that means you don't get to hassle Sam."

Curcio gave him an innocent shrug.

"On second thought, we'll take two cars."

℮

Lieutenant McNally leaned against the door of his office. Normally, he would've gone right to the second drawer and taken out a much-needed cigar, but wasn't in the mood. Nicotine was the least of his worries. He sat down at the desk and ran trembling fingertips over his eyes.

Even through his eyelids he could feel the heat radiating outward. A few minutes ago, a serious fever had given him the shaky-sweats, and now the back of his shirt was soaked. His skin felt like it was covered in tiny ants.

I felt fine this morning. Maybe it's a virus? Or food poisoning?

The fever wasn't even the worst part. An uncomfortable sensation filled his body. He couldn't describe it, but it felt prickly… unnatural.

And now to top everything off, he'd basically assaulted a fellow member of the force. Gaetani had just been asking a question.

What the hell am I doing? Why am I so angry? He rubbed a hand along his jaw. *Maybe I should take a sick day.*

He pulled a soda out of the mini-fridge behind his desk and held the cool can against his forehead. It didn't do much.

As soon as Gaetani gets back to the station, I gotta apologize to the guy.

CHAPTER 4

The loud ringing caused Sam to open his eyes. After a few moments of cloudy vision and confusion, he realized he was in his car in the school parking lot.

Did I faint? What happened?

The persistent cell phone snapped him out of his trance.

"H-Hello?"

"Where have you been?" his mother screeched.

"What do you mean? I just fell asleep for a moment in the car, I guess."

"You've been gone for three hours!"

"Three hours?"

"I must've called you fifty times! Do you know what that's like for a mother? Especially after what happened at the game. Your father is furious!"

"Tell Pop to relax, I'm awake now. I guess the game really tired me out. I fell asleep is all."

"I called all sorts of parents!" Her voice was almost a pitch only bats could hear. "I drove all over looking for you!"

"Why didn't you check the parking lot?"

"Don't you talk back to me! And now, of all things, the police are here. You have no idea how—"

Sam cut her off. "What? Why?"

"They think you hurt that player from the other team." Her voice quivered. "I told them there's no way my boy would ever hurt someone on purpose, but they're still here."

"Ma, I swear, it's all a misunderstanding."

"They want to ask you some questions."

"All I did was grab his shoulder."

"Just get back here this instant, young man!"

Sam sighed. "I'll be home soon."

He snapped his phone shut and continued squeezing until the plastic groaned.

The police? Why was everything falling apart?

Outside, only a few scattered cars remained in the lot—probably the janitorial staff cleaning up after the game. His mother hadn't exaggerated—he'd been out cold for a while.

He started to shake the groggy feeling from his head, and then groaned.

Everything's ruined.

Something moved in his peripheral vision. He twisted to get a better look.

That's it. I'm actually going crazy.

Little black swirls about the size of his palm drifted through the air. They appeared solid and floated delicately through the dark, unattached to anything, trailing in a lazy circle around the car.

Sam grasped the lever on the side of his seat and lowered the back as far as it would go. His chest thumped as he stared at the air freshener dangling from his rear-view mirror.

A few swirls passed in front of the windshield, and Sam jerked his eyes to the roof.

They'll go away in a minute. Breathe. You're just tired.

He shut his eyes and took a deep breath through his nose, exhaling through his teeth. After a dozen slow repetitions, he felt his body start to relax.

Assuring himself that he was still sane, he sat back up and examined the parking lot.

A few sweeps confirmed that the swirls had retreated into his imagination.

Giving a relieved sigh, he opened the door and stepped out into the deserted lot.

"Oh, wonderful."

His car had been trashed… literally.

While he'd been asleep, people must have walked past and shown their true colors.

Not the Grizzly green and gold.

Sam swiped at the empty soda-bottles on his roof and sent them flying across the parking lot. With a grimace, he picked off the hot dogs one by one, tossing them aside, the buzzing flies following the old meat to the asphalt. He'd hose off the globs of condiments when he got home.

Loser.

He bent down and placed a palm against the message that'd been keyed into the driver's side door.

Tonight was supposed to have been the night that he became the town hero and was whisked off by scouts for a full ride at a Division I school. It was not supposed to be the night some freaky daze came over the crowd—something only he could see. And now the police were at his house? He could be in serious trouble for something he hadn't even done.

Sam dragged a rubber trash bin over to his car. He brushed the rest of the garbage into it, and then wiped his hands on his pants, adding ketchup and mustard to the grass stains.

What the heck had happened back there? Had he just imagined the whole crowd freezing up? And what had made the cornerback drop when Sam had grabbed his shoulder? And why was he imagining little black swirly things?

Am I losing my mind?

He took the familiar route through the town's small, winding streets, and then back through the cornfields and farmhouses on near-empty roads. Two police cars, their lights dark, lined the curb in front of his house as Sam pulled into his driveway. He took a deep breath and pulled the keys out of the ignition.

"Sam!" His mother's voice made him wince. "Finally!" She flew out and embraced him. "I was so worried!" Tears flowed down her cheeks.

"I'm all right, Ma." Sam pulled out of her grip as he stepped around her and into the house. "I told you, I just fell asleep."

Three police officers—including Officer Gaetani—held coffee mugs in an awkward row on the living room couch. Sam's father overflowed the La-Z-Boy as he took long swigs of beer straight from the bottle. He didn't even look over when Sam came through the door.

"Sam," his mother whispered, "just deny everything. They can't prove that you hit that boy."

"I didn't hit him!"

The lights flickered in the hallway.

"Hush, hush." His mother patted his arm. "No matter what happens, I'll still love you and I'll always be there for you."

"Has everyone gone crazy?"

Sam pushed past his mother and went into the living room.

The police officers stood up.

"Sam."

"Officer Gaetani," Sam nodded.

"This is Officer Curcio and Officer Palazzolo."

Sam gave a slight nod to each of them before casting a look over at the La-Z-Boy.

"Hey, Pop."

His father took another long swig of the beer.

Officer Palazzolo gave a small cough.

"Right," Officer Gaetani said. "I know you probably don't want to talk about this, but we need to ask you a few things about the incident at the game."

"That's fine, but I'm telling you, something weird happened. I honestly didn't hit him. I just touched his shoulder and he fell."

"That's fine, that's fine. The thing is, though… we're going to have to take you down to the station to get your statement."

"What?" Sam's voice rose. "Why?"

"I'm sorry, son. Apparently the Skyline player is really hurt. Since you're not a minor anymore, you're just going to have to come with us and—"

"He's just a boy!" his mother said. "Can't you just talk to him here?"

"I'm sorry, ma'am, but I promise you this, I'll have him home as quick as I possibly can. You have my word on that."

"I really don't have it in me to go right now." Sam tried to keep his voice as calm as possible. "Can we maybe just do it tomorrow, after I get some sleep?"

"Sorry, it has to be now."

Sam clenched his fists and tried to hold back the scream that filled his head.

"Okay, son." Officer Palazzolo moved to the door.

"Please, can't you just let my boy get some sleep? He's only—"

Sam's father finally spoke. "Just let them take him."

"But Dad, I—"

"GET HIM OUT OF MY HOUSE!"

Sam's throat closed.

Gaetani broke the awkward silence. "Okay Sam, let's get moving, so we can have you home soon."

"Fine." Sam looked back from the front door. His mother's tears caught the light from the hallway as his father drained the last drops of his bottle.

Maybe it's a good time not to be here, after all.

Gaetani let him sit in the front of one of the cruisers. He gave Sam a sympathetic smile. "I'm sorry this happened to you. I can't imagine what you're feeling right now."

Sam stared out of the window. "If it's all the same to you, I don't really feel like talking at the moment."

Gaetani hesitated for a moment and turned on the engine. "I know you're scared, son."

"I'm not scared, and stop calling me 'son.'"

"I want to help in any way that I can. Is there anything that you want to tell me before we get to the station?"

What could he say? *Gee, Officer, some freaky voodoo happened at the game and I'm the only one it didn't affect. And my head felt like someone was hitting it with a mallet from the inside when I grabbed that guy's shoulder, but I never came close to punching him.* He wanted to scream at the world, and he wanted someone—even just one person—to believe him!

Sam said nothing.

Am I going to go to jail? No, they wouldn't put me in jail for that. Didn't anyone in the stadium see what really happened?

They reached the aging, grey police station in a matter of minutes. The other officers had pulled off the road at an all-night coffee shop, leaving just Sam and Gaetani to go in together. When Sam had been in third grade, he'd taken a tour of the department. Back then, it'd been a cause for joy—a day off from school. Now he'd rather have to re-take all his classes than face what was coming. The station house looked a lot smaller than he remembered. White paint peeled off the trim, and the wooden stairs threatened nasty splinters if he dared trip. Sam followed the officer through the metal detectors and they were buzzed through the door leading past the protective Plexiglas barrier to the rest of the station.

A stocky man came out of nowhere. "Officer Gaetani. I just wanted to apologize for what happened before. I was out of—" His jaw dropped as he stared at Sam. "It's *you*."

Sam flushed. *Guess even this guy was at the game tonight.*

"Huh?" Gaetani frowned. "Of course it's him. You asked us to bring him in."

The man's bald head shone with sweat and his eyes were totally bloodshot... no, they weren't bloodshot, just oddly red. And those hungry, red eyes drilling into him made Sam want to run.

Without a word, the man seized Sam's arm and dragged him deeper into the station.

"Sir, what are you doing?"

The Lieutenant didn't answer Gaetani. The grip on Sam's arm was cutting off the circulation.

"Lieutenant!"

"Let go of me!" Sam forced himself not to yank his arm away—he knew better than to get into an altercation with a cop.

"Sir, what are you doing?" Gaetani trailed behind them. "This is entirely inappropriate."

"Flathand," the Lieutenant grunted.

Isn't this illegal?

Gaetani clenched his fists. "I'll be right back, Sam."

Trickles of apprehension ran down Sam's neck.

What's this guy's problem?

"What happened to innocent until proven guilty?" Sam asked as the Lieutenant pulled him down the dim hallway. Stopping in front of a door, the gruff man finally let go of him long enough to reach into his pocket for a key ring. He pushed Sam forward into the dark room. Once he'd hit the switch, the lights revealed a few paper-littered desks and a row of cells along the back wall. The Lieutenant shoved Sam into one of the iron-barred rooms, equipped with a lidless toilet and a brown-stained cot with no sheets.

"What are you doing?" Sam asked.

The Lieutenant closed the metal gate. His weird, red eyes… glowed. A cold shiver of fear ran through Sam.

Am I seeing things again?

The Lieutenant twisted the key in the lock and turned to the door.

"Hey!" Sam banged on the bars. "Let me out! I didn't do anything! I swear, I didn't hit him! Just let me out!"

After the soft clink of metal, Sam heard only silence.

CHAPTER 5

O fficer Gaetani stared at the door. *What the heck's going on with the Lieutenant?* First, Lieutenant McNally had put his hands on a fellow officer—which truthfully wasn't all that bad—but then he'd assaulted the kid without reason. No reading of rights, no nothing.

Totally out of line.

The Lieutenant had always gone by the book, never leaving so much as a scrap of paper out of an evidence file. Harassing Sam like that? Gaetani hated to report him to the Chief, but—

A loud buzzing came from the front door. Late-night arrivals usually were drunken students looking for a place to crash instead of driving home—which in a small town like Stanton was perfectly acceptable, actually encouraged. He passed around the metal detectors and opened the door.

His eyes widened at the beautiful woman dressed in an elegant, tailored suit. Long, dark hair cascaded over her shoulders and her green eyes radiated intelligence. "What a fine station you have here. Very quaint."

Officer Gaetani furrowed his brow. "Thanks, Miss…?"

"*Agent.*" Her smile broadened as she held up a badge—gold, with an eagle on top. *Federal Bureau of Investigation.* The black leather holder also included her picture on an official-looking ID card. Her other hand remained buried deep in her pocket. "Agent Greenford. And you are?"

It took him a moment to respond. "Officer Gaetani."

"First FBI agent you've run into?"

He nodded and gulped. "This is a small town. We've never had any need for the FBI… at least not since I've been here."

"Yeah, we get that a lot. You'd be surprised what goes on in some small towns." She stood on her tiptoes and peeked over his shoulder. "May I come in?"

"Of course." He gave a sheepish smile.

"Thank you." Her heels clicked on the linoleum floor. "I understand that a young man named Samuel Lock is in your custody. Is that correct?"

"How did you know that? He just arrived."

She turned and flashed him a coy smile, and his cheeks reddened for asking.

"I'm afraid he has to come with me now."

"What? Why?"

Her playful look said, "Have you never heard of the FBI before?"

Gaetani almost smacked himself in the forehead. "Right."

"Now, where is he?"

"I actually don't know. Lieutenant McNally just took him somewhere. I'm actually glad you're here. The Lieutenant is acting strange. Maybe seeing some brass will set him straight."

She frowned. "Strange, how?"

"I don't know. Angry? And not following procedure. And his eyes look really—"

"Red?"

"Yeah, how'd you know?"

"Take me to him."

Now the FBI's involved? How bad did Sam hurt that kid?

Lieutenant McNally's eyes flashed up as Gaetani opened his office door. "We don't have the faintest idea where he—I have to go." He slammed the phone back on the desk. "Officer Gaetani, you know better than to come in without knocking!"

So much for Lieutenant McNally's "open door" policy.

"And who is she?"

"Agent Shelly Greenford of the FBI." Gaetani stressed the Bureau's initials.

"What the hell does the FBI want?"

Agent Greenford gave the Lieutenant a long look. "Sam Lock has to come with me."

"Sorry. That can't happen." Lieutenant McNally turned his attention to a pile of papers on his desk.

"I apologize, but this is not up for discussion. Sam will be coming with me tonight. I am sorry if this—"

"HE'S STAYING!" Spit flew out of the Lieutenant's mouth with each syllable.

"Sir." Gaetani tried to keep his voice calm, "This is the FBI we're dealing with. Now where is Sam?"

"He will remain exactly where he is!" The Lieutenant jumped up and shoved the desk out toward them. In a swift motion, he pulled his gun out of the holster and raised it toward Agent Greenford. His hand shook, and fear filled his eyes.

Gaetani froze in disbelief—his boss had a gun directed at a federal agent—while the woman smiled at the Lieutenant as he stood there armed, red-faced, and quivering. Greenford's hand twitched inside her jacket pocket and the gun dropped to the floor. Her hand twitched again and the Lieutenant fell back into his seat, which gave a loud creak of protest. He struggled in place as if bound by invisible ropes.

"Lieutenant, if you could please tell me where the young man is located. I'm on a tight schedule."

"You won't find him in time. All I have to do is wait a few more minutes."

"Less time than I thought," she muttered to herself.

"A few more minutes?" Gaetani whipped his gaze from one to the other. "What are you two talking about?"

The Lieutenant gave a smug smile and his eyes glowed even redder.

Greenford took a deep breath and did something with her pocketed hand. The Lieutenant went rigid and his jaw muscles twitched.

"Now." The woman's voice filled with iron. "I'll ask you once more. Where is Sam Lock?"

The Lieutenant gave a dry heave and moaned.

"A little louder, please."

"C-Cellblock D."

"Cellblock D?" Gaetani repeated. "That's only for *real* criminals. We haven't had to use that area in years."

"Do you have the keys?"

"Um… yes, I think so."

"Take me there."

"Sure, but what about—"

"Now, please." An urgent edge belied her calm words. The agent trailed him as he left the room. "I think running would be best."

He wasn't going to argue. "What happened back there?"

The agent kept up as he ran. "It's a secret government weapon. Classified. Civilians don't have access to knowledge about it yet."

Fair enough.

Gaetani pulled up in front of a door with no window.

"Keys." She nodded towards the door, an eager look in her eyes.

"Right." He brought out his key ring. It had been a long time since they'd used this particular cellblock; Stanton hadn't had a truly dangerous criminal in a while.

Why stuff Sam in here? It makes no sense.

He tried the rusty silver key, but it didn't quite fit. He studied the key ring and rifled through the assortment, trying to jog his memory.

Agent Greenford pushed the door open and shrugged. "Looks like he forgot to lock it."

They found Sam in the back cell.

"Sam Lock?" Greenford placed a hand on one of the bars.

"Yeah."

"Sam, you need to come with me."

"Where?"

"Somewhere safe. Don't worry, you're not in trouble, and there will be plenty of time for questions later. But if we don't get you out of here now, there could be serious consequences. You just have to trust me." She turned to Officer Gaetani. "Open the cell."

Gaetani picked through the ring, but before he could make his decision, Agent Greenford had the cell door wide open.

What the—?

Sam bolted from the cell. "Thanks. I needed to get out of there. It's been a tough night."

Agent Greenford placed a gentle hand on Sam's forearm. "You poor boy. I can only imagine. But soon you'll be out of the dark. Just know that you've done nothing wrong."

Relief washed across Sam's face. "Good to know at least one person believes me."

"Follow me." She moved surprisingly fast for a woman in heels. Greenford stopped short as they reached the front door. She turned toward Gaetani and smiled.

"Officer Gaetani, the Bureau thanks you for your cooperation."

"The Bureau? As in the FBI?" Sam asked.

"Later," she said. "Now follow me."

"It was nice to meet you, Shelly—I mean, Agent Greenford."

"The pleasure was mine." Then Agent Greenford snapped the fingers hidden in her pocket, and Officer Gaetani's mind went blank.

CHAPTER 6

"Okay." Sam followed the mystery woman past the parked patrol cars and across the lawn. She had an elegance that Sam hadn't really seen before. Probably in her early thirties, she moved with the grace of a dancer. "What's going on?"

"There's no time for long explanations. I'm sure you've been through a lot tonight, but just know that you're not alone, and there is nothing wrong with you."

"What does that mean? And why do I feel like I can trust you?"

"Because," she tossed him a quick look over her shoulder, "you're with one of your own now."

"One of my own? What's 'my own?'"

"I promise I'll explain everything once you're safe."

"Please, just tell me that I'm not going crazy."

"You're not. Just the opposite, in fact—you're about to see things as they really are."

She led him into the woods. Sam pulled in his questions with a heavy sigh; she wasn't going to give him answers until she was ready to give them. The moon cast ghostly shadows among the trees, giving enough light for him to avoid smashing his face into one of the branches.

Why does she always keep that hand in her pocket?

"So, your name is Agent Greenford?"

She stopped and turned to him. "No."

"But that's what he called—"

"I had to lie to get you out. I am not a member of the FBI. My name is May." She extended her free hand. "It's nice to meet you, Sam."

"Nice to meet you, too. Is there any chance I could have those answers now?"

"We're almost there. Just be patient and I'll explain everything."

She moved deeper into the trees, stopping in front of a mound of giant palm tree leaves about the size of a car.

She pulled at the leaves, and they came off in one piece, revealing something that looked like a giant anvil. The whatever-it-was had the dull grey luster of an old nickel, along with two doors like a car, but the front end was pointed and, having no wheels, it sat flat against the earth.

"What is that thing?"

"Trust me when I say that you are so very close to being safe. Just hop in and I'll explain anything you want to know while we go."

"But how does it move?"

"Please." Desperation tinted her voice. "Just trust me."

Sam opened the door on the passenger's side. The inside had no windows, no steering wheel, no... anything, but at least the seats had armrests. The interior glowed with a soft light that allowed him to see the beautiful artwork on the doors, ceiling, and what should have been the dashboard. The scenes depicted farmers working on huge fields with animals beside them. Sam didn't recognize the creatures, which looked vaguely horselike and towered above the farmers.

He sank into the seat, which was infinitely more comfortable and less pungent than the cot in the cell. It even accommodated his size. May took the other seat and made some motion with her pocketed hand. The lines where the doors met the sides melded together and sealed tight, leaving smooth metal. A tiny light hovered above their heads, but it wasn't attached to anything; it just floated there like a big firefly.

"Why are we sitting in here? And how is that light doing that?"

"Soon, Sam. Just hold on, we have to get out of here."

"How are we going to see where we're going?"

"We don't have to." She finally took her hand out of her pocket and Sam's eyes widened. Stretched across her hand was some sort of glove, but it was like no glove he'd ever seen before. It had the texture of a diamond, yet it flowed with her fingers like silk and caught the light with its tiny, iridescent facets.

"Nice glove."

She moved her fingers back and forth. "It's called a second-skin."

"Why?"

"Well, before I can explain the more advanced aspects, I have to tell you the basics. You see—"

The vehicle shook as if a wrecking ball had struck the outside. Sam clutched the arms of his seat to keep from being thrown from it.

"They've found us." May's eyes widened as the blood drained from her cheeks. "We're out of time."

Sam furrowed his brow at the windowless walls. "Who found us?"

Another violent impact slammed him back into his chair.

"The Tembrath Elite."

"Um, who?"

"Hold on tight, Sam. We have to get under. Now!"

"Under?" He tightened his grip on the soft armrest. "Under what?"

She thrust her gloved hand into a side compartment. Sam's gut rose into his throat as his chair dropped beneath him.

Huh? But we're on solid ground!

May closed her eyes and took a long breath.

Bone-crushing force shoved Sam back against his seat. It felt like a missile launch.

May finally let out a relieved sigh. She pulled back her gloved hand and the pressure lifted, allowing Sam to sit back up in his seat. He rotated his shoulders and stretched out his back.

"We're not out of the woods yet. But as of now, it is out of my hand." She gave Sam a wry smile. "Let's just hope they don't catch up. They shouldn't, though, since no one's as good as I am at this particular skill."

"Okay, this is getting a little too strange. What's going on? I've really lost it, haven't I?"

"Magic is real," May stated matter-of-factly.

Sam gave her a blank stare. "Excuse me?"

"Basics, remember. As far as we're concerned, that's as basic as it gets."

Sam blinked a few times before answering. "You *are* joking, right?"

"Magic is real." She grinned. "That's your first lesson. Trust me, the next lessons will be much more in-depth, but they'll make the first lesson real for *you*."

Sam slumped back down in his chair. "So I'm not the only one who's lost his marbles, then?"

"Hey." She raised her eyebrows. "You're the one who made an entire crowd of people freeze."

Sam's brows furrowed. "What do you mean, *I made* that happen?"

"Congratulations, you've had your first hiccup."

"Hiccup?"

May tapped a finger against her lips. "You know, you're right. It was much more than a hiccup. *Grip* is probably more accurate."

Sam paused. "Huh?"

"Magic... you grip it." She flexed her gloved fingers. "We say gripping, although really you can grip it, push it, twirl it, caress it, manipulate it, drape it. And of course by 'it' I mean 'Her', but we're getting ahead of ourselves."

Sam squeezed his eyes shut and wondered when he'd wake up from this dream. "Riiiiight. Magic. Absolutely."

"I assure you, this is very real."

"And currently we are traveling...?"

May touched the wall of the vehicle with her gloved hand and tilted her head. "Underground."

"Of course, underground." He threw his hands up.

She looked at him with a playful grin. "Once we hit the ocean, we're going to speed up a bit, but we still have a long trip ahead of us. If you would like, I can explain a whole lot in that time. Or, you can stay in denial, with no answers." She pointed up and the hovering light flickered. "In the proverbial dark. Your choice."

Sam sat back in his seat and let out a deep breath.

"Okay." He was too tired to fight against whatever hallucination he was having. "Explain away."

"Excellent choice. So, like I said, magic is real. However, it takes a lot to understand and use, and you won't be proficient unless you work excruciatingly hard. But I promise, every headache, every sore muscle, every long night of practice is worth it. It is layer upon layer of unfathomable glory, every flake a miracle."

With that, she took her gloved hand and placed it on his naked one. A strange tingling traveled up his arm as she squeezed. When she removed her hand, the white tape had melted off his hand, and all the scrapes and cuts from playing football were gone.

Sam looked at his smooth fingers, and then turned wide eyes to May.

This can't be real. I've gotta be dreaming. Either that, or he would shortly be needing a psych ward. He'd play along until he woke up. "How?"

"I've been studying for a long time, longer than most."

Time to start the charade.

He put on his most perplexed look and played along. "But you're so young."

She shook her head with a knowing half-smile. "I'm much older than I look. You will learn that, where we are going, looks can be most deceiving. By the way, most people feel the same when they find out. Unfortunately, you had to find out in a different way than most. I'm terribly sorry it had to happen this way."

Sam rolled his eyes. "This can't be real."

"If that's what you need to believe, that is completely acceptable. All I ask is that your 'dream-self' keep an open mind."

Sam snorted. "Whatever."

"Good."

"So where are we going, oh wise figment of my imagination?"

"That," she flicked her index finger, "is going to be a surprise, a place I don't want to insult by trying to use words to describe it."

Sam touched the image of a horse-like creature with a long furry tail in the painting next to him. "So if magic is real, how do you do it?"

"It's not so much that you do it, it's more that you use it. Magic is a wonderful thing, but tales of magic in your world don't quite capture what it truly is. Where it comes from, in our society, we call the Veil."

Sam absentmindedly cracked his knuckles. "Why the Veil?"

"You will learn that magic, or rather, what you *perceive* as magic, lies all around us like a blanket that we cannot see, but some can feel and even use it. We do not know why only some can access it and others cannot, and we assume we will never know, as we have tried for so long to figure it out. The world would be such a better place, for everyone, if all could use the Veil, but it just can't happen. In our society, some things," her face turned serious, "are just not to be tampered with."

"Don't worry, I won't tamper." Sam humphed. "How can I tamper with something that isn't real?"

"Never mind that. What you will find interesting is that you are able to access the Veil."

"You're telling me that's what happened at the game?"

Sam suddenly became aware that he was still wearing his football jersey. So much had happened, yet he had still not been able to change into regular clothes. This dream was too vivid, the details too precise.

"That was the first time you were able to access the Veil, and with it, the wondrous properties and infinite possibilities it holds. Usually, the first hiccup is triggered by an intensely powerful emotion. In your case, I'm assuming it was the desire to win the game."

Sam was beginning to feel unnerved. This was getting too real. *But it can't be, can it?*

"But if this happens to everyone the first time, why have I never heard of anything like this happening before? It seems to me that thousands of people simultaneously freezing in place would be a pretty big deal."

May looked him up and down. "So, you're not *all* brawn."

Sam gave a coy smile. "Okay, I'm going to put logic on hold for a minute and play along. Explain."

"You see," she began, "most of our kind—"

"You mean wizards?" Sam asked in the most sarcastic tone he could muster.

"If you must, we prefer 'sorcerers.'"

"Wait, why?"

"Because magic comes from a *source*."

Sam paused. "Are you serious?"

"You see," she started again, not confirming or denying, "most of our kind come *from* our kind. Two sorcerers," she smiled, "always produce a child who will be capable of accessing the Veil. It is a strange phenomenon when two flathands produce someone with abilities."

"Flathands? The Lieutenant called Officer Gaetani that," Sam said. "What's it mean?"

May flexed her gloved hand.

Sam let out a small sigh. "Right, gripping."

"We have a way of tracking these hiccups. Actually, we have a person, and you will study with him. His name is Bariv."

Sam gave her a skeptical look. "What kind of name is Bariv? Russian?"

"Names have existed for a very long time and many are forgotten. But just because they are forgotten does not mean they don't exist. In our society you will find many names that are unique. Normally, when Bariv feels the hiccups of new sorcerers, they are quite small. Things like making objects change color, or moving small amounts of water just by thinking it. We then offer to help these young people grow into their gift, but like I said, it is quite rare for new sorcerers to spring up. You are sort of a first."

"But I thought you said flathands, or whatever, *can* have magical children."

"Not a first for that. A first for what you have done."

Sam raised an eyebrow.

"You seem to have tapped into an extraordinary amount of the Veil for your first time. You made thousands of people literally stop moving, prisoners in their own bodies. It's something not even I can do."

Sam tried to hold back a smile. He could feel the hilarity of the situation bubbling up in his chest. "So what are you saying? That I'm some sort of super-sorcerer?"

"No." She shook her head. "I'm saying that you could be great if you want to be. Gripping the Veil while unfocused and unlearned is dangerous, and it can start something awful. One must work to control the power that comes from it."

Sam sighed. "Can I just wake up, already?"

"I could pinch you, but I doubt it would do anything other than sting."

Sam took a deep breath and let his muscles relax. He squeezed his eyes shut and smoothed his eyebrows with his thumb and forefinger. "So, are we flying? Does this machine, like, blast away the dirt and then float through the crevice?" The question sounded absurd to him as soon as it was asked.

"If that was the case, we would have been caught by now."

Sam rapped the metal door a few times with his knuckles. "I didn't realize my subconscious was so cryptic."

"I will tell you something concrete then." She stared at her glove. "There are three types of magic that come from the Veil. There are natural magics," she waved her hand through the air, "mystical magics, and power magics. Every sorcerer has an aptitude for one of these disciplines and they usually choose to study that path. I excel at natural magics: things that have to do with the world around us, born of this Earth, not from the minds of men. I have used my talent and mixed it with this technology to create a path for us underground. Things like dirt, roots, and rock are bending themselves to allow us passage to where we are going. They are closing after we pass so as not to leave a trace of where we have been."

30

"Of course." Sam rolled his eyes again, turning away from May in the process. For the next few minutes, the only sound in the vehicle was the groaning from the metal walls. "So what kind of magic will I be doing?" Sam's low voice just barely broke the silence.

May continued in the same jovial tone as before. "That remains to be seen, but I have a pretty good idea. It—"

Sam interrupted with a sharp exhale. "This is ridiculous."

All of a sudden, the light above them flickered and then turned blue.

"Ah!" she exclaimed. "We are past the protective borders. I think we have some breathing room. For now, at least."

She stuck her gloved hand back in the compartment and Sam felt the vehicle decelerate and begin to rise.

Then, with a loud thump and a jolt, they hit the ground.

"Here we are. Take a step outside and get a good look." She bit her bottom lip and then gazed at the painting on the roof of the vehicle. "I wish I could go back to *my* first look. Just remember, it only happens once. And whether or not you think you're dreaming, I would advise drinking in every detail."

Sam started picking the dirt out from under his fingernails. "Whatever you say."

The lines appeared around the doors again, and Sam grabbed the handle and stepped out into the sunlight. The first thing he noticed, other than the bizarre change from night to day, was how soft the grass was, like a giant green pillow under his feet. The view was incredible—a vast expanse of lush greens and clear blue streams that flowed through a thick valley.

This belongs on a postcard, he thought. *I have a beautiful imagination.*

"You're right." Sam gave a satisfied nod. "This is pretty spectacular."

She chuckled. "Sam, you're looking the wrong way. That's just our backyard."

He slowly turned around, and his jaw dropped. In front of him was a truly unbelievable sight. *Actually* unbelievable, and that was when it hit him.

He wasn't dreaming.

What lay before him was all the proof he needed, as his imagination was far too weak to produce what his eyes saw.

Magic is real.

Monstrous pillars of sandstone—each hundreds of feet high and half a football field thick—Sam counted twelve in all. They were almost uniform in shape, though different capstones created slight variations between them. One had a giant looping hole through the top—like a colossal sewing needle—another had a three-pronged tip, and one had protruding rungs.

Beneath the towers were more colorful foliage than Sam had ever seen. Continuing all the way to the giant rocks were flowers, trees, and bushes of all different hues. He looked at the treetops and saw all sorts of leaves: some were square in shape, others glowed neon red, even some blue ones that were so large they blanketed the other trees around them. It was another world; it couldn't have been the same one he had been living in his entire life.

A path in front of them meandered along toward the stones.

"Let's get moving." May took off her shoes and massaged her toes into the soft grass. "We have a little bit of a walk ahead of us."

"Wait." Sam's lungs weren't filling correctly; it was becoming harder to breathe. "This… this is real, isn't it?"

She put a hand on his shoulder and nodded. "Take your time. I know it must be difficult. But remember, this is a good change."

He leaned over and put his hands on his knees. A bout of nausea struck him hard as the world began to spin. His breathing became rapid and shallow. "I… this…"

"Here." Her tone was quiet and soothing. "A gift."

Sam couldn't see what she did, but something came over him. It started at the top of his head and made its way down through his body. It was gentle and calming, like a warm bath being poured over him. Once the sensation reached his toes, the anxiety vanished, replaced by a sense of peace, tranquility, and lastly, acceptance. All his cares melted away and he was left with wonder. Just like that, he was ready to see what lay ahead of him, magic and all.

He stood back up and rotated his shoulders. "What did you just do to me?"

"The Veil can be wonderful, can't She?" May's face gravitated toward the sun. "How do you feel?"

He took a deep breath of air through his nose and exhaled slowly through his mouth. The air felt fresh and clean. "Amazing. Kind of excited."

"I'm sorry to say that this is not a cure, only a bandage. Over the years, you build up walls against things you can't understand. That's why youth is the easiest time for the surreal to be accepted. Normally, sorcerers have their first hiccup when they are small, making the transition into our society quite enjoyable. Unfortunately, you already have quite the fortress, Sam. Let's just say I have provided you with a temporary ladder, but it won't last. You will have to learn to accept this on your own. But in the meantime, you need sleep, and this will help."

"Forget sleep." Sam's eyes shot to May's glove. "Magic is real. This is great!"

May smiled and took Sam's hand in hers. "I'm glad you think so! Just try to hold onto that feeling as long as you can. Remember, once your mind reaches a destination, it can always go back, even if it has to take a different path."

Sam's heart was pounding in his chest. "This is amazing. Show me some more magic."

She let go and turned toward the pillars. "Why don't we let the Veil show you?"

She started down the path, delicately holding her shoes, as Sam trotted behind.

"What is this place?"

"We call it Atlas Crown. It is one of many magical communities. This happens to be the one I call home."

Sam looked at the pillars again and thought that the name fit perfectly.

"Something that you should understand," May led him from open space to woods, "is that in places where the Veil is tapped, and magic is frequently used—or where large amounts of the Veil are utilized—amazing things happen."

Sam's eyes made a quick adjustment to the lesser light squeezing through the dense canopy. After a moment, he could make out a group of trees that had large, round fruit hanging from vines like tetherballs.

May twisted her head back and forth until she found what she was looking for.

"Ah!" She thrust her finger toward a colorful patch of forest sandwiched between two mounds of dirt. "Perfect example."

They tromped a few feet off the path. May had pointed toward things that looked uncannily like flowers, but could not be. Their tops were about waist high and culminated in what looked like little red faces with petals for hair. Swirling white spots took the place of eyes, and yellowish beaks protruded from where the mouths would have been.

"These are symflowers. They're not hard to find because of one certain characteristic."

"What, the fact that they have beaks?"

May chuckled, holding her gloved hand over one of them. Her fingers tilted inward and a small amount of water drizzled from her hands onto one of the petals. Immediately, the flower's beak opened and let out a low note, melodic and smooth. She moved her hand over another, and the new flower let out a higher note that perfectly harmonized with the first. She moved from flower to flower, until it sounded almost like a barbershop quartet. After kissing the flowers with small droplets, which prompted a few quarter-notes, May took her hand away and the music died down.

"When it rains, the forest comes alive with music. My favorite is a very light drizzle—it almost sounds like jazz."

Sam's jaw went slack. He felt giddy, like when he'd scored his first touchdown as a child.

33

"You see," May used a gloved finger to stroke the side of the symflower, which let out a warm purr, "this whole place is full of fantastic things. The more magic is used, the more extraordinary things spring out of the Veil. With so many sorcerers living here, there's always plenty of excitement."

Sam ran his own finger along the closest petal, but the flower remained silent. "I bet."

"Let's keep moving." She stepped over a few roots and made her way back onto the path. "There will be plenty to see on the way back, and you'll probably want to be getting some sleep soon."

"No, I want to see—" He cut himself off. In fact, exhaustion was coming quick. "Yeah, I guess you're right."

"Tapping into the Veil and using magic can be taxing, especially for the first few months. It's like running a marathon; you have to train for it. I'm surprised you didn't pass out immediately after the game."

Sam nodded. "I sort of did."

"Don't worry. I have a room all set up for you."

They continued their trek for a few silent minutes.

"Why, hello there!" May addressed a group of trees on the side of their path like they were old friends. She turned to Sam, her cheeks pinched with delight. "You'll like these!"

She pointed at the thin, zebra-striped trees beside them. "They're called zigzag trees. They don't like to be touched; go ahead and try."

"Why? What will they do?"

"Just trust me. Go on."

He slowly reached out for the tree. Just as his fingers were about to make contact, it bent backwards out of the way.

Sam startled. He tried again to touch the zigzag tree, but this time at a lower spot. The tree curled into a C-shape and again avoided his touch. Sam turned his back nonchalantly, and then suddenly rocketed at the tree as if he were going to tackle it. The zigzag split apart and Sam fell right through.

May laughed as Sam pushed himself off the ground and the tree sucked itself back together.

"They *really* don't like being touched." May winked.

Sam snorted. "Apparently not."

May tilted her head to the side, the tip of her nose giving the smallest of twitches. "Are you hungry?"

"Starved." He laid a hand on his stomach. "Do you have any food on you?"

"No." She spun Sam around. "But they do."

A pack of animals came into view. They were small and looked like black sheep. They travelled in a tight pack, reminding Sam of a small thundercloud. Each animal had three horns and a snakelike tail that twirled as they marched.

"Drecklers." May ambled over to the flock so as not to startle them, and pulled out a few tuffs of the wool-like material from the stragglers of the group. The black substance came out very easily and they didn't seem to mind.

She came back and held out her hand. "Here, eat."

Sam accepted the handful of black material and took a test bite. It was surprisingly chewy, with a consistency like licorice, but it was sweet, like chocolate. After the first delicious swallow he took a much heartier portion and the pains in his stomach quickly subsided.

"This is fantastic." His words came out sloppily in between chews.

"Dreckler cotton. It is a great sweet. Very common after-meal top-off."

Sam shoved another large chunk of cotton into his mouth. "And the drecklers don't mind you taking it?"

"They actually prefer it. Too much cotton and they get itchy."

Sam dashed toward the pack of drecklers—earning him a couple of nasty bleats—and took a few more handfuls of their cotton, which he stored in the thigh pad pockets on his pants. The cotton came out easily, without any effort at all.

After re-joining May, he gave a shrug.

She smiled. "Don't worry. You'll find plenty of it in town."

Continuing along the trail, May pointed out bushes that changed color depending on the mood of whoever passed, and gnarled vines covered in green flames, each twisting their way up various tree trunks— which May explained didn't actually hurt the tree, because the flame only gave off light, not heat.

"What are those?" Sam pointed over May's shoulder.

She turned around and then stepped back in line with Sam.

Not far off, the air was cloudy with a swarm of insects. Sam thought they might be bees, but they looked smaller, more the size of fireflies. Hundreds of them flew in their direction.

"Don't move," May whispered through still lips, having already taken her own advice.

Sam froze as the buzzing grew louder.

"Why not?" he asked softly out of the corner of his mouth.

"Echo flies. Just stay calm, do as I say, and watch."

The swarm moved closer, traveling together in tight-knit swirls. They stopped just inches shy of his face. Sam tried his best to stand completely still. Individual echo flies were uniform in color—either black, white, or grey—including their eyes. The echo flies twirled around his face, re-grouped about a yard in front of him, and started pulsating inward. Each pulse caused the group to get into a smaller and tighter formation. Certain flies came together to create distinct shapes and shadows. He first saw a nose and then eyes and then hair. After a few more throbs,

Sam was looking at himself, or at least a black and white portrait hanging in the air.

The mirror image of his face was not only the right size and shape, he could feel that it was more than an image. The flies had captured the depth of his eyes and his inner emotion. It was incredible, a truer reflection than just looking at a shiny surface.

May's voice was just above a whisper. "Now try them out."

"Try them out how?" Sam tried his best to speak through a closed mouth, but he couldn't keep his lips from moving. The black and white doppelganger mouthed the same thing he did.

He couldn't help but smile.

As his lips curled, so did the echo flies'.

Then, as quickly as they had come, they broke form and vanished off into the brush, flying in single file.

"That was incredible!"

"That was befitting, too."

"What do you mean?"

"Well," May rubbed her hands together, "that's another aspect of the Veil that I need to explain. Actually, the echo flies couldn't have picked a better time to show up. You see, not everything that comes out of the Veil is… nice."

Sam looked off in the direction the flies had gone. "So the echo flies are bad?"

"No, no, I wouldn't go as far as saying they're *bad*, it's just that with some of Her gifts, you have to be careful. It is rare, almost unheard of, for something truly malevolent to spring from the Veil here. You see, Atlas Crown, along with every other sorcerer community, is an all-inclusive deal, and most of what the Veil gives us is meant to help. We need nothing from the outside world because of what the Veil provides. Food, shelter, clothing, and even entertainment are found within. They are gifts. The drecklers and symflowers are just the tip of the iceberg. You see—"

"So where do these echo flies come in? The entertainment?"

"No." May flashed a mischievous smile and twirled a finger. "They are the vigilantes of the woods."

Sam stared, blank-faced.

"You didn't happen to see their stingers, did you?"

"No, they kind of looked like ordinary flies to me." He pulled out another tuft of dreckler cotton and shoveled it into his mouth. "Okay, maybe 'ordinary' isn't the best word, but all the same."

May's ungloved hand ran over the diamond-like covering on the other one, hovering around her wrist for a moment. "There are animals called Irukandji jellyfish. They are about the size of a fingernail. Irukandji are extremely venomous and can cause all sorts of nastiness for their victims."

Sam's words were sloppy and wet, his mouth still full. "Those jellyfish came from the Veil?"

"No, from Australia." A smirk played across her face.

"So what do they have to do with the echo flies?"

"Think Irukandji in the air. But, unlike the Irukandji—which can die from even the smallest impact—echo flies are not easily killed. The echo flies have a hard exoskeleton and live in very large swarms. They police the forest as best they can."

Sam bent down to examine a patch of twinkling, furry moss growing on the side of a rock. "How so?"

"They can see through you."

Sam cocked his head. "Like, to my organs and stuff?"

"No, they can see *through* you. They don't just mimic your appearance. They decide whether or not they see you as worthy. Once they decide your fate, they will either move with you or—"

Sam stood up. "Worthy of what?"

May smiled.

"What?"

"Using the Veil." She turned and started walking, her heels clacking together in her hand. "Come. We are getting close."

She strode toward the pillars and brushed away a few silver strands hanging down from a tree just off the path.

Sam trailed close behind. "So, you would have let them sting me?"

"Of course not. I would never have let them harm you. I could have easily kept them away."

"So, why didn't you?" Sam stepped over a frog-like creature with tiny puffed-up throat sacs surrounding its entire head like a mane.

"Lion frog," May called out, as if she had read his mind. "Watch their feet, they can stick to almost anything."

Sam was determined not to drop the subject. "So, why didn't you just keep them away? Better safe than sorry, right?"

May stopped in a beam of sunlight filtering its way through the treetops.

"Because," she gave a toothy smile, "I was curious, and I am not an echo fly."

Sam snorted. "So I passed."

"You didn't fail. However, it wasn't a test so much as an assessment. But don't worry, Bariv will have plenty of tests for you."

Sam sighed. "Oh, joy."

May smiled serenely. "I see my gift is starting to wear off. I'm sure sleeping would do you a world of good right about now."

"Agreed." Although the excitement was starting to fade, he wasn't feeling panicked like before—but he did really want to sleep.

"By the way," she gestured in front of them, "we're just about there."

A giant stone monolith filled the end of their path. Along the sides of the pillar, a stone wall reached as high as a goal post. The wall sprawled along into the forest, brush and trees growing right up against it with no obvious openings. Layers of sand rested upon the weathered ledges cut into the rock. Reaching the wall, Sam ran his finger against a crack in the stone. Where his finger touched, the rock became translucent, and for a sliver of a second Sam caught a tiny glimpse of a white room behind it.

He opened his hand and placed it against the rock. When he took it back, he could see through a palm-shaped window just long enough to make out a black door leading out of the room to some hidden destination.

Sam humphed.

"It's something the sorcerers did a long time ago."

"How long?"

May tilted her head for a moment and looked up.

"Very long."

The hair on the back of Sam's neck stood up. He could feel eyes on the back of his jersey, he was sure of it.

He quickly twisted around, only to find an empty path. Scanning the woods for any sign of life, the only thing he found was a lion frog hopping into the brush.

"You and that frog have something in common," May said.

"Hmm?"

"You're both a little jumpy."

"Very funny, but I could have sworn something was behind us."

"You have no reason to be alarmed. The higher-ups and I have taken precautions against the undesirable."

Sam focused his attention back on the glass rock.

"So how do we get in?"

May placed her glove against the stone.

A section of the rock shattered, forming an oval-shaped opening big enough for both of them. May went inside first and beckoned him to follow. Sam stepped in behind her, careful of the edges.

May laughed. "Trust me, Sam, you won't break it."

May waved her diamond-coated hand in the direction of the makeshift doorway. The shards of rock reformed themselves and sealed shut with a kissing sound that reminded Sam of fish sucking the surface of a pond.

The room was pure, unbroken white except for the black door. Sam went over and found no handle. He put his shoulder against the door, but just as he was about to push, May stopped him.

"We will go into town tomorrow. For now, you must get some sleep."

"Here?" Sam asked, looking around. He had slept in more uncomfortable places than a bare floor before, but after all he'd been through, he desperately wanted any sort of bed.

"If you would like." She chuckled. "Or…"

She pushed open a hidden section of the white wall. It opened forward, the light from the hallway only revealing a few details.

May put her hand on Sam's back and ushered him into the shadowy room. After a moment, she cleared her throat, and a light flickered on.

The inside was cut from the same rock as the walls, which gave the place a cave-like feel. A hammock of green material stretched tight between two freestanding poles. A glass ball floated next to the hammock, giving off the only light. A seat carved from a large stump filled the corner, and a large carpet woven into a beautiful tapestry of purples and yellows covered the floor. Artwork decorated the walls, drawn directly on them like cave paintings, only much more sophisticated than the primitive examples Sam had seen in his history books. A well-detailed landscape of sunflowers decorated the wall above the bed. The stars in the mural twinkled like the real night sky.

"Whisper something nice about me to the light and it will go off. The bathroom is on the right. When you get up, touch the wall. Goodnight, Sam. Travel well in your dreams."

And with that, May closed the door, leaving Sam alone.

He had a million questions to ask, but exhaustion was a powerful de-motivator. He had never spent the night in a hammock before, but at this point he was more than willing to try. After pulling out and eating a bit more of the dreckler cotton, he took off his cleats, which had accumulated more than a fair share of dirt from the forest, and he fell back into the green material.

Sam's body was cradled only by the portion of the green ropes he lay directly on. It felt like he was floating.

"May is pretty," Sam whispered.

"How pretty?" the light asked in May's voice.

"Um…" Sam had never spoken to a lamp before. "Pretty as that painting?"

The light faded and Sam was left in darkness.

It took no time for him to fall asleep.

CHAPTER 7

lue flame erupted from Vigtor LaVink's palm as he slammed it against the jade table. The outburst did not surprise the other ten Elite; it was his way of releasing anger. Vigtor lifted his arm and pointed at Saria. The scaly, black second-skin shifted with an oily ease on his hand. He had taken the skin, forcefully, from the last armor-belly to walk the earth.

"Just when we are given a gift, you let it get snatched away."

"It was May." Saria sneered. "She showed up just before we did."

"And...?" Vigtor's scowl deepened as he waited for a better explanation.

"And," Sage butted in, relieving her twin sister, "May took the boy under."

"And did you follow?"

"Yes, of course," Saria spat. "But, it was May."

"You were the one looking out of that flathand's eyes. Do you know how lucky it was to come across the boy so quickly? What happened?"

"I willed the flathand strict instructions not to let anyone know where he put the boy, but it appears that May released him."

Vigtor smiled. "She's getting better."

Crom gave a loud, throaty snort.

"Something to add?"

Crom's massive body rose from his seat. His robe didn't do much to hide his bulging muscles. Even though Crom was across the table, Vigtor had to raise his eyes with the rest of the Tembrath Elite to see his face. A full two heads taller than any of them, with power to match, Crom was the only member of the Tembrath Elite Vigtor worried about trying to seize leadership.

"We don't need him," Crom's booming voice echoed in the chamber. "You're getting weak."

Vigtor made a scooping motion with his covered hand and long rods of golden light appeared in front of him. Like arrows, the rods shot into Crom's robe and sent him flying against the back wall, pinning him there.

"I do not lose *strength*." Vigtor gave a mirthless smile. "Only patience."

This got the others' attention.

Crom flexed and pulled, but he could not get loose. He raised his second-skin—made of tanned Learox skin—and had to diminish each rod individually.

"I will admit," Vigtor pulled the others' eyes back toward him, "that I underestimated them. Bariv hasn't lost the talent. A pity he wouldn't work with us."

"And whose fault is that?" Crom asked from behind them.

A second wave of gold shot across the room and pierced the wall a hair's distance from Crom's throat. The big man didn't make a sound.

Vigtor continued. "What we need to do now is find a way to communicate with the boy."

Jintin cleared his throat.

"Let me guess." Vigtor raised his eyebrows at Jintin. "Force?"

Jintin shrugged. The man's squirrelly face and small stature created the illusion of weakness.

Vigtor shook his head. Jintin's ability to destroy was unmatched, but he wasn't known for his cleverness.

"You know as well as I do that if we tried a siege, we would lose. There are just too many of them, and apparently some have even been practicing the more nefarious arts."

Sage spoke up. "Just because May was able to break your hold doesn't mean they could keep us all at bay."

"No." Vigtor gave her a hard look. "Don't you think they are already preparing to defend against an attack? No, we need another way."

"They will not accept each other," Erimos said quietly.

The room went quiet. When Erimos spoke, everyone listened.

Luckily for Vigtor, Erimos—the man who had taught him power magic—had never wanted to lead the Tembrath Elite. He was content to sit on the sidelines and watch, offering his input when necessary. By far the wisest of them all, Erimos conserved his words, making them all the more powerful.

Erimos opened his eyes for the first time that night. They were piercing red. Vigtor knew that they had not always been that color, but red was indicative of power. In the case of the Veil, the redder the better.

Long white hair hung down over Erimos' shoulders, ending in silver tips. His face was scarred from countless years of traveling down the powerful side of the Veil. Many centuries everyone else's senior, he had discovered many aspects of how to actually use the Veil, how to access *real* power magics. He had accessed aspects people had been too scared to reach before.

"If you would care to elaborate?" Vigtor dropped his head in a respectful nod.

"They will be afraid of him. We all felt it. He will be drawn to the true methods of controlling Her. It will only make the boy join us sooner. "

Crom had finally pried himself from his magical bonds. "I can do it! We don't need him!"

Vigtor ignored Crom's comment. "Yes, they will know what awaits him. What he is capable of. Soon he will know it, too."

"Exactly." Erimos nodded. "We just have to make sure it stays that way."

"Excellent," Vigtor said. "Let's begin."

"Begging your pardon," Erimos' wrinkled hands produced an envelope from his lap, "but I already have. As simple as it is," he placed the envelope on the table, "this is how we will succeed. A small weight to tip the scales."

"It must work," Vigtor said. "That boy is the key to getting through."

The rest of the Tembrath Elite nodded at this: all except Crom.

Erimos closed his eyes once more. "I have been waiting a long time for this. Longer than all of you. Longer than most of you put together. Our purpose *will* be fulfilled."

CHAPTER 8

The championship game was heating up, the fans going wild with anticipation. Thirty seconds left and Sam took the field. Girls screamed, guys chanted, and Paul Barsky in the mascot suit started doing cartwheels. Sam waved a hand to rile up the crowd ever further. He beat his chest and hooted like a gorilla, which started the screams up again. It was the day he was to become a hero.

"Doug," Sam said, "fake sneak left and look for me in the end zone."

"But, Sam," Doug said, "you can't be on the field."

"Why not?" Sam looked around; all the other players wore black jerseys instead of the usual green and gold.

"Because that part of your life is dead." Doug pulled a black sheet of paper from his pocket. "Didn't you get the memo?"

"Memo?" Sam took the paper, which crumbled to ash. "What are you talking about?" He pulled a tuft of black cotton off the mascot suit and started chewing it.

"Get that thing off the field!" Doug shouted. "It doesn't belong here."

"Doug, just throw me the damn ball."

"But it's not a ball," Doug said. "It's you."

Sam looked at Doug's hands. In place of the ball, a black swirl filled his palm. It was just lying there, limp, as if too tired to go on. Then hundreds of other swirls drifted onto the field and attached to Sam. They started to drift upwards, carrying him out of the stadium. Up over everyone's heads, he looked down and saw blank stares on thousands of fans.

"NOOOO!" Sam jerked against the swirls.

"Did you forget your way?" The black swirls asked in unison.

"Huh?" Sam asked.

"Now jeopardous in play?"

"Let me DOWN!"

℮

Sam awoke in the pitch-black room.

"How generous is May?" asked a quiet voice.

Sam rubbed his eyes. "Uh, very generous?"

A pinprick of light appeared next to him and started to grow until the room came into view.

Sam remembered everything.

Oh no. It can't have been real.

That meant he really *had* hurt that kid and blown his football career. He started to feel the panic rising, choking him. His whole life was wrecked. The memory of being locked in a jail cell crept into his mind.

He lay there for several minutes, processing everything. A chill ran over him and his stomach tightened up. He took a deep breath and tried to remember the excitement he had felt the previous night, how ready he'd been to learn, how eager to know that magic was real and he could do it. After a couple of heavy breaths, he finally began to calm, although the knot still sat heavy in his stomach.

He had no idea how long he had slept, but it felt like only a moment. The painting on the wall had transformed overnight. Now, it showed a scene of children playing in a field, each one bearing a tiny glove on his or her hand.

Sam reluctantly extricated himself from the green ropes and got to his feet. The ball of light hovered next to him.

"Bathroom...?"

The light followed him as he made his way toward the door at the far side of his room. Sam gave it a sideways look. "Convenient."

The bathroom looked like it had been designed by an alien race, although one with pleasant taste in decor. Next to the toilet, which had also been decorated with artwork, was a small tree. Instead of leaves, however, the branches produced a soft-looking material, which Sam assumed was their version of toilet paper.

After he relieved himself, the light-ball accompanied him back into the bedroom. Sam went to the door and tried to twist the knob. When it refused to turn, he felt like the rock walls were closing in on him.

The ball of light rocked back and forth in the direction of one of the walls.

"Right," Sam remembered, "touch the wall."

After a moment's hesitation, he reached out. Instead of being stopped by solid rock, his hand passed through the wall as though it were nothing more than smoke. He pushed his arm through and felt emptiness on the other side. After taking a deep breath, he jumped through.

It seemed he was a late sleeper.

Beyond the wall, Atlas Crown was alive with movement. Morning sunlight bathed the grounds, and people smiled and waved to one another while they moved about, wearing clothing that resembled kimonos and monks' robes. Simple symbols—not the corporate logos Sam was used to—were woven into the fabric, giving Sam the impression of Native American garb. Like May and the kids in the painting, everyone wore a glove on one hand.

Nearby, a lanky, dark-skinned man held out his red glove toward the roof of a hut. An hourglass-shaped ball floated off the roof and landed among a group of kids wearing yellow gloves with green polka dots. They squealed with delight and ran off with the ball past someone wearing a metal glove—almost like a gauntlet from a suit of armor. When he swung around to watch the kids, he saw a wild-haired woman wearing a clear glove that looked as if water had been molded around her skin.

The kids ran out onto an area full of small shops, magnificent trees, statues, log cabins, and plenty of people. Rolling hills, streams, and ornamental bridges playfully entwined with the architecture. The giant sandstone pillar on the other side of town appeared to be miles away.

With a cautious smile, Sam moved closer to one of the structures, an open-faced shop selling small confectionery treats the likes of which Sam had never seen before. On the table were glossy candies the size of his arm and puffy cotton-candy-type treats that changed color from red to blue and back.

A large pond with decorative stone borders lay a short distance away. People bent down, grabbed small white things out of the water, and dropped them into pails. A few people looked his way and waved their gloved hands. He returned the gesture.

Close-cropped grass covered the ground and the folk walked around barefooted. Sam kneaded the grass with his own bare toes.

A man in a booth gave him a kind smile. "You're new."

Sam nodded.

"Welcome, young one. Come over here." His smooth, grey hair didn't move as he gestured, and Sam found himself staring at the pattern of green concentric circles woven across his chest. An enticing smell invaded his nostrils as he stepped up to the booth, where mountains of gooey pastries were spread out, buffet-style.

The man opened his arms wide. "Care to break the night's fast?"

Sam's mouth began to water. He reached into his pocket, and then remembered his wallet was back in the Carver locker room. Pulling out his hand, he gave the man a disheartened frown.

"I don't have any money."

The shop owner smiled. "My name is Fromson of the Bellamy clan. Fromson Bellamy for short." He picked up one of the larger, gooier treats. "Let me be the first to introduce you to our home." The man held out the pastry. "Eat up."

"Really?"

"Absolutely. It's a new recipe and I'm curious to know what you think." Fromson's covered hand had taken on the same sheen as the treat.

"Baker's leaf," Fromson said, noticing Sam's eyes on his glove. "Keeps things from sticking. Now go ahead, enjoy."

"Don't have to tell me again." Sam gratefully took the treat. After a single bite, half of the pastry was already gone. It was warm and delicious and…moving? The sugary icing rolled around in his mouth on its own accord, as if it were trying to hit every one of his taste buds.

"Slider buns," the man explained as he saw the ecstatic look on Sam's face. "Bet you never had anything like that before."

Sam swallowed. "Did it—"

"Yes." Fromson's glove changed to a dusty green. "It tries to make itself as delicious as possible for you. Pretty ingenious, huh? I just wrap a little bit of Her around it in sort of a triangle and… what is that you are wearing by the way?"

Sam looked down at himself. "A jersey."

Fromson pursed his lips. "New Jersey?"

"Uh… I guess it's new."

"Splendid! Wonderful!" Fromson clapped his hands together. "When I was a child, my parents told me of a distant land called New Jersey. I've never met someone from there before."

Sam pinched his lips together in an attempt not to laugh.

"No, not *from* New Jersey. It *is* a new jersey."

The man's eyes widened. "I've never heard of that magic before."

"Come again?"

The man squinted at the shirt. "Connecting a place with an article of wear. How do you do that?"

"Sam!" The voice came from behind him. "It's nice to see you're finally awake."

He turned and saw May, only it wasn't the May he was expecting to see. Instead of the sharp suit, she wore a beautiful red dress that hugged her waist and accentuated her curves. The variety of patterns on the bodice were far more complex than the shopkeeper's; May's dress had checkered patterns, birds, and flowers, along with other small symbols he could not discern. Here, she made no attempt to hide her shimmering glove.

"May!" Fromson gestured toward Sam's jersey. "Did you take a look at this? A New Jersey bonded with an article of wear!"

"My dear Fromson." She gave a small bow and took a crumbly, bite-sized pastry from the pile. "A jersey is an article of wear for physical activity in the other world."

He eyed Sam up and down. "Physical activity, huh? Think he'll be any good at our games?"

"I hope so." She gave him a grin. "I also hope Sam normally doesn't sleep this late. The arc is half over."

"No," Sam shook his head. "Usually I'm up and running by six."

"Six?" the shopkeeper asked. "Six of what?"

"O'clock."

"O-what?"

"You'll have to excuse Fromson," May told Sam. "Among other things, time is seen a little differently here."

"How so?"

"Why don't you walk with me?" She made a polite gesture toward the center of town.

Sam thanked Fromson and followed May off toward the pond.

May smiled. "How are you feeling, Sam?"

"Truthfully?" Sam polished off the slider bun and licked the icing from his thumb. "Like I just found out my whole life has been a lie."

"Not a lie at all."

"Then what?"

"A step. One level that has led you to another."

"I don't know if you realize it, but this is kind of a lot to take in."

"What a monumental step it is to take—a leap even. I had to take it myself, and my experience was a special circumstance, as well." She flashed an impish grin. "If I can do it, I think a big, tough kid like you can handle it."

Sam thought about what Coach DeGrella would say if he knew how Sam was acting. Whining was not taken on the gridiron. Then he winced as he considered what his coach was probably thinking about him blowing the game.

May held out her diamond-gloved hand. "If you'd like, I can use the Veil again to—"

Sam held up his hands in protest. "No, no, I'm fine."

"Good." May gave a satisfied nod. They resumed walking around the pond.

Sam ran his tongue across the inside of his upper lip and smacked his lips, savoring the taste of the slider bun as the last bit of icing stretched across his tongue. "So, how is time different?"

"Not different, just perceived in another way. You see, we don't have numbers for time. We have the same time as the outside world, but we do things according to the world around us. Get up with the sun, and sleep when we get tired. We don't number the hours in a day."

"So how do you know when to do things?"

"Like what sort of things?"

"I don't know... like, meetings and stuff."

"There are terms for different periods of the day, which you will learn during your training." May stopped. "Take a look at this."

47

They approached the edge of the pond and Sam leaned over the carved barrier. Staring back at him was a fish the size of a terrier, its body a bright gold with black fins. Out of its mouth came a white globule with the luster of a pearl. The ball slowly rose and finally popped the surface, sitting on top like a buoy.

Sam rapped his knuckles on the stone and the fish drew closer. "What are they?"

"Rinsefish."

"Why were people taking the white things? Jewelry?"

"No, rinsing."

"Huh?"

"Take it, it's a gift."

Sam plucked the white glob out of the water and held it in his hand. It was slimy, like seaweed, yet it held its shape.

May mimed placing it in her mouth.

Sam looked at her with disgust. "You can't be serious."

She reached down and gently stroked the top fin of the rinsefish. After a moment of this, the fish ducked under the water and swam away. "I don't know what you mean. People in your society eat flesh, so why not this?"

"Because this is disgusting."

"Just try it. I promise you'll like it."

Sam shrugged. He popped the white glob into his mouth and immediately felt a tingling sensation.

"Don't eat it," May warned. "Swirl."

The taste reminded him of lemon sorbet. As soon as it was in his mouth, the glob dissolved. Sam swirled it around—this time, on his own. After a few gurgles, he looked back at May for further instruction.

"Let it go on the ground."

He did as he was told and the white substance hit the grass; however, it didn't stay there. It seeped into the ground like ink drawn into a parchment. Where it disappeared, a small green flower sprang into existence. It happened so quickly that Sam could have sworn he was looking at a stop-motion animation.

His mouth felt exquisite, like after a trip to the dentist, but without the gum pain.

Sam took a deep breath, the air minty and soft against his throat. "You win."

"It's also used to bathe our bodies and our hair."

Sam looked back into the pond and another rinsefish gave up its white bubble.

Sam took the glob and started rubbing it on his arms. The white material dripped off him and hit the ground, sprouting more flowers.

He looked his arms up and down, noticing that his skin was so clean it almost glowed. "And the green flowers?"

"Take a sniff."

They smelled like warm cinnamon.

"Most people take the rinsers back to their homes, so when they are done cleaning, the flowers sprout and freshen up the rooms."

"Where do the people live?"

"In the towers. Think of them as apartment buildings. They circle all the way around the center of Atlas Crown. Inside the walls, where we are standing now, are the giving-huts—like Fromson's—the amphitheater, the clothing houses, the Arena, the library, and all sorts of wonderful things you will experience. You're going to love the tinker-hut." She pulled herself onto the wall and swung her legs back and forth like a young girl. "Outside the walls is where we grow our crops and teach our students."

Sam didn't know how to gracefully transition to the subject, but he needed to know. "So…why did you bring me here?"

"I thought that you would like to see the rinsefish for your—"

Sam shook his head. "I meant Atlas Crown."

May hopped down, took his hands in hers, and peered deep into his eyes. "I brought you here so we can help you."

"Help me what?"

"Learn to control and use the Veil correctly. Right now, you are a danger to yourself and others. You need to be around others like you, so you can learn how to deal with the power responsibly. I know you don't want to hurt anyone else."

Sam's mind flashed to the cornerback's blood on the grass. He pulled his hands out of May's and took a step back. "But all I did was grab his shoulder!"

"It's not your fault." May stepped up and ran a hand against his cheek. "No one is blaming you, Sam. You could not have controlled what happened to you. I'm just telling you what must happen. For now, you must stay with us."

A pleasant tingle remained after her hand dropped from his cheek. "But when will you take me back?"

"Back?"

Sam plucked the collar of his jersey. "Yeah, I have to go home at some point."

She nodded with the grace of someone much older than she seemed. "If you wish, but you just got here. How can you be so sure that you want to leave?"

"Because I have a life back home, I have my friends, school, football…" Okay, maybe he didn't have football. "Why do you even care?"

"I care deeply, for more reasons than you would understand as of this moment. I will explain more soon, but it is not in your best interest to know everything right now. Something outside of your control has happened and it needs to be dealt with. It is safe for you here. You can learn here. I am truly sorry, but for now, that is all I can tell you."

Sam scowled, but then took a deep breath to calm himself.

I'm tougher than this.

"Fine. So what's going to happen to me until it's safe to go back?"

"Well." She turned and folded both hands over the small of her back. "You are going to live with Bariv for the next few days, until the worst of it blows over. Then, after that, if you wish it, I will have a place in the north tower for you."

"So what was that room yesterday?"

"A guest room, of sorts. I wanted you to be comfortable and well rested before you saw even a small portion of our community."

"Can we at least talk about what happened at the game?"

She turned and gave Sam a look that was almost pity. "If you really want to."

Sam thought about everyone freezing, which led to him thinking about everyone booing. The knot in his stomach started to re-form. "Not really."

"Don't worry, Sam. This should be an exciting time for you. The Veil and everything She has to offer can bring you limitless joy. It is up to you to let Her."

Sam peeked over May's shoulder and noticed a small gathering of people in a circle. Voices buzzed with anticipation.

"What's going on over there?"

"Ah." She gave a shrewd smile. "Veil pushing. Or as we call it, gumptius."

"Gumptius?"

"It is a very old game. It is also one of our most popular, especially among the crowd too old for thimplist and too young for graws."

"Uh huh." Sam started toward the gathering.

He was slightly taller than most of the onlookers, but being on the outside of the circle, he couldn't get a clear view of what was happening.

He caught a glimpse of a small wooden table in the center with two people sitting across from each other, their gloved hands locked together.

"Arm wrestling?"

"Not really..."

No one really paid Sam any attention. The challenger on the right looked like he could use a few more slider buns, as his arms were more bone than anything else. Sam pegged him to be the same age as him. The boy's black robe had an even blacker X sewn into the chest. His oily hair hung limp to his shoulders, and his beady eyes stared, rat-like, at his opponent. His black glove had the sheen of tanned leather.

His opponent's bald head gleamed in the sun. A brown goatee pointed down to his thick neck. The weird symbols tattooed on his broad arms flexed as the muscles tightened beneath them.

Sam looked at May with a frown. "The little guy's going to get slaughtered."

May motioned with her head that he should watch the match.

"And push!" someone shouted from the sidelines.

Before Sam could even see what had happened, the brawny man's arm was pinned to the table. The kid sneered and pulled his hand away.

Sam was dumbstruck. "How did he do that?"

"This is a game that is not won by strength."

"Yeah, right." He started pushing his way through the circle.

"Wait, Sam!"

He reached the table. "I want a go," he told the kid in black.

The kid's gaze darted from Sam's face to his jersey. The flicker of fear in his eyes was quickly suppressed. Then the kid smirked and gestured toward the opposite seat, which Sam took.

"Nice clothes." The kid curled his lip.

"What's that supposed to mean?"

He looked at Sam's hand. "Where's your second-skin?"

"My glove? I haven't had a chance to buy one yet."

A hushed laughter escaped from the crowd.

"Buy one." The boy shook his head. "Ridiculous."

Sam slammed his elbow against the table and raised his right hand. This kid was starting to tick him off. No way he was stronger than Sam, especially now that Sam could do magic.

The other kid locked into Sam's grip. The leather glove didn't press against Sam's hand, though. Instead, a small invisible barrier blocked their palms, like Sam was pressing against a pocket of air.

"And push!"

Sam forced all his strength into his forearm. Pushing as hard as he could, his muscles strained under the pressure. The vein in Sam's bicep started pulsing, yet the kid's hand would not budge. He couldn't even get through the tiny cushion of air and touch the other kid's hand.

Across the table, the boy glared at Sam coldly.

"How—"

As soon as the word escaped Sam's lips, his hand slammed backwards onto the table. The force was stupendous; it felt like every one of Sam's knuckles had broken.

The kid lifted his arm. Sam slipped his throbbing hand under the table, nursing it.

"Next!" the boy called, and a short, squat man stepped up next to the table.

"How did you—?"

"I said NEXT!" The kid didn't look in Sam's direction.

Sam got up and let the short man take over. Beads of blood welled up on his knuckles as he made his way back out of the circle, head down.

Someone patted him on the back as he squirmed through. Sam looked up to meet the gaze of a smiling guy about his own age with curly brown hair. He carried a beautiful, curved horn—long, tan, and embossed with gold writing—in one of his hands, both of which, Sam noticed, were ungloved.

Sam attempted a smile, but failed. As he squeezed out of the ring, he saw May waiting with a hand on her hip.

She gave a heavy sigh. "What did you think was going to happen?"

"But that kid was tiny! How did he do that?"

"That *kid's* name is Petir LaVink, and he is one of the finest gumptius players we have."

Sam rubbed the back of his injured hand. "But how was he so strong? His arms were like toothpicks."

"I told you, it is not about strength. It is about ability."

"Ability to do what?"

"Use the Veil, not your muscles, to push. Now, we have an appointment to keep. It would be very rude to show up late."

His whole hand throbbed. "Where?"

"It's not far."

"With who?"

"Someone very important."

Sam sucked his teeth.

"Fine." She broke into a condescending smile. "Before you go bumbling around in things you don't understand, you need to learn a few things."

"Magic?"

"Yes, eventually."

"Can't you just take me home? I can take care of myself."

"I know you can, and I'm not worried about you, I'm worried about others, and you should be, too. It would be extraordinarily dangerous for you not to learn how to control this. Please, just trust that I want what's best for you."

Sam thought about the cornerback's screams. He managed a glum nod.

May took Sam's bruised hand and waved her diamond-like glove over it. Once again, the pain subsided as the skin healed.

"And if you go home, how will you ever best LaVink?" One side of her cheek curved into a crooked smile. "I mean, that *was* pretty humiliating. I think you need to train for a re-match to prove yourself."

Sam gave a huff. "Fine. But if I'm going to hang around here for a little while, I think I'm going need a change of clothes... and where do I buy one of those fancy gloves? And, oh yeah, where am I going to get money? I have a feeling there's no ATM around."

"We do not use money here."

Sam cocked his head to the side. "No money?"

"No money."

"How do you buy things?"

"We are a community."

"Meaning?"

"If you work hard and don't rub anyone the wrong way, you always get what you need, and usually what you want, too."

"I want one of those." He motioned to her hand. "What do they do, anyway?"

"Your second-skin is a conduit."

Sam rubbed his forehead. "I'll understand later, right?"

"You did ask." She turned her palm upwards.

He exhaled. "So, to the meeting."

"To Bariv."

CHAPTER 9

"Don't tell me this is the Veil?"

May choked back a laugh. "No Sam, this is not the Veil."

"There is no way I'm going through there." Sam snatched his finger away from the wall of gunk.

May had brought him to an uninhabited part of Atlas Crown. They were nowhere near the towers and away from any sign of people—a high contrast to the bustling atmosphere of the marketplace.

They were now face to face with a slimy, purple partition between two stone wolves, each one carved directly into the rock face. When Sam brought his finger away from the slick surface, a small amount of the purple goop came with it, which he wiped on the front of his jersey. He couldn't see anything beyond the purple, which bothered him, because May had just informed him he would have to step through.

Sam took a step backward. "I'll follow you."

"I am not needed inside. This is for you; it is a very special time. You will remember it for the rest of your life."

Sam pinched his thumb and forefinger together. He pulled them apart slowly; the remaining goop reminded him of rubber cement. "So what's behind this junk?"

"Well, once you get through—"

Suddenly, Sam was tossed through the barrier. May hadn't even budged.

He fell through the purple goo—which coated him thoroughly—and landed in a cave. It was very dark, with bare, rough walls. A small, illuminated platform caught his attention.

Thankfully, the gloppy material didn't rise with him when he stood. As the long strands peeled off his body, they crawled back to the wall like an army of inchworms, leaving his clothes crisp and clean.

Sam's footfalls echoed around him as he approached the light. He made out the shape of a young boy sitting on the raised stone platform. Candles cast dancing shadows on the wall behind him.

Sam edged a little closer. The boy couldn't have been more than ten years old. His thin, short mohawk stood up like a fin, and two tattoos graced his cheeks—a spiral on each, curling in opposite directions.

"Sit." The boy didn't open his eyes. His voice was stronger and deeper than that of any ten-year-old Sam knew.

"Bariv?"

The boy nodded.

"Really?"

"Sit."

Sam shrugged and sat down.

"When the world was a little younger, no one knew about the Veil," Bariv kept his eyes shut. "It was not empty. All the colors existed, yet there were no painters."

"Gimme a brea—"

Before Sam could finish, his mouth snapped shut. He tried to open it, but he couldn't.

"No one knew that the first artist was going to be a little girl."

Again Sam tried to move his lips, but they felt glued together.

"She was walking in a meadow, searching for berries, when she came upon a sunflower. It was a small sunflower, so she sang to it." Sam could feel Bariv's voice through the platform. "A simple, sweet song. She wished, deep down in her heart, for it to grow and then share its nourishment with her tribe. They were hungry, you see. The lyrics of the song have long been forgotten, but that is not the important part of the story. The important part is that for some reason, the flower grew," he paused, "right before her eyes."

Bariv opened his eyes for the first time, and Sam's jaw dropped. Bariv's eyes glowed an intense, bright red, blazing even brighter than the candles and tinting the whole cave. Sam could barely look at them without his own eyes getting glossy.

"The flower grew to an enormous height. The girl shook the stalk and many seeds fell to the ground, which she put into her basket. There were so many seeds that she could take only a small portion of all that fell. A single petal fell from the flower, which she picked up. From that day onward, she carried that petal around with her everywhere. She found that when it was in her hands, wonderful things happened. When streams got too thin and drought threatened, she dipped the petal in the water, and it started flowing again. When the cattle got too sick and plague threatened, she touched each one and the meat grew thick. Wonderful things happened the more she used the petal."

Sam realized his mouth was no longer sealed shut. "So what happened to the girl?"

"First, let us find out what has happened to you."

From behind him, Sam heard voices that were oddly familiar. He turned around and saw the wall light up, like at a movie theatre. Instead of a movie, though, Sam saw one very particular memory.

"This your first football, boy?" the worker at the Sports Emporium asked from high above the countertop.

"Yessir!" young Sam said. "I'm going to be the best football player the world has ever seen!"

"Ain't he a little bull," the clerk said to Sam's mother, who stood beside the little version of Sam. It felt strange, seeing himself as a child.

"My little boy knows what he wants."

"I'm going to be like the Missile!"

The clerk laughed. "Your boy knows who Bob Flywood is?"

Sam's mother shrugged, fishing through her purse for a few tens.

"One day you're going to have to come back to my shop and sign a football for me, little man. Maybe even that one you're holding now."

"I will, mister!"

The image on the wall faded, and another one took its place.

"Four catches for TD." His father flipped a big, juicy steak on the grill. "Heck of a game, boy."

It was the memory of a barbecue his parents had thrown at their house. Alongside his father were most of his teammates' dads.

"Giving you a run for your money, Pete, huh?"

"My boy is going pro." Sam's father dug into the steak with a thermometer. "Just you wait…"

Again the image faded. Next on the wall, Sam saw himself and Jenn Sardina against one of the lockers.

Jenn refused to meet his eyes as she fiddled with the necklace in her hands. "You knew it was going to happen, Sam."

The memory version of Sam turned red.

"Sean?" he scoffed. "Really?"

"Maybe you should have spent more time thinking about me, and less time thinking about that stupid game."

"But Sean is just some art dweeb."

"That may be, but he puts me into his artwork. He thinks about me. He dreams about me. All you dream about is the scoreboard."

"STOP THAT!" Sam yelled at Bariv.

"I did not choose these memories. I just provided the void; you decided how to fill it."

"Well, close it!" Sam snarled through clenched teeth.

The images continued on the wall. Jenn hurled the necklace at his chest.

Sam's fists clenched and he tried to rise, but he was lifted off the ground and pinned in midair.

"I AM THE VOICE!" Bariv's words echoed through the cave. "I was chosen to be the eyes of the Veil and I am here to make you finally see!"

Sam was lowered to the ground. Anger seethed within him.

"Those are memories that define you." Bariv's tone was quiet, yet still powerful. "But things have changed. *You* have changed." He paused. "Let me tell you another story. Or rather, show you one."

Sam's muscles seemed to melt as he was forced to relax. It was just like the whammy May had put on him yesterday when he had first realized he wasn't dreaming. He allowed himself to give in to the sensation, and again, he felt much more open to listening.

"I am very old. If I had to put a number on it, it would have to be..." Bariv started counting off silently with his fingers.

"You don't have a glove."

"A second-skin. No. Nor do I need one."

"So how do you do magic?"

Bariv traced the swirl on his right cheek. "I am a special case. Anyway, take a look at this."

Above Sam, the ceiling lit up the same way the wall had. Bariv allowed Sam to lie back to gaze upwards. At first, all he could see was an image of stars, almost as clear as if he were back on his porch on a cloudless night.

The stars began to move.

They swirled and grew and eventually took shapes and colors and forms, like celestial echo flies. Sam was left looking at another Bariv. Almost exactly the same, but the young boy was missing the spirals on his cheeks, and his eyes were bright blue. Sam watched the image of Bariv play with a small wooden carving of a wolf, making the creature gallop across the hard dirt floor of a hut. The young boy smiled as he sang a little tune that matched the prancing of the toy. A pile of grey furs sprawled along one wall. Bones carved into spears and harpoons lined the walls, while crude nets and smoked fish hung from the ceiling.

All of a sudden, a faint cry came from somewhere outside, and Sam frowned as he realized that there didn't seem to be a door in the hut. The cry startled the young boy, but after a few moments of quiet, he went back to playing. After a moment, there came another cry, this time much closer and piercing. Then a cacophony of screams—like a wild animal being torn apart—came through the walls. The young boy threw aside his carving and raced for a small mat of fur on the ground. He tossed it aside, revealing a tunnel underneath.

Bariv called into the tunnel, and two large beasts burst out. They looked like giant versions of the wolf Bariv had been playing with just moments before. He rubbed one of the dogs on the snout, and then bolted outside through the tunnel.

Bariv struggled to wade through the knee-deep snow toward the ominous patches of red. A crimson track threaded its way off into the distance, and the boy's eyes shot open in fear. He crawled on all fours, through thick powder and ice, as the red trail thickened. Finally, Bariv stood up, and the young boy's whole body began to shake.

Then came a shriek.

It was unlike anything Sam had ever heard. The noise lowered to a *boom* and resonated violently, flooding the cave. The white snow brightened until the whole image was blinding. Sam brought his arm up and covered his eyes.

As the light faded, Sam looked back up. A large white bear whimpered as it fled. Bariv knelt with his face buried in his hands, rocking gently. All around the boy, for miles it seemed, the snow had melted, leaving steam lifting off bare earth. The Bariv on the ceiling slowly took his hands away from his eyes and the red pupils glowed down at the two figures lying motionless on the brown earth.

Then the image faded.

"Were those your parents?" Sam almost felt guilty for breaking the silence.

Bariv nodded.

"But if that was so long ago, how are you still so young?"

"A few hours later, I was found. I was still lying outside, unable to speak or move. But the snow around had melted and the ground remained warm. Otherwise, I surely would have died. I was brought here. It was a much different Atlas Crown back then—not nearly as many clans—but it still had the same charm. I was given food, shelter, and a new life."

Sam looked at Bariv curiously. "So what makes you a special case?"

"I fill a niche."

"What niche?"

"Something you won't be able to grasp just yet. Before now, you were like a frog."

Sam's expression turned glib. "A lion frog?"

Bariv shook his head. "Just a frog."

"Why?"

"Because a frog surrounded by dead flies will go hungry."

"Wow... you're better at being cryptic than May."

"My apologies. I spend so much time alone I often forget how the outside world communicates." He raised both palms. "A frog has a specialized brain. It is able to snatch a fly out of the air like lightning. It filters out everything else. It is the fly and the tongue. The problem is that without motion, the frog is helpless."

"So I'm helpless?"

"No, you just weren't able to see all those dead flies around you, and trust me when I tell you they're everywhere. You are now one of the frog elite."

"Does that have anything to do with the Tembrath Elite?"

Bariv looked impressed, but also wary. "Yes, it was Vigtor being clever. Tembrath Pond is where the lion frogs congregate. I told the same story to him when he was standing here before me."

"So, can I finally know who those guys are?"

"They are fools." Bariv flicked his wrist, which glowed blue for an instant and crackled with an electric flair.

"Why?"

"You need to know a few things before you can know that."

"Still?"

Bariv snapped and more candles flicked to life around the room. At that moment, his eyes lost their red glow and became bright blue. Despite Bariv's young appearance, something ancient lurked behind his gaze—something that made Sam feel small, but at the same time, connected.

"Let's start you off simply." Bariv rested the backs of his hands on his knees. "What have you been told about the Veil?"

Sam hesitated a moment. "That it's all around and you grip it."

"Very good." Bariv positioned his hands in front of him, and a thin bolt of electricity jumped from one hand to the other with a sharp zap. "Now, I assume you have been told about second-skins?"

Sam put his hands in front of his chest like Bariv had done, but nothing happened.

"The gloves?"

"If you want to put it so crudely, yes, the gloves—although calling them such is like calling the sun a big light bulb."

"So, what do they do?"

"They are items of magical importance, made from materials that have sprouted from the Veil, making it easier for sorcerers to use Her. Without the second-skin, gripping is much harder, almost impossible. When you try to grip a wet piece of ice, it will almost always slip through your fingers. The second-skin allows focused gripping and utilization of the wondrous Veil."

Bariv made a twirling motion with his hand and a chunk of ice appeared. "It helps you make as much friction as you need to hold onto the ice."

Sam imitated the movement, but again, nothing happened. "When do I get one of these second-skins?"

Bariv twitched his pointer finger, and a piercing light erupted behind Sam. He turned to see a pedestal, about four feet off the ground, with three gloves upon it. On the left, a leafy green glove had thick vines branching along it. The center held a glove made of five thimbles connected by a thin chain to a central bracelet. The one on the right was made from skin with short brown fur.

"These are what you will use to focus. These are second-skins that I have created for choosing purposes. As May has probably already explained to you, there are three disciplines of magic that come from the Veil. First, there are natural magics, which are best gripped with the aid

of plants. The green second-skin is made from the leaf of the grampith tree.

"Natural magics are very useful. They feed, they clothe, and help us interact with the world around us. We would not survive without them. Nature is dough and you shape it to your desires—if you are skilled enough. Mountains can be leveled and water can fall upwards. Nature's secrets will whisk you away to another plane where you can realize the awe-inspiring connections we hold with the world around us."

Sam wanted it.

"Next, there are the mystical magics. The metal second-skin was mined from beneath Grus' pass and made from silver-palladium mixed by my own hand. A mystical sorcerer would use this second-skin. The mystical magics keep true to their namesake. Even I don't fully understand all that can be accomplished with this, and I have been close to the Veil for a very long time. Those who excel at the mystical arts can reach into the deepest, darkest parts of the mind and cast dreams into reality. They can navigate the vast and powerful river of time. Reap gold out of metals like a glorious harvest. Harness fear, and ride on its back until it tires."

Sam instantly forgot about the first glove.

"And last… there is the second-skin made from the hide of Sectus Remisican, the skull-wolf. This is a tool of power magics. These tools work best if taken forcibly. In Atlas Crown, we do not kill when we do not have to; however, in this particular case we had to. The power sect is a dangerous one, yet it brings with it the ability to forge oneself into the greatest ruler and purveyor of dominance. Authority is a given. Supremacy is taken. The true power sect is scarcely found here. Those who have chosen it, or rather have been chosen, usually take the road down another path, a false path that can only lead to death and misery. However, when applied for good, the power sect can be the most useful of them all. An iron body has no need for a suit. That is what the Veil is at Her heart. She is power. She holds possibilities so grand, we can never understand, only observe."

Sam felt a trace of the energy that had passed through his body at the game, the power that had turned the whole world into stone while he alone was left mobile.

"Now." Bariv's eyes returned to their fiery red. "Why don't you go try one on?"

CHAPTER 10

"Repeating that over and over isn't helping," Sam growled.

"Losing your patience will only set you back," Bariv said. "Try again, with less anger this time. You must work *with* Her."

It had been two days. Two *long* days for Sam: getting yelled at, eating some sort of slop—*well, calling it slop would be generous*—and only stopping to sleep once, and that was more of a nap than sleep.

"I'm trying, but I don't feel anything."

"To try is the first step to success; it is also the last. You need to focus on the right landing."

"That doesn't make any sense!" Sam yelled. "Stop talking like that!"

Sam ripped off the skull-wolf glove and hurled it to the ground. After days of being told the same thing, he had pretty much resigned himself to accepting failure. He'd rather go home, anyway; getting thrown in jail for assault would be better than this nonsense.

Time after time, Bariv made Sam attempt to grip the Veil and perform some particular feat. Particular turned into general and eventually general turned into anything at all. The problem was that even the simplest task involved feeling the Veil, which Sam just couldn't seem to do. They took small breaks here and there, but other than Bariv explaining a few unimportant things about the history of the Veil, it was constant monotony. Bariv told Sam to sit in a corner and meditate for hours on end. Even after a lengthy explanation, Sam still didn't get meditation or what it entailed. Although he didn't tell Bariv that—so while sitting in the corner for excruciatingly long periods, he tried to remember the pass completions for every QB he knew.

He had a newfound understanding of boredom.

"Pick that up." Bariv's eyes hardened at the sight of the second-skin carelessly tossed on the ground.

"I'm leaving." Sam crossed his arms over his chest. "I'm obviously in no danger of hurting anyone else."

"I said, pick it up." The swirls on his cheeks took on an orange tinge.

"I don't care about any of this! See *this*?" Sam plucked at his jersey. "This is what my life is about. This is what it has *always* been about, and you and your stupid Veil had to go and ruin everything for me."

After a moment of silence, Bariv spoke. "I'm sorry you feel that way."

"Yeah, me too," Sam huffed.

Bariv stood up and hopped off his platform. "I'll make you a deal."

"What could you possibly offer me?"

"Keep up the training, promise to stay here until you learn to control your power, and I will fix things for you."

Sam's eyes narrowed. "How?"

Bariv tapped the side of his head. "The Veil can do things you cannot possibly imagine, and I happen to be very close with Her."

"You... you can make things go back to normal?" Sam tried to keep the shaking out of his voice.

"There will be no such thing as 'normal' for you now, but yes, I can right what has gone wrong. No one would remember what happened at the game. No one would even remember you left."

"You can do that?" Sam's heart pounded. "I wouldn't be in trouble anymore? I could still play football?"

Bariv nodded. "If that is what you wish."

Sam thrust his hand forward. "Deal."

Bariv pointed a finger in warning. "But you must work hard while you are here, and you may not leave until it is safe."

"Safe from what, exactly?"

"It is better that you do not know the particulars. But I will tell you this: getting close to the Veil will make things safer for you. So, the harder you train, the quicker you can leave. But I must warn you, there is a right and a wrong way to use the Veil. I know you are meant for this path, yet you have a choice of how to travel down it. In the near future, you will be tempted to take the easy route, but the Veil is not about 'easy.' She is about tenacity, courage, and spirit. You can steal a gift, but remember, you will not have earned it."

Sam couldn't help but smile. "Whatever, be as cryptic as you want. As long as you make things right back home, I couldn't care less."

"Then it is decided. Now, not another word about it. We have training to do."

"How long will it take?"

Bariv thought for a moment, and then crouched to put his hands flat against the stone floor. Sam heard a small rumble coming from below them. It got louder and louder until it ended in the scraping sound of rock on rock. After a moment, a crack appeared in the stone, and a charred-looking chunk of rock popped out. Bariv was left holding a large lump of coal.

Once standing, Bariv put his hands on either side of the coal and squeezed. A blinding red light filled the cave, and Bariv's hands clapped together. When he opened them, he was holding a diamond about the size of an acorn.

"It takes power to create a diamond—sheer force. It takes control to change it back into coal." Bariv handed it to Sam. "Once you can do that, you are free to go."

Sam wondered how much a diamond like that would sell for back home.

"Don't lose it," Bariv warned.

Sam wrapped his hand around it. "So, once I can make this coal again, you'll fix everything?"

Bariv nodded.

Sam placed it in the pocket that held one of his thigh pads, the stone pressing into his leg beneath the pad. "Let's get to work."

He felt odd shaking hands with someone so short.

Sam's heart raced in his chest; he couldn't believe that he could get a second chance. He was going to work himself to the bone if it got him home faster. From here on, he was going to take his training seriously.

Who knows? Maybe this stuff could actually come in handy, once I learn how to use it.

Bariv leapt back onto his podium. "Let's try something else for a moment. Maybe I went about this the wrong way. Please, why don't you have a seat in front of me?"

Sam made his way back to the front of the stone stage where Bariv sat.

"Traditionally," Bariv said in a cool, dry voice, "I have taught all outsiders in a certain way. Most have responded beautifully to my methods, and have now integrated themselves as positive members of our society."

Sam sat down and relaxed.

"However," Bariv swayed back and forth, "I have forgotten that you are not like everyone else, and I must not treat you as such. As I'm sure May has told you, I am the one who is responsible for feeling the small ripples in the Veil when young sorcerers have their first grips. It does not happen very often in the world you come from, yet I have become acutely aware and increasingly accurate at finding those young entities when it does. You, my young entity, created a tidal wave."

"Then why can't I do any of this?" Sam twisted his head back toward the glowing podium. "I can't even grip onto the Veil. Every time I do that focusing thing you taught me, nothing happens."

Bariv rubbed one of his swirled cheeks and a strong wind passed Sam's face. "I guess for you, more contemporary methods must be pursued. Normally, one must learn to crawl before he can walk." He paused. "I think I must teach you how to run."

With that, Bariv stood up like a lightning bolt. The boy waved his hand and the skull-wolf glove pulled itself over Sam's fingers. Sam felt himself wrenched to his feet.

All at once, a loud boom thundered around him and a blast of red came toward his face. As a reflex, he held up his arm to stop the oncoming flash. Instead of pain, he felt a rush of energy across his palm, and then something warm and comforting, like a blanket left sitting in a sunbeam. The feeling caressed his forearm, made its way down to his elbow, and suddenly disappeared.

"Whoa." Sam blinked a few times. "What just happened?"

Bariv was standing with his arms out and his knees bent. "You were almost just beaten to a pulp."

Sam examined his hand. "What?"

Bariv tilted in a small bow. "I sent a scorching ball of energy at you."

"What! Why would you do that?"

"The real question is," Bariv gave him an appreciative grin, "how did you stop it?"

Sam's clenched teeth slowly turned into a smile. "How *did* I stop it?"

"That is between you and Her."

Sam's cheeks rose even higher. "No c'mon. How did I do it?"

"I assume you tapped into Her, and quite masterfully, as a matter of fact. If you hadn't stopped that energy, I would've had my hands full healing you. Might've taken weeks."

"C'mon."

"So," Bariv gave a single clap. "Now you know you have the ability. Self-fulfilling prophecies make everyone a prophet."

Sam shook his head and rolled his eyes.

ℓ

"This is pretty good." Sam munched on the crispy item Bariv had given him. "Probably the best food I've ever eaten in a cave."

"My own recipe. I usually use it as a reward for excellent training, but in this case I figured I could make an exception." Bariv gave him a sympathetic look. "You looked hungry."

"Very funny." Sam ate the next bite in the most obnoxious way possible. "But you have to admit I'm getting better."

"Yes… better."

"Hey!" Sam dropped half of his food, barely noticing when it shattered on the cave floor. "I got that rock to move at least a foot!"

Bariv looked at him dubiously.

"Okay. A few inches."

"Yes, you did. Normally, however, that is what my students accomplish in the first few hours." Bariv's eyes drifted to one of the candles.

Sam stopped eating. "Really?"

Bariv stared at the flickering light. "Hmm? Yes, but..." He bent down, scooping the small flame into his right hand. The candle went out. He went over to the cave wall and smeared the fire across the stone. The flame snuffed out as Bariv's hand came away from the surface, revealing an image burned into the stone. A thick line of black ash flowed in sort of an S-shape, with a few cinders continuing to burn along the dark streak.

Sam flexed an eyebrow. "But what?"

"Well," Bariv returned to the front of the platform, "the way you stopped my attack earlier. That was incredibly advanced. I did not hold back."

"Why did you attack me in the first place?"

Bariv jumped off the platform and poked Sam in the chest. "There was so much for you to see."

"But I could barely see it. That light was coming at me at, like, a hundred miles an hour."

Bariv chuckled and stepped back. "Instinct." He tapped a finger on his own chest. "You weren't thinking, you were doing. It was innate. You had to *see* your ability. You needed to know what you are capable of. In most intense situations, sorcerers are able to make grips that they would never be capable of in normal circumstances. I put you in danger and you overcame."

"Yet I still can't perform the basics?"

Bariv gave a tiny nod. "Precisely."

"What's the deal?"

"Basics are tough. You have to learn the fundamentals, and that takes time and practice. You have to learn how to work in harmony with the Veil or you will be limited. Remember, you can steal a gift—"

"Yeah, yeah, but I won't have earned it."

Bariv rubbed his fingertips together and a blue current played across his knuckles. "There is something else that I wanted you to see."

Sam groaned. "You're not going to show me more of my memories on that wall, are you?"

"The Veil protected you. She was there for you in a time of need." Bariv paused. "Did you know how to stop my attack?"

"No, it just happened."

"Yes." The electricity pendulumed back and forth on Bariv's forearms. "It did. You did not force it; it happened naturally, you and the Veil working together. She sees you as one of Her children. You are bonded."

Sam waited for more, but none came. "Your point?"

"Just something to remember." Bariv's eyes took on that aged sheen for a moment. "Give me the second-skin."

"Huh?" Sam clutched the skull-wolf glove to his chest. "Wait, you just gave this to me. You've got to give me more time. You said yourself, the basics take—"

"Give it to me."

Sam scowled as he pulled off the glove and handed it over to Bariv, who placed it back on the pedestal.

"Good." Bariv's hand lingered on the skin for a few moments.

Sam snorted.

"Now, it is time for you to get your own second-skin. I have a feeling that will make all the difference. These skins work for training purposes, but since they were molded by my own hand, they are linked to me, not the student. I believe you will have better success with one linked solely to you."

Sam went over to the glowing podium, picking up the green second-skin. It was light and cool to the touch. "Really? I get one already?"

Bariv snapped his fingers. The skin slipped from Sam's hand and shuffled itself back into place on the podium. "Yes."

"So where do we get one?"

"*We* don't get one anywhere."

Sam raised his eyebrows. "Huh?"

"It is you who must get it."

Sam scratched the back of his head. "But I don't know where the store is."

"Oh, dear boy." Bariv chuckled—a funny sound coming from someone who looked so young. "There is no store. You must go out and make one for yourself. Just *buying* it could never bond you with the second-skin. If you want a link to Her, you must use something from Her, and get it on your own accord. You must find the right material and make the second-skin yourself to form the necessary bond."

"Ah." Sam reached down to touch one of the metal thimbles, but found that his fingers were softly repelled. "One of those lone quest things to prove myself, huh?" Sam sighed, and then waved a playful fist at Bariv. "So what do I do now? What kind of glove do I get?"

"*Second-skin*," Bariv corrected. "And let's focus on the most important thing."

"How I get good enough to never have to listen to you drone on for hours on end?"

Bariv ignored him. "What sect of magic She will allow you to master."

"Oh."

"I think we both already know the answer to that."

Sam's eyes darted toward the skull-wolf glove. "So I have to kill something? You said power magics work best if the second-skin is taken forcibly, right?"

"It is never good to kill for greed." Bariv started pacing around the cave, his feet glowing red after every step. "In Atlas Crown, our food is given to us by the Veil. We are never hungry, as food is always available, and many in our community specialize in perfecting and transforming new recipes." He halted. "You must try the frapelcarnes made by Grun of the Sunder clan at some point. He sends me mounds of them every now and again, but I digress." His pacing resumed, as if he could think better in motion. "Creatures She sends often bear gifts to us that do not involve slaughter. Because of this, we almost never eat meat in our community, and creatures' lives are never ended—by *our* hands. Population control is taken care of by Her, because if too many of a certain creature are given, they can also be taken away."

"But you had to kill this skull-wolf thing?"

"Ahh," Bariv started moving faster, "Not every gift is meant for the initial recipient. The skull-wolf was an unfortunate poison that needed to be eliminated. Since we do not waste the Veil's bounty—as I'm sure you will see—I made the skin of the skull-wolf into something useful with my own hands."

Sam's nose wrinkled in disgust. "So, do you have, like, any leftover skin?"

"No, because you still would not have the necessary link if it was not taken by your own hand."

Sam raised his voice. "You don't make any sense. If I can't kill anything and I can't use something that is already dead, then I can't do power magic."

Bariv pointed at the candle from which he'd scooped the fire, which instantly flared to life. "Unless you know a loophole."

"Do you?"

"More of a snake-hole."

Sam furrowed his brow. "You lost me."

"It has been a long time since someone was invited into the power arts; however, you are not the first. I know of a creature that will fill the required need."

"So why snake-ho—" Sam stopped mid-sentence. "Ohhhhh."

"I am not Her eyes for nothing." Bariv gave him a somewhat smug smile. "There is actually a lot of wisdom brewing in this child-sized cauldron."

"Cauldron, huh?" Sam asked, returning the look. "Cliché much?"

"Figuratively speaking, of course."

"So this snake," Sam cracked his knuckles, "I assume I have to find the skin that it shed?"

"That *he* shed… and no."

"He? He who?"

"He who is dangerous, cunning, and extremely elusive. You know that lone quest that you were talking about earlier?"

"Uh-huh."

Bariv flashed a wicked grin. "You guessed right."

CHAPTER 11

Samuel Lock's fingertips pierced the caked mud up to his second knuckle.

"Well." Sam's face scrunched in disgust. "This is pleasant." His nose was now just inches away from the putrid material encased in the small sack Bariv had given him. Sam was in this predicament after tripping over who-knows-what in the near pitch black.

He gave a sharp exhale and pulled himself to his feet.

"Sam." He did his best to imitate Bariv's voice. "Why don't you just go right into the forest and look for an extremely elusive snake-thing? Am I going to tell you anything about it? No… I don't think that's necessary. Only one who needs to hear the truth seeks the blah blah blah. I'm going to let you figure it out on your own. Oh, and here, take this stuff. Oh, and don't be alarmed that it smells like a fart trapped in a gym sock. Why? Oh, you'll see… have fun."

He wiped off what dirt he could feel, and his hand brushed across the pocket on his thigh that held the diamond. He was back out in the woods that had captivated him so much during the day. At night, it was a different ballgame. That feeling that someone was watching him had returned. He hoped it was Bariv, as he was alone in a strange place with nothing to protect himself with—other than the moldy tang coming from the pouch he held at arms' length, which he guessed no creature would want to come near, anyway. He squinted and scanned the darkness for any signs of life, but all he could see was the glow of the green, heat-less fire from a couple of vines off in the distance.

He had no clue where he was.

About an hour ago, Bariv had taken Sam to the back of the platform in the cave and created a door in the rock that had opened into the forest. He'd conjured up the foul-smelling sack—along with Sam's cleats—out of thin air, handed them both to Sam, then shoved him through the threshold, closing the rock behind him and sealing Sam out in the woods.

Sam had trudged through the multi-colored vegetation in no particular direction, holding the disgusting stuff as far from his nose as possible and hoping that something, anything, would happen. After the nasty fall over what might've been a protruding root, Sam found himself wishing that all the trees were zigzag trees.

He slowed his pace and continued in a random direction. The one thing Bariv had cautioned him about was not to go near the protective borders. Bariv had warned him that as he got close, he would hear a low buzz that would get louder the closer he got. He'd said that Sam wouldn't be able to get past the border—as it was strong enough to keep a grotlon away from jelly-bees—and warned Sam not to try.

"Great way to treat guests," Sam mumbled.

Soft hoots came from the treetops. Sam stared into the moonlit sky, looking for whatever little creature was making the noise, until he realized it was the leaves themselves.

Sam hooted back and the sounds stopped.

"Fine, then," Sam huffed.

He kept his back toward the stone pillars and slowed to a languorous pace. The one nice thing about being out here was how clear the night sky appeared. The stars popped like firecrackers. Even on a clear night back home, when he would sit on the empty Carver field after a victorious game, the stars never seemed so bright.

In the sky above Atlas Crown, they flickered like tiny fires, set to show the world where to turn, but Sam didn't know which ones to follow.

A sudden *snap* came from behind him.

Immediately pivoting—like he'd been trained to do on the field—he held out the rancid heap.

Behind him was just more forest… endless, endless forest. As his racing heart slowed, something peculiar caught his eye. Hovering above a small bush—one with orange, tentacled branches—was a little black swirl, the same size and shape as the ones he had seen around his car and in his dream.

The swirl inched away. Sam traced the path it followed and saw more little swirls, just like the first. They looked like the ones on Bariv's cheeks, but larger.

He should have put two and two together earlier.

"Hey," Sam shouted. "C'mon out, Bariv. I know it's you!"

No answer.

"It's really okay. It makes sense that you would follow me. I'm just too clever for you."

Sam barreled his way between two of the mutant orange bushes to follow the black swirls.

"You don't have to play this game anymore. Don't worry, I won't tell anyone that I found you out!"

Sam had to quicken his pace to keep up with Bariv's swirls, which were quite spry.

"C'mon, I can see you up ahead!" Sam lied.

Sam revved up to a full sprint. *He's pretty quick for a guy with such short legs.* Hopping over mounds of blue earth and tiny creeks, Sam muscled his way onward through the underbrush.

Then the black swirls vanished.

Sam stopped short, barely huffing and puffing even after running at full speed over half a football field's worth of jungle floor.

"Man…"

The jungle around him was silent. Sam noticed, however, that it was not so much jungle anymore. All around him was a smooth, colorless, quartz-like material. The ground beneath his feet was almost like a glass floor, but with nothing underneath. Resting on his thigh, on his brand new football pants—though by now they needed to be changed, anyway—was the disgusting sack of gunk that Bariv had given him. He pulled the bag away from the formerly white material, but some of the slime, safely inside of the pouch a few moments ago, now seeped out. He almost threw up the food Bariv had given him as a training reward.

"Aww," Sam moaned. "C'mon."

Attempting to take his mind off the renewed stink, Sam bent down to examine what he was standing on. With his pinky, he flaked off a long, thin layer and held it up to the moonlight to get a better look. Something small and colorful twinkled inside.

Bringing it closer revealed a reflection of his eye… only it wasn't his eye. It was red.

Am I seeing things? Is this some weird effect of the moonlight? He stared at the red eye, which seemed to be unattached to a face.

"Bariv!" Sam shouted into the vast expanse. "I know you're there."

An eerie silence crept over the landscape. Adrenaline careened through his veins, so he took a slow, deep breath, knowing that a frantic heart would only generate frantic behavior.

There's nothing to be afraid of. Man up.

Then something soft and warm, like a kiss from fevered lips, pressed against his thigh. There, feeling the putrid material, was a long forked tongue. The ends—which were the color of raw meat—flicked about his leg, pressing into the white fabric. The viscous saliva made his skin crawl.

Too shocked to run, Sam's gaze followed the tongue to a tremendous mouth, outfitted with tremendous fangs. His body finally let him react, and he jumped, sprinting to anywhere but there.

Bariv said "snake," not "monster!"

The tongue and mouth—hopefully far behind him—belonged to what had to be by far the world's largest snake. Its body was like an oil pipeline, and its fangs could probably pierce a bank vault. It looked like a leftover dinosaur… something the other dinosaurs would run away from.

Sam's cleats clacked against the glassy surface as he took cover against the curve of what could have served as a crystal amphitheater. The quartz here was less opaque, and it looked to be a few feet thick under his feet. Underneath it, all he could see was black. His heart seemed less intent on breaking through his ribcage as he forced his breathing to slow.

Around him the crystal walls glittered in the reflected light of the too-bright stars. Intricate cracks made long shelves and designs, traveling all the way up to the natural bridges overhead. For the moment, Sam felt safe.

Then the smell caught up with him again. Running had left his nostrils free of the gag-inducing mulch that Bariv had given him; however, at a standstill, it returned with a vengeance. He still clutched the bag in his fist. Why hadn't he dropped it in his panic?

He gasped and froze as the touch against his leg returned.

The snake was again trying to lick his flesh. Its tongue curved around the corner and slithered up his leg. It made its way across Sam's chest all the way to his outstretched hand, gently prodding the bag. How the snake had managed to sneak up on him, Sam could not fathom, but nevertheless there it was. *How did it catch me?* He had no idea what to do or how to get away. He felt a mighty panic washing over him. *This is it, I am*

going to be eaten by a giant snake in the middle of nowhere. He clenched his eyes shut, and prepared for the first bite.

"I believe that is meant for me."

Sam heard the voice in the center of his head, like music through headphones. He couldn't see where it was coming from, as he was too terrified to open his eyes.

"There," the voice resonated in his brain again, *"in your hand. That is for me, I presume."*

Sam felt the tongue recede from his body.

"What the—"

"That is from Bariv, correct?"

Sam carefully opened one eye and peeked at the bag. "Um…"

"Is it for me or isn't it? I can't imagine you would have any interest in it yourself."

Sam stopped breathing as he realized where the voice in his head was coming from.

"There is no way a snake is talking to me." Sam clenched his eyes tight, shaking his head.

"Believe what you want. But I still would like to have my present, if you please."

Bracing himself for the worst, Sam stretched out his quivering hand—still not daring to look.

In one quick swipe, the bag was pulled from his grasp and the smell diminished. The creature's retreat made no sound, yet Sam knew the danger was fading; he could *feel* the presence receding.

The farther away that thing gets, the better.

Very carefully, Sam peeked around the corner.

The giant snake glided along the smooth surface, as silent as a shadow. Sam had never seen a snake—or anything, for that matter—like that one. Its scales were deep black and looked as if they were reflecting the stars, yet when it moved, the pinpricks of light remained firmly in their places. The stars were *part* of the snake. The tail gave a small flick as it rounded a bend and disappeared.

Sam took a deep, thankful breath. He transferred the remaining gunk on his palm to the wall with a long swipe. That had been a close call.

Then he remembered why he'd come in the first place—Bariv's loophole.

"Seriously?" He shuddered. "*That's* the snake? He's got to be joking."

Sam bit his lip. On the one hand, he could end up as an appetizer for that monster, and on the other, he could get some of the skin and make a faster return back to Stanton. It seemed like a no-brainer—count his blessings and go back empty-handed—but then he remembered Bariv's black swirls.

Letting out a small groan, he followed the serpent. If it would get him home quicker, he might as well try.

Besides, Bariv must still be following me, and he wouldn't let that thing eat me.

Sam cupped his hands around his mouth. "Wait up!"

He started moving faster, resisting the nagging thought that the closer he got to the snake, the closer he got to becoming a meal. For the first time in his life, Sam wished he were smaller, so then maybe his meaty arms wouldn't appear so appetizing.

"Hold on a second!"

He rounded the bend where the snake had disappeared.

Am I really trying to talk to a snake?

Against all better judgment, he kept going. Normally, millions of years of instinctual evolution would tell him to run *away* from the giant man-eating predator, but then again, he normally wouldn't be in the middle of Magictown, trying to learn sorcery from someone not tall enough to ride most roller coasters.

The snake was gone.

The empty crystalline structures loomed over him like reflective bleachers.

He tried to stop short, but his cleats skidded across the crystal for a few feet. Once he came to a halt, he heard only silence.

He'd blown his chance.

The cool flood of relief cut short as his coach's voice resonated in his mind, more forceful than the snake's vocal projection. *You gonna mess this up, too? You gonna cower there and let the world scare you into submission? You want your dolly, little girl? Gimme twenty!*

Sam grinned at the thought, and dropped to the ground. It was slippery under his sweaty palms, but he managed to execute twenty full-extension pushups.

The activity—so tied to his life back home—brought memories to the surface: the look on his father's face as Sam had been escorted out of his own house; the booing of his ex-fans at the game; his sunken dreams of a scholarship and a multi-million-dollar contract to the pros.

He had this one chance to make it all right.

Knowing one thing for sure—he was sick of failing—a strong desire took root. He had to follow that snake.

But how? Which way do I go?

Then the smell hit again, stronger than ever. Maybe it was because he had just gotten re-acclimated to a world that didn't smell like sumo wrestler, but it made him dry-heave. He hated the smell, despised Bariv for introducing him to it, and then realized it was the solution to his problem.

He would follow the stench.

He inhaled deeply, scrunched his face, and started walking. It seemed to be working. The smell drew him to the left in an almost supernatural way. *It couldn't have smelled like of one of Mom's apple pies, or a well-cooked steak on the grill, or even one of those rinsefish flowers, noooo.*

Step by step he crossed the crystal surface, hoping that he wouldn't fall through a crack into never-never land, or perhaps into the jaws of something that would look at that snake and salivate.

Letting the odor pull him, he continued on for a few minutes. The rancid smell grew more potent. Once he got back to Atlas Crown, he vowed to stick an entire handful of rinsefish globs in his nose—*if* he got back to Atlas Crown.

A few more turns, and small grains of the crystal lined the base of the walls. The smell guided him through a confusing, twisting labyrinth, where the shiny material looked less tarnished than the rest.

How am I going to get back out?

He continued on until, suddenly, he turned a corner and gasped. Sam was face to face with the massive serpent, close enough to feel its hot breath. It stared at him, eyes not twitching, scales not stirring.

Up close, Sam could see the utter beauty in the beast. Other than the fangs that could scare the white off a goalpost and the bewitching eyes, it was a striking creature. Its body was obsidian, with specks of light all over its skin, especially concentrated on its underbelly. A few cloudy spots along its scales gave the impression of distant galaxies.

74

"Is there something else?"

Sam again heard the voice reverberate throughout his head. He didn't see the snake's mouth move—nor did he expect to—but he *knew* that it was the snake talking to him.

"Y-yes," Sam answered.

"Well, speak up, what is it?"

"I guess…" Sam gulped. "I need some of your skin."

The long tongue slowly flickered from its jaws and fluttered in the air. *"Yes?"*

"Um… yeah."

The snake let out a hiss. *"How would you feel if I said I needed your skin in exchange?"*

A jolt of fear tied up his stomach. He took a slow step back. "Well… I need my skin."

"And I don't need mine?"

"I—"

"You don't even introduce yourself, and you come right out and ask me for something as precious as my skin?" The long fangs peeked out, and ropey slime dripped from the tips. *"How uncouth."*

This is it, Sam's throat felt like sandpaper. *I'm done for.*

The snake slithered forward. Its fangs protruded just inches away from his face. *"I think you can see my… point."* The voice rattled in his brain.

"I'm sorry," Sam managed to squeak.

All of a sudden, the fangs were sheathed.

"Ah well, I guess that's a start."

Sam's heart pounded so hard he thought it was going to explode. "So…so you're not going to eat me?"

What might have been a smile appeared on the snake's face. *"Of course not. I'm a vegetarian."*

Sam made a sound that was half laugh, half gasp.

"But when someone comes asking for your skin…"

"Again, so sorry," Sam said with relief. "Let's try this again. My name's Sam. I hope you enjoyed your gift."

"Pleasure, Sam. However, that gift was not for me, as much as I appreciate it."

Sam wiped the sweat from his forehead. "Then who was it for?"

The snake dipped its body out of the way. Sam could finally see where he was. They were in a cavern under a massive dome of the clear gemstone material. Behind the snake were round, green pods, just big enough for a person to curl up in, covered in layers of leaves that rested upon each other like shingles on a roof. Each pod floated above a twisting braid of tiny green roots that tethered it to the ground. They looked like balloons, but far too heavy to float or to be supported on the delicate roots.

"*For them.*"

"What are they?"

"*Cultivated by my own hand, if I had a hand, that is. I do not have a name for them, simply because they need no name. Miracles can often be best captured without the captivity that comes with a label.*"

Sam snorted. "You sound just like Bariv."

"*That is not surprising. Come, let me show you.*"

The mighty body unwound and slithered over to the looming pods. Moonlight filtered through the overhead dome, so Sam had no problem seeing the details. Curiosity replaced the last of the lingering fear as Sam drew nearer to the pod.

"*Take a peek.*"

Hoping he wasn't going to find the last person Bariv had sent out to find the snake, Sam peeled back a leaf.

Intense light burst forth from inside.

Startled, Sam let the leaf fall back in place.

"*Do not be frightened; you will not be harmed.*"

Sam again pried open a leaf, releasing the oddly bright light. The leaves tickled his cheek as he drew close and peered inside.

In the center of the spherical plant was a tiny sun—floating, pulsing, almost breathing with light. It was no larger than a closed fist, suspended in midair. Circling the sun were tiny particles of varying colors—blue, orange, turquoise, auburn—like miniscule planets in orbit. Some of the little planets even had almost microscopic rings. He felt like he was intruding on a tiny solar system, somewhere he was not supposed to be, yet he still felt drawn to watch. In an act of deep willpower, Sam pulled his head away. It took a moment for his eyes to adjust. "It's amazing."

The snake dipped its head. "*I knew you would appreciate it.*"

"What am I looking at?"

"*A plant that creates its own energy source. It is a brilliant manifestation. Absolutely miraculous of Her. They have captured my full attention for a very long time.*"

"How long?"

"*Almost a millennium.*"

Sam paused a moment. "I think that was the first straight answer I've gotten since I got to Atlas Crown."

The snake rotated its head. "*I cannot stop my obsession, nor do I have any intent to. As you have noticed, there is a self-sustaining symbiotic system inside the plant. They feed off each other. The sun gives the plant food and the plant keeps it safe. The plant feeds off the light and gets larger and grows stronger. Eventually, like everything must, the system dies. The sun expands in the most infinitesimal moment, swallowing up the tiny planets, and instantaneously crystallizes the plant. The minerals are sent in all directions and join with the other fallen.*"

Sam looked around. "Is that how this place got formed?"

"*As a matter of fact, it was,*" the voice paused. "*Then the sun implodes, and hardens into a very dense seed. The seed falls and slowly grows into a plant by using the latent and innate energy. When the energy reserve gets low, it uses it all to create a new sun. A fascinating system.*"

"That's incredible."

"*It is but one of the wonders She has given, yet it is the one I feel the most connection to.*"

Sam gestured to the pods. "You said the plants came from your hand?"

The snake snatched up Bariv's pungent bag with its fangs. Sam had forgotten about the smell, but now it was back.

"*I didn't create them, but I do watch over them and help them grow.*" The snake gestured toward the bag with its eyes. "*Fertilizer. With this, the plant has extra energy that it can put into fruit.*"

"A snake with fruit? That can't end well." Sam allowed himself a small chuckle.

The snake cocked its head.

"Never mind. What does the fruit do?"

"*Exactly what it is supposed to.*"

It pierced the bag with a fang and let the juices fall onto the various pods. The liquid seeped through, and the plant subtly changed shades.

After the bag was drained, the voice spoke. "*I know why you want my skin.*"

Sam absentmindedly put his right hand into his pocket. "You do?"

"*You are not the first to ask.*"

"Bariv?"

The voice gave a haunting laugh. "*No.*"

"Who?"

"*He never introduced himself.*"

Sam smiled.

The voice hesitated for a moment. "*I chose not to give it to him.*"

"Why not?" Sam rolled the diamond around in his fingers.

"*I have my reasons. Now. Why do you want my skin?*"

Sam thought for a moment. "To be honest, I just want to go home and play football. If I do what Bariv says, he told me he'd fix my life. So, here I am."

"*You came all this way. And my skin is some of the finest. Is that the only reason? Just to turn on your path and wander home?*"

It *was* the main reason, but something else, something deeper pulled at him.

"Well, I've been studying with Bariv. Studying the Veil…"

"*Go on.*"

"And I guess I'm suited for power magics."

"*You guess?*"

Sam thought about how he had stopped Bariv's attack and how right it had felt. The skull-wolf skin definitely had been the right pick. "I know."

"*Yes?*"

Sam gave a sharp nod.

"*Do you know what the Veil is?*"

Sam inhaled. "The Veil is where you grip magic from. It is all around us and some people can use it—"

The snake thrust its body forward, ending its strike just inches from Sam's face. A strong gust of air whizzed by.

Sam, astonishingly, didn't flinch.

"*Wrong.*"

Sam hesitated a moment. He thought about what had happened when he grabbed the cornerback's shoulder. He had tapped into something primal; he knew that for sure. Something ancient, something unique, something full of…

All pretention disappeared from his voice. "Power."

"*Yes…*" The snake retreated. "*But She is more than that.*"

Sam took his hand away from the diamond and out of his pocket. "More than power?"

The snake bowed its head low. "*She is imagination.*"

Sam frowned in confusion.

"*Does this surprise you?*"

"I just… I don't understand."

"*I know you just met Her,*" the voice said, "*but I'm sure you will.*"

Sam felt his chest tighten in frustration.

"*I will try and help you understand.*" The snake eased backwards. "*Peer again into the plant. Deep this time.*"

This time, Sam peeled back a handful of leaves and stuck his entire head inside.

"*Truly look.*"

Staring at the tiny sun didn't burn his eyes at all, unlike the times he had caught a glimpse of the real sun while attempting to catch a lobbed pass. He felt his focus being summoned inward.

"*Look deep.*"

The sun hung in the air, giving warmth and light. Giving life. Until that moment, Sam was sure he knew what silence was, but now, his head completely within the pod, the world melted away, and he truly understood. Warmth spread over his face as the yellow light drifted past his consciousness and reached deep into the crevices of his soul. The honeycombed sections of his mind filled with the sweet nectar of the tiny sun. The weight on his feet was forgotten. His muscles, tense from the second he'd entered the forest, were kneaded into complacency. The world he knew was no longer there.

"She has always been here," the voice said, although now it was much more than a vibrating noise, as it had been earlier. Now, it was part of him. He no longer felt the words, he knew them. He had always known them.

"She lives where we cannot, but we can always visit."

"Imagination?" Sam didn't speak the words; it was a conversation that he was listening to.

"Yes. The world is hidden to most. Though She is not different from the world you thought you knew. Imagination is what sets people apart. She was a part of it, the seed of a magnanimous fruit, whose flesh was consumed and whose essence was discarded. People covered themselves in self-righteousness. You were always in Her presence. You can reach Her in the place where ideas are discovered. Imagination is both cradle and grave to power. She is a cycle. She is whole."

"But why now?" he asked. "Why do I get to know Her now?"

"If you receive a gift which you are not ready to appreciate, it is not a gift; it is… a burden."

"Am I ready?"

"That is up to you. She can only give, the other side is yours."

"What about my world? What about football?"

"What about it?"

"It's all I have."

"Apparently not."

"I need it."

"Why?"

"I don't belong here."

"Belonging implies possession. Do you not believe yourself to be free?"

"I think I am."

"The key is to know."

"I feel like I don't know anything anymore."

"A clear mind is the perfect vessel to fill."

"But I can't just leave my other life behind. What about my friends? My family?"

"Family is family; that will never change, even when the world changes you."

"And my friends?"

"Friends are always left behind—it is the nature of life. A true friend will be there no matter how much time elapses."

"So I'll be able to visit?"

"When you become truly free."

"How will I know?"

"When the time comes, you will have to choose whether or not to work with Her, and it will be soon."

"When?"

The voice said nothing.

"When?" Sam demanded, but he was already on his way back.

CHAPTER 12

It wasn't quite like waking up from a dream, Sam thought, it was sort of like a dream that woke him up.

The world was fresh; it smelled new.

Sam looked back at the crystal cavern and let his hand drift to the pocket on his thigh.

Inside was a fruit. A ripe, red fruit.

Sam thought about what had just happened.

After he'd come out of the trance, everything had happened so fast. The tremendous snake sprawled on the floor, writhing in pain. Sam had run over and placed a palm against its skin. It had been burning up, so hot, in fact, that Sam'd had to pull his hand away. "What's happening?"

The serpent's voice was missing from his head. It twisted and convulsed into loops and knots. The stars on its skin changed shapes, making the constellations swirl across the scales.

The snake hissed and spat and Sam didn't know what to do. Then he realized what was going on. A portion of the skin detached from its body, bringing with it a select fragment of the constellations.

Sam tore his attention back to the present, away from the crystal cavern, as he examined what else he had been given.

Covering his right hand, fitting his dimensions precisely, was a glove. *Second-skin*, Sam corrected himself. He finally understood what Bariv had been trying to teach him before.

The snake had given him a portion of skin. The offering had looked hideously painful, but after the small section was shed, the snake had nodded toward it, urging Sam to take it. Sam had wrapped it around his hand and the beautiful skin had shaped itself to fit. It'd shrunk in some places and stretched in others, until it had become unquestionably Sam's.

Sam knew he could take it off at any moment, yet doing so was the furthest thing from his mind. It really was a second skin, maybe even a better skin.

After recovering, the snake had lifted itself up and glided toward the three pods. Sam hadn't noticed, but the plant he'd just been looking in had produced a fruit—the one currently in his possession. The snake had plucked it with its mouth and dropped it into Sam's hand before it motioned Sam toward the exit.

Now back out of the maze, he let his fingertips roll over the lump on his thigh. After pulling out the pad, he had placed the fruit securely in his slime-free pocket, next to the diamond.

I desperately need a change of clothes.

It wasn't hard to find his way out of the cave, as it felt like he had been living there for a while, like he knew the exact layout of the crystal labyrinth—though he knew that couldn't be true. Once out, he sped off, hoping to get back to town as quickly as possible and find May. Then he realized he had no idea which way the town was.

A drop of rain splashed on his forehead. The droplets started out as beads the size of sand, but quickly grew larger. His hair became saturated in a matter of seconds and cool water ran down the inside of his jersey. Normally, being stranded in a storm would have annoyed him, but this one was different. He felt as if the world was trying to wash away certain things—things he needed to let go of.

Despite the chilly weather, he felt something warm. Even as the freezing water pelted his body, the second-skin insulated his hand, trapping heat.

No, it's giving heat.

He knew it was time to try it out.

The bright pins of light on his new second-skin glowed against the smooth black scales as it was struck by rain. Closing his eyes and thinking about the tiny sun, he let his fingers curve inward toward his palm. It felt instinctual.

He could feel energy rushing through his grip like a stampede. It shot in between his thumb and index finger. It was like trying to hold onto lightning.

Imagination, he remembered.

Concentrating hard, he thought about the pillars of Atlas Crown.

Something warm scuttled through his hand down to his feet. As it passed out of his toes, he looked down. Just in front of him lay a disc of light—the same color as the light he'd seen in the pod. Flaws in the crystal ground reflected small spines of light around it.

He placed a cleat against the light.

Just as he applied pressure, the disc slid forward the distance of a stride.

He knew it would take him back because that was what he had imagined. A certain amount of pride welled up inside him. In Bariv's cave, he had been able to do a few menial tricks, but this was real. This was magic.

Like playing hopscotch, he jumped from light point to light point, traveling a good distance in the pouring rain.

He stopped to watch a bird paddling itself through the air with long flipper-like feet. A few minutes later, he stopped again to observe a flower that reflected the rain back toward the sky like a negatively charged magnet. In one spot he even saw a pack of drecklers, whose cotton was extra puffy with soaked-up moisture.

He followed the light for a good while. The rain did nothing to slow him down; he was used to harsh practices in downpours like this one, and his cleats gave him stability.

He froze at the sound of music. A friendly tune carried through the rain and reached his ears in a crescendo of lovely notes, the pitter-patter of rain providing a backbeat to the melody.

Taking a chance, he stepped away from his light and pursued the sound.

Immediately, the next luminous spot disappeared.

Oh well. I can always do it again.

He stepped through the drenched bushes and advanced toward the notes. They grew more piercingly beautiful as he hacked at weeds and tore through vines. He pushed and pulled and struggled, and the tune became more enticing. The notes were almost voices, familiar in a way.

Back home in Stanton—not being one for live music—he'd listened to whatever was on the radio. This, however, could never be captured through speakers, regardless of amps or watts.

He came to a clearing and smiled.

Sitting on a stump next to a cluster of audible symflowers, a boy played a horn. Sam recognized him as the curly-haired kid who'd patted him on the back earlier, though his hair was now plastered flat across his forehead.

Thankfully, the boy didn't notice him and continued his wonderful composition.

The boy's horn wove flawlessly among the beats, accenting perfectly constructed solos against the symflowers' background. The boy splashed his foot along in time with the music, sending jets of water into the air.

Sam's own foot was doing something very similar. He closed his eyes to listen, determined not to miss a single note. After a little while, the horn died down.

Sam craved more. He opened his eyes and found the curly-haired kid standing right in front of him. He stared at Sam with a curious expression, holding the tan horn down at his hip, the illegible writing on it brighter than before.

"That was incredible!" Sam shouted over the rain.

The boy managed a slight smile and nodded politely.

"I've never heard anything like that!" Sam's ears were still tingling with delight. "I'm Sam. Sam Lock. What's your name?"

The boy said nothing, but placed his horn on the small of his back and gave a low bow, still looking Sam square in the eyes.

"Your name?" Sam asked, a little louder this time, trying to be heard over the singing of the symflowers.

Again the boy said nothing, but he raised the horn to his lips.

A single note left the horn, and Sam instantly knew the boy's name.

Though he had no idea how—as the boy had played the horn and not spoken—Sam heard a name.

"Glissandro Thicket?"

The boy nodded.

"How did I know that?"

Glissandro jiggled the horn in his hand.

"You can speak through that horn?"

His head bobbed from side to side.

"So you're a sorcerer."

A nod.

"Don't talk much, huh?"

A silent laugh.

Sam's eyes fell on Glissandro's horn. "So is this mystical magic?"

The boy touched the tip of his index finger to his other fingers. Sam frowned. *No glove—nothing to grip into the Veil with.*

"I thought you needed metal or something for mystical magics to work best."

The boy lifted the tan horn to Sam's eye level. Golden writing that Sam could not identify ran over the surface of the musical horn.

"Ah." Sam nodded. "Can you play some more?"

The symflowers' voices trilled in the air as Glissandro looked off into the distance for a moment.

Then he shook his head.

"Why not?"

All of a sudden, as quickly as it had arrived, the rainfall dwindled. The symflowers' singing quieted as the last of the drops fell. It sounded like the batteries dying in a stereo.

Glissandro shook the water from his head and his curls perked back up.

"Well," Sam wrung the water from the front of his jersey, "it was nice while it lasted."

Looking Sam up and down, Glissandro's eyes came to rest on his second-skin. His eyes opened wide, and Sam could see he was either surprised or impressed.

"I just got it," Sam explained. "It's a long story."

Glissandro looked as if he wanted to inspect it. His eyes kept flickering from Sam's face to the snake's skin—*Sam's* skin.

Sam decided it wouldn't hurt to let him. "Go ahead."

The silent boy caressed the star-encrusted skin on the back of Sam's hand.

Sam flexed his fingers. "Pretty cool, huh?"

Glissandro gave a fierce nod. He took his horn, wiped the water off the tip, and placed it in Sam's palm. Glissandro looked at him as if to say "go ahead."

Sam placed his lips against the opening and blew.

A terrible noise came out. He imagined it sounded like a lion frog being stepped on.

Sam laughed, wiped off the tip with his jersey—though that probably made it dirtier—and handed the horn back.

"I was never good at music." Sam continued to wring out his jersey, though it didn't do him much good.

Glissandro brought the horn to his mouth and let out a few quick bursts of noise. The sound acted like air in a wind tunnel. The water shot out of Sam's clothing. He was left dry and warm, like his entire outfit had just come off a clothesline.

Sam felt much cleaner as well; the various stains and smells were no longer there. His jersey looked fresh out of the box.

Sam gave him a pat on the shoulder. "Thanks."

Glissandro nodded.

Sam noticed Glissandro's clothing was waterless as well.

"I need to learn how to do that. I hate doing laundry."

The boy still said nothing.

"Can… do you know the way back?"

Glissandro nodded and motioned back the way Sam had come. Sam turned around and saw the tip of a pillar in the distance.

He smiled. "That'll come in handy."

They trudged through the bushes toward the sandstone column.

Sam followed behind Glissandro, and after a few minutes of silence, he decided to try and get some information out of his new companion.

"So, Gliss." Sam wondered if he went by that. "Were you born here?"

The boy nodded.

"How old are you?"

Glissandro stopped, turned around, and bit his bottom lip in contemplation. After a moment, he shrugged in defeat.

"You don't know how old you are?" Sam's eyes went wide.

The boy pressed the horn to his lips and blew.

Again, Sam didn't hear any words, but he knew what Glissandro was trying to convey. The words "Age loses importance very quickly here" nestled in Sam's head.

Glissandro turned around and started toward their destination again.

"Do you know May?"

The horn played again and Sam heard what Glissandro intended.

"Really?" Sam asked. "Everyone knows her?"

Again the boy nodded.

"I guess I can see why," Sam said, remembering how stunning she was.

Suddenly, a strong surge of nausea came over Sam, and he realized just how hungry he was. He wondered how long it had been since his last meal. "Hey, anything to eat out here? I wouldn't mind some of that dreckler cotton about now."

"Hold out a little longer," Glissandro played. "It'll be worth it. Tonight is a seam."

"What's a seam?"

"It's a clan union," Glissandro played with a smile.

"There are clans? Like, Native Americans?"

Glissandro turned around and pointed to the design on his robe. It was an upside-down V with a circle above and below the tip. Turning back toward Atlas Crown, Glissandro played a few more notes. This time, Sam didn't hear any words, but the tangle of green fire-vines in front of them bent out of their path.

"You're pretty good."

Another nod.

At the next tremor of hunger, Sam remembered the taste of the slider-buns Fromson had given him earlier. *If all their food is that good, it would be well worth staying at least a little while.*

"Do you always come out here when it rains?"

"I try to."

"Why?"

"It is the only gift I can give back," Glissandro played. The notes' pitch bent upward.

"Back to who?"

Glissandro stopped and pointed his horn toward Sam's covered hand.

"The Veil?" Sam asked.

"Boys!" A voice called out. "Over here!"

Sam was glad to finally hear a voice coming into his head in the normal fashion.

May perched on the lone rock in the otherwise muddy field in front of the pillar. She waved her diamond-covered hand through the air; it sparkled as it cut through the mist. In her other hand, she held a bundled up piece of cloth.

They joined May in the muddy moat.

"Splendid, Sam." She clapped her hands together. "You've met Glissandro."

"Yeah, I heard him playing on the way back."

"Wonderful. I have had the pleasure of hearing his divine music many times. Which, if I may add, is many times too few."

Glissandro made a small bow.

May grabbed the hem of her robe and curtsied. "If you don't mind, Glissandro, I would like to have a private word with Sam. I trust I'll see you later at the seam?"

Glissandro gave a tiny wave goodbye and headed to the pillar. He gave a light toot on his horn, which made a section of stone draw back so he could pass through.

"So how did it go?" May stepped off the rock, but instead of sinking into the mud, she landed on a second rock as it popped out of the earth, keeping her feet clean and dry. "Though I feel it is a needless question, judging by what is now fitted on your hand."

"How—what...?"

"Bariv filled me in. Stopping one of his attacks is very impressive. Yet another thing I probably couldn't have done—at least not early on in my career."

Sam's voice filled with pride. "It was pretty awesome, I have to admit."

She stopped and nodded toward his hand. "And I see you have successfully negotiated with Bariv's snake."

Sam cocked an eyebrow. "His snake? Like, a pet?"

"I wouldn't say that."

"How then?"

May skated around his question. "I hope you haven't left your appetite in that cave."

Sam put a hand on his stomach. "Please tell me you're going to take me to some food."

May nodded. "Plenty of it. You are in for a treat tonight."

"The seam thing?"

"Yes." May tossed him the bundled-up cloth. "And I think this would be more appropriate for the ceremony than your uniform."

Sam unfolded the fabric and held it out. It was a blue robe like the ones he had seen people wearing around town, but this one was unadorned.

"Thanks." Sam pulled the robe over his uniform. "But how come this doesn't have a symbol thing on it?"

May made a small turn of her wrist and Sam felt a tight yank on the robe. He looked down and saw that the wrinkles had been smoothed out.

"It will make more sense tonight." May looked down at the numerous symbols on her own robe. She continued toward the pillar, stepping stones emerging under her feet like a disjointed bridge.

"You know," Sam trudged through the mud beside her, "that snake was more straightforward with me."

She tilted her head to give him a look. "Do you just want the answers *given* to you?"

Sam frowned. "I... yes?"

"Answers close paths; questions open them. I think that now is the time when you need the hunger to discover things for yourself." She put a hand on Sam's shoulder, steadying herself on the next stone, which was smaller than the others. "You can't have a quest without questions, you know."

Sam groaned. "Here we go."

"We do indeed." May pulled a small ledge out of the pillar, creating a final stepping stone as the opening widened. "Tonight you will see one of the highlights of our society. Are you ready to go?"

"Before we do, I have another question."

"Hmm?"

Sam pointed to the portion of the pillar Glissandro had gone through. "How did that kid talk to me through music?"

"All music talks to us, Sam."

Sam sucked air through his teeth. "You know what I mean."

May smiled. "I do. I was just practicing my cryptic banter, which I know you love so much."

"Thanks for that." Sam made sure that she could see the full extent of his eye-roll.

"Glissandro is an extraordinarily unique boy. I mean that literally. You see, he is mute, and—"

Sam cut her off. "He can't talk?"

"No, he never has been able to. It was quite troublesome for him as a child, though he had ways of dealing with it, things like writing in the air. However, that was most tedious work. Barring his one handicap, he was otherwise in perfect health, and though he couldn't talk, when it came to listening he was truly gifted. The ability to hear without reservation spurred his love of music. Though always rather intelligent and a quick learner, he has amazed all of us with his discovery. He figured out a way to communicate *through* the Veil with music. Beautiful music. And I haven't the slightest idea how."

Sam's curiosity was piqued. "That's incredible."

"Yes, it is."

"So he's the only one that can do it?"

"As far as I know." May nodded, her bottom lip protruding.

"So why doesn't he teach people how?"

"Think of it this way. Could *you* explain music to a deaf person?"

Sam thought about it for a moment. "No."

"Some things you just can't teach. And some things are truly your own, like what lies on your hand." May slapped a hand against the pillar. "Now how about you show me what you can do with that magnificent second-skin?"

Sam thought about conjuring the light to guide him home. "Not a problem."

He stepped up to the solid wall and placed his hand against it. Focusing his mind, he thought about the wall melting away like warm butter and let his palm rise and fingers arch.

He felt nothing. The entrance remained firm.

No monsoon of energy shot through his grasp—he couldn't feel the Veil.

"No problem," Sam said to himself, letting out a gust of breath. "Second time's the charm."

He cleared his thoughts and focused on one thing only: breaching the rock. He clenched his teeth, his fingers trembling.

Again, nothing happened.

"Well," May stretched the rock ledge to where Sam stood, "I'm sure Rona Rono will be happy to know you still have plenty to learn."

"I can do it!" Sam held up a hand. "Just gimme a min—Rona Rono? Is that a cartoon character?"

"He is a sorcerer. One of the best, brightest, and oldest in Atlas Crown. You will be one of his apprentices, and he will teach you all about Her. You should consider yourself very lucky."

Sam looked at his second-skin. "I thought I was going to study with Bariv?"

"You're not *that* lucky."

Sam gave May a disappointed frown. "Why not?"

May sighed and placed one foot in front of the other on the ledge like a gymnast. "Bariv is the first to teach those who come from the outside because he is the one who finds them. There is an important connection, like roots, between the Veil and the newcomer. These lessons are only introductory, however; he has far more important things to do than continue the education of new sorcerers."

"But you told me it's rare for two—what was that word?— straighthands to have a magical child."

"Flathands, and it is."

Sam tried to keep his voice calm, even as the scowl pulled at his face. "So he just sits and does nothing in that cave all day, then?"

May gave him a quizzical look. "There is a big difference between sitting and doing nothing."

"Fine." Sam sighed, rolling his shoulders. The robe moved with him as if it had been tailored for him. "Thanks for the robe, by the way."

She gave a curt nod. "Don't mention it."

"Now," Sam positioned himself in front of the wall and shooed May backward, "let me try this one more time."

He put his weight on his back leg and he readied himself to hit the wall. His calf muscles tensed like a jack-in-the-box. Again clearing his mind—and then thinking about turning the rock to marshmallow—he struck the rock with his open palm.

Pain shot down his forearm.

"Shoot!" Sam bit back a string of curses. "I think hitting it made the rock even harder."

May beckoned him toward her. "Think about how gumptius works. Physically, you could best LaVink easily, but that is not what magic is about. It is not what the Veil values."

"What does She value?"

"Give me your hand." Sam obliged. "The Veil values courage." May waved her diamond-skin over Sam's palm and the pain lessened.

"Cleverness."

Another swipe and the pain almost subsided.

"Creativity."

One more pass and the pain ceased.

"Focus." She let go of his hand. "But most of all, something *something*."

Sam thought maybe he had heard her wrong. "Something *something*?"

"I'm not going to spill all the secrets." She lightly slapped Sam's cheek twice. "That would close off your most intriguing path."

"You are incredibly frustrating."

"I am also incredibly excited." Her face looked frightfully gleeful. "A seam! And between two of the most influential clans!"

"Is this thing like a marriage?"

"Marriage, yes. But it is known as a seam to us."

"So, where is this seam happening?"

"I'll show you." May drew her second-skin along the stone and melted a passageway into a white room like the one Sam had encountered days before. "It's about to start, anyway."

They climbed through the hole and May sealed it after them.

May glanced at Sam's feet. "Why don't you take off those shoes?"

Sam saw the mixture of mud and vegetation he'd tracked in staining the white floor. He gave May his most innocent pout. "Oh, sorry about that."

"About what?"

Sam pointed to the mess, but where there had previously been a brown tarnish of glop, now the white floor gleamed.

May's voice took on a whimsical tone. "Something I did a long time ago."

"Does this particular obscure answer of yours have anything to do with time being different here? Because I don't think I could wrap my head around that one right now."

May gave a hearty laugh. "No, and don't worry, time is still the same, it is just seen through a different perspective." She gave his cleats an appraising gaze. "I was going to let Rona show you this—as it is his forte—but seeing as you have a hearty appetite for our world..."—the word appetite made Sam's stomach grumble—"Hand me your shoe."

Sam decided to go with it and took off one of his now spotless cleats. "All yours."

"Thank you kindly." May untied the laces. "You see, one of the most fascinating characteristics about the Veil is that you can use Her in many ways. What I am about to show you is called draping. It is extremely difficult because it is like doing a thousand-piece puzzle in your head while someone tries to poke your mind's eye. So don't get frustrated that you won't be able to do it for a while."

May closed her eyes and waved her glistening second-skin over the cleat multiple times. Sam couldn't consciously pick it out, but he noticed a subtle difference from the technique she'd used to heal his hand. A small wave of heat hit his face, like a puff from a blow dryer.

"There we are." May squeezed the cleat, and then handed it back to Sam.

Sam gave it a once-over. "What did you do?"

"Put it on."

He slipped it onto his foot. The laces immediately tied themselves to a perfect degree of snugness.

"Well, that will save me about four seconds," Sam grinned. "Couldn't you make them fly or something? Like that car thing you brought me here in?"

"I probably could." She gave a self-satisfied nod. "And if you work hard, maybe you could too someday."

"So, you can enchant objects."

"Sort of. Draping is when—after gripping the Veil—you wrap a small amount of Her around an object. You can drape an object indefinitely if you are skilled enough. Can you *wrap* your head around that?" She stuck her tongue out playfully.

"And it does whatever you want?"

"The more complicated the drape, the more complicated the artistry." She gave a dismissive wave with her second-skin. "But enough about that. I don't want to take away all of Rona's fun. We have a celebration to get to! Take those cleats off and let's get moving."

Sam took off his newly magical shoes and still-ordinary socks, aware that May and nearly everyone else *always* seemed to be barefoot.

In front of them was another black door.

"Does that take magic to get through, too?" Sam frowned. "Or is it just a door?"

"*Just* a door?"

Sam sighed. "I don't think we have time for another speech. Seam, remember?"

"You're right!" May opened the door with a gentle push. "I'll save it for the next time you are having too much fun."

Sam grinned. "I appreciate that."

CHAPTER 13

Sam spit out the rinser with a huge sigh of relief. "How long was I gone?"

May stopped her jovial humming, which she'd been doing since they'd passed into Atlas Crown. "Three days."

"There's no way they did all of this in three days."

"These are sorcerers you're talking about. And Atlas Crown has some of the finest in the world."

To Sam's surprise, it'd taken only a single rinser to rid his mouth of the foul stench that had been brewing there. Now that he could concentrate on something other than the pungent taste of death, Sam's attention was free to take in the scenery.

The center of Atlas Crown looked nothing like it had before. The various shops and shacks that Sam had seen before were stacked on top of each other—at least twenty high—in formations that looked as if they would surely fall with the slightest breath of wind, yet they stood firm. In their places, an almost unending number of festive tables overflowed with the most aromatic foods Sam had ever smelled.

Hundreds of people milled around the tables, but the majority of the crowd gathered around a beautiful mahogany stage covered with dozens of white birds—all different shapes and sizes—cooing a melody together. Two symbols—a triangle within a triangle and something that Sam thought looked kind of like an octopus—floated above the stage, circling each other, leaving trails of green and gold light. Thousands of grassy stools surrounded the stage, raised from the ground like a giant had poked the earth up from underneath.

The streams running through the area no longer channeled water. People dipped silver goblets in the red liquid and, after clanging their chalices together, gulped it down. Above them, a display of what could have been fireworks lit the sky, but instead of exploding and dispersing, the light continuously broke and reformed, creating a never-ending cycle of shapes and colors.

Throngs of happy people gathered in social groups to converse and devour mountains of delicious-looking cuisine, which spawned an envious growl from Sam's stomach. It took a good amount of effort for Sam to keep himself from diving head first onto the tables. "So, how about you introduce me to some of that food?"

"I'm afraid I have some duties to attend to, but afterwards I'll come find you."

Sam's stomach grumbled again. "Was I invited to this thing?"

May chuckled. "This is a celebration."

"Meaning, yes?"

"Absolutely. There are no exclusions at a seam. It is a glorious union of—"

Sam cut her off. "So what you're saying is that I can eat all the food I want and not feel guilty?"

"Yes, but you won't be able to—"

"Good luck with your stuff. See you later!" Sam was already off toward the nearest display, squeezing through the mob of guests.

Everyone wore robes with symbols, and Sam was thankful he blended in, though he still wondered why he didn't have anything decorating his chest. Every now and again he saw robes with the same symbols that hung above the altar. The matching symbols glowed like mini spotlights on their chests.

"Excuse me... watch out... coming through..." Sam tried his best to maneuver between the hordes of laughing guests without knocking anyone over. People gave him friendly looks and waves, but no one tried to talk to him, which worked to his advantage because the sooner he made it to a table the better.

The smells were even more potent closer to the tables. He didn't know where to start. Striped cakes were piled high next to casseroles of steaming vegetables, glazed breads, pancakes topped with fruit, roasted corn, and rice balls oozing with cheese—and those were just the items he recognized.

Gleaming metal plates, so clean that they sparkled, were stacked among the selections. He picked one up, ready to pile it as high as the stacks of shops, when he noticed the lack of silverware. He hesitated for a second, weighing the possibility of appearing rude by using his hands, but his extreme hunger demanded he put his manners on hold. He was just about to grab a handful of food, when—

"Everything looks good, doesn't it?"

"Yeah." Sam's hand hovered over the food. "This is kind of embarrassing, but—"

"You're supposed to use your hands." A smile filled the stranger's voice. "And the shells for the messier stuff. I was new once, too."

At that, he grabbed a fistful of cakes and rice concoctions and loaded a plate. He stuffed his mouth, let out an ecstatic sigh, and finally looked over at her.

Sam was used to being around pretty girls, but this one took "pretty" to a whole new level. The girl beside him looked to be right around his age, with coffee brown hair and the bluest eyes he'd ever seen. He stopped breathing as he took in her features—high cheekbones, the cute little upturn of her nose, the trace of freckles. The symbol on her black dress—the garment clung more closely to her frame than a robe—looked like a slightly unraveled knot.

She gave him a bright smile. "Good, huh?"

Sam gulped, swallowing whatever it was he'd just put into his mouth. "Fantastic. What did I just eat?"

"A rice-pack and a tumble-cake. I was never one to mix savory and sweet." She shrugged. "But who's to judge?"

"I'm Sam," he thrust out his right hand, and then retracted it as he saw the crumbs and cheese covering his second-skin.

She giggled. "Daphne. And for future reference, it's easier to hold the plate with your covered hand and eat with the bare one." She did a double take at his hand. "Beautiful second-skin, by the way."

"Thanks." Sam looked around the table for napkins. "So how do I..."

"After we finish eating," she waved her second-skin—a pink elastic material—over his and the leftovers fell to the ground and sank into the dirt, "we recycle."

Sam cocked an eyebrow. "Do you mind-read with the Veil or something?"

"No, but I remember what it was like. All of us newcomers go through the same stuff, although you do seem a little old to be so new."

Sam decided not to address that particular subject. "So you're from the outside too, huh?"

"Yup, came here when I was ten." She picked out a gooey pastry from the table and took a nibble. "American?"

"Yeah." He took another bite of his own food.

"Me too." She stood on her toes and waved to someone behind Sam. "To this day I still get chills when I think about how lucky we are. This place is like a beautiful dream."

Sam shrugged. "I guess so. I figure I'll stay for a little while."

She frowned. "A little while?"

"I'm the varsity wide receiver at my high school." Sam gave her a toothy smile.

"And?"

"Bariv said I have to stay until I can control the Veil, but once I get a few things sorted out I have a big scholarship waiting for me. I'm probably going to go pro."

An uncertain look crossed her face. "So you would leave all this for a—a game?"

"I mean, it's not just a game. It's a career. I would get a *lot* of money to do something I love. And it's not like you don't have games here."

Her expression cooled, and she no longer leaned toward him.

Sam was losing her. He needed to talk a bigger game. "Speaking of which, I'm probably going to stay long enough to beat that kid Petir LaVink at that gumptius game."

Daphne's eyes clouded with anger. "Good luck. Why don't you just break that second-skin now?"

With that, she turned away and joined up with a group of girls by what looked like a teepee—covered with a bunch of the double triangle symbols—to the left of the stage. A matching teepee on the right side of the stage had the octopus symbols on it.

Sam rubbed a hand across his face. *What did I say?* Most of the time, talk of playing pro ball got the girls in his high school to drool.

He shrugged it off and returned to the food. He polished off what was on his plate and grabbed a second helping. He devoured a slimy citrus fruit he didn't recognize, and as soon as it reached his stomach, a blue vapor misted from his nose and mouth and he felt like he had just been to the steam room, refreshed and alert.

None of the dishes had contained meat. He wondered if maybe the two families were vegetarians or something before he remembered what Bariv had said about killing. He didn't mind, however, as each dish he tried was better than the previous one. He had no choice but to try all sorts of fruits and vegetable creations. One blue fruit brought tears to his eyes, but then left his vision clear and less strained. Picking up one of the shells that Daphne had mentioned, he scooped up some stew from a decorated gourd and slurped it up. Salty and warm, the large vegetable chunks made his bare feet tingle after he ingested them, and a quick look down revealed that now his toenails were perfectly groomed. He ran a finger over the yellow bumps covering the outside of the shell—it didn't look like any sea-life he'd seen before.

Is Atlas Crown close to the ocean? Is it even in the same world as Texas?

Of all the food at the banquet, he did not see a fruit like the one the snake had given him. *Maybe it doesn't taste very good.*

"Distinguished citizens of Atlas Crown!" A voice filled the air, but Sam was the only one to flinch. "Welcome one and all to the glorious seam between Aric and Helvina, yet another uniting between the Wapawche and Hoto clans!"

People cheered. Sam gave a halfhearted yell along with the crowd.

"Please eat up, as the ceremony will begin shortly!"

As the fireworks in the sky died down, Sam went back to the buffet table. He didn't know how long the ceremony would take, and he decided to scarf down another helping, just to be safe. He picked up a piece of velvety cake, but the sweet decided to continue upward—out of his reach—like it was immune to gravity.

He frowned. *Why they would make cake so light it flies? Diet food, maybe?*

Dozens of other items parted the table of their own accord as well. Carrots soared through the air like small yellow javelins, and dreckler cotton passed by like storm clouds. The food drifted over his head, arching past the red river and right onto other guests' plates. A glowing, neon-yellow melon—which Sam hadn't tried for fear of radiation—rocketed upward and then split into many pieces, each landing perfectly on a circle of waiting plates. A splash of stew, floating along in a tight sphere, wandered past his head.

All around him, people summoned food off the tables with small flicks of their hands. It looked like a slow motion food-fight that ended entirely mess-free. Sam followed his specific piece of cake until it landed gracefully onto the dish of the rat-faced boy he recognized as Petir LaVink. Petir sneered at him and bit into the cake, mocking him with melodramatic flare, then chuckled at his small victory.

Sam cracked his knuckles and flexed his chest underneath his jersey and robe.

"Laugh now." He clenched his covered hand. "I'll wipe that smug look off your face soon enough."

He took an identical piece of the velvety cake, along with enough food to keep him happy throughout the ceremony, from what was left on the table. Picking up a silver goblet, he pushed his way through the crowd to the red river. It was at least five or six feet across and Sam couldn't see the bottom. Every twenty feet or so bridges of decorated metal crossed the river. Sam bent down, carefully balancing his plate, and plunged his goblet into the red liquid.

An old man wearing one of the glowing triangles on his chest bent down a few paces from him and dunked in his own chalice. The man winked at him. Sam gave a weak smile back.

Although the man's face was mostly wrinkles, his eyes were somehow young and bright. "Welcome."

"Thanks."

"I know who you are, Samuel."

Sam was taken aback. "Huh?"

"Be wary." The man's expression turned serious. "You are the key to the parting."

Before Sam could respond, the old man was lost among the crowd.

"Weird." Sam shook his head. He pulled his goblet out of the river. The liquid in it was not red, but clear.

"Weird," he repeated.

He tipped it out and let the clear liquid run back into the running red. Again he dipped his goblet, only to find that it once more came back clear. *What the heck?* He repeated the process a few more times with the same result.

Then someone tapped his shoulder.

Still in a crouched position, Sam turned around to see Glissandro staring back at him.

"Hey, Gliss."

Glissandro smiled and nodded.

Sam jiggled his goblet. "Why can't I get the red stuff?"

Glissandro tucked his horn into a smooth white holster and took the goblet from Sam. He dipped it into the river. He brought it up to Sam's face and revealed that the contents were clear again.

"You too, huh?"

Glissandro nodded and gave a mock frown.

"Why?"

Handing the goblet back to Sam, Glissandro placed his horn against his lips. Just as he was about to play, the loud voice spoke again.

"Accomplished citizens, humble beginners, and everyone in between, welcome. Let us all take our seats and let the seam begin."

Sam saw people cheer and clap and even jump up and down all around him. Glissandro beckoned him over to the two closest green lumps coming from the ground. Sam took a sip of the clear liquid, which turned out to be water.

Sam gestured with his goblet toward the lump. "We sit on those?"

Glissandro nodded and plopped down on the raised earth.

Sam settled down on the one next to him. The lump compressed to a comfortable fit. It was like sitting on a large pile of cotton balls.

"We are gathered here today," the voice boomed, "for another, everlasting union between two sorcerers and their long-running clans."

Rumbling cheers came from the guests with glowing symbols.

"How long do these things usually take?" Sam whispered to Glissandro.

Glissandro's eyes flashed from his horn to Sam and then he grimaced.

"Gotcha," Sam said in a hushed voice. "Can't answer—don't wanna be rude."

A look of relief crossed Glissandro's face.

"A long and wonderful relationship," the voice continued, "will continue forevermore in the love, companionship, and guidance of our community and the Veil."

Sam nibbled on a slice of seasoned bread topped with jam, but then stopped as he realized he was the only one still eating. He ducked his head and put his plate on the ground.

Up on the raised stage, the two people were getting... *seamed?* He wondered if that was the right term. The couple, dressed in black robes with both the triangle within triangle and octopus symbols, stood before... May. To Sam's surprise, it turned out to be May's voice over the loudspeaker—distorted down a half octave—although she wasn't speaking into anything. Instead, she held a diamond finger to her throat, which magnified her voice at a level volume all across the fields.

May prattled on for a while, and Sam feigned interest. She was going on about love and togetherness and gripping as one. Sam found his eyes flashing more and more to the plate of food going to waste beside him.

It would be a shame not to eat it.

"Now," May backed away from the front of the stage, "will the clan leaders please bring up their gifts."

Gifts? This could be interesting. He straightened up on his grassy stool.

An elderly woman emerged from each of the teepees, each holding something in outstretched hands. They climbed onto the stage from opposite staircases, moving curiously in sync. As they reached the podium, the white birds started cooing, and the symbols above the stage pulsed with light in time with the birds' song.

May stepped further back, along with the couple. The two women faced each other.

The woman on the right spoke first. "For the noble Wapawche clan. We present to you something very ancient that we hold very dear. It has been passed down through our family for generations." She took a deep breath. "Here is our draped reed-paper Epitom."

The assembly of guests burst into approving applause.

Sam glanced over at Glissandro with a confused look. Glissandro took advantage of the hearty sounds and played Sam a few quick eighth notes. "It is most old. It's a piece of parchment that changes shape according to what the closest person is thinking about. It's an extremely complicated example of draping."

Cool. The noise died down and Sam focused back on the stage.

"We are truly honored." The receiving elder took the reed-paper, which shifted into a shape Sam could not see. "For the admirable Hoto clan," the woman bellowed with the use of her second-skin, a featherlike material. "We present to you a droplet of pure Veil."

A hushed awe fell over the crowd. Sam heard someone in front of him say, "That must have taken a *hundred* arcs to create."

The elder on the left handed the other woman a small vial with a fantastically bright drop of something in the bottom. "It has taken a tremendous amount of effort to procure and we feel blessed to present it to you at this most auspicious seam."

The crowd did not make any noise for a moment, and Sam's gut clenched. *I didn't freeze everyone here like I did at the game, right?*

Then ear-splitting applause and confused, ecstatic shouts came from all around. Glissandro's jaw hung open. Even May looked impressed.

Sam cheered along with the crowd, taking advantage of the hectic moment to sneak a piece of doughy bread from his plate.

Glissandro had his horn in hand, blasting loud notes into the air. Up on the stage, the Hoto clan elder's eyes were wide as she stared at the vial in disbelief.

What could possibly shock a community of sorcerers who can do things like enchant stone walls and make people float in the air against their will? Sam—still stealthily chewing the bread—looked at Glissandro for an explanation.

Glissandro caught Sam's eye and blew a single note. "I'll explain later."

The audience settled down and the ceremony continued. The elders both retreated with their gifts and the young couple again became the focus. May continued with her monotonous speech on love and magic and magical love and loving magic and Sam again got caught in a web of his own thoughts. *What's "pure Veil?" Why does May seem to do everything in town? What the heck does the Tembrath Elite have to do with me?*

"Congratulations to both clans!" Sam shook himself out of his rampaging jumble of thoughts as May waved to the crowd. "And congratulations to you both. You may now fuse the symbols!"

Fuse the symbols? Not kiss the bride?

The couple waved at the guests and then looked at each other. They both thrust their respective second-skins straight into the air, pointing at the glowing symbols above them. Slowly, the couple moved closer to one another. As they came together, so did the symbols. At last, as their hands touched, the symbols joined in an explosion of white light. The blast thinned and became thousands of silky strands careening through the air, like a weeping willow of brilliant threads. Each separate filament rained down and landed in the outstretched hands of each guest. Sam—emulating the crowd—thrust his second-skin out and let a shining fiber land in it. Somehow, the light had a bit of weight to it. As the radiance diminished, he saw a tiny white berry in his hand. It was the size of a plump blueberry and had the waxy sheen of an apple. All around him, people were holding out their berries, waiting for something.

Next, May cried out, "To Helvina and Aric!"

The couple's black robes were now white.

"To Helvina and Aric!" the crowd chanted back.

Everyone threw the berries into their mouths. Sam did the same.

As he swallowed, his whole body tingled in delight. It was like a week's worth of endorphins all at once. He was struck with a strong desire to dance. Since he considered himself a terrible dancer—especially after his coach's "ballet will improve your dexterity" fiasco—the urge was all the more bizarre.

Sam, still concentrating on how vital and healthy he was feeling, missed the memo for a standing ovation. The stool beneath him began to sink back into the earth. Green lumps all around him retreated back to whence they came. He rode his chair down, until he was left sitting with legs outstretched on the ground. His fingers now level with his plate, he felt powerless to resist the urge to chow down again. Sam didn't know how it was possible, but the food tasted even better than before.

He lifted himself off the ground and looked around, wide-eyed. People's plates cruised through the air like tiny flying saucers from an old 1950's sci-fi movie, piling up in neat stacks on the tables.

Glissandro was no longer where he'd been a moment ago. People all around Sam were laughing, hugging, and cheering. The mood of the seam infected him, and he too felt abnormally chipper.

People drifted into large circles, like a large magnet pulled them into formation. *Huh? What's going on?* Sam backed away.

Sharp blasts of cheery music came from the stage. Smack dab in the middle of the line of musicians, Glissandro played his horn. Sam continued to shy away from the oncoming circle and backed up against the stack of shops, careful not to nudge them at all.

One by one, the other musicians joined Glissandro in perfect harmony. Sam didn't recognize any of their instruments. A middle-aged woman with her hair in a bun held a round piece of wood with strings extending from every side like a mane. She let her second-skin pace through the fence of strings, emitting a pitter-patter sound. A beefy man held a brass horn that looked sort of like a trumpet but had three bells, each pointing in a different direction. Beside him an Asian man tapped a drum that looked like a fat lightning bolt.

It sounded to Sam like the big band music his grandfather used to play on the record player, but with a strong syncopated backbeat. The urge to move grew stronger, as if his feet were late for an appointment. The circles of people started to rotate together in some sort of dance. Sam's mind was perfectly content with watching this happen and enjoying what was left of his goodies, but his body wanted to join in.

Oddly enough, he felt his jaws chewing in rhythm to the music.

"I'll show you how to do it if you want," a tiny voice squeaked next to him.

Somehow he'd failed to notice the girl in the bright purple robe standing beside him. On her hand was a matching second-skin, with a purple, ceramic glaze. The bird symbol on her robe looked as if it might fly right off the fabric. She was not unattractive, but very small and fragile-looking, not the type of girl he usually talked to. She looked to be maybe a year or two younger than Sam. Her hair was pulled into a tight ponytail, with a yellow mushroom crimping it together.

Sam waved a dismissive hand. "I'm fine with just watching. I was never good at dancing."

"Me neither." She looked at him with a big, hopeful expression. "But we could fumble around together."

"I don't know." Sam rubbed underneath his chin and felt the rough stubble that had grown over the last few days. "I think I just want to watch."

"Okay." Her eyes were now pinned to the grass.

Sam looked into the dancing wreaths of people and saw Daphne not too far off with a giant smile across her face, laughing and matching footwork with the same group of girls from the teepee. Something about her intrigued Sam, something besides her looks. Maybe the fact that she danced with the fluidity of the Grizzlies' offensive line when they performed a buttonhook play—which was about as smooth as it got.

"You know what?" Sam gave a confident smile. "I'm sure I could get the hang of it."

The girl's eyes lit up. "Really? You want to try?"

"Sure… as long as you don't make me look bad." The urge to dance was actually starting to win over Sam's inhibitions. "I'm Sam."

The girl stepped in front of him and gave a deep curtsy. "Cass… Cass of the Pyx clan."

"Nice to meet you, Cass."

She looked at him with a bashful expression. "You can call me Cassiella, if you want."

Sam repressed a smile at the odd introduction reversal. "I'll do that."

Cassiella let her eyes meet Sam's. They were a soft green, with some real depth behind them. Sam wondered if perhaps, like Bariv, she wasn't as young as he'd guessed.

"So, do you want to go dance now?" She clutched her hands to her chest.

Sam pushed off the wall. "Yeah, but what exactly do we do?"

"Just join the circle and follow the person next to you. There are no set steps or anything, they just make it up as they go along." She looked down as she giggled. "You can follow me."

Sam gestured forward, feeling uncharacteristically giddy. "Lead the way. Let's show these people how to move."

Cassiella took Sam's hand in hers, leading him toward the closest group.

"Actually, hold on." Sam tugged at her hand. She stopped short and turned as she blanched.

"Nothing's wrong," Sam assured her. "Can you just answer something for me before we go?"

She gave a timid nod.

"What's so great about pure Veil?"

"Oh!" She slapped her forehead. "You're new, you wouldn't know."

Sam grinned. "Hence the asking."

Cassiella gave a nervous laugh. "I—I guess… I…" Half of her face scrunched in concentration.

"Maybe you could just explain what it is?"

"You see…. well, I… umm…" She pursed her lips and then tapped them with her index finger.

"How 'bout just a brief summary?"

She hesitated for a moment, her eyes back on the soft grass. Then she gave the most innocent shrug Sam had ever seen. "Anything, I guess."

Sam felt his legs itching to dance. "What do you mean, 'anything?'"

"It's kind of like… if you are trying to grip or drape or anything that is too far out of your skill, you could use the pure Veil to do it without breaking your skin."

Sam grimaced. "Breaking your skin?"

"Your second-skin. Like the one you have." She peered at his star-covered hand, her eyes growing wide with wonder. "What exactly is that, anyway? It's lovely. I've never seen anything like it before."

Sam flipped his hand over so she could see all of it. "It's from that giant snake in the woods."

Her face went blank. "What giant snake?"

"Bariv's snake."

Still no recognition.

"You know," he moved his hand back and forth in a serpentine manner, "talks without actually talking, grows crazy plants with suns in them, its scales look just like this." He wiggled his covered fingers. "The *giant* snake."

Her eyes widened. "Did you get it in Grus' Pass?"

"What? No." Sam felt his face getting red. "Right out in the woods over there."

"Sorry, Sam." She tucked her chin against her chest.

"Its… fine. I… just, how 'bout we go dance with everyone?"

At that, she finally relaxed a little. "Follow me."

He grinned, but he couldn't help but think about the pure Veil. *What does she mean, "anything?"*

Cassiella suggested the circle closest to them, but Sam shook his head and gestured to a different circle. She didn't ask why they ended up in the ring with Daphne and her friends. The circle graciously opened with a cheer as Sam and Cassiella entered. Everyone except Daphne. Sam ended up squished in between Cassiella and Fromson of the Bellamy clan.

Fromson clapped a heavy hand on Sam's shoulder. "Sam, my boy!"

"Hello, sir!"

Sam looked over at Daphne, but failed to grab her attention.

They moved around the circle and alternated kicking out their feet and bobbing their heads from side-to-side. Sam felt incredibly silly, but kept going, hoping to catch Daphne's eye.

Fromson pointed at one of the building stacks. "That's my stand all the way up top!"

"Is it?"

"Yep. Did it myself, too. Figure if you own a stand, you ought to be able to stack it." He stuck out his chin. "Hope it doesn't topple over! It would be a shame if I couldn't give out my new tender benders. Came up with the recipe this morning."

Sam followed the next step, which involved putting his hands together and rocking his shoulders back and forth. "I'll have to stop by tomorrow and try it."

"I'll save the first one for you." His lips twitched into a coy smile. "If you let me take another look at that New Jersey of yours again."

"Deal."

Sam frowned; Daphne was too busy gabbing with her friends to notice him.

"Watch yourself, Sam." Cassiella's shoulders shot back and forth like alternating pistons.

"Watch wha—"

In one swift motion, his body lifted into the air, along with the rest of the dancers.

"Whoa!" His whole circle, along with the others, rose into the air like it was just another step in the dance.

"Sorry!" Cassiella smiled, the mushroom that bound her hair fluttering. "Forgot to mention that!"

"What's happening?" Sam felt the blood drain from his face.

"The band!" Fromson laughed.

Sam had been too focused on the ascending crowd to notice that the band had changed tunes. This one was loud and peppy. Over on the bandstand, Glissandro winked at him.

"It'll be fine," Cassiella squeaked. "Uh, you can let go if you want."

Sam's hand gripped her shoulder like a vice. He immediately let go. "Sorry!"

She gave him another bright smile.

Sam started to laugh. "This is incredible!"

"This is just the beginning, my boy!" Fromson shouted.

It *was* just the beginning. The different circles floated and rotated until they were gathered into one giant tube, starting at the ground and rising almost as high as the stone pillars. Above and below Sam's circle other rings of people danced. Each ring swirled in the opposite direction from the ones above and below it. Sam noticed the newlyweds rising through the tube. They waved and blew kisses as they passed each row, and a pack of white birds circled their feet. When the couple reached Sam's row, everyone around him called something that sounded like "Meet-a-coil-oval-seen." He didn't even try to join in on that one.

The couple rose higher and higher on a platform of light until Sam could no longer see them. Then a sudden chill ran through his body, like being dunked into the deep end of a pool.

Everyone let go of the people on either side of them and lifted both hands like they were coming to the top of a roller coaster—right before the plunge. The rings disbanded, and Sam was tossed backward, tumbling head over heel toward the ground. As he got closer to becoming a sticky human pancake, he felt his body slow down, like a bungee cord had been wrapped around him. He ended up gently touching down next to the original members of his circle.

Daphne laughed and hugged her friends.

"Forgot to mention that one, too." Cassiella winced as they landed. "Sorry."

"Don't mention it… actually, I take that back. Please do mention it."

She laughed and looked up at Sam. Her eyes were big and round, with specks of green reflecting the moonlight. After a moment, she blushed and tore her gaze away.

"Well, that was interesting," Sam tried to sound like his heart wasn't jackhammering against his ribs. "But I think I've had enough excitement for one day."

"Do you…" Cassiella blushed a deeper red. "Do you maybe want to go for a walk with me? I could show you around if you want."

"I…" Sam looked over at Daphne. "I was hoping to…"

"Sam!" May zipped toward him.

Sam waved. "Hey, May."

Her dress fluttered in the night breeze. "I hope you've been enjoying yourself."

"Too much." Sam's heart was finally slowing down.

"That's nice to hear. It isn't easy to raise everyone up like that." She turned to Cassiella. "What a pleasure to see you!"

Cassiella curtsied and grinned.

"I hope you don't mind, Cassiella, but I have to borrow Sam."

"Oh." Cassiella's expression weakened. "I understand." She took two fingers and drew them across her heart. "Travel well, May."

May copied the gesture. "And you."

Cassiella scampered off behind one of the building stacks.

"What was that?" Sam asked, putting two fingers on his heart.

"Just an old custom." May gestured behind them. "Let's go this way."

Sam and May moved away from the crowd, toward the rinsefish fountain.

Once there, Sam leaned against the railing and peered into the dark water. As soon as he peeked his head over the banister, several rinsefish rushed toward him. Dozens of little white globules reached the surface and bobbed like little buoys.

May rapped her knuckles against the stone. "They know that after the seam, people are going to want to freshen up."

"How do they know? Don't fish have really small brains?"

May tilted her head in thought. "You know ants?"

"Um, yes. I know of them."

"Did you know that some ants build separate sections of their hills to place their dead? So the toxic fumes of decomposition don't harm the rest of the community."

Sam cocked an eyebrow. "Really?"

"Really." May smiled. "And I'm not a scientist, but I think ants have much smaller brains than fish."

"I think it's safe to assume." Sam's grin widened. He reached down and selected a rather large white glob. He popped it into his mouth like candy and again savored the cleansing feeling—it had been a disgusting couple of days.

"Togetherness." May's voice had a dreamy quality. "It's the most important thing in the world. It's why we are programmed to be social creatures, why we live in communities. Just like ants, the most amazing things happen when we look outside of our own capabilities. One finger can't even lift a pebble, but a pair of hands…" May swallowed hard and looked away.

"There's no 'I' in team," Sam spit out the cleanser and a small flower grew where it hit.

May went to pick out a white glob herself. The rinsefish pushed the white blobs toward her with their heads. As she plucked one from the water, the fish shied away. "No, I guess there isn't."

Sam tried to sound sincere. "Good job with the ceremony, by the way."

"Thank you. I've seen so many—led so many—yet they never get old. If anything, they give me the vitality to keep going for so long."

"How long have you been doing them?"

May spit out the rinser in the most elegant way possible. "Would you like to know why you couldn't drink the wine?"

Normally, Sam would have again been irritated at her circumvention of his questions, but he *was* curious. "Is that what the red stuff was? Is it because I'm not old enough?"

May's eyes twinkled. "It's because you haven't gone through Omani."

"What's that?"

"It's a coming of age ceremony. When you are ready, you will have to accomplish a series of tasks. Then, you will be seen as an adult under the Veil."

"What kind of tasks?"

"I'm not sure what they would entail." May shrugged. "It's not up to me."

Sam knew he probably wouldn't get any more information about that out of her. "So what was the deal with the pure Veil? And breaking second-skins?"

"That would be best explained by Rona. You will be having a session with him tomorrow. Get some sleep; you have a long day ahead of you."

Sam sighed. "Another one, huh?"

"Yes, and you look exhausted."

"But I want to go talk to—" Sam glanced back, trying to catch a peek of Daphne.

"I'm afraid I have to insist that you get some rest. Cassiella will still be around tomorrow."

"No, not—"

"Anyway," she interrupted. "Goodnight, Sam."

"But I—"

May snapped her diamond-encrusted fingers. Immediately Sam felt incredibly tired. She snapped again, and his body rose and shot through the air. He was flying… again. In a matter of moments, he was back in the guest room, lying on his back, cradled in the green hammock. The light bobbed above him.

Sam let out a yawn so large that his jaw hurt. "Talking to May is like talking to a wall."

The light remained quivering in front of him.

"A really pretty wall."

The room went dark and sleep took him.

CHAPTER 14

Crom's learox skin was the last in the line of second-skins. Ten other second-skins were equally spaced across the plateau, all on the hands of the Tembrath Elite. Each one was different—except those of Sage and Saria, who were both using horned totum-screecher skins. Vigtor had taken each skin from its previous owner with pain and fear, which made them all the more appropriate for their current purpose.

"We won't get another shot until the next time the full moon is missing from the sky," Crom grunted.

Sage sneered. "We all know the necessary conditions."

Crom stood up straight, towering over the rest of the Tembrath Elite. "If you and your sister weren't a small step from useless, then maybe—"

"You thick-headed oaf," Saria interrupted. "Maybe if you had the brains to do even the smallest of natural magic—"

Crom waved a giant hand. "Who needs it? When did natural magic ever—?"

"Silence," Erimos uttered.

All eyes turned toward their most senior member.

"Crom is correct. Remember this. We have only the smallest window. Let us begin now."

"Yes!" blurted Jintin.

"Now don't go and blow us all up," Sage warned. "Remember what happened last time."

Jintin's eyes looked especially beady in the dark. "Your ear grew back fine. Erimos knows what he's doing. Now if it was Crom…"

Crom balled his second-skin into a fist. "Shut it."

Jintin looked down, suddenly fascinated with his toes.

"Now," Vigtor broke in, "I have gone through the trouble of getting these skins for you. Let's not make me get more. We have the correct tools and the skills to use them. Tonight is the night we get through."

Jintin squealed.

Crom flexed, the muscles in his shoulders bulging like mountains. "Shut it."

"No, you shut it!" Saria clucked. "He can speak if he wants."

"No, he can't," Crom spat. "When I tell someone to be quiet, they do it!"

"You don't have that kind of authority."

"The rest of you wouldn't even get close without me!"

"But you can't do anything else," Sage jeered.

"You worthless piece of—"

"Come now, Crom," Jintin's eyes narrowed to slits, "There's no 'I' in team."

"How dare you use a flathand saying when you speak to me!" Crom started to advance on Jintin. Erimos made a barely perceptible twitch with his pinky finger and Crom froze in place. Erimos shuffled him back into line like a chess piece.

Vigtor tipped his head to his teacher. "Thank you, Erimos."

Erimos opened his eyes. They were blazing infernos of red.

"Everyone prepare for their rip," Vigtor commanded.

The space where they stood—the flat stone on the peak of the dead mountain right above Dami Sanctorum—grew silent. The Veil was thinnest there; no one knew why, but Vigtor presumed it was because the desolate land around it had been abandoned for many years.

Every time they attempted their rip, it seemed that the life around the mountain recoiled a little further.

The wind whipped up dust and powdered bone. Black clouds huddled above, hiding the stars. The world was waiting.

Erimos bound their essences, and Vigtor began his rip.

As soon as he began, pain shot up his arm. He was at the beginning of the line and he had begun the course of action. He knew what She would throw at them. The Veil was determined to stop their rip at any cost.

Vigtor's second-skin—a saber-beak neemia skin—started to crack and peel. It flaked off and brown tufts of fur spun out over the cliff, drifting down into the dark. His fingers twisted into unnatural positions, resembling the gnarled branches of a tree. His cries echoed through the crackling air as he left a gash in Her as deep as he could.

Thunder roared, and the wind picked up.

After ripping Her, Vigtor fell to the ground, twisting in agony. He felt the next member in line scream in anguish. His hand was red and raw where the neemia skin had torn and fallen off, useless.

Down the line, the members pulled and screamed, each one toppling to the ground in turn as their second-skins ruptured. Erimos was the only one not to make a sound. The agony each felt was a necessary consequence—a pain they all shared now that their essences were bound. Vigtor couldn't feel the actual pain each member felt as the Veil retaliated, but he could feel the *presence* of their agony.

The sky was bleeding—the black clouds had unleashed their burdens, and the water came down red and rancid, like they were being bombarded with the juices of the recently decayed. The wind surged, tearing away anything in its path. If it weren't for Erimos' drape keeping them grounded, they would have been knocked into the abyss.

Vigtor felt each step closer to Crom's turn—the final rip. Crom hadn't exaggerated before: they all knew he was their most vicious member when it came to getting through.

They had focused long and hard since their last attempt, making subtle changes to the line, altering their second-skin choices. Vigtor had even taken these particular skins in a more ferocious fashion than ever before, another necessary sacrifice. The more depraved the kill, the more powerful the skin. Everything was about to be unleashed. At last, the *true* power would be theirs to manipulate.

This was why Vigtor had formed the Tembrath Elite. This was their purpose.

Sage fell. Saria fell. Jintin fell.

Vigtor watched, eagerly waiting for Crom.

The Veil hit their anchor like an avalanche. Crom roared as his muscles seized.

Vigtor could feel both Crom and the Veil writhing in pain. She had held against them for too long.

The toxic wind carried vile fumes into the darkest recesses of their lungs. She always had nature throw something new at them, but She was weak. She wasn't the real power.

Just a little more. So close.

The clouds were now red, the vile water like a ruby waterfall. The harsh wind—blowing like sandpaper against their skin—couldn't sweep them away, so now the sky was trying.

The red river beat their bodies, attempting to carry them off the edge.

Crom struggled. His frame shuddered and started to buckle, as he howled into the downpour.

Just a little more.

Then Crom's second-skin burst into flame.

So close!

Instead of putting out the fire, the red rain fed it. The blaze grew and swallowed Crom, crackling his flesh. With everything that the Veil was, She had still been unable to break the protective drapes the Tembrath Elite had placed on themselves. She could break bones; She could char flesh, but She could not kill them. Vigtor's hand throbbed as if knives twisted within his palm. The other Elite still writhed in agony. The pain was real, but it could do no lasting damage.

Crom's deep voice boomed across the plateau, echoing off the surrounding mountains, like they were screaming back. In the distance, what was left of the tiny green trees ripped from the ground, leaving nothing but a brown canvas across lifeless earth.

The flames around Crom changed color, becoming pure white, and the torturous sounds he made drowned out everything else. The dark clouds reflected back the white light from the sizzling flames.

"Do it!" Vigtor tried to scream, but he could not hear his own words.

Flashes of lightning—possibly Her last-ditch effort—arced down from the clouds and pierced the flames.

Crom's screams changed pitch.

The sky suddenly went dark.

Silence.

CHAPTER 15

"Uh," Petir grimaced, his eyebrows nearly touching, "you must be lost, kid." Sam looked around. He didn't think he was in the wrong place; it was exactly as May's light had described when it woke him. "Walk the perimeter of Atlas Crown until you get to the three-pronged pillar. There will be an opening for you. Go through, and continue straight until you get to the Valley. Rona Rono will be waiting for you with his other apprentices."

Day was just breaking and Sam stifled a yawn. He hadn't seen anyone else in town and assumed no one else was awake yet. The bobbing light had interrupted his dream just before dawn. If Sam hadn't been used to getting up early for practice, he probably would have wrapped his second-skin around the light and squeezed until it exploded.

Under his bare feet, the emerald soil massaged each step. Past the patch of vibrant green was a vast expanse of wondrous landscape. Almost symmetrical mountains framed a valley of pale green, almost yellow vegetation. The further up the mountain Sam looked, the darker the shade of green. At the very top, the trees looked almost black. It looked like someone had taken a brush and meticulously painted the flora.

Running through the mountains—ruler-straight and almost exactly centered—flowed the bluest river Sam had ever seen. He saw the spots where the river started and where it ended, which—based on Sam's past knowledge of rivers—was not supposed to be possible. It looked like someone had cut out a section of a river and plopped it down in the valley, like some optical illusion. Circles of water—whirlpools—frothed within the main body like a necklace of pearls. The circles flowed without disturbing the water in the main channel—which didn't seem to fit with what Sam knew of physics.

Sam approached the small group of people. "I'm exactly where I should be." Sam rubbed the remaining sleep from his eyes. "Deal with it, twerp."

"C'mon, Rona." Petir's expression looked like he'd been kicked in the stomach. "You can't be serious."

Petir, along with four other kids—Glissandro, Cassiella, Daphne, and a fourth he didn't recognize—sat cross-legged in front of an older man, whom Sam assumed was Rona Rono.

His new teacher had skin the color of dark chocolate and two hoop earrings in each ear. The symbol on his white robe looked like the outline of a bull's head. A golden headband decorated with large gemstones rested on his shaved head. He looked to be around the same age as May, and muscles bunched under the white garment. His second-skin—the color of a tiger-eye gemstone—reminded Sam of a ring his mother sometimes wore.

"Petir," Rona's thick African accent added a lilt to the words, "I expect you to treat our new apprentice with respect. And I also expect to be addressed by my proper title."

"But *Master* Rona," Petir whined. "He's basically a flathan—"

"Enough." Rona brushed away Petir's words with a dismissive gesture. "Sam, please come join us. Sit down."

Glissandro waved and patted the ground beside him. Sam gave him a nod as he plopped down next to him, bouncing a few inches off the ground as he landed on the strangely springy earth. Daphne gave Glissandro a wide-eyed look of disbelief. Cassiella smiled and opened her mouth, but then dipped her head and giggled. The beautiful, mocha-skinned girl Sam did not recognize wore a white robe with a bull-symbol like the one Rona had on. Her black hair was tied back with ribbons of gold, and Sam's brows shot up as she met his gaze with sparkling, orange eyes.

"Welcome, Sam." Rona clasped his hands in front of him, and sat as though his spine was a rod of steel. "My name is Rona of the Rono clan, but since you are my apprentice, it is tradition that you address me as Master Rona."

Sam nodded. "Nice to meet you, Master Rona."

"May has informed me that you know Glissandro, Petir, and Cassiella already."

"We danced together last night." Cassiella's face turned red.

Sam scratched the back of his neck, looking to the side. "Um, yeah."

"I'm surprised," Daphne matched Petir's sneer as she looked at Sam, "considering dancing isn't a competition."

"Daphne." Rona gestured toward her. "And this is my daughter, Zee."

Zee flashed a dazzling smile at him. "You can call me Zawadi, if you would like." She had a lighter accent than her father.

"Nice to meet you, Zawadi."

"Sam, now that we are all acquainted, May has asked me to spend some time answering your questions."

Petir groaned.

Sam picked the first one that popped into his mind. "People keep mentioning that second-skins can break?"

"He doesn't even know about *that*," Petir whined. "How are you supposed to prepare us for Omani when you have to spend time—"

"Enough." Rona's voice was a tad firmer, but remained pleasant. "You know as well as anyone, Petir, to teach is to learn. Which, as you know, will help you with Omani. So how about you start thinking positively?"

Petir grumbled something indecipherable.

Rona held a hand up to his ear. "I didn't quite catch that, Petir."

"Sorry, Master Rona," Petir muttered a little louder.

Rona smiled—his teeth were impressively white, as well. "That is an excellent question, Sam."

"Thanks." Sam looked over as Glissandro also nodded in approval.

Rona rested his index finger under his bottom lip and thought for a moment. "The best way to answer that is... it's like biting off more than you can use."

"Chew," Sam corrected him.

"Sorry?"

"The expression is 'bite off more than you can *chew*.'"

Daphne rolled her eyes.

"Well, you can probably chew it," Rona nodded, "but you surely could not use it."

Sam hesitated for a moment. "Huh?"

"Let me give you a demonstration."

Rona lowered himself into a crouch. The banded orange and black skin on his hand hovered just above the ground. His fingers curved inwards as a plant grew. It started as a tiny bud inching its way above the ground, and grew to the size of a bonsai tree in seconds. Like a puppeteer, as Rona stood up, the plant grew taller. It was the same color as the green earth they were sitting on. The plant produced broad, blobby leaves as it expanded to about shoulder height. All in all, compared to the plants Sam had seen around Atlas Crown already, it was rather dull-looking.

"This is the Solowunda plant." Rona returned to a perfectly straight stance. "But we call it the practice plant." He tucked his tiger's eye glove into an invisible pocket of his robe. Plucking off one of the bigger leaves, he placed it on his upturned palm. The leaf began to mold itself to his hand, slowly constricting, with the sides sealing themselves together where they met, forming a perfectly fitting second-skin, like green spandex.

"Now watch." Rona raised his covered hand and faced the sky. He muttered something under his breath and took in a lungful of air. Clouds stained the clear blue sky, rolling above the valley from all directions as if Rona had called them over.

One smaller cloud, in the shape of an eagle, raced down toward Rona's hand. The closer it got, the smaller and denser it became. Rona brought his palm down as the cloud came into contact, pulling the vapor into it, and then held up a tiny ice sculpture crafted to look just like an eagle about to take off.

"This is a grip I can handle, and do very easily." Rona held the eagle between his thumb and forefinger and flipped out his palm for Sam to see. "Notice my second-skin is still intact."

Sam brought his hands apart to clap, but stopped when he saw no one else was doing it. "That was awesome!"

Rona gave a satisfied nod. He made the ice-eagle float through the air and stop just in front of Sam. As Sam reached out and took it in his second-skin, a sudden burst of energy rushed across his palm. The surge passed harmlessly through the little sculpture. He stared at the sculpture and thought about turning it back into a cloud. Without so much as a warning, the eagle burst into thousands of shards, pelting everyone with slushy shrapnel.

Sam grimaced. "Sorry!"

The other apprentices wiped the ice crystals from their clothing. For some reason, far more ice particles were scattered around them than could have possibly come from the small eagle.

Glissandro puffed a small note into his horn and large chunks of ice shot from inside the bell. Cassiella had a small cut on her forehead, which Zawadi sealed with a wave of her covered hand, and then looked at Rona with a sly smile.

"I don't know what happened." Sam held up his hands defensively.

Rona gave him an appraising look. "How about that."

Daphne looked at him curiously.

"Anyway," Rona waved his hand, causing all the ice to melt and seep into the ground. "Like I was saying, *that* is magic that I can use."

Sam was wondering what he had done to make the ice explode, when Rona tucked his hands in at his sides, fist clenched, and bent both knees about ninety degrees. Considering the white robe, Sam couldn't help but think of the kung-fu movies he used to watch. Rona thrust out his hands and began performing some sort of dance. His arms swirled through the air and his body shifted with ease, like the air supported his weight as he moved.

Then he struck toward the sky.

Sam felt heat push past him. The others didn't seem to notice.

Rona's hand shook, vibrating like a string that'd just been plucked. Sam saw the green material start to turn brown and wither away. Beads of sweat appeared on Rona's head, rolling down and catching in his golden headband. Tension pulled at his cheeks, and his eyes went wide with the struggle. More of the second-skin drifted away, leaving Rona's hand covered with a brown, veined skeleton of the plant. The rest of the second-skin trembled and then popped off.

The tension left Rona's body as he sat with a limp sigh.

Sam leapt up. "Are you okay?"

Rona chuckled. "Yes, yes. Just a little tired."

"What just happened?"

Rona let out a small huff of air. "I just tried to move the moon."

Sam's jaw dropped. "The moon?"

"It's the big grey thing in the sky." Sarcasm filled Petir's voice.

Sam tossed him a dirty look. "I know what the moon is."

"Then you know what an impossible task it would be," Rona interrupted. "Please Sam, take a seat. I am perfectly fine.

"When a grip is too much for you to handle," Rona began, already regaining vitality. "It will destroy your conduit to Her. This holds true for draping, as well. But you should not worry too much; only hard concentration and a stubborn will for an impossible task will cause your second-skin to break. Normally, when you pursue a grip that is out of your proficiency, your concentration will break before your conduit. Even so, we always use the practice plant during these sessions—though it won't give you nearly the results of your true second-skin—so that we don't chance destroying the conduits that are precious to us." He paused, tipping a finger in Sam's direction. "That is, when we attempt to do magic that is far beyond our capabilities."

"I understand." Sam looked from side to side. "So what exactly am I doing here?"

"This is your gift to society, Sam. The citizens of Atlas Crown will make sure that you receive everything and anything you will ever need, and in return, you are studying the Veil to eventually take over for them, and provide for future generations."

"So what are we learning here?"

Rona tilted his head. "I teach natural magic."

Sam felt his stomach constrict. "But Bariv said I'm suited for power magic."

The others let out a collective gasp.

Daphne's body tensed, like she was ready to run away. "Why would you *want* to do power magics?"

Sam felt his second-skin grow warm. "It's not exactly what I *want*, but it's apparently what I'm meant for."

Daphne raised an eyebrow. "But no one new here has excelled at power magics since..."

"Don't worry, Daphne," Petir said. "From the looks of it, he won't actually be able to do any of it."

"Sam," Rona leaned forward, "how about we take a walk together?"

"But who—"

"This way, Sam." Rona stood up, ushering him toward the funny river. "Apprentices, I want you all to work on growing your own practice plant. I want…two arms tall with ten leaves, equally spaced. Glissandro, you know what to do."

Sam trailed behind Rona until they stopped at the water's edge. Up close, Sam could see that the water seemed to come from under the earth, like the river was a closed loop. A little ways downstream, a shell jumped from the water in front of him. It was large—the size of a conch—but swirled like a snail shell. It traveled through the air to Glissandro's outstretched hand.

"Sam," Rona kept a slow pace, "you might not want to spread that information just yet."

"Why not? Shouldn't I be proud of it? Bariv said it's really rare to do power magics."

"I have heard about what you have done," there was an solemn air to Rona's words, "and I, too, believe that power magic will be your path."

Sam felt a twinge of relief.

Rona continued, "I'm terribly sorry that you have come to us at such an advanced age. Let me take a moment to explain a few things about our society, which, knowing May, you probably did not have the luxury of hearing—not that it's her fault, as she is very busy."

"Thank you." Sam threw his hands up in relief. "I've been waiting for someone to let me in on what this place is. Right now, I'm still all jumbled. I was basically kidnapped and brought here in a car that travelled under the earth; I ran into a bunch of flies that formed my face; I've been lifted off the ground by magic—multiple times—and I've seen a miniature sun inside of a plant, which proceeded to talk to me—only it wasn't talking, more like—"

"Slow down." Rona gave Sam a curious look. "What miniature sun?"

Sam sighed. "Bariv's snake took me to that cave made of crystal, where he had that pod with the little sun inside."

Rona furrowed his brow. "I know the crystal land of which you speak—we tend to stay away from it, as the crystal breaks very easily and below it, there is only an abyss. But I'm sorry, I'm not aware of any connection between Bariv and a snake."

Sam couldn't believe it. This was the second time someone had told him they didn't know about Bariv's snake. *Could I have dreamt it?* His hand moved to the bulge under his robe where the fruit lay. It was real, so the snake must have been real. For some reason, Sam's instincts told him not to show Rona the fruit. "The snake is how I got my second-skin."

"I have never seen any material like it," Rona admitted. "How did you get it?"

"The snake gave it to me. He talked for a while and then shed it."

Rona held out his hand. "May I see?"

Sam placed his palm on top of Rona's.

Rona examined it, and then spoke almost as if addressing the skin instead of Sam. "A taste of the night sky. What wonders might we see from you?"

"Huh?"

Rona let go of the skin. "I think you might have met Karundi Kai."

"Who?"

"We have a legend in Atlas Crown about a snake we call Karundi Kai. It is said to be the cleverest of all creatures that She has bestowed upon us. The story goes that She gently peeled off a sliver of the heavens, rolled it in Her palms, and shaped it into a serpent. Karundi Kai is massive and cunning and beautiful, but no one has seen it in many, many years—some say never. There have been sightings of a black tail whipping around corners like fire, and even reports of big flanks of starred skin melting away into the ground, but this is all hearsay."

Sam wiggled his fingers. "I'm telling you, I saw it and talked to it."

Rona's face became serious. "I believe you. I am concerned, because it is also said that Karundi Kai will only present itself when the world needs its words, words that can change everything, when it is time for…"

"For what?"

Rona's voice dropped to a whisper. "A new era."

Sam's throat went dry.

Rona slapped him on the back and laughed. "But that is also hearsay." His face lit up. "It is a beautiful skin, so consider yourself extremely lucky. But stay away from the crystal land, you might not get so lucky next time."

Sam nodded. "Sure thing, coach."

Rona frowned.

"I mean Master Rona." Sam felt odd using the title.

Rona smiled brightly. "Very good." He pulled his own second-skin out and wrapped it around his hand. "All mysteries aside, I will begin our lesson on the division of magics. In Atlas Crown, almost all of the sorcerers have been chosen to use natural magics. It has been this way since our community was founded. This is not saying that they cannot do other magics, but for the most part, the majority of what they excel in—including myself—are grips and drapes of the natural world. Natural magic is a wondrous feat. It is how we are able to feed, clothe, shelter, and occasionally heal so many."

"So most of the town helps with all that?"

"Yes. There is a small sector of sorcerers, however, whom She has chosen to become authorities in the area of mystical magics." Rona tapped a finger under his lip again. "I would say…two percent."

"Two percent!"

Rona gave a satisfied nod. "I believe that is a fair assessment. It is rather rare for the Veil to give the gift of the mystical arts. Glissandro is one of the few, though he has not gone through Omani, so his path is not yet set in stone. She proportions the different talents based on how much need there is in the community. She is remarkable, you know. When someone passes on and joins Her, She inspires someone else to take their place."

Sam looked over to where Glissandro played a bright little melody toward the ground. "Why are there so few mystics?"

"Because they live very long lives, extended so they may study their art deeply and wholly. I regret to say that I know frightfully little about mystical magics. Those who are chosen for the mystical side tend to surround themselves with their own… and keep to themselves. The authorities of the mystical magics are known simply as 'The Mystics,' of whom there are always three. Atlas Crown is very lucky to have them here."

Sam was almost afraid to ask. "What…what about people who are chosen for power magics?"

Rona gave Sam a steady look, and something hid behind his expression. "Here, there is only one."

Sam leaned in. "Me?"

"No." Rona grinned and slapped Sam on the shoulder. "You are still too new. I speak of Bariv."

Sam thought back to their session in the cave. "That can't be."

"It wasn't always that way. There used to be a few who lived with us."

"Who?"

"Bad men." Rona hesitated. "No, misunderstood men. *Misguided* men."

"Why aren't they here anymore?"

"They are no longer welcome." Rona adjusted the crown on his head. "Outcasts. They decided to pursue something that was not good for the community and we have banned them."

Sam gulped. "*All* of them?"

"All of them."

"Forever?"

"Until they give up their pursuit."

The knot in Sam's stomach moved to his throat. Right then, he wished he could be back on the gridiron, chasing passes and waving at pretty girls. "What did they do?"

Rona waved away the subject. "I have said too much about them already. May would not be pleased."

Sam took a deep breath, yet it did not squash the frustration. "This is stuff I need to know, Rona!"

"*Master* Rona," he corrected. "The most important thing you need to understand is that power magics are not evil, though some may hint that they are. It is just that we have had some trouble before. Regardless of what people may say, you need to remember something. Bariv has already gone down the same path you now embark upon."

"Yeah, but if he's the only one—"

"He is one of the most important people in our society—maybe *the* most. People often forget about Bariv's position because he lives in seclusion. He deals with the newcomers and with May, but only rarely has contact with anyone else. New sorcerers always come to Atlas Crown because of him. They have the option of traveling to other communities once he has prepared them. Bariv is a special case. He doesn't need to leave his cave for anything. Not food, not clothing, not the company of others. He is the Conduit to the Veil. The only one in existence."

Sam felt kind of foolish asking, but for some reason he needed to know. "Doesn't he get lonely?"

Rona smiled. "It is nice that you care."

Sam felt flustered. "I—"

"She is all the company Bariv needs."

"May?"

Rona shook his head. "The Veil. Now why don't we go back and see if we can't get that extraordinary second-skin to show us its worth?"

Sam knew better than to press his questions. "Okay. But I want to know one thing."

Rona gave him a comforting smile. "Of course."

Sam moved closer and lowered his voice. "Aren't the others much more advanced than me? I mean, I just got here and we're meant for different things. Why am I learning with them?"

"Learning natural magics will compliment and help you control the power inside of you, which is what I've been told you want. It will help prepare you to leave us." Rona give him a dubious look. "That *is* what you want, correct?"

Sam gave a sheepish nod. He'd known the man for about five minutes, and he already felt like he was disappointing him by wanting to leave.

Rona's smile got even bigger and he rubbed his hands together. "We'll see about that. I know more about you than you think. Besides, I only teach the most promising students: the ones who will be of greatest use to our society."

"Yeah, exactly."

"Yeah." Rona winked. "Exactly."

Sam felt a mixture of confusion and pride as they walked back to join the group. He wasn't sure which emotion fit the situation.

The other students stood next to their practice plants. Everyone's plant was exactly what Rona had asked for—except for Glissandro's.

Instead of a plant two arms tall with ten equally spaced leaves, Glissandro frowned at a knee-high bush with green berries.

There was no trace of disappointment in Rona's voice. "Don't worry, Glissandro, you'll get it."

Glissandro smiled without showing his teeth.

Rona waved his hand over Glissandro's mess. It sank back into the ground with a small crunch. "The bright side is that you don't need it to practice, anyway."

Sam gave Glissandro a curious look.

Glissandro waved the snail shell.

"Right." Sam snapped his fingers. "So you don't break your horn."

"You catch on so quick!" Cassiella chirped.

"Here we go again," Daphne muttered to Zawadi. "It seems she's picked another one."

Sam frowned at Daphne's choice of words.

Rona began to assign the other apprentices various tasks for the morning. He told Petir to coax a nearby group of four-winged butterflies—though Rona called them pygma-floaters—into flying in a straight line through his legs. Each of the pygma-floater's sets of wings were a different color. Sam saw orange-green, blue-maroon, and white-black pairs. When they fluttered, the top and bottom pair changed colors, creating the illusion that they were spiraling through the air.

Glissandro was instructed to mark an ordinary stone from the riverbank with his clan symbol and then toss it into the river. His task was then to fish it out as many times as he could. It sounded sort of easy to Sam.

Daphne, Cassiella, and Zawadi were teamed up to complete a task. Rona told them that somewhere in the Valley he'd hidden an amorberry, and if they found it, they could keep it. At the sound of this, the girls moved away from the others, giggling.

Sam turned to Glissandro and lowered his voice. "What's an amorberry?"

Glissandro played a few soft notes through the snail shell. The tone the shell made sounded like a cross between one pig oinking and another pig squealing. This time, the words in Sam's head were scratchy and raw. "Very rare. If they can find them, girls use their juice as perfume. They supposedly attract men and can get us to do things we wouldn't normally do."

Sam heard Cassiella softly bargaining with the other girls for it.

Sam gave a nervous cough. "Do they work?"

"They're very small and odorless until they're squished, that's why they're hard to find, even with the use of the Veil." Glissandro shrugged. "So I don't think you have anything to worry about."

Sam grinned and nudged Glissandro a few times with his elbow. "Not that Daphne needs it."

Glissandro gave Sam a puzzled look. "No one *needs* it."

Rona pointed out an especially green patch of dirt to Sam. "Let us start in that spot over there. It's a particularly bouncy patch."

Sam nodded.

"We will begin by putting you in a concentrative stance," Rona bent his knees almost to right angles. He left his hand with the second-skin out, palm up, and tucked the other hand in a fist, resting the back of his knuckles against his thigh. "Like so."

Sam copied him.

"Very good." Rona straightened up and put his fingertips together. "I see you have strong legs."

Sam nodded and slapped his thigh. "Like iron."

"That will help. First step," Rona circled around Sam. "Close your eyes."

Sam did as he was told.

"Hold this stance as long as you can."

Sam's legs were strong from all his conditioning, so he figured holding it would be a breeze.

Rona's voice got quieter. "The Veil has always been right there in front of you, waiting. She is not what you think, Sam. She is not just a source of what you would call magic. She is our protector. She is and always will be the reason for our survival. She holds within Her limitless possibility for us to explore the depths of our hearts and minds. She can recognize emotion and bring forth love. She is adventure and home. And… Sam, open your eyes for a moment."

Rona gave him a solemn look.

"She is not your enemy."

"I didn't say She—"

"Just remember," Rona's voice was stone. "She is not your enemy."

"Okay, I get it."

Rona nodded. "Very good. You may close your eyes again."

Rona continued to circle him. "What you did before, with the ice sculpture. It was lack of concentration. Normally, a beginning apprentice wouldn't have that much access to the Veil. You do, which has led Bariv, May, and me to believe that you are meant for power magics. This does not mean that you will be naturally great at grips and drapes. You will still have to build your skill, but it does mean that you will have more of Her to work with. This is a good thing, but it also means that you will have to concentrate exponentially harder than the rest of my group. Can you do that?"

Sam didn't hesitate. "Yes."

"Very good." Rona clapped him on the back. Sam didn't move from his stance. "Strong legs. That will help."

"Why?"

"It is like training while wearing extra weights. If you can do it with an extra variable, then you can do it more easily without."

"So what are we going to do?"

Rona tapped Sam's forehead with his index finger. "You are going to practice containing your mind. You need to keep it close when it tries to wander off."

Sam tapped the same spot Rona had touched. "Not a problem."

Rona closed Sam's outstretched hand and guided it to his other thigh. "For now, just hold a picture of the practice plant in your mind."

"For how long?"

"Perfect question. Let's find out."

Sam heard Rona walking away and opened one of his eyes.

"Eyes closed," Rona called. "The last time I checked, I did not look like a practice plant."

Sam grinned, closed his eye, and pulled an image of the practice plant into his mind. After only a few moments, Sam found that it wasn't going to be as easy as he'd thought. Every time he got a clear picture of the plant in his head, it broke up and went black. He tried to hold the fleeting image, but his mind really wanted to wander free. It snapped to thoughts about home, about football, about the snake, about Daphne—whose image he didn't discard right away—and basically anything but the green plant.

He kept trying for a while, but his mind won in the end. He was thinking about college girls when he heard a grunt in front of him. He opened his eyes and saw Rona smiling at him.

"How's it going?"

"Very good, Master Rona."

"Oh, really?" Rona looked suspicious. "How long were you able to keep the image?"

Sam sighed. "Honestly? Not very long."

"I appreciate the honesty. Stand up straight."

Sam got out of the stance and shook out his legs. They were getting a little tired.

Rona rotated his neck. "There is a reason I am teaching you this, Sam. This is the first step in the best way to use the Veil. Not the only way, but the best way. This way will leave you free of restrictions. Think of you and Her as a team, and the clearer you are in what you need, the better things will work. If things in your mind are muddled, then your grips will be muddled. Communication is key. Understand?"

Sam shrugged. "Sure."

"You can even think of it like your football. The best way to work with your team is to be precise with your directions, no?"

Sam stretched out his lower back. "Right."

"Think clearly, and try not to get frustrated. It only makes things harder." Rona turned to walk away. "Try again."

Sam tried again, doing only slightly better the second time.

After what felt like an eternity, Rona returned. Sam dripped sweat, and his leg muscles quivered.

"Take a seat." Rona pulled out a gold chalice and handed it to Sam as they settled on the ground.

Sam looked in—empty.

"Take note." Rona did a slight grip and waited. In a moment, a globule of water rushed though the air and landed in the chalice. "From the river."

Sam raised his brows and looked into the chalice. "It's clean?"

"Of course."

"Thanks." Sam finished the water in one gulp.

"More?"

Sam shook his head.

"So," Rona took the chalice back, "any better this time?"

"A little."

"How about a small task, then? Or would you like to practice honing your mind some—"

"A task is good," Sam interrupted.

"Very well. I have just the thing." He pulled out two more chalices. They were both gold, like the first, but the three ranged in size from the small chalice Sam had drunk from to one that was almost the size of a pitcher.

How the heck did they fit inside Rona's robe?

"Your task will be to fill these chalices with water from the river. However, you may touch neither the water nor the chalices once I have set them down. Start with the smallest and work your way up. Any questions?"

Sam raised an eyebrow. "You don't think that's a little much for my first day?"

"Not at all. Water is the easiest element to manipulate. Sometimes it travels as ice, sometimes water, sometimes a cloud. It is used to being all places."

"But what if I break my second-skin?" Sam looked at a belt of stars across his thumb's knuckle. "I don't think the snake would give me any more."

"Assuming you could even find it again. No, I think it is best if you grow a practice plant."

"But how?"

"I know you can feel Her; I saw it with the ice sculpture. She is there. You just have to connect. Think about Her, feel the energy, and concentrate."

Rona placed the chalices a few feet away and sat down on a flat rock to meditate. When Sam approached to ask him a few more questions, a force halted him, like he'd walked into a padded wall. Rona, with his eyes still closed, shook his head.

Instead of getting frustrated, Sam laughed. If Rona didn't want to help him, then he obviously thought Sam didn't need help. It was a compliment. Pride welled up inside of him.

He picked a spot. "Okay, here we go."

Sam waved his second-skin over the ground. He concentrated on trying to feel the Veil. After minutes of mind-throbbing deliberation, he still felt nothing. He tried hard to focus only on the Veil, but his mind had its own agenda.

He got into the stance Rona had showed him and thrust his palm out. His knees were squared off into perfect right angles, and his back was like a steel beam. It was exactly the way Rona had showed him.

Even so, he felt nothing.

Deciding to change his strategy, he resolved to think about the plant instead of the Veil. He closed his eyes and pictured a small sprout. In his mind's eye, he watched the tiny plant spring from the ground. Miraculously, he felt the rush of energy under his fingers.

I got it!

So as not to let it get away, he imagined the plant getting larger. In his head, it got taller and broader and sprouted dozens of leaves. The rush of energy grew, and he gripped Her tighter so She wouldn't slip away. She pulsed through his fingers like a freight train. At last, Sam saw the practice plant fully grown in his mind. It had ten evenly spaced leaves on each branch and was shoulder height. He felt the last of the energy pass through his fingers, and with a sigh of relief, he opened his eyes.

There, beneath him, was indeed a plant, but it was only large enough to shelter a few ants—baby ants.

Sam looked down at his pitiful creation. The sprout poked just far enough out of the green soil to mock him.

Sam was about to stomp on it, when he heard Rona next to him.

"It is a fine start." Rona's words seemed genuine, which only made Sam feel worse.

Sam snorted. "It's a fine failure."

"Failure is only permanent if you let it stick around."

Sam groaned and rolled his eyes.

Rona chuckled. "May told me you'd like that one."

Sam didn't think it was funny. "Well, did she also tell you that I couldn't even do the simplest of grips?"

Rona nodded, his smile growing frustratingly big.

Sam gave Rona an irritated stare. "So, can you teach me something that I can do?"

"No."

Sam threw his hands in the air. "Does that logic make any sense to you?"

"Pushing yourself *to* your limits defines who you are. Pushing yourself *past* your limits defines who you can be."

Sam sighed and rubbed out a kink in his thigh. "Did May tell you to tell me that, too?"

"No, that one was mine. She doesn't hold the monopoly on good sayings, you know." Rona gave him a calming pat on the shoulder. "I've also spoken to Bariv."

"So?"

"So, I trust that he knows best, especially if you are meant for the same path of power magics. For now, why don't you use one of Daphne's leaves for a practice skin? I think you might do better with the river than you think."

"Okay. But how should I even start?"

"Let me ask you this. What do you think the Veil is?"

"I—"

"You don't have to tell me," Rona shook his head so fast his crown almost fell off. "You are my apprentice, yes, but *She* is where you find answers. Use Her."

"I'll try." He paused and looked up at Rona's smiling face. "So, water into the chalices, huh?"

"Just follow your submarine of thought."

"*Train* of thought," Sam corrected.

"But Sam," Rona said with a sly smile, "trains can't go underwater."

Sam grinned and made a mental note never to correct Rona.

Rona went back to his rock, and Sam wandered over to Daphne's plant. Reluctantly, he pulled off his own second-skin. Sam felt sort of nauseous after he tucked it away into the pocket of his robe. Without the twinkling black skin, his hand looked like it belonged to someone else.

He plucked one of the larger leaves from Daphne's plant and let it wrap itself around him. After it formed a second-skin, Sam felt like he'd dipped his hand in green paint.

I like my own second-skin better.

The other students were busy with their tasks. He saw the girls holding hands and traversing the valley together in a ring, stopping at certain points. She was too far off to be sure, but Sam thought he saw some sort of bird on Daphne's shoulder.

He joined Glissandro at the riverbank.

"Hey, Gliss."

Glissandro smiled.

Sam wiped a bead of sweat off his forehead. "How'd you do so far?"

Glissandro pinched his lips together and held up a finger.

"Well, at least you accomplished something. Did you see my practice plant?"

Glissandro grinned and nodded.

"Yeah, I know." Sam swirled his hands in the air. "Now watch, as I mysteriously make water jump from the river." He laughed and looked over at Glissandro. Instead of his new friend joining in, Glissandro looked like he'd just heard a terrible secret.

Sam looked from side to side, but saw nothing unusual. "What is it?"

Glissandro shook his head and went back to playing his horn.

Sam spent the rest of the morning standing next to the river, trying his best to make anything at all happen. Both his lips and the chalices remained dry. Every once in a while, when he needed a break, he looked over at the other apprentices to see how they were doing.

Petir kept stomping the ground in frustration and throwing clumps of green dirt at the practice plants.

Note to self: remind Petir of this failure in later arguments.

The girls had dug and refilled at least a hundred holes in the valley over the past few hours. Daphne really had gotten her hands on a bird, which looked tropical, and the group followed the bird around, magically digging in the spots where it pecked the ground.

After Glissandro had succeeded a second time, he sat next to the flowing water and carved symbols into the shell with his marked pebble.

Sam plopped down next to him and extended his legs, letting the current run over his feet. "What's that for?"

After a few more short scrapes, Glissandro gave a satisfied nod and blew a long, beautiful note through the shell. With the modifications, it no longer sounded like a tortured pig, but more like a French horn.

Sam gave a sigh of relief. "Nice."

It had been hours since he'd felt even the slightest trace of the Veil. The others, including Rona, carried on without bothering to check on him. Sam understood; he didn't expect he'd accomplish anything, either. Peeling off the green skin and fitting it on his other hand didn't attract the Veil any better.

At this rate, I'll never get home.

Giving up for the time being, Sam sighed and flopped down on his back. After a few minutes of staring at the sky, he rolled over into a push-up, losing himself in the familiar rhythm of exercise. At least pushups were something he could do very well. It was on rep thirty that he glanced over and started laughing so hard he crumpled to the ground, knocking the wind from him. Next to him, Glissandro had joined in on the pushups, only he had both arms behind his back and was doing armless pushups. Every time he went down, he blew a small toot on the snail horn in his mouth, which pushed him back upwards.

A louder note sent him flying to his feet. Sam was still laughing when he stood up beside him, wiping the tears from his eyes. "I need to learn how to do that. My friend Doug would think it was a riot."

Glissandro waved to an invisible crowd and took a bow.

At the mention of Doug, Sam flashed back to the football field—the field where he could be again, if only he could focus.

No—thinking like that wasn't getting him anywhere. He forced himself back to where he was, and he blurted out the first thing that crossed his mind. "Why does Rona wear that crown? Is he the king or something?"

"He *was* a king," Glissandro played.

Sam's brows shot up. "Really?"

"A tribal king in Africa."

"Seriously?"

"Yes. A long time ago." Glissandro played a series of long, low notes. "He and his people lived in a territory where the tribal groups were always in battle. They were trained for constant combat."

"That explains his physique. He could probably put up well over three hundred."

Glissandro frowned. "Three hundred what?"

"Never mind." Sam inched forward, sinking most of his calves underwater. "Go on."

Glissandro played a trill. The note stopped, but the words kept showing up in Sam's head. "He was originally the shaman for the tribe. He was able to heal all their injuries, even the serious ones. He used a special staff for healing—a staff made from a small tree that had come from the Veil. This meant that Rona's tribe lost fewer soldiers in battle, which in turn meant that they had more men to fight in future encounters. All agreed that it was best if they made Rona king. Rona made an excellent leader; however, he refused to take the life of another man. This eventually led to his downfall.

"Even though he refused to kill, he went into battle every single time, healing his fallen warriors right on the field with his staff. He was petrified of dying—not because he was afraid, but because he didn't want to leave his young daughter alone—but still he went. His tribe won each fight and soon all surrounding tribes feared Rona's. They grew larger and became extremely powerful."

Another trill, this time higher. "There was a man in his tribe who saw Rona's mercy as weakness. This was a greedy man, a bad man. Now that the tribe was so powerful, the bad man wanted control. He came up with a plan. He snuck into the territory of a rival tribe, where he was captured and taken to the tribe's leader. In exchange for his life, the man gave up the secret to Rona's magic powers—his staff. The man was set free and he snuck back into his territory.

"The next night, the rival tribe declared war against Rona's. As always, Rona went into battle, but the bad man hid in the woods. The rival tribe had a plan. Instead of attacking the warriors, they all attacked Rona. Rona tried to fight them off, but there were just too many. They broke his staff and beat Rona nearly to death. They would have killed him, but Rona's warriors were able to save him—just barely—and win the battle, defeating the rival tribe. Rona's tribe lost an extraordinary number of warriors. Since there was no one to nurse Rona back to health, he went into shock and fever all through the night. Miraculously, he survived, but remained unconscious.

"The bad man was able to take power and became the new king, since Rona remained in a coma for some time, powerless. Now that word had gotten out that Rona had lost his magic, the other tribes attacked. Rona's tribe began to dwindle in number. They got desperate and began looking for someone to blame. Not wanting to have the tribe's wrath focused on him, the bad man suggested they sacrifice Rona's daughter to the gods in the hopes that they restore Rona to health and power. The members of the tribe were losing family—which meant they were losing their sanity. In the end, they decided that the bad man's plan was the best course of action. In the middle of the night, they snuck into Rona's dwelling and stole his daughter. All she could do was scream.

"Since none of the tribe wanted to murder the child, they decided to let nature do it for them. Close by, lions hovered around the carcass of a recent kill. The tribe threw Rona's daughter to them, and she was viciously mauled. She was near death when Rona showed up. His eyes blazed red and he actually flew through the air to come to his daughter's aid.

"The lions backed off at the sight. As Rona reached his daughter, he pulled her close to his body. The lions circled back toward them, preparing to attack, but Rona looked at his daughter's broken body and let out a ferocious roar. In an instant, all of the lions and all of the warriors lay dead. Rona was left holding his daughter's body, watching her die in his arms."

The words stopped coming.

Sam threw his arms out. "What happened?"

"Sorry." Glissandro let out another trill. "Didn't make that one long enough. What happened was that May found him. She healed his daughter, but when she was running her hand over the girl's face, the girl asked her to leave one scar. Rona started crying. He assumed May was an angel. Rona thought she was there to take them to the other side, but instead, she brought them here."

Sam felt his chest constrict. "How did she find them?"

"Bariv," Glissandro played. "He realized something was wrong when Rona stopped using the Veil. He sent May to see what had happened."

Sam looked over at Rona, sitting peacefully on his rock. "How are they both still so young?"

"What do you mean?"

"Rona and Zawadi. They're still so young—and where's Zawadi's scar?"

Glissandro's long, slow notes sounded like a lullaby. "The Veil gives certain people prolonged life, like Rona. Zawadi is our age. Rona calls Zawadi his daughter because he leads the Rono clan. He calls all of the Rono girls his daughters."

"But why does *Rona* have prolonged life?"

"Necessity," Glissandro played.

Sam turned back to the river, and let his eyes drift over the water for a little while. He looked over at Rona meditating on the rock and wondered if the man sitting there with a calm smile was really the same man who had gone through all of that.

After a few silent minutes, Sam stood up and pounded his fist into his palm.

Rona's a genuine hero—not just a football hero, a real hero.

If it took Sam all afternoon, he would get that water into the chalices.

He settled into the stance and concentrated on the smallest of the three cups. If Rona could survive all that he had gone through, surely Sam could do this small task. He'd frozen all movement in the football stadium; he could definitely make a little water jump. Bariv had shown Sam that he could use the Veil. Maybe he was just trying too hard. In the cave, the Veil had come naturally, like they were a team.

He thrust his palm over the bank of the river.

Sam thought about what May had told him earlier.

The Veil values courage.

A small charge jolted underneath his fingers. Sam opened his eyes and watched the water. He thought about Glissandro's ability to talk through music.

The Veil values cleverness.

He thought about Fromson of the Bellamy clan's pastry.

The Veil values creativity.

His hand began to shake. Sam thought about May draping his cleats and how she told him it was like doing a puzzle with something distracting you.

The Veil values focus.

He thought about the echo flies creating an image more in-depth than a mirror ever could.

The Veil values something... what was it?

The air around him felt warm.

The Veil values something extraordinary!

Sam watched as three drops of water arced from the river and landed in each of the chalices. In his mind, he had envisioned all three filling to the brim at once. He stared mournfully at the inside of the chalices.

He took a deep breath and tried to bury his frustration. Holding out his palm again, he tried to focus on the Veil. Nothing came. He was never going to get home at this rate.

He felt like kicking the smallest chalice into the river.

"It just takes time," Glissandro played. "You'll get it."

"You *don't* get it." Sam clenched his fists. "I need to be good at this."

Glissandro looked at the river. "Why?"

"Because I have to get home! This isn't what my life is supposed to be!"

Glissandro carved another notch into his shell. "It just takes time."

"Just because you can do it doesn't mean I can. I don't know why I'm wasting my time with this stuff!" Sam rubbed a hand across his face.

Glissandro shook his head, still staring out at the water. "It's not wasting. The Veil will always be with you now. You have to learn to embrace Her possibilities or cope with Her burden. I hope you choose the first, but either way, it just takes time."

Sam's heart sank. "Just leave me alone! You don't know what it's like to keep failing."

"The truth is, you don't know what it's like to *really* fail."

Sam scowled. "Just go away."

Glissandro shrugged and followed the current away from Sam. As he played a long note, a stone popped out of the water and into the bell of his shell. Glissandro shook it out, examined it, nodded, and tossed it back in.

Sam knew it wasn't Glissandro's fault, but he was in no mood to apologize.

Why can't I do this? It doesn't make sense. May said I'm supposed to be great.

He looked over at Rona, still and silent on the rock.

What would Coach DeGrella say if he saw Sam failing like this?

Again.

He stepped up to the chalices and cracked his knuckles. He thought about the Veil. She was surrounding him, an entity that provided life and power.

Rona's words reverberated in his mind. *She is not your enemy.*

He thought about working with the energy, about Bariv's snake and the tiny sun, and about how he'd felt while his head was in the dome.

He felt it—a strong rush under his fingers.

Here we go.

The water needed to fill the chalices. His desire took over, and he stared hard at the river, willing the water to jump. The energy pulsed through him.

Again, three drops of water rose and fell into the cups.

That's it? Sam felt like screaming,

The energy hadn't left. It was still there, teasing him. Burdening him with a potential he didn't want. Insulting him. Mocking him.

His head started to pound, and he focused all of his anger and frustration as he thrust his hand deep into the energy. Desire seethed through his heart, and he ripped out what he wanted. She would not control him. He grabbed more. The energy struggled to get away, but he held firm. He dominated the power; it was *his*.

He willed the water to move, and he felt the energy join with the river. *So much power.* With one huge pull, he tore the energy away.

And with it, the river jolted.

The roaring current halted. Huge whitecaps formed along the surface. The water rumbled. As quick as a breath, the river overflowed the banks, rushing past Sam's knees, almost knocking him over before he felt the energy dissipate.

The river… was flowing backwards.

The water that had escaped returned to the river, sweeping the chalices away and joining the rest of the current in the opposite direction. Sam stared with wide eyes.

Rona grabbed his wrist. "Not like that." Rona's eyes burned with a mixture of fear and disdain. The calm smile was gone. "*Never* like that."

CHAPTER 16

"Sorry," Sam said. "I just—"

"*Never* like that."

Rona let him go, and Sam pulled his arm back.

"Okay," Sam tried his best to sound apologetic. He was a bit taller than Rona, but his teacher's gaze made him feel like a small child. "But, what did I do wrong?"

Rona took a deep breath and the intensity melted from his face. "She is not your enemy." Rona sounded like he was pleading. "You must work together."

"I will."

Rona leaned forward, lowering his voice. "You may be strong enough to do what you have done, but it hurts Her. I promise, She will come to you. You don't need to force Her. It will only lead to limitations. There is a right way and a wrong way. The wrong way might bring quicker results, but it is not real. That is the wrong type of control. Your emotions can affect everything, and you must control yourself, not Her."

"Rona!" Petir called. "What happened?"

Petir and the others ran toward Rona and Sam.

Rona brought his face close to Sam's and lowered his voice. "You did not do this—I did. Understand?"

"But—"

Rona grabbed Sam's shoulders, fear outlining his dark features. "I did this to the river. Not you."

Sam swallowed hard. "I understand."

Rona broke away from Sam, turning toward the others. "*Master Rona*, Petir!"

The rest of the group stared at the now-backward river. It flowed gently now, as if nothing out of the ordinary had happened. Rona reached out, curled his fingers, and the three chalices rose from the river and set themselves at his feet.

"I was just showing Sam the power that can be found in natural magics." Rona gestured toward the water. "No need for alarm."

Glissandro's eyes went to Sam's practice skin. Sam looked down; the green skin had several tears across it. He was able to tuck it into the pocket of his robe without anyone else seeing.

Zawadi nodded. "It's true, Sam. Natural magics can do the most extraordinary things. There is one natural sorcerer in the Gobo Highlands who can stop volcanoes from erupting."

Petir gave a drawn-out sigh. "I still think that's a rumor."

"It's true. I heard it from a reliable source."

Petir shook his head. "He could just go to a regular mountain, cause the earth to shake, and claim that he stopped the volcano. Who can prove him wrong?"

Zawadi shrugged. "I believe it."

"While we're all here," Rona said, "how about a meal?"

Petir ripped off his practice skin, stole a quick glance at Sam, and then pulled on his leathery second-skin. "It's about time."

Rona picked up the chalices—now filled with water—and led the group to a spot near his meditation rock. Pulling out a basket, he laid out a varied assortment of fruits—including the glowing neon melon—as well as vegetables, bread, and pastries—but no meat.

Sam ate his food in silence. He rolled the different fruits and breads around in his mouth without tasting them at all. All he could think about was the river.

How did I do that?

Rona gave the group some post-project pointers while they ate, but Sam didn't get most of it. "—feel as free as a grassglider and persevere like the legendary Viking sorcerer, Framholsven the Tenacious."

Sam shook his head and took another bite of fruit, and then swallowed hard when he realized Rona was talking to him. "This group does not only learn how to use the Veil; it is also responsible for learning what has come from the Veil. We train in the mornings, but each afternoon we search the areas surrounding Atlas Crown for new gifts from the Veil."

Sam gave a perplexed frown.

"As May has probably told you," Rona began, "in areas close to where the Veil is used often, unique plants and animals occasionally sprout up. As this new life is ever-changing, we need young sorcerers from the most advanced groups to document what comes out of Her and what of it we can use."

Sam shook the thought of the river from his mind. "Shouldn't it all be usable?"

"She gives us what we need, and often what we want, but don't be deluded. The world does not revolve around us alone."

Cassiella jumped in. "We start at the area beyond the tri-pronged pillar and do a reconnaissance around a third of Atlas Crown. It'll take us about sixty days to completely investigate the locale—and that's a fast pace."

Sam wasn't planning on staying that long.

"This is not the only group that documents these gifts from the Veil. But," Rona nodded, "since I teach the best students, I expect more thorough results from this group than from the other two. My students always have the most new discoveries at the presentation ceremonies."

Sam could see that, although Rona didn't outright say it, he would not be satisfied if this bragging right was taken from him. Sam admired that about him.

They set off, skirting the mountain on the left, bringing Sam toward the spot where they'd stopped the day before.

Glissandro walked next to Sam. "—and that's a quillflower." He pointed to something that looked like a sea urchin on a stick. "We don't find new life every day, but we try to."

When his friend wasn't looking, Sam ditched the tattered practice skin behind a bush and pulled his snakeskin on.

They passed through a field of blue grass where Sam could clearly smell the ocean—the salt even stung his eyes. He looked around for water.

"Joker-grass." Glissandro played in triplets. "Tomorrow the field will probably be brown and look dead. They go from ocean to desert a lot. I've even seen some of the grass grow to look like a cactus."

"If it ever turned normal green, this would be a great place to have a catch."

Glissandro gave him a curious look. "What are you trying to catch?"

"A *football* catch. Toss it back and forth, you know, work on your arm... but I think it's probably safe to assume you don't have football here."

Glissandro shook his head.

Sam shrugged. It didn't matter. Once he learned how to control the Veil, he would have all the time in the world to have a catch.

He took another sniff and closed his eyes. He pretended he was on the beach and let the gentle ocean breeze wash over him. He and Doug waved to a group of pretty blonde girls going by in their bikinis and—

"How dare you sit around while your room is such a pig sty?"

Sam was pulled from his fantasy by his mother's voice. It was quiet, but undeniably hers.

Sam looked over at Glissandro. "Did you hear that?"

Glissandro looked down at his horn and then placed a finger behind his ear.

Sam heard his mother grumbling off in the brush. He followed the sound away from the field and into the woods. The sound originated in a small shrub full of silver fruit.

Sam stared. "What the—"

"SAMUEL PETER LOCK! YOU WASH THOSE DISHES THIS INSTANT!"

There could be no mistake; it was his mother's voice.

Glissandro appeared beside him, his face overflowing with anguish. "It's the fruit."

"A fruit that happens to sound exactly like my mother?"

"It's the defense mechanism." He stuck a pinky in his ear. "Each person hears the sound that annoys them the most."

Sam took one step closer to the fruit.

"DON'T THROW THAT THING AROUND INSIDE THE HOUSE!"

Sam covered his ears. "Let's get out of here!"

Glissandro nodded—he'd placed his horn in its holster and now had both pinkies in his ears.

They ran back across the field to catch up with the rest of the group.

Once they were a safe distance from the nagging fruit, Sam let his hands drop to his sides. "So, what'd you hear?"

Glissandro stopped short. He took a deep breath, and blew the most horrendous note Sam had ever heard. It was obnoxious, out of tune, and really loud.

Sam scrunched his face in disgust, and Glissandro stopped playing.

Sam felt lightheaded. "That was awful!"

"I know," Glissandro played, a pensive look on his face. "That was the first note I ever played through this thing. I guess it will haunt me forever."

"Me, too."

Glissandro laughed silently.

Sam let out a slow breath. "I'm not sure which is worse, hearing my mom's nagging or Petir's whining."

Glissandro moved his hands up and down like a scale.

"I know." Sam let his head hang. "Either way, I lose."

They caught up to the others making their way down a dirt path. Daphne was leading the way.

Sam winked at Glissandro and moved to catch up to Daphne. "So," Sam put his arms back and stretched out his chest, "wanna hear about the time I caught seven for seven?"

Daphne gave him a blank look and continued walking.

"How 'bout the time I froze a whole crowd of people without knowing it?"

She huffed and elongated her steps.

"What's your problem?" Sam quickened his pace.

"I have no problems." Daphne flicked her hair out of her face. "I am perfectly content with everything the Veil has done for me."

"Fine. Then what's *the* problem?"

She made a motion with her second-skin and a few vines moved from their path. "The problem is you."

"What about me?"

"I don't think it's worth my breath. By the time I explain it to you, you'll probably be back on the football field, far from here. Or worse."

Sam felt his tone become harsh. "Hey, I'm stuck here. It's not like I have a choice."

"You just answered yourself, you know." Her voice dripped disdain.

"Just come out and say it. I get enough riddles from May."

She stopped short, and the others gathered round.

"You know what? I *will* tell you." She turned and looked him in the eye. "Since your brain is probably full of useless things like sports statistics, I get that you don't have the capacity to see what the problem is."

Sam shrugged. "So, tell me."

"For starters, let's look at your word choice. You're *stuck* here."

Sam gave her the most patronizing look he could. "Yeah, May and Bariv told me I can't leave. So yes, I'm *stuck*."

She poked him hard in the chest. "You've been given a gift most people only ever dream of. I'm sure you—like every other kid—grew up wishing magic was real. Well, guess what? It is! We live in a beautiful community where everyone supports each other with love and companionship, where everyone is family and you don't have to hide what you are from anyone—not like on the outside." Daphne's eyes burned and her cheeks turned red. "Here they would accept you with open arms, and you get to explore the wonders of the Veil and learn how to do amazing things. Yet you're going to give it all up for a—a game."

Sam stepped back. "You don't understand. It's not *just* a game. Doing magic and stuff isn't the only thing people wish for, you know. Being a professional football player is something that a lot of people dream of, myself included."

"And you'll play for a while, and then what? A game eventually ends. Here, everything is new and exciting. The Veil protects us, nourishes us, entertains us—it is truly a blessing. You stand there with your second-skin and basically mock us all. Your life could *mean* something. Instead you're just going to end up being a statistic in another naïve boy's head."

Cassiella looked like she wanted to jump in and defend Sam, but she stayed silent.

Sam rubbed his hand over his second-skin. "Even if I leave, it doesn't mean I can't come back after my career."

Daphne's cheeks were now bright red. "So now we're so unimportant that you can just postpone your gift?" She imitated Sam's voice. "'Thanks a lot, I'll take that later. No, what you have to offer isn't good enough for me.'"

"Real smooth," Petir whispered.

Sam clenched his fists. "No one was talking to you." He turned back to Daphne. "That's not it." Something vibrated under Sam's feet. "It's just that I *have* to take the football opportunity now, because I'll never have it again."

She looked at him with fiery scorn. "Who says we'll even want you back?"

Sam's temper rose, along with the vibrations. "Hey, I'm doing everything right here. I'm not hurting anybody. I'm doing everything May asks. I'm playing the game."

"Game?" Daphne's blue eyes had turned from a serene lake to hurricane waters. "THIS... IS... NOT... A... GAME!"

"It's an expression!" The tremors intensified. "Why do you even care?"

"I don't." She turned her back and continued walking.

Sam watched her stride away, fists clenched at her sides, and he felt something stir. He wasn't used to girls calling him out on things. The last time it had happened, the necklace he'd bought his ex had ended up on the school linoleum.

"Good," Sam huffed. The shaking underneath him subsided and he turned to look at the others. Zawadi's eyebrows were almost intermingled with her hair. The smug smirk on Petir's face was more potent than when he'd crushed Sam's hand at gumptius.

Cassiella looked ready to cry.

"Let's keep moving," Sam said, as if nothing had happened. "I want to get started with that documenting."

Glissandro came over, gave Sam a strong pat on the back, and followed after Daphne. Sam turned to follow him, leaving the others behind, with Petir cackling to himself at the back of the group.

Sam didn't feel like talking; a lump had settled into his stomach. Even when they passed a sloth-like creature using the paw on the end of its tail to crush walnut shells, Sam decided to keep his mouth shut. *What do I care what she thinks? Just because she's beautiful doesn't mean that she can act like a—*

"We're here," Zawadi declared.

Sam raised his eyes. In front of him hovered thousands of tiny green birds, or... *butterflies*? The tiny wings fluttered as they clouded the canopy, letting only a small amount of daylight reach the ground. Squinting, Sam realized that they were not, in fact, birds or butterflies, but leaves.

While in the air, they moved so fast and erratically that they were tough to make out, but as they landed, Sam could see them more clearly.

The leaves were V-shaped and had a waxy sheen. Once on the branch, it looked to Sam as if they actually attached to their landing strip, becoming part of the tree. On a few branches, some of the leaves rapidly turned gold and then yellow, orange, and finally brown. Once they had gone through the spectrum of colors, they gracefully fell to the ground and crumbled.

"They are divvy trees." Zawadi gestured, and a leaf flew down and landed on her second-skin. She touched it with a gentle breath and it flew away. "But they are not what we came here for."

Sam stared up at the trees; the air above him was a chaotic mess of green. When his eyes relaxed, the scene shifted, making it seem as if the leaves were actually dancing. "What did we come for?"

Zawadi pointed to Sam's left.

About twenty feet away from him was a devious-looking plant. It had more thorn, spike, and needle than anything green. The height of a medium-sized dog, the main body was black and pulsed with a sappy discharge, and Sam could feel its radiating anger. Two pods protruded from the trunk like mutated eyes.

Sam peered closer at it. "Doesn't look very useful to me."

"We found it yesterday," Cassiella said. "It's new to the world, or at least, it's new to Atlas Crown."

Sam scratched the back of his neck. "So I guess now we have to figure out what it does."

"You catch on so quick." Petir's voice pitched higher with sarcasm.

Sam ignored him, turning back to Zawadi. "So, what do you know so far?"

"Not much, but we do know it does not like us."

"How do you know?"

Zawadi approached the plant, stopping at a line of stones on the grass about ten feet from it. The plant's eye-like extensions whizzed in her direction and some unknown orifice made a hissing sound, like water trapped in a burning log. When Zawadi moved closer, the plant's spikes extended.

Sam joined her behind the stones. "You're right. It doesn't seem to like you."

"No," Zawadi agreed. "We haven't tried getting closer than that, in case its spines can be projected."

"I still say we lift it out of the ground and examine it that way." Petir tossed a stone up and down in his second-skin.

"And I still say that if we do, it might die," Daphne answered. "You know how delicate these plants can be."

"Doesn't look too delicate to me," Sam immediately regretted saying it, as he realized he was making Petir's point.

"Actually," Zawadi gently removed a divvy leaf from her hair, releasing it into the air with a kiss, "some of the Veil's most fragile plants have the toughest exteriors."

"Makes sense." Sam licked his lips. "I know a few girls like that. Have you tried to use the Veil?"

"Yes," Zawadi flourished her second-skin—the same tiger's-eye color as Rona's. "However, anytime we try to use Her, the plant knows. The more we grip, the angrier it gets."

"We haven't come across anything like this before," Cassiella said in a hushed voice.

"We'd like to get some spines, or a sample of the sap, but we need to figure out how." Daphne kept her voice empty of inflection.

The others stood around looking pensive, all except Glissandro, who had a little smile on his face.

"So," Sam nudged one of the stones with his foot, "the closer we get physically, or through the Veil, the more defensive it becomes."

Zawadi confirmed with a nod.

Sam thought for a moment, and then turned toward the group. "It's like a lineman."

They stared at him, not understanding.

"Pardon my ignorance," Zawadi said. "But what's a lineman?"

"It's a position in *football*." He stressed the last word for Daphne's benefit. "To get to the quarterback, the spines or sap, you have to first get through the linemen, the big scary shield."

More blank stares.

"Well, usually the linemen look impenetrable," Sam puffed out his chest to comic proportions. "That's why you have to throw them off their guard."

"And what do you propose?" Petir taunted. "You don't know anything about our world."

Sam smiled and tapped a finger against his head. "But I do know strategy."

"What do you suggest?" Zawadi asked.

Sam surveyed his surroundings and came up with a plan.

"One person can't get to a quarterback. You have to work as a team." Sam sized up their opponent. "I think we have to go at it from different fronts."

Cassiella was almost jumping up and down. "So, go at it from different sides?"

Sam bobbed his head from side to side. "In a way."

Though the plant had no visible ears, Sam still thought it was best to get into a huddle to discuss the strategy. They gathered round, and Sam spoke in a hushed tone.

Petir hovered a few feet outside of the circle with his arms folded over his chest. "That won't work."

Sam wondered if he'd even heard the plan at all. "Well," Sam flipped his palms up, "from what Daphne said, your plan would kill it. So why don't we just give it a shot?"

"It sounds like a great plan!" Cassiella looked at Sam with wide eyes. "You're so brave!"

"It sounds like a dangerous plan," Daphne said, although Sam thought she sounded a little impressed.

"Only dangerous for me." Sam shrugged. "I'm willing to take the risk."

"And if you get hurt? What about your football?" Daphne spit the word.

"If I get hurt, then May can heal me. She's done it before."

"Actually, I can heal you." Zawadi gave Sam a coy smile. "I'm getting quite good at it. I plan to become an Allu Shaman one day. They're the healers who deal with the worst injuries and ailments. Rona started teaching me how to heal when I was young, even though we're not *technically* supposed to know how until after Omani."

"I don't know if this is the best idea." Daphne turned to Zawadi. "I know you're getting better, but if he got really hurt, then—"

"It's perfect!" Sam clapped his hands together, eliciting a loud hiss from the demon-plant behind them. "How 'bout we do this thing?"

All eyes turned to Daphne.

"Fine." She huffed a sigh. "But if anyone gets seriously hurt—"

Sam cut her off. "You all just keep your distance and we'll be fine. Besides, I bet Zawadi can handle anything that comes our way."

Daphne sighed again, and then shrugged.

"Thank you for your confidence, Sam." Zawadi gave a slight bow. "Let us begin."

Cassiella ran back the way they'd come as the group took their positions. After a few minutes, she returned, looking petrified.

Glissandro was in charge of their first point of attack. He whipped out his horn and started playing as loud as physically possible. Sam had no idea so much noise could come from such a little instrument. He clapped his hands over his ears and moved into position.

Just like he'd asked him to, Sam could feel Glissandro attempting to speak to the plant. Words cluttered the air like divvy leaves. Sam couldn't make them out, but he could feel them rushing all around. It was like he heard the words, then instantly forgot what they were. The plant swiveled its spines toward Glissandro and opened its eye-pouches as wide as they could go. The crisscrossed bristles on the pods looked uncannily like eyelashes, while the center of each pod held a blood-red circle glossed over by a syrupy substance.

A foul stench smacked Sam's nostrils, making it necessary to take a hand off one of his ears to plug his nose.

Ugh! Compared to this, the pouch Bariv gave me was like potpourri.

The others also pinched their noses. Sam hoped they'd still be able to perform one-handed.

Cassiella and Zawadi were next.

With a look of great relief, Cassiella took out two silver fruit from her pocket, and Sam heard his coach screaming about pansies. Sam's original plan had been for them to levitate some dirt or rocks into the plant's pods, but Glissandro had suggested they use the annoying fruit instead. His thought was that, sometimes, other plants would bend toward a symflower while it played. He hoped that the opposite might also be true.

Sam thought it was worth a shot.

The silver fruit whirred past and landed in each pod. Bristles snapped together, and then opened wide, trying to heave the fruit out. Just as Sam had hoped, the fruit stuck to the sticky substance inside. The plant thrashed about, but couldn't get the fruit off. Any sympathy Sam might've felt for the demon-plant died when another wave of the nasty stench hit him.

Next was Daphne. When Sam had suggested her task, he wasn't sure if it was possible. But he figured if she was able to call that bird to help her search for the amorberry—which he wasn't entirely sure they hadn't found—maybe she could do something similar again.

Sam was now in position and looking up. Above him the flock of flying leaves blocked his view of the sky. All of a sudden the leaves changed course, bombarding downward. They swarmed Sam like bees around their queen, gravitating toward his body.

Daphne was actually pulling it off.

The leaves closed in around him, forming a tight cyclone of flashing green. Then they started landing on his body. Sam waited until he had an entire outfit made of green camouflage, and then started inching toward the demon-plant. The leaves didn't have any weight behind them, but they still felt funny—like he was less aerodynamic—and he moved slowly so as not to shake any of them off.

The rest of the leaf armada swirled about, creating chaos. Hissing and flailing, tortured by the silver fruit, the thorny plant didn't see Sam come up from behind. Sam reached out his emerald arm. With his second-skin, he gripped one of the large thorns and plucked it out with a firm pull.

Instead of ejecting the barbs deep into Sam's abdomen or whipping him with its tentacles, the plant shriveled up and folded in on itself. As it slipped under the earth, the hissing grew in pitch, like a teakettle getting too hot, and eventually sizzled out when the plant disappeared.

Glissandro stopped playing the ear-shattering noise, and thankfully the smell left with the plant. Daphne stopped influencing the leaves and they all fluttered back up into the trees.

"I got it!" Sam shouted as the leaves drifted away. His heart thumped hard in his chest and he felt that old comforting feeling of victory. It was the first time in Atlas Crown that he had truly felt at ease.

Having the large thorn in his hand made him nearly burst with pride. The plan, *his* plan, had worked.

But just like at the game, the shouts and cheers weren't forthcoming. He looked at the others' mournful faces.

"Look!" Sam waved the thorn. "I got it!"

"Yeah," Petir scoffed, "but now we have to search the whole forest."

"But I got it! Right here!"

"Good job, Sam." Zawadi smiled, though her tone was a tad dampened.

Sam felt the bubble of pride deflate. "Is there something that I'm not getting here? The plan worked. You all were great!"

"Thank you, Sam, it was a fine plan." Zawadi bit her lip. "You were great as well."

"It was a great plan!" Cassiella interjected, though it looked like her smile was forced.

Sam arched his eyebrows. "Then what's the problem?"

Daphne sighed. "The problem is, one thorn isn't enough to study."

"It's a start." Cassiella forced her smile even wider.

Sam examined the thorn. "So, let's go find the plant again."

"You don't know anything," Petir huffed. "It's going to take days to find it again. And even then, we know *you* can't touch it or you'll send it away. Why don't you leave the plans to us, flathand?"

Zawadi's mouth hung open in shock. "Petir!"

Daphne was about to say something, but Sam cut her off. "Fine. You all can do it yourselves." He threw the thorn into the ground, where it stuck like a flagpole. "I'm out of here."

He looked around but couldn't see any of the pillars past the dense brush. Glissandro motioned with his head to the right, and he and Sam stormed off toward the city.

◉

The Tembrath Elite stood just feet outside of the borders of Atlas Crown.

Jintin reached out a finger, which crumpled on itself as it touched the invisible barrier.

"This thing cannot hold us." Jintin prodded the air again. "We should just break through and ransack the place. I've been working on this new drape where—"

Vigtor silenced him with a wave. "Did you forget about the Mystics?"

"They probably wouldn't notice," Jintin retorted. "They're so isolated up there that they wouldn't even feel it."

Vigtor clenched his teeth. "But Bariv would."

Jintin thought for a moment. "Bariv is one bird in an otherwise deserted sky."

Vigtor smirked. "When did you get so elegant in your speech?"

Jintin's proud expression showed that he hadn't caught the subtle insult.

"Besides," Vigtor ran a finger against the barrier, "I wouldn't call this place deserted. Even the clearest sky could just mean that the bigger birds are waiting on the ground. You know what the Mystics can do."

Jintin's expression darkened. "Let them try."

Vigtor looked straight into Jintin's eyes. "You are a fool."

Sage pounded her fist against the barrier. "I can't believe we are actually stooping to this."

Saria took her sister's hand. "We all started as beginners, too."

"Yeah, but him?"

Erimos put a hand on each of their shoulders. "He has done something that hasn't been done in a very long time."

Sage's eyes narrowed. "But that doesn't mean that he's qualified to join us."

"We need him." Erimos stared her down. "So yes, it does."

"Everyone move aside and let me begin," Vigtor said. "I'm going to need space and silence."

"How do we know they won't detect this?" Crom's tone was skeptical, as usual.

"When I was here," Vigtor pushed them back further, "I came across one. No one realized it was there except me. I studied it for months, and eventually I was able to re-create it."

Sage took a moment to step back. "Will it work?"

Vigtor placed his second-skin against the invisible barrier. "It might take some time, but yes."

"But who will stay with it?"

Vigtor didn't hesitate. "Jintin."

"Me?" A nervous look crossed Jintin's face. "Why?"

"Because it seems that you are unafraid of the Mystics, and if *this* plan doesn't work in time, then we do your plan."

Jintin immediately regained his composure. "If it doesn't work, I've been planning this grip where—"

Crom mumbled something.

Vigtor's head snapped up. "I didn't catch that."

"Waste of time," Crom boomed.

Vigtor's face darkened. "If you have a better plan to get the boy to come out, then by all means, enlighten us."

Crom's nostrils flared. "The *boy* is a waste of time."

"I'm growing impatient with your attitude. You know, in all likelihood, the boy will have enough access to Her that he can replace you as final. Either stop wasting my time with your foolish insecurities, or we will toss you out."

Crom's face grew murderous. "You try it without me and I'll cut off your—"

"No need for threats." Erimos' voice carried through the air like smoke. "Let us begin."

"Clear a space," Vigtor commanded.

As the rest of his group backed away—Crom moving away with sullen slowness—Vigtor began his drape. Balancing wind in a vacuum was a tricky weave, and even for most natural sorcerers it would have been nearly impossible to do, but for Vigtor, it was like riding a bike—a swirling, black, vacuous bike.

After a few arduous minutes, it was there before them. With a circumference just big enough for a body, it was the perfect size for trapping. Vigtor had created a tunnel which would bring someone under the protective border. It currently sucked air in, and Vigtor added the finishing touch by crushing and tossing in a few kolo buds—which would bring someone faster than a jelly-hive brings a grotlon. He waited a few moments for the kolo to pass through, and then with a few powerful passes of his second-skin, the air changed directions and began to blow out.

Sage peered over the edge, her hair getting flung by the wind. "Why can't we just go through it?"

"Because the most powerful protections—the ones against us—are still in place. We still can't get in, but *they* can most definitely get out."

Sage cackled.

"Stop that," Crom snapped.

The darkness twisted with the air, making a black vortex in the ground. The daylight did nothing to illuminate the inside of the tunnel. They couldn't see the opposite end, either, but it was out there somewhere, waiting to catch its prey.

Vigtor handed Jintin the envelope.

"Signal us when it happens. When someone comes through, the vacuum will be on this side, so watch where you step. I trust you can handle this?"

Jintin placed the envelope in the pocket of his robe. "Yes."

"Good." Vigtor moved close, his mouth just inches from Jintin's ear. "You'd better," he whispered, "because if you don't, you're going final next time… and I don't think you want that."

Jintin gulped.

CHAPTER 17

After about half an hour of walking in silence, Sam and Glissandro were back in the heart of Atlas Crown. Since Sam had only seen a small portion of Atlas Crown so far—and that was mostly the forest—Glissandro assured him that he hadn't really had the chance to understand the extent of the wonders they kept guarded inside the walls. In fact, Glissandro told him, it would be a long time before Sam could really grasp what their town was truly like.

In an attempt to lift Sam's spirits, Glissandro brought him to a restaurant unlike any food establishment Sam had ever been to. It was essentially a huge water slide down a long hill. Along a smooth, stone channel, water flowed on a continuous loop, just like the river. As the guests slid down the hill, waiters threw refreshments into their oncoming mouths. Sam watched as happy children and adults alike took the ride with relish. It was hot out and the line for the restaurant was long, but moving quickly. After the descent, Sam watched the people magically dry their clothes, although some children left themselves saturated.

"I still don't understand how this place doesn't use money," Sam said as they took their place at the back of the restaurant line. In front of them, a man hummed a simple tune. He had a second-skin on each hand, one white and one black. "Why work at all if everything is given to you?"

"Everything is not given to you," Glissandro played, shaking his head. "If you don't contribute to the community, then the community will not give back. Take this place, for example. This group contributes what they love. For this season, they run this food-slide, which they've been doing since I was a kid, and for the winter they'll do something different—I'm hoping for stew-skating. Since the Veil allows us to do what we want, it's not really working, but it's still contributing. That's the sad thing about the outside world, the fact that most people don't get that luxury."

"How do you know that?"

Glissandro smiled. "I've spent time there."

"What?" Sam's voice cracked in surprise. "Where?"

"Alaska," Glissandro played a simple pip.

"Alaska? Why?"

Glissandro traced the gold inlay on his horn with a finger, and after a moment brought it to his lips. "Because there are places in the outside world with magic, too."

"I haven't seen any."

Glissandro looked off into the distance with a wistful smile. "I went to see the Aurora Borealis."

Sam repressed a chuckle. "That's not magic."

Glissandro played an innocent slur. "Why not?"

"Because… it's just light hitting the clouds in a funny way, or something like that."

Glissandro gave him a blank stare for a moment. "Are you sure?"

Sam thought about it, but couldn't remember if he had actually learned that in class, or if he'd made it up. "I guess not."

Glissandro played something that sounded like ambient whines. "I was under the impression that solar wind excites the atoms, which emit light when they return to a ground state."

Sam gave Glissandro a skeptical look. "How in the world do you know that?"

A thin wisp of a smile appeared on Glissandro's face. "Just because I can't talk doesn't mean I don't listen."

Sam conceded with a sharp nod. "Fair enough."

"I took in everything I could learn when I was on the outside."

The man in front of them turned around. His close-cropped hair was flecked with grey. "I was born in Puerto Rico, you know. There's magic there as well. There's a whole bay that lights up like there are blue fireflies under the water."

"Oh, sorry," Glissandro played, "this is our head grower, Fernando of the Ojowakeepsawej clan."

Fernando lifted his second-skins and compressed the air in front of his chest. "Ojo for short."

Sam stuck out his hand. "Nice to meet you."

Fernando gave his hand a quick shake, but his eyes lingered on Sam's second-skin. "Nice to meet you, too…?"

"Sam, Sam Lock."

Fernando's eyebrows drew together. "I don't think I'm familiar with the Lock clan. Which community are you visiting from?"

"He's from the outside," Glissandro played.

Fernando's eyes widened. "Are you the boy that the Tem—" He cut himself off. "The football player?"

Sam pulled the collar of his robe down, revealing the top of his jersey. "That's right."

Sweat formed on the man's head that hadn't been there a moment ago.

"Welcome, Sam." His eyes darted around wildly. "I—well—you see…" He shaded his eyes and looked up at the sun. "Oh, I totally forgot, I have somewhere to be. Head grower duties and all. Stop by my tower whenever you like; we'll make a meal out of it." He dashed out of line and scurried off.

Sam sniffed his shirt for residual odors.

Glissandro shrugged. "Have you ever seen the Aurora Borealis?"

Sam shook his head.

"The swirling lights, the performances." He played softer. "Don't tell anyone this, because we're not supposed to use the Veil on the outside unless it's an emergency, but the light played along to my music. I asked it to dance and it did—all night."

Sam slapped a hand on Glissandro's shoulder. "That's cool, but it's not magic."

"Of course it is."

Sam wiggled the fingers under his second-skin. "The *Veil* is magic."

Glissandro shuffled to the edge of the slide. He looked back at Sam with a simple smile and dropped down into the water. When Sam followed, the server tossed him a tight ball of liquid that broke apart in his mouth as a smoothie that tasted of mangoes and coconuts. After that, Glissandro dried Sam off with a powerful trio of notes and took him to the library.

It wasn't the stuffy, neglected place Sam was expecting.

The library itself was a tower that spiraled its way skyward, almost as high as the pillars, but it was made entirely out of books. The only part of the tower that wasn't books was the ramp inside.

"The ramp's floor has writing on it, too," Glissandro played. "And the books are all protected with drapes. You can only pull them out with a grip, but you can do so from the ground. This way, the wind doesn't destroy anything."

Several citizens approached the base of the library, paused for a moment, and then books would jiggle their way out of the tower and into their hands. They all smiled at Sam as they passed and some even exchanged pleasant greetings, but still, no one seemed all that interested in getting to know him.

"Writing is a highly prized skill in Atlas Crown," Glissandro explained. "Sometime in their lives, everyone strives to add something to the library. The newer books are placed at the top, and the older books can be found deep within the earth—the viewable portion of the library is just the tip of the iceberg." Glissandro pointed out the hole from which the underground books emerged. "The library has so many books that the passage down reaches all the way to the center of the earth. The oldest book at the bottom was not even written by human hands, but by the Veil Herself. Down in the dark depths, there are books describing—in detail—how the Veil draped Herself across the whole world as a gift for everyone to use. Also, the books on darker magic are kept far below. If you go down far enough, you might even come across a chinoo reading one. But don't join in reading with them, or you might become one. Or at least that's what my clan mother used to tell me."

Sam tried to pull out a book near the bottom of the tower, but it wouldn't budge. Glissandro played a birdsong melody, and the book popped out and landed in Sam's hands. He opened to the first page, but the book was written in a language he didn't recognize. "What's a chinoo?"

"A chinoo," Glissandro played, " is a made-up creature that the elders talk about to keep children from pursuing evil grips. To do wicked grips, you have to reach far into the Veil, much deeper than if you are using Her for good. The story goes that, a while back, some children became fascinated with evil grips. Despite the love their parents bestowed upon them, the children kept reaching deeper and deeper to use the Veil for gradually worse things. Eventually, they reached so far in that their souls fell past Her and they left their bodies behind. They were then doomed to walk the earth soulless, which of course leads to horrible physical deformities."

"Like what?"

"It's just a fairy tale." Glissandro touched each finger to his thumb. "Playing of, you're in for a treat later tonight."

"What?"

"You'll see. It's worth the surprise."

Sam tried to put the book back into the empty slot, but it felt like it was already filled. He looked over at Glissandro, rolling his eyes.

Glissandro played the book back into the tower.

Sam prodded the book, which didn't budge. "So, what's next?"

"Are we done with the library?"

"I'm not a big reader."

Glissandro thought for a moment. "Want to see the bird zoo? No reading involved."

Sam shrugged. "Why not?"

Glissandro's mouth curled. "We tend not to write on the animals."

"No, I meant—" Sam laughed and dismissed it with a wave. "Real funny. The bird zoo sounds good to me."

Glissandro led the way back through town.

"Does everyone spend time on the outside?" Sam asked as they strolled through the stands.

Glissandro shook his head.

"So why did you go?"

"Sometimes, when people struggle here, they go live on the outside or with another magical community for a while. I've done it; Petir's done it, and a lot of other people our age, too. Most of the time they come back. Except a certain few."

Sam thought the end of Glissandro's song sounded a tad weak. "Anyone in particular?"

Glissandro looked nervous. "I'm not the person to tell you that."

"Why is everyone so secretive with me? Is this about those Tembrath guys?"

Glissandro tore his eyes away and sped up the pace. "We're almost there."

Sam grabbed his arm. "Just tell me! I'm gonna find out sooner or later."

Glissandro looked over Sam's shoulder. "Listen," he played very quietly, "if I told you, May would not be happy with me. If you want answers, I'll take you to the Mystics tonight. They'll have no problem with explaining what you want to know. Please don't make me be the one to tell you."

Sam let go of his arm. "Tonight, then."

Glissandro gave him a thankful nod.

@

The bird zoo didn't have any birds in it.

It didn't have anything in it; the place was just an area with raised platforms of many different colors and little patches of a black, rubber-like material.

Sam pinched his lips in confusion. "I don't get it."

"Stand on one," Glissandro played.

Sam went up to a large golden platform and took a step onto the black rubber.

A bright trill came from underneath his feet.

Sam looked down, and then back at Glissandro. "I still don't get it." "Just wait."

The same loud trill came from beyond the stone border of Atlas Crown as a giant bird soared over the wall. The size of a small plane, its plumage matched the golden color of the platform. A sparkling gold trail marked its path as it drifted on the wind without flapping its wings. It sailed down and landed right on the gold platform, its shadow covering Sam.

Glissandro nodded toward the bird. "Pet it."

The bird's beak made a toucan's look like a joke. Marble-like eyes glared at Sam while it preened its feathers.

"No way." Sam started to back away. "It'll bite me."

"It might bite you if you don't pet it."

Sam put out a hesitant hand and stroked the underbelly of the bird. It gave a soft coo.

Glissandro mimicked the coo. "Pretty neat, right?"

"Yeah. But where are the other birds?"

The bird ruffled its feathers and flew off with a powerful burst of wind that almost knocked Sam over.

Sam's eyes stayed on the bird. "Was it something I said?"

Glissandro gestured for Sam to step off the platform. "You have to give them your full attention. That's why they come, you know."

"For the attention?"

"Absolutely. We don't force them to be here. Why else would they come?"

Sam moved from patch to patch, seeing which birds would come to what podiums. Some birds didn't appear, but the ones Sam did get to see were spectacular, especially a pair of brown ones that dove in and out of the earth like it was water.

"So, this treat I'm in for," Sam rubbed his hands together, "will Daphne be there?"

"I believe so."

"What's her deal?"

"What do you mean?"

Sam shrugged. "I don't get her."

"That's exactly the reason why you won't."

Sam sighed. "You too, huh?"

"Sorry." The humor dropped out of his expression. "But you have to understand something about her."

"What?"

"Just like in gumptius—which you also jumped into unprepared—you can't go in thinking bravado and muscles will get you what you want."

Sam puffed out his chest and buffed his fingernails against his robe. "They haven't hurt me before."

Glissandro rolled his eyes. "You are no longer on the outside. Daphne isn't the type of girl who's going to be impressed with that. She's very close to the Veil and has worked hard to be so." Glissandro grinned. "She's also really popular."

Sam rocked his index finger pointedly. "But she came from the outside, too."

"That is true. But it also strengthens my point. She's seen both sides."

Sam gave a quick huff. "I guess."

"And besides, Daphne's pretty, smart, and very good with the Veil. Plus, she wants to be head grower some day."

Sam flexed his bicep, giving it a few taps with his finger. "You saying I don't have a shot?"

"I'm saying you can't aim for the moon and expect to hit a star."

Sam stepped away from the green platform.

That bird wasn't coming.

They left the zoo and made their way toward the outskirts of town. At their destination—a giant stage carved directly into a rock face—they ran into May.

She greeted them with her ever-present smile. "I've got some news for you."

It turned out that over the last few days, she had healed the cornerback, and managed to have the Mystics somehow alter the memories of everyone in Stanton to think Sam was not at the game, but rather in the hospital with tonsillitis.

"No way!" Sam's voice overflowed with excitement. "If you weren't so old, I'd kiss you right now."

May gasped. "Bringing up a lady's age!" She looked ready to burst into tears. "After all I've done for you?"

"Sorry," Sam grimaced. "I didn't mean—I—You're really pretty. Like REALLY—"

"I'm going to cut you off there." She released a warm smile. "It is actually an honor to be as old as I am."

Sam ran a hand through his hair. "How did they do it?"

"That is between them and their many years of study. I could never do it, but then again, neither could anyone else. Your case was exceptionally complicated, and they were stretched to their limits, but it is done. However, they did want me to inform you that altering all the photographs was a particularly difficult job." She winked.

"So it's all forgotten?"

May gave a delicate nod. "Yes."

"And my parents?"

"They think that you are at a special training camp for a college football team. They also sent me back with a letter, which is currently in your room."

"This is incredible!"

Standing next to him, Glissandro gave a feeble smile.

"However," May's expression sobered, "I still have to insist that you stay here for a while longer."

This immediately put a damper on Sam's celebration. "But now that they don't think I choked, I still have a shot. And that kid isn't hurt—"

"I know," her voice was gentle, "but for your own safety, you will have to stay here." She gestured to the stage. "Haven't you fallen in love with the place yet?"

"It's great, it's just—"

"I did you a favor by asking the Mystics to alter memories, which we only do in the most dire circumstances—because of which, I now have to bring Delphi an avocado and nettle-melon sandwich every sunrise for twelve arcs. The last thing I want to do is dampen your spirits, but it is for your own good. So please, do me a favor and stay put."

He was too excited to argue. "Sure."

Glissandro's smile turned bold.

Sam surprised himself—he actually wasn't too heartbroken about staying a little longer. He would drink in all the exotic things Atlas Crown had to offer and then return home to a wonderful welcome. An odd thought darted across Sam's mind. "But Bariv told me that he would fix everything for me when I learned to control the power."

"That *is* the reason why you have to stay. We can't have you hurting more people."

"So why did you fix everything now?"

"The longer we waited, the harder it would be for the Mystics to work. More recent memories to sift through, I guess, but I could be completely off mark. They actually got started the minute you got here."

So Bariv lied to me? Why would he do that? Sam decided he didn't care. Everything was fixed: they'd given him his life back. "I can't believe they pulled it off."

May's eyes glinted. "So you're a believer now? I thought all of this was imaginary."

Sam's grin reached from ear to ear. "I said *can't* believe."

May returned the expression. "My mistake. I guess I hear what I want to hear. It seems we still have our work cut out for us, then."

Sam wanted to jump up and down, but thought better of it. He pulled his eyes off May and looked over at the stage. It was large enough to comfortably hold a herd of elephants, and a small army of people from different clans scurried on and off, tending to the decorations. "A play?"

Glissandro played a melody that somehow echoed around them. "Tonight will be a reenactment."

"Reenactment of what?"

Glissandro played a barrage of descending notes. "The beginnings of magic."

"What are they doing to the stage?"

"They have to create the set, the costumes and the items, all before rehearsal."

"Can we take a look?"

Glissandro gave Sam a wicked grin and shrugged. "Why not?"

Sam snorted.

Glissandro pointed his horn toward the sky. "But since it's getting dark we won't have long before the show."

"May, do you want to—"

Sam stopped, as May was no longer standing next to them. "Where'd she go?"

"May is the busiest member of our community."

Sam rubbed the bottom of his chin with his second-skin. The scales felt warm and soothing against his skin. "Yeah, I've been meaning to ask about that. What does she do, exactly?"

"May is the reason for our stability. She's our liaison to the outside world, along with the other magical communities."

Sam clucked his tongue. "Full plate."

"The fullest."

"I'm surprised she gets so involved with all of the new recruits."

"She usually doesn't."

"So why is she on my case so much?"

Glissandro craned his neck. "Look, they're almost done setting up."

"Let's go take a look."

The closer their proximity to the stage, the more confused Sam became. They were building the set by hand. No objects flew through the air; no one was using the Veil to weld beams together; no costumes were sewing themselves—it looked too normal.

Sweat and dirt stained the workers' robes as they used hammers, saws, and pulleys to build the scenery. No power tools—which Sam admitted would have been weird to see being used by sorcerers—all the bangs and slams came from manual labor.

An older woman with a mortar and pestle mashed berries into colorful spreads that other people applied to the actors' faces with slow and careful strokes of tiny brushes. Another, even older woman next to her pulled a needle and thread through a black, leathery material.

"It's not real hide," Glissandro played. "It's from a plant."

"I don't understand. Why aren't they using magic? They could set everything up so quickly."

"This reenactment is very important to us. When they put on fictional stories, there are all sorts of drapes and grips, but for this, they work with their hands."

Sam watched as an older man molded black clay into a ball. "Why is it so important?"

"It is the beginning. It's the story of how we discovered the Veil. Our entire way of life would crumble without Her. To show our appreciation, they do not use Her to create anything. She makes life easier, so they purposefully make preparations difficult for themselves, both to show our appreciation and our respect."

All of a sudden, a purple curtain fell in front of the stage. Sam recognized it as the same material that separated Bariv's cave from the rest of Atlas Crown.

"Rehearsal. They don't want anyone to see them practicing." Glissandro gave a bashful smile. "And to be fair, that barrier doesn't count as using the Veil. They planted it there long ago."

"That stuff is a plant?" Sam grimaced, remembering the unsettling feeling of passing through it.

"Well, technically it's the dead material of the plant, like fingernails, but—"

"Actually," Sam winced, thinking about the wet goopy feeling of it on his skin, "let's just leave it at that."

"Good," played Glissandro, "because I think the light's just about low enough."

"For what?"

Glissandro gave him a knowing look. "Gumptius."

At the mention of the game, Sam thought of Petir's pompous face.

"Why does it need to be dark? People were playing in the day before, remember?"

Glissandro's closed lips starting trembling, like he was repressing a laugh.

Sam threw his hands up. "I didn't know how to do it!"

"Of course. That's what it was." Then he bent double in a silent guffaw.

Sam punched him in the arm. "Yeah, it was."

Glissandro eyed Sam's second-skin. "So, you want to give it another go?"

Sam grinned. "Uh… I think I'll just watch this time."

They didn't have to go far to find the matches. The scene was a lot livelier than earlier, with crowds of cheering spectators split into different circles. Small beacons of light flashed at different intervals within each circle.

Sam stood on his toes, trying to peek into the matches. "What's going on?"

"You saw people *practicing* gumptius last time. This time, people are competing."

Sam shaded his eyes as a few intense bursts of pulsing yellow came from the closest circle. "What's with the light?"

Glissandro nodded toward the circle where the yellow eruptions occurred. "Let's squeeze in, so you can see for yourself."

They nudged their way through the thick crowd. Sam was again taller and broader than most, so polite maneuvering was a challenge.

Once in the front row, Glissandro bent to one knee and motioned for Sam to do the same. Sam shrugged, and then took a knee.

In front of them, the rock tables and stools looked to have been pulled straight out of the ground—as they still had craggy edges and soil residue clinging to them. One side of the table held a bunch of symbols, one of which Sam recognized as the double triangle from the seam.

Two young men stared at each other from across the table. Though roughly the same age, one of them had considerably more facial hair than the other.

"Good," Glissandro played over the racket, "this one hasn't started yet."

The two opponents sat down with dramatic menace, and the surrounding ring of people grew so loud they drowned out the noise of the other matches.

The man on the left stretched his fingers by pulling them toward his wrist, and then made a tight fist. The other rolled his neck and shook out his shoulders.

Glissandro played a loud blast. "It's for show."

"I'll have to come up with something intimidating, then," Sam shouted, but Glissandro didn't hear him.

The challengers' second-skins came together, and the match began. At first, the players' hands stayed stationary in the center of the board. The only thing that changed was their expressions. Sam could see a small pocket of air between their hands, like what had happened in his match with Petir.

What's that for?

In a matter of seconds, the man on the left was panting for air, and his rival's face was redder than a symflower.

Then a glow formed around their hands. It started out soft, almost imperceptible, but swiftly grew stronger. Layers of light pulsed from their locked skins. A twist of blue spiraled off into the distance, and small clouds of green sprouted and hovered above them.

All of a sudden, a white light shot into the sky like an electric beanstalk, and Sam saw a hand pinned to the stone. The clean-cut kid had lost—both the match and his second-skin. The ropey material lay unraveled on the table.

The circle howled with delight.

The winner waved his second-skin over the table, and the symbol from his chest appeared, burned onto the side of the table along with the others.

Sam nodded toward the scorched stone. "Keeping score?"

Glissandro nodded.

The opponents bowed to each other and a new challenger stepped up.

"Why did his second-skin break?" Sam asked Glissandro.

"He pushed too hard." Glissandro pointed two fingers at his eyes and then back at Sam. "Not enough focus."

"That can happen here, too?"

"It can happen anywhere. But don't worry, most players make new skins before they enter a match. They don't use the second-skins they are truly attached to."

Sam looked down at his own second-skin, which he'd sort of forgotten he was wearing. "Good to know."

They watched a few more matches and joined in on the cheering. Sam felt himself rooting for someone to take down the scruffy kid, whose name he'd learned was Galio.

After Galio took down yet another challenger, a girl with a bendy bark-skin, they decided to move to a different circle.

"That kid was really good." Sam stretched out his arms once outside of the mayhem. "That was nuts when the rock started cracking."

"He's one of the best." Glissandro pulled at his chin. "He's growing that beard until he loses one of the tournaments."

Sam craned his neck to catch a glimpse of Galio. "He's undefeated?"

"Yes… but he hasn't accepted Petir's challenge yet. I expect when he does, Galio's face is going to be smoother than that rock before it was cracked."

"Is Petir really that good?"

"The best."

Sam stretched out his fingers and made a tight fist like Galio had done. He gave Glissandro his most arrogant grin. "For now, maybe."

Glissandro pointed a warning finger. "Just promise me that you won't jump into any matches tonight."

"Don't worry, Gliss. I want to make sure I'm ready before my grand entrance, anyway. I want them talking about me long after I leave."

Glissandro gave him a brittle smile.

At the next circle they ran into Daphne, laughing and giggling with the same group of girls she'd been with at the seam. As soon as she saw him, she stiffened up.

Sam tried his best to sound casual. "Hey."

Daphne countered with an even more indifferent, "Hey."

"You going to introduce me to your friends?" Sam put on his most dashing smile.

One of the girls behind Daphne blushed, while the others giggled.

Daphne turned from Sam. "You all know Glissandro."

The girls giggled and waved. Glissandro's face went red and he gave a quick nod.

"This is Sam," she made a frivolous gesture in his direction, "but you don't have to worry, he probably won't be here much longer. He has a *football* scholarship to get to."

"Oooh," one of the girls simpered. "What team?"

Daphne shot her a look of contempt.

"Not sure yet." Sam gave his most apathetic shrug. "I have a lot of options to choose from."

Daphne gave Sam a look that screamed, 'Oh, brother.'

Sam grinned. "You girls mind if I talk to Daphne alone for a second?"

Daphne went wide-eyed. "But—"

"We'll meet you in there, Daphne," one of the others cut her off. She had a remarkable tan, flawless skin, and her brown hair had the slightest trace of red streaks. She beckoned for the other girls to follow her, throwing a look over her shoulder. "Oh, and Glissandro, I need to talk to you about something. I simply cannot get the upper notes to work on my sugar flute. Think you can come with us and give me some pointers?"

Glissandro's face turned an even brighter red, and he gave another silent nod.

"Great!" The girl gave Sam the type of smile that could melt ice. "We'll see you in there, Sam?"

Sam mustered up a winning smile. "Count on it."

Glissandro walked off with the snickering girls, leaving Sam and Daphne alone.

Sam rubbed a thumb against the palm of his second-skin. "I wouldn't have thought you the type."

"What type?"

"To be here, watching a game. Aren't all games beneath you?"

Daphne flicked her hair. "I'm only here because my friends wanted to come."

"I wouldn't have pegged you as a follower, either."

Her words burst out like a firecracker. "I'm not!"

Sam held up his hands in mock-surrender. "Okay, okay. You're not."

She crossed her arms. "Why do you even care?"

"I don't know. Maybe if you acted like a human being and actually enjoyed this, we could watch it together."

She lifted an eyebrow. "Together?"

"Well, I'm new here. I don't know any other places I could take you on a date."

Her eyebrows tried to escape into the stratosphere. "A date? You're joking, right?"

"Do they call it something else here? A loose stitching?"

"Are you making fun of us?"

"Geez," Sam tried on a smile, "it was a joke. Lighten up."

Daphne put a hand on her hip. "Your jokes are about as lame as your grips."

"Ouch. Well, maybe you should teach me some of each. We could make that our date." Sam shrugged. "And if it goes well, I know something I could teach you about…"

Her cheeks instantly flushed. "You don't know the first thing about me."

"I know you were able to cover me with tiny flying leaves, *and* you were able to use that bird to find the amorberry."

A glint of humor touched her eyes. "*Failed* to find the amorberry."

"Whatever, it was impressive nonetheless."

Daphne tilted her head and gave him a skeptical look. "I know your type all too well, and I don't know what you are hoping to get with one date, but—"

"Who says it just has to be one date?"

"Wait," she spoke in faux confusion, "don't you have to go back for your football scholarship?"

"C'mon… one date."

"In case you don't understand subtle hints, let me spell it out for you. Not. Interested."

"How about we just go watch the gumptius together?"

"It's not *the* gumptius, it's just gumptius. And why can't you just leave me alone?"

Sam shrugged. "You intrigue me."

"If I intrigue you more than the Veil, then you must have gotten tackled on your head more times than I thought."

"You don't get tackled *on* your head. You just get tackled."

A tiny trace of a smile appeared on her lips. "Let's just go watch the match."

Sam made a pointed gesture. "Only as long as you sit next to me at the reenactment."

"Don't push it."

The next circle of people was significantly larger than the one Sam had come from, but he and Daphne were able to find Glissandro and the group toward the front. This time, Glissandro didn't suggest they kneel. The energy in the crowd was verging on explosive. Everyone was on their toes—someone was even on Sam's toes—trying to get a peek at the upcoming match. Sam saw all sorts of symbols and ages in the crowd.

"What's the big deal?" Sam shouted to Glissandro.

His friend nodded toward the table.

To Sam's dismay, Petir stood at one end of the stone slab, his arms raised high above his head. Already, a bunch of black X's were scorched into the side of the stone. Behind Petir, an entourage of other kids with X's on their robes patted him on the back and led the cheering.

Sam ran his hands down his cheeks, tugging the skin. "*He's* the big deal?"

"Not just him," Glissandro played over the rising commotion.

From out of the circle came a young woman. She was a little older than Sam, and stood about half his height. She wore something like a kimono with patterns that shifted along the silk, and on her head were a pair of makeshift goggles and a bowler hat.

Daphne's head jolted back, her eyes going wide. "Sparks!"

Sam furrowed his brow. "Who?"

"Crealynne of the Orbus clan, but everyone calls her Sparks. She's one of the best, but she hardly ever plays. She's studying to go through the

Omani for mystical magic, so she spends most of her time in meditation."
Sam thought there might have been admiration in her voice.

Sam gave her a quick nudge with his elbow. "How do you know so much about a game that you hate?"

She slapped his arm with the back of her hand. "You don't have to like the game to know about Sparks."

"Why do they call her Sparks?"

"You'll see." Daphne turned back toward the table.

Sparks gave a little bow to Petir, who did not return it. She daintily sat down and pulled out a rectangular metal dish.

Sam tapped Glissandro on the shoulder. "What's that for?"

"She makes a new second-skin before every match."

Sparks pulled out a tiny yellow gourd. Taking off the cap, she poured its contents evenly across the tray. What came out was grey and sticky looking, sliding across the dish like molasses. Sparks dipped both sides of her hand into the mixture and let the sludge drip down her forearm.

"Liquid steel," Glissandro played.

"Liquid steel?" Sam asked. "Wouldn't it burn her?"

"She's found a way to keep it cool."

Instead of hardening, the steel stayed limp and pliable around her hand, like salt-water taffy. She held out her hand for Petir and the crowd hushed.

"You aren't going to beat me." Petir pulled off his green practice skin and pulled on the black leathery one.

Sparks' voice was vibrant and oddly melodic. "The most beautiful vibrations are sometimes found in dissonant groupings."

"You're out of practice," Petir sneered. "And you don't even make sense."

"A sense can be distorted by a lack of connection." For some reason, she looked over at Sam. "And without a connection, everything is dark."

"Let's just get this over with." Petir reached around and slapped the scorched X's on the side of the table. "I have plenty more people to beat tonight."

This spurred a round of cheers from the "X" pack.

Sparks still looked at Sam, the goggles enlarging her eyes. He felt like she was staring through him, just like the echo flies.

"Hello!" Petir snapped his uncovered fingers. "Let's go."

Sparks turned her gaze back to her opponent and they put their hands together. A dramatic pause stilled the commotion, until…

"Now!"

A roaring cheer noted the beginning of the match. For the first few seconds, nothing happened; their hands just seemed to sit together, like they were still waiting for the go-ahead. Sam watched as Petir's facial expression went from arrogant to apprehensive. His cheek muscles strained with effort. Sparks, on the other hand, looked as stiff and unflinching as a wax figure. The kids behind Petir attempted to rile him up.

"You can beat her!"

"Crush her hand!"

It was actually working. Sam watched Petir start to move Sparks' hand down toward the table.

"That's it!"

"Almost there!"

Then Sam saw how Sparks had gotten her nickname.

Crackling sparks shot from the back of her second-skin like someone was taking a chainsaw to sheet metal. Handfuls came from under her bowler hat and flooded her face, and Sam realized what the goggles were for.

Their hands went back to the middle.

The match went on like that for a while. Petir would gain a little advantage, and then Sparks would set it back with an eruption of fresh flickers of electricity. Storm clouds, their electric bellies buzzing, formed above them. Frustration pulled at Petir's face as he screamed. The stone table began to shimmy from the ground, and the sparks turned from yellow to blue.

Sam thrust his fist high into the air. "Go, Sparks!"

She looked over at Sam. The black of her pupils took up the entirety of each eyepiece. "The connection will break!" She screeched.

Her hand slammed backward into the table and the liquid metal burst like a water balloon, coating all of the spectators in shiny splatter.

The match was over. Petir had won.

Sam watched in horror as the conceited look returned to Petir's face with a vengeance.

Petir burned an X across the entire surface of the table, his face aglow. After looking at his clan members, he gave an apathetic shrug.

His assembly of followers lifted him onto their shoulders and sent layers of red flares into the sky.

"Oh no," Sam dug his fingers into his scalp, "I'm sure we won't hear the end of this."

Glissandro played a mournful dirge.

Sparks jumped away from the table and pulled on a shiny platinum second-skin. She waved her hand in an elliptical motion and the wayward liquid silver was sucked off of everyone's clothing and gathered in a ball against her palm. She took one quick look at Sam, before zipping through the crowd without a word to anyone.

Petir had his flunkies place him back on the earth, although Sam knew he had left his head in the clouds.

"I've never seen Sparks freak out like that," one of Daphne's friends said. "I wonder what happened."

Sparks' cold gaze flashed in Sam's mind's eye. "So we're not going to see Petir get beat today, huh?"

"Not unless you want to try." Petir was standing just inches away from Sam. "That's right, I saw you over here. Why don't you get over to the table and let me humiliate you again?"

The onlookers grew silent, waiting to see what would happen.

Sam looked over at Glissandro, who gave him a disapproving glance. Sam grit his teeth. "I... not today."

"Oh, what a surprise," Petir's mocking tone dripped like acid. "You really can't do anything, can you?"

Glissandro waved his arms across his chest in warning.

Whispers permeated the crowd.

"Who is that?"

"I haven't seen him before."

"He's handsome." The last whisper came from one of Daphne's friends.

Sam felt adrenaline pump into his veins. "I'll play you another day."

Petir scoffed. "Big loolabird on the outside, but here you're just pathetic."

Sam took a calming breath. "Another time."

"Yeah, you probably don't need me slamming your hand into the table and making it any *flatter*."

A collective gasp arose from the mob.

Sam felt something snap in his head. A seething anger built up in his chest as he stepped uncomfortably close to Petir. Being that Sam was a full head taller, he had to look down to give Petir a menacing glare. "You know what? You're on, you little dweeb."

Petir looked back with an arrogant grin. "That's more like it."

The crowd spread apart, giving them a path to the table.

As Sam made his way over to the rock chair, fresh waves of energy came over him. It was the same thing he'd felt at the football game. Right on cue, the pounding started in his head. He looked back at Daphne, who gave him an agitated scowl.

Petir's eyes swarmed with arrogance. "I can't wait to see that second-skin split apart."

The crowd was still quiet, not sure how to react.

Sam felt his fingers twitch with excitement. "I'm going to tear you to pieces, you little—" Then he looked down at his hand.

The stars were twinkling almost as brightly as Sparks' emissions. Countless stories stretched across his palm. It was infinite space wrapped around his knuckles. Thinking about the inside of the snake's pod, he looked back at Daphne and smiled. The pounding in his head started to subside, and he felt the energy begin to dwindle.

Sam turned and faced Petir. "I don't have to prove anything to you." He got up and walked away from the stone table.

"Pathetic!" Petir yelled. "Why don't you just go home already? No one wants you here."

Sam stopped, took another deep breath and let the residual energy drain away as he approached Daphne. "Let's go to the reenactment."

She gave him an appraising look. "Fine. But still no guarantees that I'll sit next to you."

"Deal."

@

They weren't the first two at the theatre, but the now-raised seats on the slanted earth were still rather empty. Glissandro had hung back with Daphne's friends to try and show them some grips involving music.

The purple curtain was still down, shielding the stage.

Daphne suggested they reserve a few seats up front, so they went down and picked a good spot in the middle of the row. The seats were raised by the thousands, like at the seam, but this time they had backs to them and reclined.

Daphne touched a few of the seats around them, and the grass turned from green to red. "So people know that our friends are going to be sitting there."

Sam motioned to the stage. "Have they done this before?"

Daphne sat down, crossing one leg over the other. "The reenactment?"

"Yeah."

"They have, but it's different every time."

Sam paused and then sat next to her. "Why?"

"Because it was so long ago that no one knows the real story."

"But Bariv told me there was the girl with the sunflower petal…"

"That's about the only thing that stays the same."

Sam prodded the seat next to him with his second-skin, but it stayed red. "How is it a reenactment if they don't know what happened?"

"They know the gist. And that's the fun of it: the mystery keeps it exciting."

"I guess." Sam settled against the back of the seat and locked his fingers behind his head. "What did they reenact last time?"

Daphne looked up at the stars. Moonlight glinted off the silver specks scattered within her bright blue eyes. A tremor of desire traveled through Sam's body.

"Rona came up with the last story. It was brilliant. What happened was, the little girl was being chased by evil spirits. Her mother had just died and the spirits had been haunting her ever since, taking away both her joys and disappointments in life. They entered her soul and sliced away the ends of her emotions. She was left cold and emotionless, because when you can't feel the highs and lows, the middle means nothing. They were chasing her around, trying to drag her to the underworld. Then she came to a river and became trapped. The evil spirits closed in on her from both sides. Cassiella actually played the part of the main evil spirit—which was kind of funny. All of a sudden, a giant sunflower grew right before her eyes. A single petal flew off, and the little girl held it out like a shield against the demons. The light coming from the petal grew and grew, until all of the demons were banished. Then she ate the seeds from the sunflower and could feel again. She used the petal as the first second-skin."

Sam paused a moment to take it in. "Pretty powerful story."

Daphne gave a serene nod. "The Veil is pretty powerful."

"Then why is everyone scared of *power* magics?"

At this, Daphne's eyes fell to the ground. "It's not the magic."

"Then what? It seems to me like somebody freaks out every time the subject comes up."

"Let's just talk about something else."

Sam shrugged. He didn't push the subject, especially since Glissandro had promised him answers from the Mystics. "Like what?"

"I don't know." She held her pink second-skin in front of her face, examining it like a normal girl would examine her fingernails. "Don't you have a million questions about us? I know I did when I got here."

"I've got a question."

Daphne waited. "What?"

"Do you have a boyfriend?"

She sighed, but Sam was sure he could hear a smile beneath it. "Out of all the questions in the world. You could ask about our past, our customs, our heroes, our foods, anything. And you ask that?"

"Right now, I think it's the most important thing."

"You really are a jock."

"Regardless, I stick by my question."

She bit her bottom lip. "No… and I'm not looking."

"Perfect, because that's exactly when you find things."

Daphne rolled her eyes. "You're ridiculous. Right now, I'm just interested in the Veil. And you should be, too."

"The Veil can't keep you warm like I can."

She raised her palm and curled her fingers inward. A flame blossomed in her hand. "You were saying?"

"So what about your family?" Sam shrugged and changed the subject. "Where are they?"

She straightened out her hand and the flame died out. "I don't want to talk about that, either."

"Why not?"

She paused for a second, refusing to meet Sam's gaze. "I just don't."

Sam saw her eyes start to gloss over.

"Sorry, I won't pry."

"It's okay." She swallowed hard and then forced a smile. "So, did you catch my mention of Cassiella before?"

"Yeah."

"She's got a thing for you. She couldn't stop talking about you when we were searching for the amorberry."

He shrugged. "That's cool."

"So…"

Sam stretched and put his arm around the back of her chair. "So what?"

"Are you going to do something about it?"

"She's not my type."

Daphne looked offended. She slapped him playfully on the chest. "She's wonderful."

"I don't know if you noticed, but I wanted to come here with *you*, not her."

Even in the darkness, Sam could see her face turn red. "I'm going to go get some snacks."

Without looking at him, she got up, and Sam was left alone with his thoughts. *Wonder what my parents are doing? Dad was so angry when I left. The next time I see May, I'm giving her another hug for fixing everything. Wonder what the NFL's policy would be on second-skins—I don't ever want to take this off.* He peeled up the section on his wrist and took a sniff.

Still clean.

"Hey there," Glissandro plopped down on the grassy seat next to him. "I see your aim has improved."

"I see you've been aiming, yourself." Sam grinned.

Glissandro gave a shy smile. "I don't know what you're talking about."

"I think you do."

Glissandro's face was red again. "Good choice not to face Petir. You would have broken your skin."

"Thanks for all the confidence."

Glissandro gave Sam a mischievous smile.

"It was tougher than you think." Sam stuck out his hand and curled it into a fist. "I'm a competitor and when you don't compete for a while, it kind of itches."

"So tonight I'll race you up the mountain."

Sam raised an eyebrow. "What's up the mountain?"

Glissandro stared at Sam for a silent moment. After a few beats, he played a low moan. "Answers."

Daphne's friends filed into the seats around them. As they sat, the grass turned from red back to green. Chairs all around flickered from red to green as they were claimed by the rest of the town, and Sam couldn't help but think of Christmas.

Do they have Christmas in Atlas Crown?

"Big turnout," Sam said to no one in particular.

"This is about more than entertainment," said Daphne's friend Helenia, the tan one with the sugar flute. "And the reenactments are usually really good."

Helenia had an enticing smile, long legs, and a pumpkin-hued second-skin. She gave Daphne a run for her money for best-looking sorcerer. As she took the seat closest to Glissandro, he turned a shade of red Sam hadn't thought possible. Glissandro went to play his horn, and then paused, his fingers tightening around it.

"Are there even enough seats?" Sam asked Helenia, giving Glissandro time to compose himself.

Helenia brushed a loose strand of hair behind her ear. "They can always make more."

"Plus, there's a lot of people acting." Glissandro kept his eyes on the seat in front of him. "I think half the town tried out for this one."

Sam stared at the stage, drumming a beat on the seat in front of him. "Who came up with this story?"

"Not sure," Helenia said. "They usually keep it a surprise until the end."

Glissandro played a soft, dissonant note. "I just hope it's good."

Helenia's eyes opened wide in recognition. "I bet it was a Wapawche." She slapped Glissandro's knee. "They wouldn't miss this opportunity."

Glissandro looked down to where Helenia's hand lingered on his knee. He went to play something, but all that came out was a wet buzz.

Sam couldn't help but chuckle. "Why the Wapawche?"

"Rona's last show was a huge hit," another one of Daphne's friends, Nina, said. "I'm sure the Wapawches spent weeks coming up with something to outshine him. They can't stand to be outdone."

Sam stopped his drumming and gave Nina a curious look. "I thought this place was all smiles and working together and stuff, what with the Veil and all."

"Just because we have the Veil doesn't mean we're not human," Daphne sat back down in the seat next to him. "Dreckler cotton?"

"Don't mind if I do." Sam pulled out a sizable portion.

"The Wapawches are always looking to prove why they're the best clan." Helenia performed a grip that created a mirrored surface along the palm of her second-skin, which she held up to her face. She pulled out a pink string bean, squeezed it and spread its contents on her lips, leaving them glossy. "They can't stand that none of their children are in Rona's group."

Sam couldn't stop staring. "Why?"

"Because nine times out of ten, people in Rona's group end up doing great things. It's universally known that he's the best teacher." Nina mirrored Helenia's actions with her own bean, a slightly darker shade. "Not just in Atlas Crown. That's why we're so proud of our Daphne."

Daphne blushed.

"Speaking of Rona," Helenia touched up the corners of her mouth and put her hand away, "how did you manage to get into his group, Sam? I've been trying for years."

At the chance to impress her, Sam decided to tell her the truth. "Back at my football game, I had my first grip and—"

"The Rono clan wants him," Glissandro interrupted. "Rona wanted to keep him close and give him a bit of training before the ceremony."

Helenia's eyes lit up. "Really?"

"What are you talking about?" Sam asked. "I thought it was because—"

"He's just being modest." Glissandro shot Sam a look that said, 'drop it.'

"You're lucky." Helenia tapped the butterfly symbol on her chest. "You should display that symbol proudly after Omani."

Nina gave a skeptical scoff. "When was the last time the Rono clan took an outsider?"

"Look," Glissandro played, "it's about to start."

Sam heard the squelching curtain before he saw it. Someone dressed all in black prodded the purple goop with long electric strands from his second-skin. The curtain folded in on itself, rising to the cave ceiling.

"That should be the last magic until the end," Daphne told him quietly.

Sam leaned forward. "Who is that?"

"The conductor," she whispered. "He's our head grower, F—"

"Fernando?"

Daphne gave an impressed nod.

Something up front made a low, droning noise as the conductor made leisurely passes through the air with his pointer finger. A slight tremble of hand drums joined the drone. The ominous score echoed through the theatre.

"Why aren't you playing?" Sam whispered to Glissandro.

The side of Glissandro's mouth curled into a crafty smile. He pointed at his eyes and then back at the stage.

The sound grew brighter. A musician hidden in the rafters made tiny pings, like fingernails against hollow metal. Some horn blasts caused a few audience members in front of Sam to jerk upright in their seats.

The first actors came on stage. He had never been one to go to any of the school plays—or any plays, for that matter—but nevertheless, he felt a smile forming on his lips.

Before Sam knew it, the curtain dropped for intermission.

Sam's eyes hadn't wandered from the stage for the entire first half, even though the reenactment had been composed of few words and mostly music. The story had been completely different from the one Daphne had told him. This play was—if he had understood correctly—about the Veil having an evil sister, who tortured the actors by setting beasts upon their crops, setting fire to their homes, and tormenting the children.

The most exciting part for Sam, however, had been when the black fruit showed up on stage. Sam never thought a fruit could be scary, yet every time one popped up, he'd felt some panic. Right in the middle of the happier musical compositions, when the actors were dancing and singing, a black fruit would grow and all the noise was sucked away. The actors grabbed their throats and stomped, but no sound would come.

Every time the fruit showed up, Glissandro winced.

The first act had concluded with one of the actresses eating the fruit in an attempt to bring the sound back for the others. Her face had contorted in pain, and she fell to the ground, accompanied by a low, sad chord that died out as Fernando waved at the purple curtain, which dropped in front of the stage.

"Wow," Daphne said, after the applause had receded.

"I didn't see that coming." Nina's cheeks were wet. "What a powerful scene."

"Those fruit aren't real, right?" Sam asked, chomping away at a mouthful of dreckler cotton.

"I don't think so," Daphne said. "But whoever thought that up has a twisted imagination."

"But brilliant!" Helenia flipped her hair back. "The Veil having a wicked sister, it's so good. Poor Rona, I think the Wapawches actually outdid him."

"We still don't know if She has a evil sister," Glissandro played.

Helenia scanned the crowd. "I think it's safe to assume."

Glissandro kept his eyes on his feet. "Maybe. But we won't be sure until the end."

Daphne picked at the small pile of dreckler cotton she had left. "I almost didn't recognize Cassiella."

"Was that her?" Helenia asked. "The Veil's sister?"

Daphne nodded. "She plays a convincing villain."

"She does." Nina put on a devilish smile. "I always knew she could be sneaky if she wanted to."

"So, just to be clear," Sam repeated. "Those fruits aren't real?"

The girls started giggling again.

Daphne wrinkled her nose. "You know, you're kind of a big chicken."

Sam raised an eyebrow and cracked his knuckles. "Would a chicken have snuck up to that monster plant and grabbed one of its thorns?"

Nina's eyebrows lowered. "What's a chicken?"

Daphne ignored her. "No, but a chicken would definitely turn down a gumptius challenge. What's the matter, Sam, scared of breaking your skin?"

The girls giggled even louder, but Sam didn't find it so funny. Immediately, he felt his face grow hot.

"I don't blame you." Nina combed her hands through her hair. "Petir would have definitely broken your second-skin. He would have broken any of ours."

"You don't understand." Heat filled Sam's tone. "I could have beat him. Earlier today I made a whole riv—"

Glissandro cut him off with a blast of noise.

The whole audience went silent and turned around to see what the commotion was about.

"Sorry," Glissandro played softly, his head down and his eyes pinned on the ground in front of them. "Wrong note."

A few people close to them laughed, and conversation returned to normal.

Glissandro gave Sam a small shake of his head.

"What was that about?" Nina asked.

"Nothing," Sam huffed.

The next few minutes were filled with conversation about the play, which Sam mostly stayed out of. He didn't look at Daphne, even when she tried to engage him about the part of the play where the lizard permanently attached itself, like a leech, to one of the townsfolk. He still couldn't believe she would say something like that in front of her friends. Sam gave her short, one-word answers and hoped she'd leave him alone.

Thankfully, Fernando came back onstage, conducted a short piece, and then prodded the curtain back up.

Sam wasn't nearly as interested this time.

The scene started with Cassiella rampaging though the town and yet again torturing the townsfolk. Out of the corner of Sam's eye, he saw Helenia slip her fingers on top of Glissandro's hand. Glissandro went stiff as a board, but after a few seconds he turned his hand over so their fingers could intertwine.

Glissandro's eyes flickered over to Sam's face. Sam gave him a quick wink and flashed a thumbs-up against his stomach. Glissandro gave the smallest of nods and relaxed his shoulders a bit.

Sam turned his focus to the stage and was instantly drawn back into the story. The music was loud and clamorous, with a lot of off-tempo drum hits. He watched as the Veil's sister stole children, draped the land to stay barren, and drank the clouds—Sam couldn't figure out how they pulled off the effects without magic. She even tossed out the black fruit like grenades.

"I'm sorry," Daphne whispered in Sam's ear.

Sam kept his eyes forward.

"Just talk to me for a minute," she said a little louder.

Sam turned his attention away from the play and onto her. Glissandro and the others were still engrossed in what was happening on stage.

She gave Sam an apologetic look. "I shouldn't have said that."

"No, you shouldn't have."

"I don't know why I did, it just came out."

"Yeah, well, you're the one telling me to get closer to the Veil, and not be a dumb jock. Make up your mind."

Someone on stage let out a thunderous cackle.

"I know, I know. I'm sorry."

Sam took a deep breath through his nose. "Make it up to me."

"How?"

He broke into a wicked smile. "How about a date?"

She gave Sam an incredulous look, which he countered with an innocent shrug.

She paused for a second. "Fine, but I get to pick the place. I bet the bird zoo might get you to reconsider leaving."

Sam thought about the golden bird and smiled. "Maybe."

The next scene got even more intense, when the Veil's sister put a black ring around the sun and only let a pinprick of light through. It immediately became winter and the townsfolk started shivering and dying from the cold. The music faded, leaving the stage deathly silent. The actors huddled together, trying to hide from the evil force around them.

Sam felt Daphne slowly slide her hand under his.

He tried not to act surprised like Glissandro, but he felt his heart start to beat faster.

Her fingers gripped tighter.

Sam let his eyes drift over and look at her face. She was staring at the stage, biting one of her knuckles, and Sam squeezed back.

Back on stage, a young girl entered, played by someone he did not recognize. She was dressed in a plain, simple tunic, and moved with purpose. Her hair was decorated with small flowers, which connected to a golden wreath around her neck.

"Get out of here, Sister!" Cassiella cried to the new arrival.

The girl walked over and wrapped her arms around one of the freezing townsfolk. Immediately, the townsman's shivering ceased and his shoulders relaxed.

"I said get out of here! They are mine! Don't interfere, you wretched girl!"

Booming percussion accompanied the last three words.

The girl held strong.

"I'll banish you!" Cassiella squealed. "You'll never get to see them again, even from the shadows of the forest."

The young girl beckoned more people to join the embrace. They all came together, and the warmth spread through the community.

Sam's eyes left the stage. He couldn't help but look over at Daphne, even if it meant missing some of the reenactment. He was used to contact with girls, but Daphne brought out something different in him. She made him feel sort of insecure, which was something no girl had managed to do since middle school.

"I'll—" Cassiella stopped short. "I'll—"

Sam looked back at the stage. Cassiella was facing the audience, and was looking right at him and Daphne. Something was definitely wrong. "I'll—"

One of the actors closest to Cassiella started whispering a line out of the corner of her mouth. Sam was close enough to the stage to see the shiver run through Cassiella's body.

"I'll never let them see the sun again," the actor whispered to Cassiella, a little louder.

Cassiella turned toward her sister and got back into character. "I'll never let them see the sun again!"

The Veil finally spoke. "You can't control them forever!"

Cassiella pointed toward the sun, constricted by darkness. "I can and I will! You cannot win!"

"For now," the young girl said calmly.

"FOREVER!" Cassiella's voice was surprisingly strong. "Now leave, before—"

Sam was in the middle of visually tracing the curve of Daphne's cheeks when, again, Cassiella stopped mid-sentence. All of a sudden, Daphne's hand jerked away from his.

Cassiella was staring at them again. Even from a safe distance, Sam could see that her eyes looked glassy and unfocused.

"Now leave, before I don't give you another chance," whispered the young girl.

Cassiella jumped back into the scene. "Now leave before…" her eyes drifted toward Sam, "before…"

"You should go," Daphne whispered frantically.

Sam talked out of the corner of his mouth. "What, why?"

"I think we hurt her."

"…before…"

"But—"

"Just go," Daphne said quietly.

Sam tried to take her hand. "Come with me."

She pulled away from him, tucking her hands in between her legs. "I don't think you understand what's going on here. Just go."

Cassiella's voice got weaker and was barely audible. "…before…"

Sam gave a hopeful smile. "See you tomorrow?"

"Fine," she made a shooing motion. "Just go, quickly."

Sam swiftly got out of his seat and did his best to hunch as he made his way through the aisle.

Cassiella's voice broke through the silence. "Before I don't give you another chance!"

Deciding it was best not to look back, Sam crept away from the amphitheater. As he snuck off, he heard the play get back on track—Cassiella included—but it didn't stop the hundreds of eyes curiously looking at him, as if wondering why he'd leave during the best part.

Sam picked up the pace and was out of earshot and close to the gumptius tables in a matter of minutes.

Confused and alone, Sam looked back at the mass of people. He couldn't make out what was happening on stage, and he felt a surge of disappointment. The town had no streetlights, only moonlight, which left Atlas Crown bathed in a soft glow.

"Think you can take me?"

Sam turned around and saw Glissandro already sitting at one of the rock slabs, his hand outstretched.

He wondered how Glissandro had gotten there so quickly, especially since Sam had been moving pretty fast.

"You don't have a second-skin," Sam said.

"No?"

Glissandro made a high-pitched whistling sound with his horn—a tone Sam hadn't heard him make before. From the inside of the bell came dark smoke. It twisted though the air and made its way to Glissandro's hand, leaving it covered in a thick, dark mass. After the smoke settled, Glissandro played small peeps, which shot tiny morsels of light against his hand, landing on the hardened smoke. A few more notes, and Glissandro had a second-skin that looked almost identical to Sam's, constellations and everything.

Sam held back a smile. "I stand corrected."

"No, you were correct," Glissandro played. Sam noticed the smoke starting to dissipate and the little stars fell to the rock table.

"Still pretty cool."

"You know what's not cool?" A shrewd smile crept onto his face. "Leaving during the middle of my play."

"Hey, I didn't want to leave, it's just…wait, did you say *your* play?"

Glissandro played a quivering note and more black smoke snaked from the bell of his horn. The smoke gathered in front of Sam's chest and coagulated into a black sphere that looked just like the fruit from the play. "I worked excruciatingly hard on it, too. You'd better have a good reason for walking out."

"I… um…"

Glissandro stared at him.

"Well, you see…"

The last of Glissandro's tiny stars fell to the table, twinkled, and went out.

"I really needed to use the bathroom." Sam brushed a hand through the black fruit, causing the smoke to break apart and dissipate.

"Ah." Glissandro gave a fake smile of relief. "And Cassiella's freak-out had nothing to do with it?"

Sam felt his face get warm. "I wouldn't necessarily call it a freak-out."

"So you and Daphne are going to the bird zoo, huh?"

"How'd you know?"

Glissandro touched each finger to his thumb again. "Words are a type of music, too, you know."

"And you're the master of musical words."

Glissandro clicked his tongue.

"You sly dog." Sam rocked a finger at him. "I have to be more careful with what I say around you."

"Or less careful." Glissandro winked. "Maybe I could pick up a few pointers."

Sam gave him an exaggerated wink back. "I think you were doing just fine."

Glissandro's cheeks grew red.

"I didn't know it was a secret." Sam sat down at the table across from him. "Especially because of the amount of drool that came out of your mouth when she sat next to you."

"Hey!" Glissandro stabbed out a note. "I didn't drool."

Sam held up his hands. "No judgments."

"Did I really drool?"

"Enough to make a symflower scream."

Glissandro silently laughed.

"What were you thinking, leaving the play?" Sam asked. "I feel like you of all people would want to see the end."

Glissandro shrugged. "I already know how it ends."

"What happens?"

Glissandro bit his lip and squinted one eye. "I don't know if I should tell you," he played. "You did leave, after all. Very rude."

"C'mon. How does the Veil beat Her sister?"

Glissandro tapped his lip.

"C'mon…"

"I don't know… it's such a well thought-out ending."

"Fine." Sam cracked his knuckles. "How 'bout we play gumptius? If I win, then you tell me."

"I have a better competition."

"What?"

"Go."

With that, Glissandro jetted away from the table, running at full speed.

Sam cupped his hands around his mouth. "Where?"

He could barely see the back of Glissandro when he heard the response.

"To get you those answers."

CHAPTER 18

Sam took a giant step backward. "Unless there's a titanium-enforced bridge, there's no way I'm going across."

Glissandro laughed. "You really are a chicken."

Sam shook his head. "Your eavesdropping ability is starting to be a problem."

"It's only a problem for you."

In front of Sam lay the mountain, only before he could get to it, he had to get across the abyss. A seemingly bottomless moat—with no visible bridge—surrounded the mountain. He gauged the distance to be about five yards across. Bright glowing dots lined both sides, like the lights on a runway, showing where the land ended and where imminent doom began.

Sam shook his head in disbelief. "Why have a giant nothingness blocking the way?"

"Beats me," played Glissandro. "You assume I know everything."

Sam picked up a pebble and threw it into the moat. He waited a few moments for a soft plunk, but it never came. "How do we get across?"

Glissandro played a sharp note. Starting at their feet and traveling to the right, a wave of light traveled through the dots on both sides of the chasm. "Follow me."

Sam walked a few paces behind Glissandro, staring at the little glowing things the whole time. "What are they?"

"Worms."

"Why are they there?"

"So people don't fall in."

Sam thought about the pebble. "Really?"

"Kind of. They like the vapors, too."

Sam stopped walking. "What vapors?"

"Take a whiff, but make it shallow."

Sam moved over to the edge, peeked his head over—careful not to lose his footing—and inhaled.

It was like horseradish, gnawing at the inside of his nostrils and finding its way up to his brain. It left him lightheaded, and Sam quickly retreated.

"They *like* that stuff?" Sam rubbed his palm against his nostril.

Glissandro gave a somber nod. "They're not the only ones."

After silently trekking along in the dim light for a few more minutes, Sam could finally see their destination—a small bridge about a car-length wide, lined with the glowing worms.

"Not the most welcoming sight," Sam said.

"As you'll find out, the Mystics like to be alone with their thoughts. They don't mind visitors, but they want to make sure you actually need their advice. For example, this bridge moves to a different spot every night."

"That's inconvenient."

Glissandro silently chuckled. "Not if you like your privacy."

Sam stared at the empty air between them and the mountain. "Can't people fly across? I mean, May and Bariv both lifted me up easy enough."

Glissandro shook his head. "The focus it takes to fly is extraordinary, not to mention the danger if that focus breaks. Not many people in Atlas Crown can do it."

Sam huffed. "Well, that's lame."

They reached the bridge. It looked sturdy enough, but it was a long way down into the blackness.

"You first," Glissandro played.

"Why me?"

"Don't you want to hear the ending of the play?"

Sam paused. "And?"

"Aren't we racing to the mountain?" Glissandro played the sharp note again, and the dots on the bridge glowed brighter. "There's your opening."

Sam frowned at the bridge. "That ending had better be worth it."

Glissandro shrugged. "You'll just have to find out."

Sam tilted his head back and held his hand above his face. The second-skin meshed well with the night sky. As soon as he peered at his hand against the heavens, the spots of light on his second-skin grew brighter, as if to match their stellar counterparts.

Sam took a calm breath. "I don't know what to do."

Glissandro played the worms brighter. "You need to decide whether or not to take this path."

"That's not what I meant." Sam let his eyes drift up to the stars. "I was talking about staying in Atlas Crown."

Glissandro gave a tight nod. "I know."

For some reason, whether it was the lingering lightheadedness or the cool night air, Sam was in a sharing mood. "So what do I do? May fixed everything back home. They won't hate me."

"But will *you* hate you?"

Sam picked up another pebble and tossed in into the moat. "How could I hate me when I'll be doing what I love?"

Glissandro touched each of his fingers to his thumb.

Sam copied the motion. "Why do you keep doing that?"

Glissandro stayed silent for a second, and ran his fingers over his horn. "When I was younger, I was different from everybody else. Everyone else could speak, but I couldn't. No one picked on me, but that made it worse, because that meant I had no one to direct my disappointment at—nobody but myself. I hated being different. It was easy enough to get my message across: I drew words in the air with my second-skin. They came out sparkling gold, but I was still not the same. It wasn't even the talking that bothered me; it was the singing. I heard others use their voices to create beautiful music, and I couldn't. I tried to sing, but I ended up choking. I spent a lot of time in the woods and in the library by myself, thinking. One day I went deep into the library, deeper than I'd ever been, and found an old, moldy book in the wall. There was nothing special about it, and I don't know why, but I knew I had to read it. Most of it was in a language that was spoken before my time, but some of it I could understand. That book taught me some dangerous things, one of them being how to do a dark drape. I knew it was against the rules to change yourself with the Veil, but I wanted to sing, more so than I wanted to follow the rules.

"I went into the woods and reached far into the Veil, farther than I had ever gone before, and attempted to drape myself. I vomited because the pain in my head was unbearable. When I opened my eyes, there was a terrible creature before me. A skull-wolf, something I'd only read about and seen pictures of, but recognized immediately. It sank its teeth through my second-skin and deep into my hand. It was excruciating. It tried to drag me away, so I grabbed the horn on the bottom of its chin with my other hand and kicked it in the face to try and get away. I fell back, along with its horn. The skull-wolf ran away and everything went black.

"When I woke, May was standing over me. The Allu had healed my wounds, but the poison had already taken its toll. Some things can never be changed back to how they were. To this day, I cannot feel anything with my right hand. I touch my fingers together to see if the feeling will ever return, even though I know it won't."

The silence rang through the night.

Sam slid his hands into the pockets of his robe. "That's terrible."

Glissandro's eyes flickered to the sky. "Not really. Because of it, I have this horn, and I learned an important lesson."

"What?"

"Don't read books."

"Amen." Sam gave a strong snort. "Really, though?"

Glissandro stayed silent for a moment and stared at the moon. "I think by the end of all this, you'll learn it, too."

Sam sucked his teeth. "So you're going to play cryptic with me, too?"

"If someone had told me that trying to drape myself would cause a skull-wolf to steal my sense of touch, I probably wouldn't have made that mistake."

"Exactly."

Glissandro dipped his horn through the air and played long, stringy notes. Golden letters started dripping out of his horn and spread across the air. After a few scrawls, Sam was looking at a word sitting in mid-air.

EXACTLY

Sam peeked over the words at Glissandro. "So you're not going to be much help here, huh?"

Glissandro played something long and wistful, and the worms on the bridge started glowing bright green.

"Thanks." Sam looked over at the bridge and was smacked with a powerful sense of nostalgia. It was like his entire past sprawled in front of him, hovering over the void—memories of his mother and his team; parties with past girlfriends. He thought of elementary school, where he'd thrown wet clay around the art room and begrudgingly played the trumpet. The memories shifted to his homecoming date… May's smile… the proud look his father wore as he polished his old trophies. Then the rush of memories and emotions started thinning, and he thought about Rona's story of Karundi Kai.

Sam took a deep breath and stepped forward. "Well, here goes everything."

Cautiously, he took a step onto the bridge. The faint horseradish smell in the air encouraged him to get to the other side quickly.

Once he was again on solid land, the air itself changed—becoming warmer, almost balmy. Thankfully, the mountain was mostly barren, with most of the vegetation near the top, so climbing it wouldn't be too taxing. Dark grey, grainy material covered the ground, sloping upward from where he stood. As he took a few steps, his feet sank a few inches into the substance, like he was walking in sand.

This might be harder than it looks.

Glissandro noiselessly appeared next to him.

Sam dug the heel of his foot into the land. "It's a long way up."

"If you look behind you, it's a long way down."

Sam peered over his shoulder and saw endless black. "Up it is, then."

They climbed the deserted mountain in silence. Every few minutes, Sam would feel like he had to say something and then decide to hold back. Glissandro seemed comfortable with the silence, and Sam didn't want to break it. As for himself, he was all too comfortable with the physical exertion. It was the first time in a while that he'd felt a burn in his legs. Nothing could clear his head better than good, old-fashioned muscle pain.

Something dark shifted in the distance—distorted, like the way heat changes the air above a grill. Sam thought about meat again and felt his stomach groan.

As the whatever-it-was moved down toward them, Sam looked to Glissandro. Already frozen, Glissandro whispered, "Stand still."

Echo flies, Sam realized.

Getting a good foothold against the gradient, he paused.

Not only was this swarm bigger than the last he'd seen, it was faster, too. The flies reached them in only a few heartbeats and split into two fluid clusters. The group in front of Glissandro throbbed into a mirror formation, and the other clouded around Sam like the divvy leaves had done, landing on his face and ears. Several settled on the back of his neck, the tiny hairs on their feet prickly against his skin.

Though he'd passed the flies' test last time, he did his best to stay still.

They gathered on Sam's second-skin like it was rotten meat. The collective buzz grew louder, and he felt himself getting nervous. Worried that even moving his eyeballs too hastily might get him stung, he cast a cautious look over at Glissandro.

The other swarm had already organized themselves into a perfect Glissandro, horn and all. The echo fly version of Glissandro had the magical instrument to its lips.

"Don't move," he heard Glissandro play, "I think I might be able to send them away." Glissandro's notes had a metallic echo, which Sam realized was the echo flies' version of his music.

A blast of music sent a serious gust of wind at Sam, but the flies remained plastered all around his body. Sam thought about how much damage May had said they could do. He shuddered as goose bumps sprouted all over his arms.

"Hold on," Glissandro played. "I'll go get help."

Again, the swarm echoed Glissandro's notes in a metallic tone.

Sam watched as the flies from the duplicate Glissandro fell apart and started joining their brothers all over Sam's body. The buzz in his ears began to crescendo. The rising tension from the swarm flowed into him like electric current. The noise became too high-pitched to hear, and Sam braced himself for their attack.

All the flies dissipated.

Moving in-sync, like a school of fish, the echo flies reconvened about a yard in front of him. They throbbed inward and started to form a shape that was not Sam, but more like a bunch of curved lines.

After a few more pulses into formation, Sam recognized the shape—a giant version of what he'd seen outside his car and in the woods.

A black swirl.

Just as quickly as they'd come, the flies broke free and disappeared into the darkness. Sam felt his stomach descend from his throat as they left.

Glissandro blinked a few times, his jaw slack. "I have no idea what just happened."

Sam mumbled something like "me neither" to Glissandro, but he wasn't paying much attention. The dream that he'd had the first night reverberated in his mind.

Sam couldn't gauge the time it took to finally reach the top of the mountain. Glissandro hadn't said anything further about what'd happened, which was one of the many qualities Sam was beginning to value in his new friend. Most of the people Sam had surrounded himself with back in Stanton were loud and obnoxious. It was a nice change of pace to be able to hear himself think, although what he was thinking filled him with unease.

Glissandro played a fast note. "Watch yourself."

Sam looked up just in time to stop himself from running face-first into something big.

The huge something was wider than his house, and a quick look upward revealed it to be a tree. The gigantic branches splayed in different directions, bearing the largest leaves Sam had ever seen. It marked the end of the barren section of the mountain. Beyond it, the forest was thick and wild.

An illuminated message had been carved into the tree. After a moment, Sam realized that the words weren't, in fact, carved in, but rather growing out of the bark, and the tree itself created the light.

Sam read aloud. "Those looking for change are already receiving it."

Glissandro ran his fingers along the large sheets of bark. "It's their last-ditch attempt to stay left alone."

"What does it mean?"

"It's an old proverb."

Sam stepped back and scratched his head. "Yeah, well, it doesn't answer my question."

Glissandro motioned around the tree. "Then let's keep going. We're almost there."

The message on the tree faded away, and a new message appeared.

Those who ask questions can't avoid the answers

Sam looked over at Glissandro. "Another old proverb?"

Glissandro stared at the message for a moment. "I think it's a little more than that."

Sam rounded the tree's enormous circumference and continued upwards through the trees. All were close to uniform in shape and size, and Sam wouldn't have looked twice at any of them back home. Besides the giant message tree, the sights were less than exciting, considering all that he'd seen since coming to Atlas Crown.

Sam clucked his tongue. "Kind of a boring mountain."

Glissandro didn't respond.

Sam wondered if it was taboo to call something boring. "All I mean is that for a place where the Mystics live, I expected more mystical stuff."

"Like what?"

"I don't know," Sam patted one of the bland trees, "but May told me that the more you use the Veil, the more stuff sprouts. I guess I figured the mystical magic would send out some pretty wild stuff."

Glissandro nodded. "You're right, it can."

"So, why's this place so dull?"

"The Mystics rarely use the Veil."

Sam stopped moving. "You're kidding, right?"

Glissandro plucked a leaf. He held it next to his ear and rubbed it in between his fingers. After giving a satisfied nod, he placed the leaf gently on the ground. "Well, rarely for us."

Sam rubbed two fingers against his temple. "This place gives me a headache."

"You see, the Mystics live a lot longer than most, and they really don't use the Veil that much. For the most part, they study Her."

"Kind of a let-down."

"Sorry to hear that," a voice called out from behind them.

Sam jumped around. A shrouded figure ambled toward them, the hood of his robe concealing his face. He had no second-skin but clenched something in his fist.

"But," the person stepped into a patch of moonlight, "I'm glad to see you taking an interest in the Veil."

"Greetings, Delphi." Glissandro made a bow so low that Sam was surprised he didn't topple over.

"Must I remind you again that you don't have to bow?" Delphi let his hood fall back. "No need to lower yourself for an old fool."

Glissandro bowed even lower.

Delphi sighed and shook his head.

"Hey, I know you." Sam pointed at the old man's symbol. "You talked to me at the seam, at the wine river."

"Indeed." Delphi mimed knocking back a drink. "Quite the celebration."

Sam frowned. "What are you doing all the way out here?"

The old man chuckled. As he laughed, the wrinkles on his face creased deeper, leaving Sam wondering how old Delphi really was.

Delphi gestured around them. "I should ask you the same thing."

"Delphi is one of the three Mystics," Glissandro played, still bowed at an extraordinary angle.

Sam's eyes went wide as he realized the old man was the Mystic that May had mentioned earlier. He decided to make a low bow himself. "Oh, hi."

"Please, stand up straight," Delphi said with a hurried gesture. "It reminds me of how my height has abandoned me for younger shoulders."

Both boys straightened.

"I hope you are here to regale us with some music." Delphi closed his eyes and took a deep breath through his nose. "Do you sing, Samuel?"

"No." Sam almost choked on his answer.

Delphi tipped his head, his eyes still shut. "If you're sure. Although, your voice says otherwise."

Sam shook his head. "I'm sure."

Delphi opened his eyes, revealing some disappointment. "I must then assume you have a question for us, Samuel?"

"You can just call me Sam."

Delphi gave a solemn nod.

Sam cleared his throat. "And, yes. I do have a question. Who are—"

"For *us*." Delphi wagged his finger. "Not for me."

Sam raised an eyebrow. "There's no one else here."

"Ah," Delphi's face lit up, "then we must find them."

"More searching," Sam grumbled. "Do you have any idea where they could be?"

"About three hundred and sixty-eight paces up, and…" he squinted, "seven over."

Sam was taken aback. "Kind of precise."

Delphi shrugged. "They could have moved."

Sam felt another eye-roll coming on. "So, what were you doing out here?"

"Late-night snack." Delphi opened his palm, revealing a handful of little berries. "The garden May keeps for us seems to be producing more and more succulent fruit every day. She still hasn't planted any avocados, though. Alas, it's how she maintains power over me." He picked out a berry and tossed it in his mouth. As he bit down, instead of making a popping sound, the fruit crackled.

Glissandro played an ascending trill. "Will you lead us to the others?"

"I have one condition." Delphi licked his lips.

Sam tried his best not to groan. "What?"

Delphi ran the back of his fist across his mouth. "My legs don't much like walking without a little tune behind them." He turned to Glissandro. The moonlight made his grin look rather ghoulish. "A very serious condition."

Glissandro played a classical tune that reverberated throughout the forest. The trees seemed to amplify the sound, making it much fuller, as if hundreds of musicians played along with him.

Delphi started up the mountain and beckoned them with a wave.

After three hundred and sixty eight paces up and seven over—Sam noticed they stepped to the beat of Glissandro's song—they reached the other Mystics.

Sam didn't know what he'd expected from the Mystics, but it sure wasn't what was in front of him.

They occupied a very plain stone plateau, with three rocking chairs on it. The one in the middle was empty, but in the chairs on either side a man and a woman, both with greying hair, held silver chalices. The man was of Asian descent and the woman was about as pale as they come. They swayed back and forth, staring at Sam as he approached. Neither of their symbols matched the one on Delphi's chest, and neither had a second-skin on. Sam hadn't seen them before.

Glissandro let the notes die out as they reached them.

As soon it was silent, the sitting man said, "Please, finish it." His tone was gentle and soothing. The way he said it made Sam wish he could actually sing well, just so he could be the one performing for the old man.

Glissandro happily obliged, and coaxed the last part of the song from his horn.

While he played, Sam eyed the Mystics. Besides the robes, they looked like normal older folks, dignified yet frail. The woman could have even passed for Sam's grandmother—minus the giant foam finger his grandmother always carried with her.

The surrounding clearing also looked normal. No colored leaves or strange animals—it was just standard woods.

"Wonderful," the man said as Glissandro finished the song. "You don't come here enough, young man."

Glissandro played a bashful bend. "You all have more important things to do than listen to my music."

"Quite the contrary." The man rocked back in his chair. "And Samuel, it is nice to finally meet you in person."

"You know me?"

"We should." The woman chuckled. Sam couldn't place her accent, but the way she said "we" sounded more like "vee." "We've seen enough of you to never forget."

"I've only been here for a few days," Sam felt his face scrunch, "and I've only met Delphi once."

"We have seen you in memory, young man." The woman tapped a finger against the side of her head. "And we have made plenty of people un-see you."

"That's right." Sam snapped his fingers. "I can't thank you enough for that."

The man gave a slight nod. "You're welcome."

Sam felt slightly embarrassed that he hadn't thought to bring a gift or something. "Is there anything I can do to repay you?"

The two sitting Mystics looked at each other and grinned. They both got up and started walking away.

"Was that rude?" Sam whispered to Glissandro.

His friend just smiled.

Sam watched the old sorcerers bend down at the end of the stone platform. They dipped their chalices into something, carefully carried them back, and then plopped back down in their chairs.

"What name do you see when you look at me?" The woman asked. "What" sounded more like "Vut."

For some reason, a name popped right into his head. "Margaret?"

"Margaret!" The woman shouted in delight. "Haven't been her before!" She drained the liquid in her cup.

"And me?" the old man asked, beaming from ear to ear.

Again, a name surfaced, but it didn't seem right. "Frank?"

The old man looked over at Margaret, who stuck out her bottom lip and nodded.

"That's the one!" He tipped his cup to Sam and then emptied the chalice into his stomach.

Sam looked to Glissandro for an explanation.

"Now that you're here," Glissandro played a soft drone, "don't ask me."

Sam turned to the sitting Mystics. "I'm sorry, but I don't understand."

The woman was smiling. "Every hundred years or so we change names. Keeps things fresh, you see. Now, I'm Margaret. Thank you, Samuel."

"Frank." The name passed through the old man's lips as smooth as a breath. "I could definitely be Frank for a while. I knew a Frankzi back in the Eryu straits."

Sam gave Delphi an inquisitive look.

The third Mystic shrugged. "I think I'm going to keep Delphi for a while."

"An alter trombenick." Margaret gave a wave of her wrist. "He never takes a new name."

"You let me give you new names?"

"We *asked* you," Margaret corrected. "Now, I would consider us even for the whole memory-erasing thing."

Sam paused for a moment. "I need to ask you a question."

"Down to business." Frank rocked back and forth. "I like him already."

Sam felt the muscles in his right arm tense up. "Who are the Tembrath Elite?"

"I'll field this one." Delphi joined the other Mystics in the chairs. A chalice already waited beside his seat; he scooped it up and drained it. "The Tembrath Elite are a group of power sorcerers with a single objective. They are attempting to get past the Veil."

Sam couldn't believe that he had finally gotten a straight answer, though it was not the answer he was expecting. "Why?"

"Because—"

Margaret cut Delphi off. "My turn. They think that the true power can be found behind Her. For most dark drapes, the hurtful uses of the Veil, the sorcerer has to reach very deep. Dark drapes and grips tend to be the most powerful. Because of this, they assume that the Veil is covering up a source of energy even grander than Her." She waved a hand. "Narishkeit, I say. If it was grander, then She would not be able to hold it back. "

Again, they had given him a straightforward answer. Also a weird word.

Sam felt his chest clench. "Does everyone in town know this?"

Delphi spoke. "Yes, this is why the Tembrath Elite were cast out. It was put to a vote, and came up nearly unanimous."

Sam's heart started beating faster at the thought of his next question. "What do they want with me?"

Delphi and Margaret both turned to Frank.

Frank sighed. "They haven't been able to reach their objective, so we assume they want you to join them."

Sam felt his heartbeat pounding in his wrist, just under his second-skin. "Why *me*, though?"

Delphi went to go fill his own chalice from the reserve. "You have an uncanny ability. What happened at the football game was no mere feat; you may just be the missing link."

"But I don't want to join them." A wave of nausea washed through his stomach. "I just want to play football."

Delphi returned and raised his glass. "Lucky us."

Margaret licked her lips. "Any other questions, darling?"

"If I'm so powerful, why can't I do simple grips? And why—"

Margaret finished his sentence. "Can you do powerful ones? Things that would be improbable for others to complete?"

Sam nodded.

Margaret stopped rocking as a flicker of fear crossed her face. "Out of anger, you can summon the strength to dominate Her energy completely. So can the Tembrath Elite. It is a curse upon those chosen for the power sect. It's what makes them the most dangerous of sorcerers. This is not the correct way to use Her, however. She is there to work with you. Without Her cooperation, you will be limited. This is what frustrates the Tembrath Elite most. It's why they can't accept Her, why they look beyond." She gave him a calming smile. "The Veil can help or hinder, but She is powerless against people using Her. She can be a healer or a weapon, a builder or a destroyer, a blessing or a curse. But it's not up to Her. She is the path, but you have the choice of where to go with Her."

So that's why Rona got so upset.

"It is up to you to succeed." Margaret gave Sam a motherly look. "It is all about the decisions you make."

Sam felt his temper rising, and his head pounded again. "This isn't fair. I didn't ask for any of this. Can't the Veil just leave me alone?"

"Calm down, Sam!" Glissandro played a harsh blast of noise. "Don't speak like that!" The energy in the clearing changed, and for the first time, Sam saw frustration in his friend's face. He was looking at Sam with disdain, like Sam's presence was a bitter taste.

"It's fine, Glissandro." Frank continued rocking. "Remember, Sam has only just arrived. It must be a lot to take in. Why don't you let us talk to Sam alone for a moment?"

"I apologize for letting my temper get the best of me." Glissandro pulled his eyes away from Sam. He drew two fingers across his heart. "Travel well."

All three Mystics copied the gesture.

"Glissandro," Margaret's tone was firm, "I think tomorrow shall be the time."

He bowed, turned on the spot, and walked away with stiff strides.

Margaret stopped Sam following. "He'll be waiting for you. Let us continue, just the five of us."

As Sam watched his friend disappear into the trees, he tried to shake the feeling of disappointment. First Cassiella, now Glissandro: not the best day for his new friendships. He looked back at the Mystics, who were watching him curiously.

Wait, doesn't she mean the four of us?

"I'm sorry I snapped." Sam sighed. "In fact, you have been the most honest out of everybody I've talked to here."

"We try to be." Delphi nudged the rock with his toe, causing his chair to rock back and forth. "Also, if you tell people what they need to hear, they tend to leave more quickly."

Sam caught the subtle hint in his words. "So why were you so vague at the seam?"

Delphi rocked in silence for a moment. "I'd had a little too much to drink."

Sam wasn't sure if Delphi was kidding, but he felt like he had already worn out his welcome. At least he had gotten some of the answers he was looking for. "I'm sorry to take up so much of your time." Sam bowed. "I'll leave you alone now."

"I don't believe we're finished here." Margaret stopped rocking. "I think you have another question."

Sam nodded. "Could I come back to Atlas Crown? Later in life, I mean. After football?"

Frank cleared his throat. "So you have made your decision, then?"

"It doesn't matter if I did or not, May wants me to stay for a while. But I was just wondering. I mean, I passed the echo flies' test, so obviously I'm worthy to be here or whatever. So can I come back?"

Margaret's eyes focused on something in the darkness. "It is not up to us."

"Who, then?"

"If you leave," Frank checked the bottom of his chalice, "who will bring you back?"

Sam started to say something, but then stopped himself.

"Whatever your decision," Frank said, "it has been a pleasure, Samuel."

"You can call me Sam."

"Oh." Frank looked hurt.

"Samuel is good, too."

The joy returned to the old man's face.

"Thank you for everything." Sam left to find Glissandro, leaving the Mystics to their thoughts and drinks.

It only took a few moments of wandering to hear the music. A horrible song filled the air, full of dissonant notes and off-key pitches. It scraped Sam's ears like nails on a chalkboard. He almost didn't want to follow it.

"I don't know why you got so mad," Sam said when he found Glissandro leaning against the wide message tree.

Glissandro started playing louder and more obnoxiously.

"Whatever," Sam yelled over the racket, "I can get back by myself, anyway."

Glissandro stopped playing the noise. He played a sharp note and Sam's hand involuntarily rose in front of his face.

"Look deep," Glissandro played.

Sam was forced to stare at his second-skin.

"And tell me what you see."

Sam let out a gruff *hmmph*. "Snakeskin."

Glissandro shook his head. "Then that's all you're ever going to see." He holstered his instrument and started down the mountain.

CHAPTER 19

Sam woke up.

"May is a hard worker."

The light went on, and Sam saw the letter from his parents on the table next to his hammock. A lipstick mark smudged the seal, and an orange stain—probably from some flavored snack chip—stained the corner. After getting the silent treatment from Glissandro the whole trip back, he'd been too emotionally drained to read it when he'd seen it there last night.

Now it was morning. Sam was about to slide a finger through to break the seal but decided against it.

If today's going to be anything like yesterday, I'll want some comforting words from brainwashed parents to come back to.

The events from the mountain rushed back into his head. The Mystics had given him answers, and they'd made Stanton safe to go back to. He would still be the king there, and when he left and the Tembrath Elite came to him, he could tell them to find someone else. It was as simple as that.

But he still felt an embarrassing coat of depression.

Sliding out of the hammock, the tenderness in his quads barked at him. He bent down to stretch out the morning soreness and felt pressure against his thigh.

He'd forgotten about the fruit Bariv's snake had given him. Taking it out of his pocket, he held it up against the light. The perfect red fruit now had a bruise on it. The flaw was small, the size of a thumbprint, but it was there, and it was leaking.

That's just fantastic. Why did I put it in the same pocket as a giant diamond?

The trickle of juice coming from the fruit was tantalizing in a peculiar way. It was glowing, which by now wasn't an oddity in itself, but the glow seemed weirdly familiar.

Normally, he wouldn't drink something that had its own light source, but the juice dripping down his thumb emitted the most fantastic smell. The scent brought on something like déjà vu, but different. It smelled almost like a flash of events that had occurred over his lifetime. It took him back to his first touchdown, the sun-warmed grass and rubber scent of his mouthpiece. No, maybe it was his first kiss, Jenny's perfume and the sweet, passionate smell of young lust. A few more memories passed through his mind, but he still couldn't fit the scent to any one of them. Whatever it was, he yearned to taste it, and his stomach rumbled.

He placed the fruit in his diamond-less pocket and licked the juice off his hand.

"Hmm." Sam smacked his lips. Maybe it was all of those memories? He'd eat the rest later at lunch and try to decide.

He went through the smoky wall and entered Atlas Crown. This time, however, he wasn't late or early. All around him, people exited the pillars and set up the shops. Waking with everyone else kind of made him feel like a part of the works.

His stomach grumbled even louder.

He tried to burp to release some of the now-building pressure. The small belch he got out did nothing to ease the rumbling noise. He put a hand on his abs and felt his stomach vibrating.

All of a sudden, his stomach felt light, like it wasn't there anymore. Then his head felt light. The weightless feeling traveled down the back of his neck, his spine, his waist and then all the way to his still-grounded feet.

He burped even louder, loudly enough to attract glances from a few townspeople.

Then he felt warm.

It wasn't an unpleasant sensation, but it was overwhelming. It wasn't like he was burning, but rather like his whole body was sitting the perfect distance from a roaring fireplace. His *whole* body, inside and out.

A gurgling noise came from his throat.

"Umm, help," Sam managed to get out. "What's happening?"

Some of the closest people started moving toward him, at a pace that showed they were concerned, but not in a panic. A young girl and her mother got there first.

"Are you hurt?" the woman asked calmly.

"I," he involuntarily made the gurgling sound again, "ate this—"

He couldn't speak anymore; whatever was taking place in his body had stolen the entirety of his concentration. He couldn't focus on anything but the warmth.

The heat entered his head and feet simultaneously, and then moved to his chest, gathering there before making its way down his arm and settling in his second-skin. The pressure and heat built around his fingers, and his hand started to shake.

The woman waved her second-skin over Sam's forehead, but it did nothing.

Just as Sam thought his hand was going to fold in on itself, he felt a surge of emotion.

The Veil. It was magnificent. But this time it wasn't like the rush of a train, it was like the whole earth was rotating under his hand and he was trying to hold on for dear life.

BOOM.

☙

After the explosion, Sam could see only red light. Atlas Crown was no more, and all that remained was bright, intense red. His body was immersed in a shimmering red universe composed only of surging power, and Sam was a part of it.

"Sam" was no more. He was now part of a limitless energy, power that he could never have fathomed.

Then the red started collapsing in on itself.

White light stained the edge of the red as it folded down countless times.

Sam cowered back as the red crashed upon him and into his second-skin. The skin was red and the stars were red. He felt himself dissolve into his hand, and eventually disappear altogether.

Then all was silent.

Suddenly, everything become solid again, like his soul had been thrown back into his body. He opened his eyes.

It was dark, but Sam could see dirt in front of him. The first thing he checked was his second-skin. Relief flooded through him when he found it intact.

"Whoa." The memory of the red place started fading away, like it had all been a wild dream. He tried to hold onto the sensation of all that power, but it was useless. "What was that?"

He ran his hands over his body to make sure he wasn't hurt. He didn't feel any pain, and everything was still intact. It was like nothing had happened.

He turned in place. All around him was more dirt and roots. Light filtered in from above, and he realized he was in a hole, like a large well.

"Are you down there?" a voice shouted from above.

After a cough, Sam was able to yell. "Yes!" He ran a hand over his throat, glad to have control over his voice again.

"Don't move!" the voice shouted.

Like I could go anywhere.

It only took a moment for his body to start lifting out of the hole.

Fernando set him on his feet. "Let me take a look at you." His second-skins twitched at his sides. "Does it hurt anywhere?"

"No." Sam looked himself up and down. "I'm fine."

Crowds of people stared wide-eyed at Sam, apparently waiting to see if something else was going to happen. Sam held still as Fernando waved his two second-skins across his body, leaving a trail of small tingles wherever the skins passed. A sense of calmness engulfed him, like it had with that spell May had put him under.

Then Sam saw something that made his stomach churn worse than before.

The mother who'd been trying to help him before cradled her daughter in her arms. The girl's forehead dripped blood. The mother's eyes were closed as she brushed her second-skin over the little girl, muttering something that sounded like a prayer. Sam saw blood seeping through the girl's robe, as well.

He burst away from Fernando and ran to them. The pleasant, complacent feeling waned as soon as he broke from Fernando's grip.

Sam's breathing was frantic. "What happened?"

"Please," the woman's voice was calm as she made a pass over her daughter's face, "give us some space."

"How can I help?" Sam dropped to his knees next to them. "What can I do?"

"SOMEONE CALL THE ALLU!" The woman cried out.

Fernando sent a spiraling black mist into the sky, which let out a firecracker sound three times as it hit its pinnacle. The black swirled into a circle cut through the middle by an arrow pointing down to their location, where the little girl was turning sickly pale.

The woman looked at Sam with pain in her eyes, a kind of pain Sam had never seen before. "Some space... *Please.*"

That one word pierced him deeply. His heart crumbled.

He stumbled backward and searched for a friendly face, but the crowd gazed at him with cold suspicion. Even Fernando looked uneasy. All Sam wanted to do was run.

It was the football game all over again.

He ran like he was being scouted. He passed the rinsefish fountain, the library, and a bunch of buildings that seemed to be defying gravity. He ran by people sitting cross-legged on blankets in small circles, and around a patch of fire that a few sorcerers were making stand still. As he sprinted, he aimed for the three-pronged pillar.

Suddenly, he heard the one voice he would stop for.

"Sam!"

May was actually flying toward the place Sam was fleeing, determination in her eyes. She tore through the air like a missile and settled to the ground in front of him.

Sam bent over, putting his hands on his knees to catch his breath.

May bent down to lock eyes. "What are you running from?"

"I… did something." Sam tore his eyes away and looked at the ground.

"What happened?"

Sam sucked in as much air as his lungs could hold. "I hurt someone. A little girl."

"On purpose?"

"Of course not."

"Who?"

"I don't know! It was this young girl. I just woke up and went outside and then I, like, felt something weird and there was this energy and…"

"Go on."

"It exploded around me. It was like what happened with the cornerback after the game, only worse. I ended up in a huge crater, and when I was pulled out, the girl was bleeding."

"Sam." She placed a hand on his shoulder. "It's okay."

He felt his face get hot. "It's not, she—"

"She will be fine." May lifted Sam's chin up with her finger so they were face to face. "Healing is one of the first things the people in our community learn after Omani. I see that the Allu Shaman have been called. They are the best healers in the world and they can get anywhere in Atlas Crown in a matter of minutes. Everything will be fine. I promise."

Sam felt heat behind his eyes, making them glaze over. It was something he hadn't felt in a long time. He felt a single teardrop roll down his cheek. "You didn't see the look in her eyes."

"The little girl?"

He didn't want to remember the agony in the mother's expression. He'd never seen that kind of pain before, let alone caused it. On the football field, he'd seen agony from twisted knees, torn ligaments, and even a broken bone or two. But the mother's pain transcended physical; it made him feel cold just to know it existed.

"I don't belong here." Sam wiped the tear away with his knuckle. "I just want to go home."

"I'm sorry, Sam, not just yet. Now more than ever, you need to learn how to control your abilities."

"Then when?" Sam shouted as he stood up. "I know about the Tembrath Elite. I know that they want me to join them, to help them get past the Veil. So when are you going to let me go? When they all die?"

May stayed silent for a moment, her face solemn. "I'm so sorry, Sam. It's just too risky right now. We can't afford—"

"Whatever!" Sam spat. "I should have known you were a liar from the minute I met you, *Agent Greenford*."

May looked down at her second-skin. "A few more days. I'll sort things out."

"Yeah, right," Sam said with a snort.

"I am not a liar, Sam." Fear widened her eyes. "But there is a reason I have remained vague with you."

"Two days." Sam clenched his teeth. "Not a minute more."

"Fine." May gave him a gentle nod as she turned to go.

"FINE!"

He ripped off his robe and threw it on the ground. He still had the jersey on underneath, proudly displaying his number. He took off his second-skin and shoved it into the pocket on his thigh. One-of-a-kind or not, it was doing more harm than good.

He gave up on the idea of joining the rest of his group and ran until he was deep in the woods. He sped past a troupe of rainbow-colored rodents, a giant spider-web in the shape of a tree, and round birds that looked like puffer-fish, floating on tiny wings in the air. He stopped for none of them. When he did finally halt, it was because of the ringing in his ears.

I must be close to the borders.

He kept moving in the direction he was going, and the ringing got louder, until it was like a smoke detector going off inside of his head.

He reached out a hand and felt the invisible barrier stopping him. He wondered if trying to smash through it would do anything, or if it would be like the pillar wall.

The ringing made him feel unbalanced and dizzy, like he was about to fall over. He backed away from the border and the annoying sound diminished.

This is ridiculous; I'm a prisoner.

He stared at the border for a few minutes, trying to decide what to do. *Maybe I could go underneath?*

"You can't get through!" a voice called out from behind him.

Sam closed his eyes and breathed in through his nose. He stood still and pretended not to hear. He hoped that whoever it was would just leave him alone.

Unfortunately, he could hear the footfalls getting closer.

"Sam?"

He exhaled and turned around, and then his jaw dropped.

It was Cassiella, but not the Cassiella he remembered.

She was ravishing. Her hair was no longer held back by the yellow mushroom, but hung delicately at her shoulders, playfully dancing in the breeze. Her skin had a slight glow to it, and her eyes were almost too beautiful to look at. Instead of the shy girl from before, her aura had become confident and sexy. She was the same girl, but it was like something had been dulling her good looks, something that she had escaped from.

"You won't be able to get through."

Even her voice was enticing. *What changed?*

"Why not?" Sam felt the anger in his chest slide away at the sight of her. "I seem to be very good at breaking things lately."

"That's some serious magic." She sauntered up and gently placed a finger on his chest. Her eyes were so stunningly bright that he almost had to look away. "It can keep out very powerful people."

"Yeah, so I'm told."

"I was on my way to Rona's lesson and I saw you running." She smiled and locked her hands behind her lower back. She bit her bottom lip, which sent a lustful shiver through Sam's body. "I couldn't keep up, but I used the Veil to follow your steps. I hope you don't mind."

Sam was about to say that in fact he did mind, but the way she was looking at him...

"No," Sam shrugged, "it's fine."

"Good." She bent to the side and looked behind him. "What are you doing out here?"

"I just... needed to get away."

She flashed a smile at him. It made Sam go weak in the knees.

"Mind if I get away with you?" Her voice was almost suggestive.

He felt a certain stirring. "I guess not. Want to sit on that log over there?"

She giggled. "That's not a log."

"What are you talking about?" He picked up a small stone and tossed it underhanded at the log. As soon as it made contact, a reptilian head popped out of the hollow. Four legs—complete with nasty claws—emerged from the rotted holes on the sides. The creature's beady eyes glared at Sam before it skittered off.

Sam almost felt like laughing... almost. "Note to self: don't sit on turtle-logs."

"Actually, they don't mind so much. When I was a kid we used to ride them around, but they don't like being woken up."

Sam sighed and shook his head. "This place makes no sense."

Cassiella flicked her hair. "You just need to give it more time."

"I think I gave it plenty."

"How about we take a walk?" Instead of being meek, her question was full of confidence, and Sam was powerless against it.

He gave an agreeable shrug. "Okay."

"I know you've been having a tough time." She ran a hand through her hair.

"No, I'm fine."

"...Sam."

Again, he felt powerless. "I just want to go and play football. This place is great and everything, but I think it's time I got back."

"But you haven't even seen anything yet."

Sam thought about the look in the mother's eyes. "I've seen enough."

"You can't just run away when things get tough."

"You can when you're as fast as me."

Cassiella stopped and looked him square in the eyes. The change in her was unnerving. "Football is a game, right?"

"Yes, but it's more than—"

She cut him off with wave. "And from what I heard, it's very physical?"

"Mental, too."

"Even better," she smiled. "And you love doing it?"

Sam nodded.

"More than anything?" She asked in a playful tone.

"Anything."

"Then I have a question for you." She gave him a steady look. "What happens if you get hurt?"

Sam didn't like to think about that circumstance. "I won't."

"Very optimistic. But seriously, what happens if you do?"

Sam shrugged. "Then I heal and keep playing."

She wagged a finger at him. "But it would take time to heal out there, yes?"

"Well, yeah."

She twirled and then opened her arms wide, gesturing to everything around them. "It doesn't take long to heal in here. In fact, the Allu can do it pretty much instantly."

The mother's eyes flashed in the back of his mind. He pushed the image away and swallowed hard. "Yeah…"

"All I'm saying is that it wouldn't hurt to have a few sorcerers on your side."

"I could just do it myself."

Cassiella suppressed a laugh. "No, you can't. Only others can heal you."

Sam looked her up and down. She was gorgeous. He couldn't understand why he hadn't seen it before. *Maybe I didn't give her a fair shot.*

"So it would be beneficial not to leave right away and to make a few friends." She winked. "Am I right?"

Maybe he was being too rash trying to leave right away. It would be good not to burn any bridges, though he might have sunk a few of them already. "You're right."

"Good." She gave a satisfied nod. "Now let's go to Rona's lesson."

Sam scratched the stubble on his chin. "I might need you to make me a practice plant."

"Sounds good to me." She twirled again, the hem of her dress spinning out hypnotically. "This way."

"Let's walk a little more." Sam felt the last of the anger drain away. If the Allu really could heal instantly, then the little girl was probably fine. "They won't care if we're a little late, right?"

She bit her bottom lip again. "So you're saying you want to spend more time alone with me?"

Sam did his best nonchalant shrug. "Maybe a little."

Cassiella smiled, curtsied, then led him along the perimeter.

"So, how did the reenactment end?"

"I was defeated," she said, walking in front of him.

"How?"

"The Veil got everyone in the whole community to sing at once, and when I was distracted trying to steal everyone's voices, She unblocked the Sun and used the light to banish me."

Sam paused. "Sorry that I made you freak out like that."

She flicked her hair back, which billowed easily through the air now that no mushroom held it together. "I have no idea what you're talking about."

Sam decided to drop the subject. "You were pretty good."

She turned around and started to walk backwards. She tilted her head down and gave a slight bow, flourishing her hands outward.

Sam gave a few soft claps. "Glissandro knows how to write a good story."

She stood up straight but continued stepping backwards. "He was always a believer that words are a type of music. A good story can make a good song."

"So." Sam felt the buzz from the protective borders creeping back into his ears. "Where are you taking me?"

"I don't know." She placed a finger on her lips. "I just feel like walking this way. That's the best part about this place. Sometimes there's no reason for it other than 'just because.'"

She moved with a grace that Sam had never seen before. A faint glow gleamed from behind her, making her stand out. She somehow made Daphne seem ordinary.

Why didn't I see this before?

Sam raised an eyebrow. "Is there something different about you?"

"I have no idea what you mean." She tossed her hair. "Maybe you're opening your eyes for the first—"

Her words were cut off as she disappeared.

It looked to Sam like she had fallen down a hole or something.

He rushed over to see what had happened. The air around him was being pulled into the hole, like the opening was a giant vacuum. Light did nothing to penetrate the darkness, like it was being swallowed along with the wind.

Sam's stomach tightened.

"Cassiella!" He called down. "Are you all right?"

No response.

He got on his knees and leaned forward, bracing so the air wouldn't suck him in.

"CASSIELLA!"

Still nothing.

Without thinking, he dove in after her.

A second later, however, a giant blast of air forced him back out. He tumbled backward as he landed. As soon as he stopped rolling, he reoriented himself and then ran back to the hole.

Now, instead of sucking in air, it was blowing it out.

"Cassiella!"

He again tried to jump in, but the air coming out threw him backwards with tremendous force.

"HELP!" he shouted, but he realized no one was around.

He took a second to gather his bearings and try to pick out a landmark that he could remember. The only noteworthy thing he saw was a pile of rocks that looked like someone had stacked them. Deciding that was the best he would do, he ran as fast as he could toward the three-pronged pillar.

CHAPTER 20

Jintin jumped out of the way. "That was quick."

Vigtor flared his nostrils and took a deep breath. Even after years of traveling through the Veil, it still managed to leave his breath thin. "Are you implying that I would take my time with this?"

Jintin turned defensive. "No, it was just…"

"That I didn't have to come?"

Jintin sneered. "I could have done it myself."

"Really?" Vigtor smiled, his tone lighthearted. "When did you figure out how to correctly harness people's minds? Because I'm sure I would have noticed your development of that particular skill. Did you have a run-in with Delphi while out here? Did you have a sudden epiphany after three hundred years of static wit?"

Jintin lowered his voice. "At least my harness wasn't broken by May."

Vigtor moved close to Jintin's face. "I didn't catch that."

Jintin's eyes lit up. "Thanks for coming, boss?"

"Better." He stepped back. "Did you perform the cloaking drape?"

Jintin looked uneasy. "Yes."

"Why the uncertainty?"

"Will it really keep the Mystics blind? You know what they'll do to us. I don't want to end up thinking I'm a—"

"It will be fine." Vigtor waved his second-skin, and the air around it grew dark. "You know our magic always prevails. Why do you think they haven't found us yet?"

Jintin nodded. "Do you really think this is going to get him to come out?"

"Erimos thinks so, so yes, I believe it will work."

Jintin looked unsure. "But they're just words."

"To you, any words are just words. But if Samuel is anything like the rest of us, which I believe he is, a feeling of isolation will have already taken hold. I think this will be just the thing to push him over the edge." Vigtor locked his hands together. "Now stand aside and let me see her."

Jintin did as instructed and revealed his captive. The girl was small and young. She was very attractive, however… almost too attractive. It triggered Vigtor's suspicion. Robes bound her hands and feet and cloth spilled out of her mouth.

Vigtor grabbed a tuft of her hair and took a quick whiff. "Amorberry."

Jintin nodded. "Thought she seemed a little too appealing. I had trouble tying her up. Had to close my eyes."

Vigtor scoffed. "Tying her up. You really need to learn some subtle drapes. This is just so cha wo-wakan."

Jintin sighed. "You know I never learned Lakota."

Vigtor shook his head in disappointment. "Just so flat."

Jintin's nose twitched. "I didn't want her to end up in a million pieces. Who knows when the next person would have come through?"

The girl's eyes widened.

"Finally, something intelligent escapes your lips." Vigtor looked deep into the girl's eyes. "Trying to impress someone, are we?"

She gave him a poisonous glare.

Vigtor ripped the cloth from her mouth. "I asked you a question."

She spat at his face.

With a simple flick of his finger, the saliva stopped in the air. "Not very nice."

"I know who you are, you demon!"

Vigtor didn't like how her voice penetrated him. He decided to take away her allure. An upward thrust of the wrist did the trick. All particles of the amorberry dispelled into the air.

There we go. The girl now looked weak and feeble. *Much better.*

"You'll never do it!" Her eyes were murderous. "You never have and you never will. You're weak!"

Even without the amorberry, he was starting to like the girl. She had pluck. "No?"

"You think you are any match for the Veil? You weren't even a match for Bariv when he cast you out!"

Vigtor saw her hand twitch behind her back. The girl pinched her lips together and gave Vigtor a look so intensely vile that it could have held off a stampede of trample-feet. A rumbling sound came from somewhere behind him, and Vigtor turned just in time to stop the boulder from crushing his face.

It took almost no effort to stop the giant rock, but if he hadn't turned, his head would have been split open.

He shoved the girl onto her stomach and ripped off her second-skin. After he burned the purple material with a simple grip, he turned to Jintin with a menacing gaze. "You left her second-skin on?"

Jintin held his hands up defensively. "No, I took it! She must have had another one!"

Vigtor pointed a shaking finger at Jintin. "I'll deal with you later."

"It's not his fault you're a coward!" The girl screamed. "You're a delusional, scared little boy. No matter what you do, you're always going to fail! You're pathetic!"

Vigtor grabbed the girl by the shoulder and sat her up straight. He brought his face close to hers and gave a predatory grin. "We have a secret way. Or rather… we will."

She clenched her teeth and her lips trembled. "The Veil knows all. You can't hide any secrets from Her."

Vigtor caressed her hair. "You're mistaken, little one."

She turned her head to the side, the vein in her neck thick with anger. "Just get it over with."

"What?"

"Whatever you want with me."

It would be effortless for him. People were so simple. He had even gotten so good at harnessing that he could do it over the flathands' phone devices, though he despised using them. "What makes you assume it's you I want?"

"She will protect me."

"She won't be in charge for much longer." Vigtor closed his eyes and curled his fingers.

It took only seconds.

When he opened his eyes, the girl stared at him absently. She looked good with red eyes.

"Now." Vigtor handed her the envelope. "What do you know about Sam Lock?"

@

"Rona!" Sam pushed through the fire in his legs. "RONA!"

The group hovered around Rona, who was showing them something on a small white dove.

"Rona!" When Sam finally reached them, the group separated and stared at him.

"Master Rona," Rona corrected. "What's wrong, Sam, and why are you late?"

"Sam thinks he can do whatever he wants." Petir crossed his arms and put on his favorite sneer. "Isn't that—?"

"Shut up or I'll knock your head off."

"I'd like to see you—"

"ENOUGH!" Rona's thick accent came through even more when he yelled. "What happened, Sam?"

Sam took a deep breath. "Cassiella, she's gone."

"Oh." Petir threw a hand over his chest in fake shock. "Just like you at the reenactment. I can't begin to stress how rude that was, by the way."

That was all Sam could take. He put all his weight on his front leg and struck at Petir as hard as he could, intending to bury his knuckles as deep as possible in the little punk's face.

Petir held up his second-skin and stopped Sam's fist inches away from his infuriating smirk.

"So angry," Petir tsked. "We don't like that here."

Sam wanted nothing more than to pound the little freak's guts into the ground. He reached into his pocket to grab his second-skin and—

"I said ENOUGH!" Rona thrust his palm out, separating Sam and Petir. "What do you mean, 'gone?'"

"She fell." Sam still scowled at Petir. "Through this hole in the woods."

"And you couldn't get her out?"

"I tried to go after her, but this hole was weird. It was like a vacuum that was sucking up air, and then when I dove in, the air reversed and threw me out."

A look of panic crossed Rona's face.

Petir whipped a skeptical look to Rona. "*That* sounds real."

"For once, would you just be quiet!" Daphne snapped.

That finally shut Petir up.

Rona released the dove. "Where did this happen?"

"By the border. I can get us back." In his panic, Sam hadn't realized until that moment that Glissandro wasn't there. "Where's Glissandro?"

"He's off with the Mystics today," Rona said quickly. "Now hurry, lead us there."

@

It was harder then he thought it would be to find the pile of rocks. After what felt like miles of running, they finally came across the stack.

"Over here!" Sam ran up to the hole, which was sucking in air again.

Rona pulled him away from the vacuum. "She fell in there?"

"Yeah." Sam pulled against Rona's grip. "She didn't see it; she was walking backwards."

"You must have tried *really hard* to go after her," Petir said. "That air is *really* pushing out hard."

Rona stepped around Sam and knelt down right next to the hole, running his finger along the rim. "It wasn't like this when you left?"

"No, I swear."

"Step back," Rona warned. "I don't want any more of you falling in."

Petir snorted. "Falling in? Sam probably pushed her."

Sam ignored him. "What do we do, Master Rona?"

202

He placed his second-skin over the hole. It trembled a little before he pulled it back. "She is not in there. I am not familiar with this magic, but because of the airflow, I assume there is an exit. Let's hope it is not too far away."

Sam inched toward the hole. "Let's go in after her."

Rona thrust a hand up in refusal. "Only as a last resort."

"But—"

Rona brought himself to his full height. "That is final!"

Sam paused. Deciding not to press the issue, he took a step back. "So should we split up and look?"

Rona gave a solemn nod, his expression grave.

Zawadi bowed as she walked backward. "I'll go find May."

Rona nodded. "Go."

"Can you do some sort of grip to find her?" Sam's eyes refused to leave the hole. "There's got to be something."

"Unfortunately not; there are too many people in Atlas Crown to feel her, and too many places for her to have gone. But I *can* do this." Rona got into a stance and thrust his palm toward the sky. Above them, clouds swirled, forming giant letters in the air. He thrust his hand even higher, and lightning struck the clouds, making the puffy letters crackle, furiously bright.

FIND CASSIELLA OF THE PYX CLAN

"When someone sees her," Rona said, "they will send a message up. The good news is that this natural phenomenon must have come from the Veil, and it is rare for something to come from Her that is truly harmful. The Mystics can do what I cannot, so they should find Cassiella soon. Delphi is very good at that sort of thing."

They waited for what felt like an eternity.

Rona kept staring into the sky, the sweat beading around his crown as time passed.

"Shouldn't they have found her by now?" Daphne shifted from foot to foot.

Rona gave a stoic nod.

At this point, Sam itched to just go ahead and dive in the hole. "What do we do?"

"If the Mystics can't find her, then there is something unnatural taking place. Something dark."

Sam nervously cracked his knuckles. "Meaning?"

"We search by foot."

"The whole town?" Petir's jaw dropped. "That'll take days."

A sound like a wire being whipped through the air whizzed above them. After a sudden crack, three symbols appeared over Rona's clouds. Sam thought they looked like Chinese characters, but more fluid.

Rona looked up at the symbols and sighed. "The town *and* the outskirts."

"Everywhere?" Petir grabbed his greasy hair. "But that could take—"

"It doesn't matter," Sam interrupted. "We have to find her."

@

Back inside the pillars, all of Atlas Crown was on alert. Everywhere, people called out her name, scoured buildings, and organized search parties for the Atlas Crown outskirts. Sam noticed surprisingly few sorcerers using the Veil to find Cassiella. One lady with a maroon robe draped Cassiella's name onto pieces of smooth bark and lay them on a small pool of water, trying to create some sort of directional compass. She tried with a few different types of bark, but they all ended up the same, spinning out of control and splashing water everywhere.

After a few hours, the hunt inside the town started to dwindle as the search parties focused on the outskirts, checking the woods and other surrounding land. At sunset, some of the older sorcerers created balls of light for everyone—not unlike Sam's lamp—allowing the search to continue. Sam ended up in a group with Daphne and Rona. The three of them scoured the woods for hours on end, creeping through the dark, calling out to Cassiella. Rona had warned them to be careful where they stepped, because the vortex Sam had found might not be the only one of its kind. Every minute felt like an hour and every hour felt like a day, and as it got later, Rona seemed less confident and more concerned.

"Can't Bariv feel her through the Veil?" Sam's fingernails had dug deeper into the skin of his palm over the last hour. "I mean, he can feel new sorcerers all over the world. Can't he find one girl?"

Rona's voice was tired and full of grief. "No. Bariv is able to detect new users of the Veil. He tracks fluctuations in the Veil. There is too much magic here. Always."

A brilliant idea popped into Sam's head. He wondered why no one had thought of it yet. "What if everyone stopped using magic? Couldn't he find her then?"

Rona looked at Sam with kind eyes. "A fine idea, but it is not just people who use the Veil here. Everything that springs from Her is in constant harmony with Her for survival."

Daphne directed her light into a small hollow in the earth made from an uprooted tree. Save for a few scuttling insects, it was empty. "What if we can't find Cassiella tonight?"

Rona did not hesitate. "Then we search until we do."

Daphne lowered her eyes toward the ground. "But what if…"

Rona halted. "What?"

The words burst forth from Daphne. "What if the hole ended up outside of the protective borders?"

Rona sighed, sending his light skyward, which caused a few creatures to scurry off and make a mumbling sound, their furry bodies retracting into the canopy. "Don't think I haven't thought of that. If she does not show up by sunrise, I will go into the vortex after her."

"I'll do it." Sam tried to sound braver than he felt. "Right now."

Rona placed a hand on Sam's shoulder. "Very noble of you, Sam, but while it's dark out, it would be very dangerous to take that chance. We will wait until first light and, if you like, we can go together."

Sam nodded. "But what's so dangerous about the dark?"

"The dark is a wonderful place to hide," Rona sent his light into a crevice made by a boulder that had been rolled out of the ground. "And a terrible place to be hidden."

"But why can't we just let the protective borders down and all go check together?" Sam did his best to sound inspiring. "We could get a whole team together."

Rona turned away from Sam, staring off into the woods. "We only open the borders if it is of the utmost necessity. If we do not find Cassiella tonight, it will be considered."

"But if we all go together—"

"Sam," Rona's voice was soft but firm, "it is something that you cannot understand."

Sam clenched his second-skin into a fist. "Because of the Tembrath Elite?"

Rona tried to hide his surprise, but Sam heard the change in the tone of his voice. "Who told you about them?"

"The Mystics."

Rona sighed. "They have always been too quick with their answers."

Sam stifled a yawn. The day had taken its toll and his body begged for some rest. "At least they were honest with me."

"There is a balance between the need for honesty and for caution." Rona stepped around a patch of quilted moss. "A balance that they often tip."

"Yeah, well, why shouldn't I know?" Sam fell in at Rona's side. "It's not like I want to join up with them."

Rona nodded but kept his eyes forward. "I know, but they are not what you should be worrying about right now."

Daphne performed a grip, and the earth absorbed the puddle blocking their path. "We should focus on finding Cassiella."

A change in the sky filled Sam with relief. "I think we just did."

Above them, dazzling words floated over the Chinese-looking characters, bright enough for everyone in the entire area to see.

CASSIELLA IS SAFE NOW
AND WITH THE PYX CLAN

Rona bowed to the letters. "She always comes through."

Sam let himself finally breathe again. *She's safe.*

Daphne ran over and hugged Sam tightly, her silky hair brushing against his forearms. He inhaled her scent and thought it was the most wonderful smell he'd ever come across. A shiver ran through his body. *Did she actually did find the amorberry?*

Rona looked up at the stars. "I think it's time we have a nice, long sleep." He winked at Sam. "I think we can let lessons start a little late tomorrow."

"Sounds good to me," Sam said as Daphne broke the embrace.

"I'll see you tomorrow." Daphne gave Sam a bright, but tired, smile.

"But," Sam stole a quick glance at Rona, "I was thinking we could do something."

She raised an eyebrow and gave Sam a "you-must-be-joking" look.

"I mean, now that Cassiella's found," Sam lowered his voice, "do you want to come—"

She turned away before Sam could finish his sentence. "I'm going to find Cassiella." Daphne bowed to Rona. "Goodbye, Master Rona."

Rona returned the gesture, and Daphne took off toward the town.

Sam sighed. "At least Cassiella's safe."

"And that is what matters." Rona gave him a smile filled with relief.

Sam felt the fatigue tugging at him again. "I guess I'll turn in for the night as well."

Rona stared into the distance. "I trust you know your way back?"

"You're staying here?"

He nodded again.

"Alone?"

Rona smiled and shook his head no.

@

The town had a peaceful aura around it. Even though most people had gone to sleep, Sam could almost feel the good cheer resonating in the air. That is, of course, until he reached his room. Of all the people to find there, Sam couldn't think of anyone he would've liked to see less.

Petir leaned against the pillar, waiting for Sam. His dark attire stood out against the sandy stone.

Sam's good mood took an immediate turn for the worse. "Not now."

Petir didn't scoff or snort or even huff. He just looked at Sam with steely eyes. "I have something to tell you."

"What, that you're sorry for being a prick to me?"

Petir's expression remained serious. "You deserve every bit and more."

Sam went to pass him, but Petir stepped in his way.

"I'm not in the mood for your attitude right now," Sam loomed a good six inches above Petir. "Get out of here."

Petir clenched his teeth. "Don't you want to know what happened to Cassiella?"

As tired as Sam was, he did in fact want to know. "You saw her?"

"Yeah. Right here, as a matter of fact."

Sam was baffled. "What was she doing here?"

"She wouldn't say. Mostly she just cried. She wouldn't even open her eyes and look at me. She was probably coming to tell you off."

Sam felt the anger rising again. He was getting tired of all of this. "For what?"

Petir's hand started to shake. "For leaving her in the hole."

"What do you mean, 'leaving her?'" Sam's jaw tightened. "I had to go get help."

Petir's gaze was unyielding. "That's not what she told me."

"Well, that's what happened."

Petir blocked off his path again. He held his leathery second-skin up and pointed at Sam, his hand shaking with cold fury. "She said you were the one who created that hole."

Sam's body went rigid. "What?"

"Cassiella told me that you tried to do some grip to impress her, but instead you created that thing."

Sam grabbed the front of Petir's robe. "That's not what happened."

"She said she tripped and fell in." Petir grabbed Sam's wrists. "She ended up outside of the borders, but then jumped back in and came out on our side again. She said it only took a moment, but when she got back, she saw you running and called to you, and you weren't even running toward the town."

Sam felt a pounding in his head. He gritted his teeth and closed his eyes, trying to calm himself, but he could feel his anger growing, calling forth a furious energy that surged through his body.

Sam opened his eyes at the sound of Petir's yelp. Petir stared at the red blisters covering his bare palm.

Sam shoved Petir away. "That's a lie!"

Petir held his injured hand against his chest. "I talked to May. She said she'd seen a hole like that before. It can only be created from power magic."

Sam's head throbbed with thundering intensity. "Shut up!"

Petir turned away, keeping his hand pressed hard against his robe. "Better be careful; we usually cast out people who do power magic. I'm sure May is deciding your fate right now." He stormed into the night.

The room was dark and Sam was in no mood to say something nice about May. He blindly pulled out his second-skin and forced it over his hand. It felt cold and alien, like the deep anger that churned within him. The ground under him started to shake, and the snakeskin felt different on his hand; instead of conforming perfectly to his fingers, it pulled tighter in places and seemed rough to the touch.

Why can't the damn room just have a light switch?

A shock rippled within the snakeskin. Out came red beams that attached to the ceiling, hanging there like fluorescent streamers that kissed the room in a red glow.

Why would Cassiella lie like that? I thought she wanted me to stay. And May—how could she just expect me to keep living here forever? She took my freedom away. They're all liars.

He wanted out. Plain and simple, he wanted nothing more than to go back to the way things had been before that last game. Back to his old life…

He snatched up the letter from his parents, ripping it open. His mother had written in her usual flowery handwriting, full of praise and kisses, about how proud they were of him for being selected for the special football camp, and how his father just couldn't stop bragging to all their friends. It said how much they missed him, and how much they couldn't wait to go see his first professional game.

Sam crushed the paper in his fist before casting it to the floor as the anger within him grew. *More lies.* His mind flashed to the woman whose daughter he'd hurt. *Is the little girl even okay?* He didn't know—didn't know if he'd seriously injured yet another person. The stupid Veil had come into his life and messed everything up.

He hadn't asked for any of this! He'd been on his way to becoming a star. Rage seethed inside him, and his hands shook with frustration as little red flickers fizzled at the ends of his fingers.

Another letter stared up at him from his hammock, crisp and clean. As he ripped it open and pulled out an official-looking document, his heart began to pound; embossed in the top right corner was the logo of his first-choice college football team.

Dear Sam,

We are pleased to inform you that you have been accepted to—

He almost dropped the letter as he scanned the rest of the information with wild eyes. All his anger deflated, replaced with joy. His dream—all there on a single piece of paper.

He'd done it.

"They want me." The letter shook in his hands. "Full ride."

He felt like shouting it out, and then realized he was in a dark, ominous room… all alone. No one in the entire town would care about this—about what this meant to him. Well, Glissandro might, but who knew how he felt after their last encounter. Sam was on his own.

I've got to get home. Pulling out the diamond Bariv had given him, Sam clutched it in his second-skin and held it up. The diamond refracted the red light into pale little slivers that danced along the walls. Sam looked deep into the crystal. If he could turn the diamond back into coal, then he was free. It represented what kept him their slave: the threat of hurting others, *really* hurting them. If he could control his power, then he could go home and play football for the rest of his life. No being held hostage, no lying sorcerers, no worrying about if he would spontaneously combust… just football.

He curled his fingers around the stone and concentrated. If this worked, it would be the last thing he'd ever have to do with the Veil. After this, he'd never hurt anyone with magic. If he could harness the power, then he could banish it deep inside him, send it somewhere dark, where it would never get out again.

Energy rushed through his grip. His fingers closed tighter at the thought of all his future fans… the parties… the women. His knuckles creaked. *Meat… fast food… real beds.* Vibrations traveled through his arm, sending his entire body into violent shaking.

Coal. Turn to coal. Set me free.

He pictured the lumpy black rock Bariv had pulled out of the ground. *Bariv. Liar.*

The stone shifted in his grasp, sliding across the scaly skin, rotating in his fist, burning within the grasp of his second-skin.

Coal. Coal.

Something definitely was happening. He squeezed his eyes shut. He *knew* he could turn it back. The Veil struggled against his fingers, but he held tighter, controlling Her. He ripped into Her, making Her do it. She tried to escape but he refused to let Her go. He didn't care anymore. He didn't care whether it was the wrong way or the right way. It was his life: She wouldn't control him. He would control Her. He was strong enough.

The stone throbbed as though trying to escape, but Sam wasn't about to let it go. A strong jolt passed through it, and the heat disappeared as it stopped moving. Sam opened his eyes. He retracted his fingers and revealed what lay in his palm.

A black lump of coal.

Victory filled his heart. *I did it!* He could control Her. He was finally free.

The coal disintegrated. A layer of ash coated his palm, dulling the little stars. He blew on his hand, and most of it puffed away. He rubbed the remainder against his pants.

He made his decision.

Finding his cleats in the corner of the room, he put them on. The laces still tied themselves, but Sam wasn't thinking about magic. He was thinking about the cheering fans, college girls, parties, and fame.

He'd never feel lonely again.

Sam scooped up the college letter and headed out.

He knew exactly what he had to do. He couldn't get through the borders, but he could go through the vortex. Petir had said that Cassiella had ended up on the other side, so that was exactly where he'd go.

Bright plants and drapes lit up the now silent structures of Atlas Crown. It looked even more beautiful now that Sam had made his decision.

Just like when he'd met Glissandro, he focused on his destination, the pile of rocks deep in the woods. He felt the Veil and again forced Her to obey. An icy feeling dragged from his second-skin to his feet, and again, a light blossomed beneath him, although this time it was dimmer. He ran with the light as his guide.

Sam was thankful no one wandered around at this time of night; he didn't want to see anyone he knew.

It would be awkward if he had to say any goodbyes.

It didn't take long to find his way back. The moonlight acted as a beacon, working with his own magic, leading him to the pile of rocks. And there, only a few yards away, was the vortex—his way out.

RIIIIIBIT.

Sam startled back as a lion-frog jumped off the rock pile, nearly hitting Sam's face before landing not-so-gracefully on the ground and hopping off into the bushes.

He thought about when he had first come through the pillar, and that feeling of being watched struck him again.

"Who's there?" Sam's voice was gravelly and low.

Again, no one answered, which made Sam feel even less at ease. Someone was definitely out there, hiding in the brush.

As the lion-frog made its final jump, Sam saw them again.

Black swirls hovered over the bush, making their way toward the nearest tree.

"I don't care anymore, Bariv. No more games! If you have something to say, then say it!"

Hearing an abrupt movement in the bushes behind him, Sam twisted around. Something black moved against the silhouette of a tree.

"Play your games with someone else! I'm done!"

He took a running start and jumped into the swirling vortex.

@

There he is, Vigtor felt the corners of his lips pull into a smile, *just as expected.*

The boy tumbled out of the vortex and landed clumsily on his feet. He was large for his age, very muscular, and surprisingly still wearing a football uniform. Vigtor looked over at Jintin, who nodded.

So, this is Sam. The key to getting through.

Sam's second-skin twitched at his side. "Who are you?"

"Sam," Vigtor kept his voice calm, "my name is Vigtor, and unlike everyone in there, I am going to be completely honest with you from the beginning. But first tell me, were you followed?"

"You're them." Sam's eyes flashed from Vigtor to his companions. "You're the Tembrath people."

"Elite," Crom snarled.

Vigtor knew it'd been a mistake to bring Crom along. "Sam, this is very important. Were you followed?"

"No, but—"

"Good." Vigtor beckoned Sam forward. "We need to move right now. I'm sorry I don't have time to explain things to you right away, but I promise, as soon as we get back I'll answer all of your questions."

"You know," Sam gave a derisive snort, holding his ground, "that's the exact same thing that May said to me when she took me there. I don't want to join your group, so let me get going."

Vigtor considered harnessing Sam's mind. *The boy will be more useful—more powerful—if he does it of his own free will.*

"Sam." Vigtor kept a soothing tone. "You have been lied to and brainwashed. I'm the only person who can get you home. I'm sure that soon, someone will realize that you are gone, and they will come after you. They'll hold you in there forever when they catch you."

"To keep me from joining you." Sam's eyebrows arched in suspicion.

"Yes, but they have not told you the truth about us. They will keep you prisoner. We will help you get free. Don't you want to get to your football scholarship?"

Sam hesitated. "Why should I trust you?"

Vigtor took a step closer. "Look at your hand."

The stars on his second-skin radiated a glorious amount of light.

It was a skin Vigtor did not recognize. *Which plant did the material come from? Surely they wouldn't have let him take it from an animal? Surely they weren't that stupid...*

Then it registered. It had been so long since Vigtor had laid eyes on that particular skin. He forced himself to hide his surprise.

"Power recognizes power." Vigtor held out his own second-skin and produced a red glow in the crevices between the armor-belly scales. "You are and always have been a part of our family. If I wanted, I could force you to come with us. But I am asking, because I have the utmost respect for my family, and trust you will make the right decision."

"I don't know…"

"I'm not sure if you realize this," Vigtor pointed behind Sam, "but Atlas Crown is on an island. Right now, we are far out at sea, and there are no other inhabitants. The sorcerers have draped it so it cannot be located by flathands, by sight or by machine. You are trapped here… unless you come with us."

Sam gasped, and then sighed. "And you can get me home?"

"Yes, but not right away. That is the first place they will look for you."

"All I want is to play football."

"And you will. Now close your eyes." Vigtor secured his second-skin around the boy's wrist, and together, they went into the Veil.

CHAPTER 21

Sam didn't want to do that again anytime soon. It felt like his body had been put through a blender, mixed around for a while, and then molded again into human shape. Whatever had just happened, it wasn't right.

He felt blood dripping from his nose even before he opened his eyes.

"Don't worry," a voice said, "it gets easier."

Sam's eyes felt like they were swollen shut. He lifted a hand to rub them and a sharp ache, like a tender bruise, came from under his arm.

"What just happened?" Sam's tongue felt bulky and foreign.

"A true power magic," the voice said. "We entered the Veil and traveled within Her. It's the quickest way to travel."

As Sam's eyes adjusted, he took in his surroundings. *Underground.* Thick, ancient-looking stalactites stabbed the darkness above him. *A cave, maybe?*

A circle of ominous figures stared at him hungrily in the dim light.

"Where are we?" Sam tried his best to sound brave. *Trapped. Trapped underground... with the Tembrath Elite.* He recognized the man in front of him as the one who'd introduced himself as Vigtor. His dark hair and the goatee on his smug face were both speckled lightly with grey.

"Dami Sanctorum." Vigtor inhaled through his nose. "One of our areas of domestication."

Sam squinted, trying to get a better view of where they were. "Are we in a cave?"

"Yes, but before we get to that..."

The figures moved eerily toward him, as if gliding. *Maybe May had been right to keep me prisoner...*

Someone shot sparks into the air. They were all sorts of colors and made firecracker sounds as they broke apart and festively lit up the cave.

The figures around him started cheering.

What the—?

Once illuminated, the cave wasn't as gloomy as it'd first appeared. The area was filled with comfortable-looking furniture, tables full of food—including meat!—golden suits of armor, a roaring fireplace, and piles of books on shelves.

The people surrounded him, welcoming him with bright smiles and handshakes.

"I'm Sage." A middle-aged woman in a blue dress took his second-skin in both hands. "And this is my twin sister, Saria."

An older, less greasy version of Petir came after the sisters. "Jintin. Such a pleasure. I'll teach you how to—"

"Dralis Banseer." A squat, bearded man patted Sam on the shoulder. "Hacheto welo. Welcome."

"Give him some room." Vigtor pushed through the others. "Come over here, Sam."

He led Sam to a plush recliner near one of the walls.

"Sit and relax. I'm sure you've had a trying day."

"Thanks, Victor." Sam didn't need to be told twice. He plopped down and tossed his legs up.

"Vigtor," the man corrected him.

Sam nodded. "Got it."

Vigtor snapped his fingers and the woman who'd introduced herself as Sage brought him a plate piled high with all sorts of meat.

Sam attacked it, biting a large chunk off a chicken leg. The meat dripped off the bone, and he sighed with delight.

Jintin thrust a goblet of dark red liquid into his hand.

Sam took a generous swig, his eyes going wide. "Wine?" *Do they know I'm underage?*

Jintin gave an eager nod. "The best. We make it ourselves."

The others pulled up chairs around him and started digging into their own feasts. They all seemed so happy and asked Sam so many eager questions about himself that he didn't know where to start.

Vigtor pointed his second-skin into the air, made a quick rotation of his wrist, and lively music started up from somewhere in the cave.

"So, tell me about football," someone said. "How do you play it?"

"What was it like growing up without magic?"

"There's no substitute for meat! The body needs protein!"

"You look so strong! How much can you put up?"

Sam laughed and ate and drank and, for the first time in a long time, felt at ease.

After polishing off his second plate—the food was ten times more delicious than what he had eaten in Atlas Crown—he sighed and sat back, and then noticed something that made his heart jump. "Is that a football?"

Vigtor motioned to Jintin, who picked it up and tossed it to him—it was a wobbly throw, but on target. Sam caught it with delight.

"Especially for you." Vigtor raised his goblet. "Thought you might want it. We even created an area outside for you to practice."

Sam rolled the ball around in his hands. It was brand new. Whoever these people were, they seemed to want to make him comfortable.

They all talked and joked for what must have been an hour, until Sam finally felt the pangs of fatigue hit him.

As if he had read his mind, Vigtor called for everyone to let Sam get some rest, and the others filed out with a few more "so nice to have you heres."

Vigtor stood up. The light formed little arcs on the scales of his second-skin, and Sam wondered what it was made of. At a curl of his fingers, a large mattress layered with plush comforters and pillows came from somewhere in the dark and floated next to them.

A real bed! It's about time.

"Goodnight, Sam." Vigtor gave a knowing smile. "If you need anything, just give a shout. I'll be in the next cavern over."

Sam's whole body ached to turn in for the night. "Thanks, especially for the football."

"Not a problem, Sam. Get some sleep."

Sam bit his lip. "Um, where's the bathroom?"

Vigtor laughed. "Almost forgot." As he turned to leave, he made another motion with his second-skin. A section of the cave floor split apart, and a square stall rose up from the ground.

Sam hopped up and went in, and then sighed. It was the perfect end to a great night. In front of him was a real toilet, with rolls of actual toilet paper.

❂

Glissandro always hated passing into Bariv's cave. The purple sap managed to get into recesses of his horn he didn't even know existed. His notes would be sloppy for hours until the gunk finally freed itself.

That morning, however, he didn't care what happened to his horn.

The football he'd made for Sam was tucked underneath his arm. It wasn't perfect, but Glissandro had fastened the skin from hemsith bark, so it would cut through the air with ease.

As he reached Bariv's platform, he saw that the Conduit was not sitting in thought, as usual, but was rather performing complicated grips. His hands flowed through the air, causing ripples. Stone cracked and re-joined under Bariv's feet. A strong wind came from behind Bariv and almost pushed Glissandro to the ground.

Glissandro put his horn to his lips and played as loud as he could. "We're organizzniing—"

He stopped, looked down the bell of his horn, and shook it furiously. A purple blob fell out and slithered away.

He tried again. "We're organizing a search party for Sam Lock!"

Bariv made a circular motion with his hand, and the mayhem halted. "He's gone." Bariv's eyes blazed red.

"What do you mean, gone?"

"He left. This morning."

Gone? How could he be gone?

"How do you know?" Glissandro asked. "Couldn't he be trapped somewhere?"

Bariv glared at him. "The vortex closed."

"So?"

Bariv did another grip and two black, swirling holes appeared on either side of the cave. "I know that magic very well."

Another quick grip closed each vortex with a low whistle.

What is he talking about? Cassiella passed through the vortex, and she's fine. "I still don't understand. Where could he have gone? It's not like he swam away."

Bariv shook his head. "That vortex was no accident. It takes a comprehensive understanding of power magic to create one and destroy one. Since I am the only one here—with the exception of May, perhaps—who can do it, it was created by an outside force."

Glissandro gasped. "The Tembrath Elite?"

Bariv nodded. "He's with Vigtor now. They traveled through the Veil together."

Glissandro's heart sank. "Why didn't you stop him?"

"In truth," Bariv splayed his arms, causing a strong wind to howl around the cave, "I probably could have, but it's more complicated than that."

Glissandro felt heat rushing to his head. "What do you mean? How can you let—"

"We could not keep him prisoner. It would have only led to resentment."

Glissandro put a hand against his forehead. "But he can't go with them! What if…?"

"If it is in his heart, then he would have done it anyway. We have to trust that he'll make the right decision."

"THAT CAN'T BE YOUR DECISION!" Glissandro's notes shook the whole cavern. Dust and particles rained down. "WE HAVE TO FIND HIM!"

Bariv curled his fingers. A wave of the purple goop rushed through the air and attached itself to Glissandro's horn, coating it inside and out.

"Just as we have shrouding borders, the Tembrath Elite have their own. I am blind to where they took him." He sighed. "Are you calm?"

After a moment, Glissandro nodded.

Bariv snapped his fingers and the goop flew away.

Glissandro buzzed a clean note. "What can we do?"

Bariv sat down and closed his eyes.

"Pray for Her."

CHAPTER 22

"You're getting better," Sam called across the field.

Vigtor tossed a tight spiral over forty yards. "After three weeks, it would be a shame if I wasn't!"

Sam was still getting used to the image of Vigtor, dressed all in black, tossing around a football. It was an odd sight, as if he had stumbled upon Crom bottle-feeding kittens. The hot sun beat down on the field, and Sam wondered if Saria would bring them that lemonade soon.

Sam threw the ball back, a perfect spiral that cut the air with dangerous precision. "Still, I have teammates who don't throw as well as you."

Vigtor stretched out his hand, and the ball halted between them and shot straight into the sky. Sam bolted forward. The lines they'd drawn on the grass were a little off, but nevertheless, the field was just about regulation.

The ball started to fall and Sam was under it in time. He had gotten even faster since he'd arrived at Dami Sanctorum. In the three weeks he'd been there, not only had Vigtor taught him how to *really* use the Veil, he'd encouraged Sam to practice football for when he returned to Stanton.

In one fluid motion, Sam cradled the ball against his forearm and tucked it against his body. He started toward Vigtor, his head low. They'd practiced this often, and Sam built up as much speed as possible for what would happen next.

Vigtor did a grip, and the air in front of Sam started to compress, like an invisible spring. He kept inching forward, his quads screaming. He'd almost reached Vigtor when the pressure became too much and he stumbled backwards.

"Closer every time." Vigtor held his thumb and forefinger about an inch apart.

Sam twirled the ball on the tip of his index finger. "Which means you'd better make that grip better, or you're gonna end up on your back."

Vigtor smiled. "Sit down, Sam. We need to talk."

Sam tossed the ball in the air, and then caught it one-handed. "Why? We're just getting warmed up."

"Don't worry." Sam saw an eager look pass through Vigtor's eyes. "We're not finished yet, but the time has come for you to know something important."

Sam threaded the ball between his legs in a figure eight motion. "What?"

"Will you just sit!" Vigtor quickly composed himself, bringing back a smile. "I apologize, but this is very important."

Sam shrugged and sat.

Vigtor took a deep breath and then began pacing back and forth. "Sam, it is about time you learned why we exist."

"I already know."

Vigtor stopped pacing and looked at Sam with a serious expression. "You do?"

"Yeah." Sam drummed his fingertips on the football. "The Mystics told me."

Vigtor paused. "What did they tell you?"

"That you guys are trying to get through the Veil."

Sam wondered why it had taken Vigtor so long to bring it up. For the weeks he had been with the Tembrath Elite, no one had mentioned it. They were very careful to skate around the subject whenever Sam was around. They treated him well and taught him all about power magic, but they still hadn't talked about what they'd been banished for.

Vigtor nodded. "What else?"

"That's kind of it."

Vigtor stroked his goatee and stared at Sam pensively. "Did they tell you why?"

Sam thought back. "Something about a better power behind it."

"I've taught you a lot since you came here, no?"

Sam closed his eyes and plunged his fist deep into the Veil. He thought about how magic had to be taken forcibly—you had to go to it, not wait around for it to find you. You had to be violent, and show some backbone. He merged what he wanted to happen with the energy coming to him. Every time, he felt something deep inside him scream with delight as he manipulated the world around him to fit his desire.

He knew he'd succeeded before he even opened his eyes.

He tossed the football behind him and heard it snatched out of the air.

Sam turned around and watched the doppelganger version of himself sprint off down the field, the ball tucked tight. He was a fuzzy version of Sam, always out of focus, but solid. It was a grip that Vigtor had taught him early on—a difficult power magic—but once Sam had learned the *true* essence of the Veil, power magic became like second nature. As the doppelganger reached the other side of the gridiron, he faded back into the energy he'd come from, and the football dropped to the ground.

"Yes." Sam gave a shrewd grin. "A lot."

Vigtor returned the smile and pressed his hands together in front of his face. "I have yet to teach you the most important thing."

"I don't want to break through the Veil." Sam turned and stared out over the barren land. "If that's where this is leading."

Vigtor snapped his fingers and Sam's face was forced back to Vigtor's. "Listen carefully. I need you to understand why we are trying to get past the Veil. As you've already figured out, only a select portion of humans can use the Veil."

"Right."

Vigtor's smile had an edge to it. "Do you know why?"

Sam shrugged again.

Desire penetrated Vigtor's gaze. "Because the real power is behind Her."

"Yeah, but—"

"There is a reason She is called the Veil. She is a mask, a fine linen covering the soul-stirring art that is behind."

Sam hadn't thought about that. "What's She covering up?"

"You have seen that the further into the Veil you dive, the more power you find."

It was true. "Yes."

"That is because the *true* power is trying to break through. It wants the world to know it exists. We just have to create a path."

Sam cracked his knuckles. His second-skin felt warm to the touch. "But what will happen if you get through?"

Vigtor's expression was deadly serious. "Peace will spread throughout the world."

Sam thought he'd heard wrong. "Huh?"

"The Veil does not have enough power for everyone in the world to use Her. If everyone on earth could use Her for their own gain—which they would—She would no longer exist. She would be used up in a heartbeat, as She is just not grand enough. That is why only a select group can use Her."

Vigtor did a grip, and a knife-thin sheet of rock sprang from the ground between them and hovered in the air. "She is a thin layer of oil covering the ocean behind Her. Unfortunately, the water cannot break through the oil. Someone needs to dive in."

Another grip, and the pane of rock split with a loud crack. Vigtor stepped between the two floating pieces and helped Sam to his feet.

"And you're sure you need me?" Sam stepped back as the pieces fell to the ground.

Vigtor placed a paternal hand on Sam's shoulder. "Yes, Sam, we do. The whole world does. Imagine this. If everyone had access to the exact same resource, greed and jealousy and crime would disappear overnight. With all that energy, people could grow unlimited food, and world hunger would be sated. With one true power that everyone could agree on, a power that actually helped them, religious battles would no longer be necessary. People could clothe and shelter themselves. People could find love, peace, and harmony, because hatred and malice come from wanting what you don't have. All the basic needs would be met. The world would be united under one power. Music would flourish, art would blossom, and people could spend their time at their leisure. And what do most people do in their leisure time?"

Sam's heart was racing. "What?"

Vigtor bent down, picked up the football, and handed it to Sam. "Watch sports. Sam, you could help bring a world utopia. You could be its greatest champion. Everyone would know your name. And after you assist with setting the human race on the path to a golden age, you can play football, and everyone in the world will be watching."

Sam felt dizzy. "But why are the sorcerers in Atlas Crown against this?"

Vigtor swung an arm through the air and created a tiny mirage of the pillars and walls of Atlas Crown. "The place itself, not just the people, screams elitism. Atlas Crown: the kings of the whole world. They sit high and mighty and let the rest of the world rot and bring about its own destruction. They don't want everyone else to have what they have. They are selfish. They have grown fat on their own narcissism. They don't even communicate with flathands. Did you not notice how everyone was frightened of you there? I bet that when you started to get angry, they draped you with a calming feeling. Am I correct?"

Sam recalled the serene feeling that May, Bariv, and Fernando had placed over him. "How'd you know?"

"They did the same to me. They took away your free will. They wouldn't let you feel what you were meant to feel because they don't want anyone ruining their precious way of life. They don't think about others, only themselves." Vigtor lowered his voice. "Do you understand?"

Sam thought about it: the lies, the looks of panic at the mention of power magic, the isolation. Although he still didn't feel like part of the group here, at least they treated him with respect. "I guess."

"They kept you prisoner." Vigor seethed, a black anger shadowing his eyes. "You were lucky to get out of the king's dungeon. They were scared you would escape and make everyone equals." Vigtor held his hand over the tiny Atlas Crown. Bariv's face appeared underneath, as if he were wearing the pillars as a crown. The face trembled with a cruel laugh, his eyes brimming with evil.

"The king's worst fear is for himself to become a subject, especially after neglecting those whom he was supposed to rule." The crown broke apart and Bariv's face faded away. "The people will rise and those of Atlas Crown will become just like everyone else."

Sam's head throbbed. *Could it be true? Could they really be conspiring to keep the rest of the world fighting, while they sit around and have reenactments and feasts all to themselves?* "So you're saying if I help you get through, we could really do all that? World peace and everything?"

Vigtor opened his hands wide. "There is no limit to the joys the world will feel. Togetherness is the reason we are born, and it is the reason we live. The whole world will be united and true happiness will abound in everyone's hearts. We can be the ones to do that. We just need to unleash the masterpiece that the Veil is hiding."

Sam stayed silent for a moment, rubbing his second-skin against his temple. "Can I think about it?"

Vigtor gave a swift bow. "Absolutely. It's a lot to take in. But think quickly, because we act early next morning, before dawn breaks."

Sam almost choked at the haste of it. "Why so soon?"

Vigtor made the pieces of rock slide back into the ground, leaving the field pristine once again. "She is thinnest right after the full moon."

Saria stepped out onto the field. "Lemonade?"

Vigtor looked into Sam's eyes as he called out to Saria. "I think we could both use a refreshment."

Saria handed them both cold, frosted chalices. "How's the practice going?"

Vigtor winked at Sam. "I think he'll be ready in no time at all."

Sam chugged his drink and handed the glass back. At the entrance of the cave, Crom stood, arms crossed, staring at them. He was the only one of the Tembrath Elite who had remained aloof during Sam's time with them.

"How about a few buttonhooks?" Sam handed the empty chalice back to Saria.

Vigtor took the last sip of his lemonade. "Work on your own for a while. I'll join you in a moment."

Sam nodded at Saria, thanked her for the drink, and then ran off to the other side of the field.

What Vigtor had said made sense, but something still nagged at him. He would have to think it over that night. *It's not like me helping will get anyone hurt. It is called the Veil. That means it's hiding something beautiful, right?*

Could he really help save the world from itself? Vigtor had been honest with him so far; Sam couldn't see a reason not to trust him now.

And everyone in Atlas Crown did seem a little bit elitist. Could it all be true? Was he really the key to everyone's happiness?

He'd sleep on it, but for now, he had training to do.

@

Vigtor watched as Sam physically exhausted himself. It was good—the endorphins would make everything easier. When the time came, he was confident Sam would do his part.

Saria's hand went tight around Sam's chalice. "Did you do it?"

Vigtor held his cup upside-down, letting the last drop trickle out. "Yes."

"And will he be the last?" Saria asked eagerly. "Will he be the one to finally break through?"

A pause. "Yes."

"You're sure?"

"I am quite a convincing storyteller."

Saria smirked. "You always were."

Vigtor flexed his fingers. The armor-belly skin was still coarse and dark. Bariv's snake had refused to give him its skin, but it didn't matter. Perhaps second-skins would no longer be necessary after they broke through.

"Tomorrow," Vigtor grabbed the Veil, delicately smiling as She ran across his palm, "we will meet the real power, and when we do, the true kings will emerge."

CHAPTER 23

Glissandro stomped through the woods. *It's hopeless.*

Bariv and May had been holed up inside the cave for over a week now, trying to figure out a way to stop what was to come.

Fear had paralyzed the town after May had spoken. *Sam is with them now.* Everyone knew the Tembrath Elite's plan. May had the other magical communities around the world on high alert, but Glissandro knew it wouldn't do much good. If the Tembrath Elite could hide from the minds of Atlas Crown, then chances were they'd remain hidden.

People skittered through their daily activities, hurrying home when they were done. No dancing, festivals… or music. People were scared, and Glissandro didn't think them wrong to be.

People should be celebrating the Veil. If this is the end, then we should at least go out with honor and courage.

It was raining, and he was off to find the symflowers for one final session. He had psyched himself up and made a promise to at least try and be happy for a little while. He headed in the direction of his favorite patch of symflowers.

It was funny: for the last few days, whenever Glissandro had played, the tone of his music had been different: richer, deeper, more vibrant… And it wasn't just the tone. His words felt more mature, more important. They were more potent, too. He had to be careful so as not to vibrate too much of Her, as the results could be unpredictable. It was like learning to play for the first time. Now, every time he played, he again felt the first shock and spiritual wonderment of magic. During the day, he scoured the fields for closed flower petals, and gently coaxed them open with music.

Not everything beautiful in Atlas Crown needed to hide.

At night, he traded his time between meditation and going to watch the greeter-owls as they scratched pictures into tree trunks. He waited until after they had finished decorating a tree and tried to figure out what they were drawing. Lately, they seemed to be trying to draw circles, or maybe spirals?

What will happen when the Tembrath Elite get through the Veil? No one knew for sure, but Glissandro had an idea.

The Veil would cease to be.

One crack, one flaw, and the power behind Her would take over. The animals would disappear, the plants would die, and he would be mute once again.

If only he'd done things differently.

He played loud, anything and everything he could, beautiful and raw. His lips got puffy and sore, but he continued playing. He stirred up every creature he could find and played each one a personal song. He turned rain into ice and back to water. He played a hymn for the griffin-bugs as they chopped up plants to bring back to their silk-dens. He lifted boulders high above the canopy and brought them gently back to earth. He uncapped the Geyser of the Ancestors and called the winds from deep below, creating sullen wails as the air escaped. Many of his actions held no reason; he just wanted to feel alive. He wanted to interact with the world before it was too late.

The rain only made his music grander. His hair was so saturated that it was almost straight. His robe was more water than cloth, and struggling against the extra weight strained his muscles, but it didn't bother him. His feet sank into the mud, and tiny, rough stones scraped his toes.

To his right, a pride of lion-frogs hopped in and out of a large puddle, their manes inflating once they reached the surface and keeping them afloat. Releasing a gust of air, one soared a few inches off the surface, propelled by its own breath.

Glissandro played a low note, and they all puffed up completely. He stepped into the puddle with them, wanting to share in the joy they felt. He had a quota of happiness to fill.

Everything's changing. It would all change. Yes, he'd had his brief stint in the outside world, but this was home. This was what he knew and loved. It had been glorious, but it was going to end.

He couldn't blame Sam. He wanted to, but he knew it wasn't Sam's fault. Sam had been marked an outcast the second he was chosen by the Veil. He could use Her, but he would ultimately be used against Her.

Glissandro thought back to the rainy night with the symflowers when he'd first spoken with Sam. Even through the heavy rain and music, Glissandro had heard him approaching—as Sam had all the stealth of a grotlon around jelly bees. Though unaware, Sam had been part of the music that night.

Glissandro remembered the goofy smile on Sam's face as he listened to them play. A smile like that didn't happen upon someone with hate in his heart; it was a smile of pure love and simple joy: beautiful things that the spiteful could never embrace.

If only I could go back to the night on the mountain and explain myself better, maybe Sam wouldn't have left.

A rustle came from somewhere behind the bushes, flinging droplets of water. Glissandro got into a crouch, and his knees dipped into the puddle, the water freezing his skin. The lion-frogs had stopped croaking and seemed to be waiting for something to happen. A dark body moved in the shadows just a few paces away, big and bulky.

Then, just inches above the brush, a few tiny black swirls hovered in the air, and then moved gracefully back down out of sight.

They triggered a memory. He'd seen that shape before, but on a much larger scale. Up on the mountain, before they reached the Mystics, the echo flies had made that symbol.

A flash of black appeared in the corner of his eye, and he heard a low growl behind him. Like a cat, Glissandro twisted gracefully. More floating swirls drifted through the air, the rain doing nothing to alter their path.

A dark figure lurked behind a boulder. Before he could react, it stepped out and revealed itself. Something went off inside of Glissandro's head. He knew exactly what he had to do—knew the instant he locked eyes with the creature.

It wasn't over yet. He'd seen those eyes before.

Glissandro howled through his horn, shooting a massive message into the sky.

GET MAY NOW!

@

Something was glowing under Sam's bed.

He looked around. No one else was awake, or if they were, they were doing the same thing as Sam: preparing for the big event. At some point earlier in the night—he didn't know when, as he had yet to see a clock—the gravity of the situation had finally struck him. He could really make a difference in the world. He was going to help them break through the Veil.

It actually wasn't all that hard of a decision to make. When Vigtor was teaching him to take the Veil and use it as he wished—which made a lot more sense than what Bariv had tried to teach him—Sam could feel something more, something massive lurking just around the corner, waiting to come into the light.

On the football field, he used his mind, but mostly he followed his gut. Intuition had always been his closest teammate. He never *really* thought about the path to the end zone, it just unfolded, like it was always there.

Right now, he was headed down a path, but this time he could do more than put numbers up on a scoreboard.

Bluish light trickled through the mattress. After staring up at the ceiling the whole night thinking, he'd gotten up to use the bathroom and had seen the tiny light leaking out. He crouched down and lifted the corner of the comforter.

Bright! He shut his eyes and let the fabric cover it again. Behind his eyelids, an imprint of color remained, like he'd looked directly into the sun. *A face.* A beautiful, delicate face smiled at him: sharp cheeks, lustrous hair, and piercing eyes. The image remained for a few moments before fading.

When he picked up the comforter to get another look, the light was gone, but he saw the fruit he'd stored there on the first day. Thinking back, he didn't know why he'd hidden it instead of throwing it away, but it'd felt like something he had to keep, even if only for sentimental reasons. He reached under and pulled out the gift the snake had given him.

Sam had tried not to think too much about Atlas Crown since he had been with the Tembrath Elite, but when he did, it was mostly about the mayhem and disturbance he had caused. Maybe he hadn't fit in because he was meant to de-throne them all. He was an enemy. He was *meant* to bring out the power that would save the world, and Atlas Crown just stood in the way. If he wasn't meant to do this, why would the Veil have even come to him in the first place?

Atlas Crown wasn't all bad, though. If not for his fate, he probably could have been good friends with Glissandro and would have eventually won Daphne's affection. And he *definitely* would have beaten Petir at gumptius. Heck, it could still happen. After they got used to everyone being able to use the real magic, why couldn't all that still happen? Things wouldn't change for them all that much, besides becoming intertwined with the rest of the world. And wasn't that the point of existing, to make connections? May had said something like that.

Without the strange light, the fruit looked kind of normal, like something he could pluck off a tree back in Stanton. Of course, it wasn't normal. He remembered the voice that had penetrated his head... no, not penetrated. It had already been there, lying dormant.

When the time comes, you will have to choose.

He'd wanted an answer, but had gotten none. This was the choice he had to make, and it would be one he could not turn back from.

It took some time, but the decision was made.

He put the fruit in his pocket.

"You're awake."

Sam popped up. Crom hovered menacingly above his bed.

Sam smoothed out his jersey. "Finally speaking to me, huh?"

227

The big man grinned and showed his teeth. Discolored, they all came to tiny points. The man was so large Sam didn't even come up to his chest. "You're young." Crom's voice had a hint of an accent. *Russian, maybe?*

"So?"

Crom pointed to his chest with a broad thumb. "I'm much older."

"… And?"

Crom's grin fell dangerously close to a sneer. "You should respect me."

Sam frowned at his tone. "I don't even know you. This is the first time you've even acknowledged my existence."

"They think you're so great, but you're still nothing." Some spit flew from his mouth and speckled Sam's forehead. His breath smelled like rancid meat and stale beer.

Sam wiped the arm of his jersey across his forehead. "What's your problem? What did I do to you?"

Crom bent further over the bed, his face just inches away from Sam's. "It should be me. It's always me."

Sam refused to back away. "What's always you?"

"The last one. It should be me that breaks through, not you. You don't even know—"

"The time has come," Vigtor interrupted. Sam hadn't seen him sneak up.

Sam shot Crom the dirtiest look he could dig up. "Now?"

"She will be weakest very soon." Vigtor cleared his throat. "We must strike."

Crom backed away, but his eyes remained locked on Sam's.

The Tembrath Elite convened in the main room. Vigtor pointed his second-skin at the large hearth in the corner, and a roaring fire came to life.

Sage and Saria came over to Sam, and each laid a hand on his arm.

"Are you ready?" they asked in unison. One of their voices was slightly higher, but Sam couldn't tell whose it was.

"Yes." Sam nodded. "But how'd you know—"

"It's your destiny, Sam." Vigtor's smile was like a beacon of light. "Of course, the choice is yours, but we all knew the minute we met you that you were meant to do this. You are fated to be one of us."

Sam felt oddly proud. He really did feel a connection with these people. He still couldn't wrap his head around it, but he was about to be part of something bigger, something that was going to happen very soon.

"Let's do it." Sam pounded a fist into his palm.

The cave erupted in cheers, lights, and music. Everyone gathered around Sam—except Crom, who slunk back to the shadows.

"Give us a minute." Vigtor tipped his chin at Sam. "We'll meet you up there."

They waved as each took a turn disappearing without a sound.

Vigtor picked up the football and tossed it to him. "You made the right decision."

"It feels right." Sam tossed it back underhanded.

"I'm sorry that Bariv and everyone else skewed your mind before you met us. It must have made the choice more difficult."

"I'm not going to lie; I was pretty confused for a while."

Vigtor tossed the ball back; Sam returned it.

"You must do what comes naturally." Vigtor waved the ball toward the ceiling. "You must not fight against yourself. Make a decision and then stick to it, whatever comes your way."

Sam nodded. "I'm used to that."

"Good, because you will need to remember that when it happens, especially because you will be going last."

Sam caught the ball, tucking it under his arm. "Yeah, what does that mean?"

"Because none of us are actually strong enough to break through ourselves, we must build off one another's work, like toppling a building. Pulling one support won't bring it down, especially if the structure can quickly rebuild itself, but if you get them all…"

Sam's stomach tightened. "So how do we do it?"

"We get into a line. Before we start, our essences will be linked. Erimos takes care of that."

Sam frowned at the name. Erimos made him uneasy. His eyes were red like Bariv's, but Erimos looked far older. He'd been pleasant enough to Sam, though, going out of his way to give him some pointers when he'd been training with Vigtor.

Sam put the football on the mattress. "So what do I have to do, exactly?"

"When the rest of the line has done their duty, you will finish the job. Get the last support. Since we will be linked, you will know exactly where to reach. You must use all your strength. She is strong, but together we are stronger."

The knot in Sam's stomach wrung tighter. "This doesn't seem at all wrong to you?"

Vigtor snapped his fingers and the fire in the corner dwindled. "This is what you have to fight against." As the last of the flames flickered, Sam could see the intensity in Vigtor's eyes. "You must not battle yourself. You need all of your concentration on your one task."

"So, I just rip as hard as I can?"

"Essentially." He paused. "You know, you are the best student I've ever had."

This eased Sam's anxiety a bit. "Yeah?"

The fire was on its last flickers, and shadow was cast upon Vigtor's face. "I have instructed most of the Tembrath Elite, and you've embraced power magic faster than any of them."

Sam was flattered, but he had to ask. "It's funny that the people in Atlas Crown are the elitists, but you guys call yourself the Tembrath *Elite*."

The final flame died, casting the cave into darkness. "I thought the irony was appropriate."

Sam paused and bit his lip. Were they really about to do the right thing? "I guess it is."

"Now." Vigtor held his voice steady. "We mustn't be late."

Sam swallowed hard. "But I don't really know what to do yet."

"Instincts, Sam. They will be your greatest ally. Now hold your breath; it will make it easier."

<p>

It was easier, in fact: this time passing through the Veil only left him with a ringing in his ears and a numbness in his feet. "Where are we?"

"We have emerged from our place of hiding under the mountain." Vigtor filled his lungs with a deep breath through his nose. "We now stand upon it—the peak of Dami Damascus."

The first thing Sam noticed was the smell—dry, earthy, and dusty, like he'd wandered into the middle of a western. The mountaintop was barren, the entire peak a cracking, grey plateau. Wind whipped off the edge, taking particles of dirt and dust with it. It sounded like the mountain was trying to whistle, but couldn't quite get the technique right.

Air raced past his body in a furious hurry, tugging him toward the edge with invisible fingers. The full moon hung at the horizon, looking closer and brighter than Sam had ever seen, and bathed the mountaintop in a soft glow.

Erimos hunched over, waving his second-skin over the land. The rock faded to a lighter shade of grey, and Sam felt gravity increase, like he was wearing weighted clothing... or had an anchor tied to his feet.

Vigtor pointed toward the sky. Waves of red energy emanated from his second-skin, pulsing outward and pushing the wind with them. The waves went right through Sam, but as they passed, the wind stopped stinging his face and everything became calm.

Vigtor kept his hand held high. "Let us not waste any time. Start the formation. Sam, you're at the end."

The rest of the Tembrath Elite queued up behind Vigtor, perfectly straight and spaced a few feet apart from each other. Crom snarled at

230

Sam as he swept by. As the group got in line, their demeanors began to change. The pleasant, cheerful faces they'd been wearing for the last few weeks melted away, revealing a deep, primal longing in their eyes. They watched the moon like animals about to rip the meat off a fresh carcass.

Doubt twinged in Sam's gut. "Don't fight it," he said to himself. "They want the best for everyone. It's all worth it in the end."

The Tembrath Elite stood in silence as they watched the moon dip toward the horizon, their eyes going more feral with each passing heartbeat.

What did I get myself into? I don't even know them. What am I doing?

The last of the moon disappeared, and darkness surrounded them.

From the place where Sam had last seen Erimos, a pulse of power whipped around him, and Sam felt his body being taken over.

It was awful.

The only way to describe it was that his essence had been stolen and mixed together forcefully with the others'. Who he'd been no longer existed; now only his mind existed… and the rest of the Tembrath Elite.

Hate. Greed. Lust. Sam now knew what they meant to do—what *he* was going to do. They'd misled him. They wanted the power to come forth, but they were going to use it to take over. He could feel the hundreds—no, thousands—of years of yearning. They wanted power. Not just over Atlas Crown… over everyone.

It was vile. Sam felt like his mouth was full of metal. He wanted to scream, but his voice was no longer his; it was theirs, together. He was lost in the ether, somewhere in his body, but he couldn't do anything.

He still saw out of his eyes, still felt the scraping of the wind against his body as it returned, but he was part of Vigtor now, part of the Elite.

He tried to cry out as his body moved to the back of the line, but nothing happened. He could feel their thoughts, their giddy malice, their desire to take the Veil and break Her.

It was so *wrong*.

No wonder May had tried to keep him from this.

Vigtor began. Sam could *feel* him, as they were a team in the fullest sense of the word. Vigtor controlled the others like they were extensions of him, extensions of his power.

Sam could feel Vigtor grasping the Veil and defiling Her. They were ripping out Her soul, and Sam was one of the murderers.

He wanted to throw up, he wanted to bend over and rid himself of everything they had fed him, everything they had taught him. He wanted to purge it all.

He felt Vigtor fall to the ground; the first blow had been dealt.

The wind picked up, aching to flay their skin and end Her suffering. Sam wanted Her to succeed. He wanted to get tossed off the mountain.

One by one, they fell. Each time, Sam felt the Veil cry out in pain. It brought tears to his eyes. He was helpless against it. He kept trying to scream, trying to shout out, but nothing came. He could only watch as everything beautiful was destroyed.

Erimos, Sage, Saria—they were all down, each one taking a little more of Her. They stole Her beauty and tossed it to the ground.

Sam wanted to die.

Only three Tembrath Elite were left: Dralis, Crom… and himself.

He included himself in that number, and despised everything he was. The Veil called out to them, She pled, She begged, She threw everything She had at them, but they kept going.

Dralis was now the commander. She threw lightning bolts at him, threw monstrous, hurricane winds, but the Tembrath Elite were one now.

She was no match for them.

Dralis decimated Her. They were getting so close now. She was torn apart and bleeding rain. She dripped from the sky in terrible, thick sheets.

Dralis fell.

Only Crom and Sam were left.

Sam needed to get away. He needed to be rid of all of this. He needed May, needed Bariv, needed *anyone*. The fallen Tembrath watched him; he felt their eyes on him, but he also felt them staring out from his own eyes. Their power was exponentially greater as one. They slithered around his soul, binding his will to theirs.

He would do anything if he could just get out. He could see Her true beauty now. As they tore Her apart, he could see Her perfection being stripped away.

He tried to bury his mind away, hide his soul so he wouldn't be part of this, but yet he was there, his fist being guided.

Crom roared.

Great lashes of fire stretched from the sky, trying to burn Crom to ash. Sam could feel Crom's fury, his all-consuming lust for power. It was easy for Crom: he thrust his arm, slashed at Her, and came away victorious.

Crom fell.

Sam was alone. He was standing, unable to control himself, when it happened.

Everything died down. A hushed silence coated everything, like She had given up fighting.

Around him, the wind had ceased—no fire, no lightning, just calm.

With all his might, Sam summoned up everything he had, and broke the hold. "I won't do it!"

Vigtor stood up. He pulled out a second-skin from his robe. It was a scaly, black one, like Sam's without the stars. None of the Tembrath

Elite had the second-skins they had been wearing. They were all broken, tossed along the mountaintop.

"Don't fight it," Vigtor snarled. "Think about all of the people we can help."

"You're a liar!" Sam's eyes burned. "You don't want to help anyone. You want to rule everyone."

Vigtor's mouth contorted into a vile smirk. "It's the best way to help everyone. People are weak. They need to follow."

"It's wrong!" Sam stumbled backward. "The Veil needs to be there."

The rest of the Tembrath Elite glared at him as they pulled out new second-skins.

"You're all weak." Sam backed toward the cliff. "I felt it. You don't have it in you."

Vigtor's eyes burned. "The Veil will be broken, and you will do it."

Sam took another step back, now only a few feet from the ledge. "I'll die first."

"You have no choice, boy. We've been waiting for thousands of years. You really think we would let you have any choice in the matter?" Vigtor pointed at Sam. "No, this is too important to be left up to chance."

Vigtor's face contorted as he and the rest of the Tembrath Elite gripped into the Veil and took over Sam's body.

Sam tried to fight against it. They clawed at his insides, creeping up his spine and into his brain. He tried to push back, but they were too many. He lost himself.

He couldn't speak, only watch as his hand thrust deep into the Veil. His muscles ached as he tried to pull back, but the force of the Tembrath was too much.

Just like that, it was over. It had only taken an instant.

He had broken through the Veil. He felt the other side, and it was hot, like sticking his hand into an open flame. He pulled back.

Sam felt his body become his again, and immediately was hit with the greatest wave of nausea he had ever felt.

He hunched over and grabbed his stomach. His throat felt dry and raw. He tried to say something, but his voice was missing.

Vigtor slapped a hand on Sam's back, laughing wildly with vile enthusiasm.

Cheers fired all around him. Not like the cheers he had heard in the cave, but *real* cheers. This was the sound of a murderer who had finally squeezed the life out of his victim.

Suddenly, a furious push from underneath shoved Sam into an explosion of light.

He looked around, confused. He wasn't on the mountaintop anymore; he floated in a sea of white. It was pure, the most wholesome and unsullied place Sam had ever been. Sam couldn't hear any sound, but it wasn't frightening. It was home. The pain was gone, and he felt whole once more.

"Where am I?"

"They do not know what has been done," a voice spoke. Sam had never heard a more perfect sound. Every word massaged his very core. "It must not be allowed to happen."

"Who are you?"

"Exactly who you think I am."

Sam didn't need any clarification. He let his head fall. "I'm sorry."

"Don't be." The voice was surprisingly calm despite the circumstance. "I have seen your heart: they left you no choice."

He searched around, but saw only white. The voice seemed to be coming from everything and nothing at the same time. "I wish there was something I could do."

"There is. If I break, our world will fall. The power I hold back does not want to work with our world. It wants to destroy it and bring new life, terrible life."

Sam tried to take a deep breath, but then realized he didn't need to. "What do I do?"

"Things are already happening. You need to help May."

The corners of the perfect white started to stain red. Something was trying to get in.

"May? How?"

"One of my children has already presented you with the tool. Give her the fruit."

Sam put a hand against his pocket. "I will, but—"

"There is no time, Samuel. If you succeed, we will meet again."

Sam straightened. "I won't let you down."

The voice laughed, and the sound made all of Sam's insecurities disappear. It made him a man. "I know you won't."

Tears pricked Sam's eyes. He never wanted to part from Her, but he already felt himself sliding back into his body, back to the chaos.

Sam stayed hunched over, his head dizzy, as the ground started to take on a red tinge. Taking a deep breath, he stood up.

The sky was splitting apart in hundreds of places. Dark red oozed from behind the cracks. The air rumbled with electricity.

The Tembrath Elite watched in awe as a new power emerged.

The rumble got louder. The sky kept splitting, like cracks in ice, spidering their way further across the horizon. More red light oozed out of the cracks.

Sam knew just by looking at it that it was an abomination—this light was tainted; this light wanted everything gone, wanted to bathe the world in a new order.

The Tembrath Elite were still shouting when the sound was stolen. All of it. Vigtor tried to call out, but nothing came.

The red light burned Sam's skin like a heat lamp. A furious itching attacked his whole body.

Joy dribbled off the faces of the Tembrath Elite, replaced by worry as they grabbed their throats. They tried to talk to one another, tried to do grips, but nothing happened.

From the red cracks in the sky, swarms of ominous creatures emerged. Their wings were riddled with veins, and their skin had a slimy sheen. Other figures dropped out of the cracks closer to the earth—large hulks, teeming with muscle, black and bulky.

Sam's heart sank. *Where is May?*

The Tembrath Elite huddled together, wide-eyed.

Sam didn't have to know exactly how, but he knew that the natural world was about to be destroyed. There would be nothing left; everything he loved would be wiped out.

Then, just as he was going to surrender all hope, he saw the swirls.

Little black beacons of hope hovered near one of the larger breaks in the rock. Sam knew they must be there for a reason. They floated to him, surrounding him, and their presence gave him comfort. He just wished he knew what they meant.

Then Sam saw her rush past in a blur. *May!* She'd found him.

He watched her aim the diamond second-skin toward the cracking sky and brace herself.

He tried to call out to her, but he knew it was useless. The red light grew hotter.

More people ran toward him. Behind Glissandro were Bariv, Daphne, Rona, Cassiella, Zawadi, Petir, and a few older people he did not recognize. Panic filled their eyes as they stared at the red cracks.

Sam turned back to where May attempted to grip into the Veil. Her face tightened with despair.

Then the words from the white place filled his mind. *The fruit.*

His pocket was giving off light again. He pulled out the fruit and finally recognized where he'd seen that shade of light before—in a glass vial presented at the seam.

Pure Veil.

He raced over to May.

The fruit's bright light counteracted the red, cooling his skin.

May met his gaze with sadness in her eyes. She lifted her hand, and let it fall.

Sam thrust out the fruit, and a small glimmer of hope flashed across her face.

May took the fruit, kissed Sam on the cheek, and then took a large bite out of it. Her face radiated pure ecstasy. She took another bite, chewed fast, and handed the fruit back to Sam with a nod of thanks.

She was glowing as she moved, a beautiful white aura. Her diamond-hand shimmered, scattering refracted light. Every place it touched, the red light vanished.

The cracks in the sky grew larger as a deep rumble resounded through the earth. Bigger and more menacing creatures started to emerge—winged monsters ripped through the sky, while other creatures with hundreds of legs fell to the ground like cockroaches escaping a hole in the wall. Some even looked human. The sky peeled further. Soon, there would be no more cracks, just a different sky, a damned sky.

May stood out like a white wall against the crashing doom. The glowing sheen around her expanded, engulfing everyone on the mountaintop.

The rumble shifted into loud, snapping cracks.

May held strong, her diamond-skin outstretched.

More sound returned. Next came singing, like angels humming a soft prayer, growing louder and louder—the music of heaven.

You can do it.

The white light poured out, almost blinding. The music rose, and May's body began to shudder. It was too much for her.

The cracks started to close. Very slowly, the fractures sealed up.

Despite her convulsing body, May smiled.

The music erupted into a choir of voices, all singing May onward. Even the Tembrath Elite looked on with awe.

She was going to do it.

May gave one final heave. After an explosion of light and sound, she fell.

CHAPTER 24

Samuel Lock's fingertips pierced the soft grass up to his first knuckle. He was lying face down on a bed of soft green.

Sam had watched May's body fall with grace, like hands were gently laying her to rest. As soon as she'd struck the stone, an explosion of white had knocked them all over. In seconds, a thick layer of green grass had covered the plateau, and a whole army of trees had grown in an instant and circled them.

May lay on her side, peaceful.

Sam rushed over to May, cradling her body, ignoring the pain in his arm.

His voice was no longer gone. The sky was back to normal, and the sun was rising.

She had saved them all.

"Hello, Sam." May smiled, a small trickle of blood coming from her mouth.

Sam felt the tears coming. He tried to hold them back. "You did it."

She stroked his arm. "We did it."

Sam sniffed. "How'd you find me?"

"Something special came out of the Veil when you did your first grip." Her voice was joyous but feeble, as if it would fail at any moment. "I'm sure he will let you meet him soon."

Sam's words burst out. "I didn't want to break Her, I swear." The tears broke through. "They made me—"

"Hush. I know." She ran her fingertips across Sam's cheek. "As soon as they got Cassiella, you had no choice."

"What do you mean?"

"They took over her mind and made her lie. Plus, they gave you that letter." She coughed and her hand fell to her side. "They knew exactly how to nudge you out."

Sam held back another wave of tears. "I'm so sorry."

Her voice weakened to a whisper. "You don't need to be. You're still a boy; we all know you never meant to hurt anyone. Promises of saving the world can be very persuasive."

Sam nodded.

"I'm so glad I met you, Sam." The light from the rising sun illuminated her face. "You are going to do extraordinary things. It has truly been an honor." She coughed onto the back of her hand, which came away bloody.

Sam shed a steady flow of tears. *She's dying.* "You can't go."

"It's my time. Do not weep, for I have been around long enough."

"But I need you."

She smiled. "Death is such a funny thing."

Sam couldn't understand how she was so calm. "How so?"

"Because everything changes, even death."

Sam sniffed again, rubbing his nose with the back of his sleeve.

"This is one mystery I am happy to explore." She brought her hand up and held it in front of Sam. Her second-skin had cracked and pieces peeled off her hand. The last patch fell away, revealing a yellow petal hidden against her palm, covered in radiant dust.

A yellow sunflower petal, as vivid as if it had just been plucked.

Sam wiped the tears from the corner of his eyes. "It was you?"

May beamed and nodded.

He chuckled between sobs. "You were the one who started it all? You were that little girl from all the stories?"

Another nod. "Take it." She pressed the petal into his palm. "Remember me."

Her white glow started to fade.

"I will."

"It was wonderful knowing you, Sam, even if only for the briefest of periods."

He smiled. "You can call me Samuel."

She laughed. "So, you're taking to our customs already."

Sam swallowed hard against the lump in his throat. "I still have a lot to learn."

"You will."

Sam took two fingers and drew them across his heart. "Travel well, May."

She took his hand and smiled. "And you."

With one final gaze deep into his eyes, she was gone.

CHAPTER 25

Bariv stretched out, letting the sun wash over him. "Do you like your new room?"

Sam nodded, but kept his eyes on the pond. "It's great."

"So, I hear you and the rest of Rona's students are back to normal."

"Yeah, as normal as can be expected, considering we almost saw the end of the world." He dipped his hand into the water and swirled it around. "But I have many more apologies to make."

Bariv sat down on the bench beside the rinsefish pond. "You made the right choice."

Sam chuckled. "Don't worry, I have no reservations about that. I know in my heart that this is where I'm supposed to be."

Bariv bent over the stone and reached down, just barely able to reach the water's surface. He dipped his finger in, and dozens of rinsefish swam up, nudging their rinsers toward him. "And your parents?"

Sam raised an eyebrow. "Don't you guys have some sort of protocol for that?"

"We do." Bariv sat back on the bench without taking a rinser. "They can come live here if you like, or we have other options."

Sam tried to picture his father in a place like this. "I think maybe 'other options' are best."

In the days since the incident, Sam had been adjusting to his decision. It wasn't even really a decision: after all that had happened, it felt more like destiny. He was going to live in Atlas Crown and learn the craft of magic—the right way. He had a lot to do already. Despite what Glissandro played and what Cassiella promised in between her own apologies, Sam still felt responsible for everything that had happened.

Sam flicked the surface of the water. "Still no sign of Crom or Erimos?"

"We have the other Tembrath Elite here waiting judgment, but no, Crom and Erimos have not been seen since the events at the top of the mountain."

"What will happen to all those creatures that came from behind the Veil?"

"They will die, as they are cut off from their energy source. Do not worry though; I already have a team of sorcerers making sure they remain where they are until they perish."

The day was bright and the community bustled again. Although no one came over to speak with Sam or Bariv, most of them waved or gave small bows. Sam wasn't in the mood to socialize, anyway.

He just hoped they would eventually forgive him.

"I met Her, you know." Sam sat back down next to Bariv.

"I know." Bariv gave a boyish smile. "She is quite fond of you."

Sam ran a hand across his second-skin. The stars on it seemed extra bright that morning. "When can I talk to Her again?"

Bariv took a diamond out of his pocket and handed it to Sam. It looked exactly the same as the first one Bariv had presented him with. "In time."

Sam took the diamond and placed it in his pocket. "I still can't believe that May was the first one to discover magic."

"Not many people knew, actually. She didn't find it necessary to share. I also think she rather liked watching the different reenactments. She used to tell me, 'just because it didn't happen that way, doesn't mean it couldn't have.'"

"She was amazing." Sam pinned his eyes to the ground.

"You'd think more people would have guessed from her robes, though."

"Hmm?"

"Since all clans come from her, she honors the clans that have died out over the years by keeping their symbols alive on her robes."

Sam rubbed his temple and let out a deep breath. "I'll never be able to forgive myself."

"She never blamed you."

"But—"

Bariv cut him off with a pointed finger. "There he is again."

Sam turned and saw the panther. Or at least, "panther" was the best way to describe him. He paced back and forth a few yards away. Lean and muscular, his sharp blue eyes looked exactly like Sam's. Tiny black swirls adorned his sleek black coat—the same ones Sam had been seeing since the football game. As the large cat moved, swirls flowed off his body and lagged behind in the air. They drifted along until they eventually reached his coat again and latched on.

Sam held his hand out, but the panther kept its distance. "I still can't believe he led you guys right to us."

"To *you*." Bariv's tone was coy. "You know, I didn't find out about my snake for *years*."

Sam watched the graceful cat move closer. "So just us, huh?"

"As far as I know." Bariv traced the swirls on his cheeks. "And I know a lot."

Sam pulled his hand back. "I still don't understand."

"Things come out of the Veil when we use Her. When I saw my parents' deaths, and when you were at the game, we both caused something new to be created. It does not usually happen. When it happened, we were so closely linked with Her that we pulled out something closely linked to us."

The panther crouched low to the ground. The creature was more the size of a lion, its body thick with muscle. "How did he know to go to Glissandro?"

Bariv nodded toward the panther. "I assume he's been watching you for a while now. He knew you were in trouble. You two are connected, very strongly, in fact. He is here because of you, and you are here because of him. The relationship will grow stronger over the years; at least, my own experiences lead me to believe so."

The panther pounced on some invisible prey. Black swirls arched off its coat and through the air.

Sam's words escaped as a whisper. "He's beautiful."

"Truly." Bariv gestured around them. "Just imagine what you'll see when you actually take the time to see our town properly."

"First I want to train up. I don't want to ever be used like that again."

Bariv sat back, leaving his feet dangling off the ground. "Relax and take your time. The power is behind the Veil, and I know the Tembrath Elite will not try to reach through again."

"So, what do I do now?"

Bariv pointed again toward the panther.

It stared up at Sam now, only inches from him. It fixed gentle teeth around Sam's second-skin and pulled it away.

Sam wasn't afraid of the creature, but it hadn't yet spoken to him like Bariv's snake. He'd tried talking to the cat a few times since returning to Atlas Crown, but it seemed to be following its own agenda.

The panther dropped the second-skin on the grass and lowered its head.

A single swirl drifted off its coat and came to rest against Sam's palm. As he watched, the swirl sank deep into his skin. Sam curled his fingers and felt the rush of the Veil against his palm.

Bariv clapped a hand on his shoulder. "First, we honor May, and then I think it's time that you became my first *real* student."

The panther dashed off into the distance.

Sam relaxed his hand and felt the brush of the Veil subside.

He picked out a rinse-fish glob from the pond and wiped it against his palm, making sure the swirl didn't wash away.

It stayed, making Sam wonder if the panther had just given him a permanent connection to the Veil.

Bariv pointed a finger at the swirl on his cheek and nodded.

The white glob dripped off his hand and hit the ground.

To his surprise, a cinnamon flower did not grow.

Instead, it created a tiny sunflower.

THE END OF BOOK ONE

Acknowledgments

First off, I'd like to thank my fantastic editor, Kate Kaynak, who has a tremendous talent for showing others the magic in themselves. Thanks to my family and friends and God.

Thanks to Rich Storrs, Vicki Ciaffone, Alex Bennett, Danielle Ellison, and everyone over at Spencer Hill Press: my writing family that redefines what it means to be a publishing company. Thanks to Katie Radzik for such great preliminary editing and copy editing. Special thanks to (the amazing) Stephanie Radzik, Jenn Sardina, Brian Keegan, Matthew Elmes, Josh Darfler, Justin Curcio, and everyone else who helped support and shape this novel. And thank you Shaul Hendel, M.S, L.Ac, who managed to save me from myself.

This is not like my first book, written mostly for the fun and excitement of it. This novel kept me alive, kept me going. It was, at the same time, my escape and my path back to life. I took my passion and wrapped myself so tightly around it that I forgot where I ended and the story began. This is not just the story of a football player turned sorcerer. This is the place where I rediscovered who I was.

We all go through hardship, and we all have our ways of coping. In these pages, you will find the best and worst of me, which I'm sure many of you can relate to. You can see my strengths and insecurities; my faith and failures; my relationships and my demons. This novel is the cross product of so much pain and hope, and eventually, hope won.

I sincerely hope you enjoyed this book.

Dan
September, 2011

About the Author

Photo by Kaitlyn Elissa James

Daniel A. Cohen was just your average business student. Microeconomics, finance, marketing… you name it, he had to do a PowerPoint presentation on it. One dark and stormy night, he was bitten by the radioactive realization that memorizing business jargon could possibly be the most boring activity known to man.

After gaining eagle-eye vision, abs that could grate cheese, and a talent for imagining things (including his cheese-grating abs), he wrote his first novel and began his epic battle against the formidable business jargon. He continues to fight the good fight by playing saxophone and writing YA fantasy, forever hoping his Veil Trilogy will help inspire others to join his cause.

Find out more at **www.spencerhillpress.com**.

Made in the USA
Charleston, SC
16 May 2012